IRRESISTIBLE IMPULSE

Also by the author

ROBERT K. TANENBAUM

IRRESISTIBLE IMPULSE

A DUTTON BOOK

DUTTON
Published by the Penguin Group
Penguin Books USA Inc., 375 Hudson Street,
New York, New York 10014, U.S.A.
Penguin Books Ltd, 27 Wrights Lane,
London W8 5TZ, England
Penguin Books Australia Ltd, Ringwood,
Victoria, Australia
Penguin Books Canada Ltd, 10 Alcorn Avenue,
Toronto, Ontario, Canada M4V 3B2
Penguin Books (N.Z.) Ltd, 182–190 Wairau Road,
Auckland 10, New Zealand

Penguin Books Ltd, Registered Offices:
Harmondsworth, Middlesex, England

First Printing, November, 1997

Copyright © Robert K. Tanenbaum
All rights reserved

REGISTERED TRADEMARK—MARCA REGISTRADA

ISBN 0-525-94310-2

Printed in the United States of America
Set in Plantin
Designed by Leonard Telesca

PUBLISHER'S NOTE
This is a work of fiction. Names, characters, places, and incidents either are the product
of the author's imagination or are used fictitiously, and any resemblance to actual
persons, living or dead, events, or locales is entirely coincidental.

Without limiting the rights under copyright reserved above, no part of this publication
may be reproduced, stored in or introduced into a retrieval system, or transmitted, in
any form, or by any means (electronic, mechanical, photocopying, recording, or
otherwise), without the prior written permission of both the copyright owner and the
above publisher of this book.

To the ones I love,
Patti, Rachael, Roger, and Billy T.

ACKNOWLEDGMENTS

Again, and yet again, all praise belongs to Michael Gruber whose genius and scholarship flows throughout and is primarily responsible for the excellence of the manuscript. His contribution cannot be overstated. He is alter ego and truly lifetime partner.

None of the prosecutorial experiences dominating the central core of these books could have occurred without Rick Albrecht and Mel Glass, who gave me entry into the DAO. The former, an outstanding prosecutor and trial lawyer, had the wisdom to guide me through the process; the latter, the best of all the DA's, blessed me with his knowledge as well as by his incredible example.

And special heartfelt gratitude to Mike Hamilburg, who for fifteen years has represented me with the utmost integrity and loyalty.

And to Georgia di Donato, who still shows enthusiasm and wonderment after listening scores of times to the tales of Marlene, Karp, and their band of merry men and women. Such is the nature of confidential executive advisors!

ONE

In the early hours of the 5,742nd year since the creation of the universe, Dr. Mark Davidoff, M.D., stood in the crowded, marvelous, immense nave of Temple Emmanu-El on Fifth Avenue, and belted out *"Ain Kelohanu"* in a lusty voice, and thought that so far the universe was working out fairly well. He was young (young-ish), healthy, and rich, an internist like his father and grandfather before him, possessing all his hair, a Jaguar Van den Plas, a ten-room condo on Central Park West, a wife and two blossoming Davidoff-ettes. Around him standing and singing were his people, in whom he was well pleased, the upper crust of Jewish New York, a group as prosperous and secure as any Jews had been since collapse of the caliphate of Cordova.

The song and the service ended. Davidoff crowded out with the rest, for the temple was packed for Rosh Hashonah, the beginning of the High Holy Days, when it was appropriate for Jews of Davidoff's degree of religiosity to seek solidarity and, it might also have been, exculpation for countless Sundays of Chinese food, countless Sabbaths at the office or on the links.

He knew many of the people milling around the cloakroom, and there was considerable hand shaking, and "good-Yonteff"-ing, before Davidoff, enclosed in camel-hair coat and cashmere muffler, was able to leave the synagogue and emerge out into the bright, crisp day. He was about to walk down the avenue, to where he would stand a better chance of finding a cab home, when he heard his name called and saw the very last person of his acquaintance he would have expected to see standing in front of Temple Emmanu-El on Rosh Hashonah.

Vincent Fiske Robinson stood out in that particular throng like a Hasid in Killarney. He was tall and slim with a face both sculptured and sensual, set with sky blue eyes and decked with fine blond hair worn swept back from a widow's peak. Mark Davidoff had blue eyes and blond hair too, but not, of course, *that* kind of blue eyes and blond hair. Davidoff moved through the crowd and held out his hand. Robinson's hand in his felt hot and damp.

"Vince. Long time no see," said Davidoff with an uncertain smile. "What are you doing here?"

"I came to see you, man. I called your apartment, and your wife told me I'd find you here."

"Yeah, I didn't figure you were thinking about conversion . . ." Davidoff began in a bantering tone, and then stopped, automatically checking out the other man with a diagnostician's eye. Robinson seemed flushed and overheated despite the chilly air. He looked as if he had dressed in the dark—he was wearing grubby jeans, a worn blue button-down shirt, and sneakers, over which he had thrown a lined Burberry. "You okay, Vince?" Davidoff asked.

"Yeah. No, actually, I'm in a bit of a mess. Actually, a gigantic mess. The thing is, could you do a consult for me? It would really help me out."

"A consult? Vince, it's Rosh Hashonah. Can't it wait?"

"Actually, no, it can't," said Robinson. "It's personal. My nurse, one of my nurses, actually, she's my girlfriend . . . she's in my apartment, very sick, very, very, sick . . . I was . . . could you, you know, take a look at her?"

"Vince, what is this? You have an emergency, call 911, get her into a hospital . . ."

"No, actually, I don't think that would be appropriate in this case. That's why I came here."

Davidoff was about to refuse when he registered the desperation in Robinson's eyes.

"Please, Mark. I really need your help."

This was new and, Davidoff could not help feeling with a little thrill of self-satisfaction, not a mien that Vincent Fiske Robinson had ever adopted with Mark Davidoff when the two of them had been at Harvard Medical School together. For a brief period the two students had shared a group house in Cambridge, during which Robinson had given Davidoff numerous unspoken lessons about the difference between New York Jewish aristocracy and *Aristocracy*. There was no actual anti-Semitism, of course, not that you could put your finger on, only a humorous, casual condescension. That Davidoff studied hard and got top grades, while Robinson did not seem to study at all, but eventually received the same degree, and got a good internship, too, was also the subject of considerable comment on Robinson's part, charming comment, for Robinson was certainly the most charming man in Davidoff's experience. Even when he had pissed you off, and made you feel like, for example, a grubby Jewish grind, it was hard to remain angry with him. Unaccountably, on this cold New York street corner, an image from a dozen years past flashed across Dr. Davidoff's mind: spring in Cambridge, a Friday, the Friday before the dreaded human physio exam, himself surrounded by books and notes, glancing up from his desk as Robinson pranced by, swinging a lacrosse racket, a white sweater draped around his neck, and a pale laughing girl with a blond pageboy haircut draped on his arm. Somehow, the current situation, Robinson begging Davidoff to help him out of a mess, balanced out that long-ago scene on some cosmic and inarticulable scorecard.

So Davidoff smiled and said, "Sure, Vince, I'll have a look at her. Let's go."

Robinson lived on the East Side, of course, a duplex in an old brownstone in the Sixties off Madison. They walked there in silence.

"Shit, Vince!" he cried when he saw the woman in Robinson's

bed, and felt sick himself. She was a lovely woman, or had been. Pale hair framed a fine-boned face, with a wide, inviting mouth. Davidoff found himself thinking once again, just for an instant, of the laughing girl in the Cambridge hallway. He cleared his throat to gain control of his voice, and said, "When?"

"This morning. She was, um, like that, nine, nine-thirty."

" 'Like that'? You mean *dead*, Vince. That's the term we docs use for a person in this condition. How long was she sick?"

"A day, a day and a half. She was fine Friday. We went out for dinner, came back here, went to bed, and mooched around Saturday morning. We were going to go out biking in the afternoon, and she said she wasn't up for it; she said she felt feverish, headachey. I thought, flu. Saturday night she started spiking a fever. One-oh-three, one-oh-four. I couldn't bring it down. I gave her a shot of penicillin Sunday morning. Sunday afternoon she was sick but coherent. We joked, you know, we're playing doctor. Jesus, Mark, she's twenty-eight! Never been sick a day. I figured, viral pneumonia, liquids, bed rest, antibiotics to keep the secondaries down. Sunday night I went to bed in the guest room, and I came in to see how she was, seven, eight this morning, and she was in coma. I panicked, and . . ." He made a helpless gesture.

"Okay, so let me understand this: you wake up, find your girlfriend dead, and your first thought was to come get *me* for a *consultation*, I think you said? Right. We've consulted. She's dead. I agree. So, what's going on here, Vince?"

"It's . . . I need a certificate, Mark," said Robinson. He was looking off into the distance, his eyes shying from both the dead woman and the other man. "I want you to declare her."

"You want me to *declare* . . . ?" Davidoff felt the first stirrings of anger. "Ah, Vince, correct me if I'm wrong, but didn't Harvard give you one of those nice posters with the Latin? I got mine framed. Why the hell don't *you* write out the goddamn certificate?"

Robinson gave him a brief look, in which Davidoff read both despair and shame, and then turned his face away again. "I'm involved with her, Mark, you know? And, well, I've been giving her things."

"Things? What kind of things?"

"Oh, megavitamin shots, diet stuff, stuff to help her sleep. She was a troubled person."

Davidoff took a deep breath and bit off what he was about to say. He went over to the bed and examined the dead woman's arms and thighs.

"This is a junkie, Mark," said Davidoff, his voice now quaking with rage. "What the fuck are you trying to get me into?"

"She's *not*, she *wasn't* a junkie! I told you, she was a troubled girl. I was trying to help." He turned to face Davidoff, and he seemed a different person from the elegant figure Davidoff had envied for a dozen or more years. He was literally wringing his hands, and his eyes were wet and red rimmed. "She has a family, Mark, you know? A mom and dad? I just . . . I want her to go out decently. I loved her. Mark, I'm begging you . . . do you want me to go down on my knees?"

Davidoff believed that he would have. He felt a wave of loathing, and an intense desire to get out of this apartment, away from this man, and, what was worse, he felt a tincture of self-loathing too, because some part of him was enjoying the sight of Vincent Fiske Robinson brought low.

They stood that way in silence for what seemed a long time. At last Davidoff let out his breath in a huff and said, "Okay, shit, give me the thing and I'll sign it. I presume you have one."

"Yeah. God, Mark, I can't tell you how much I appreciate this."

"Viral pneumonia, huh?" said Davidoff as he cast his eye down the single-sheet form that Robinson handed him. "Why not?" He signed his name and dated the death certificate in the spaces provided.

"Well, Vince," he said, handing over the paper. "I wish I could say it was nice seeing you, but . . ."

"Thanks a million, buddy," said Vince, the famous perfect smile appearing for the first time that afternoon. "Look, I'll call you, we'll have lunch."

Davidoff said nothing, nor did he offer to shake hands. Outside the apartment, in the fresh, cold air again, he took several deep breaths. Vince Robinson had never called him for lunch before, although they had been working in the same city for at least a decade. He doubted Robinson would call him now, and found that he was glad of it. He would have been even gladder had he observed the expression on Robinson's face as he walked out.

There were only four people who were allowed to interrupt, by a phone call, a bureau meeting of the Homicide Bureau of the New York District Attorney's office: the district attorney himself, John X. Keegan; the bureau chief's wife; a detective lieutenant named Clay Fulton; and the chief medical examiner of the City of New York.

"Excuse me, guys, I got to take this," said Karp, the bureau chief, to the twenty or so people assembled in his office as he lifted the phone and punched the flasher.

"Butch? Murray Selig," said the voice.

"What's up, Murray? I'm in a meeting," said Karp.

"Yeah, sorry, but I thought you should hear about this one personally."

Karp turned to a fresh page on his yellow pad and poised his pen over it. "Okay, shoot."

"The dead woman is a nurse, Evelyn Longren, twenty-eight, cause of death, viral pneumonia. All right, that's the first thing. Pneumonia, they call it the old man's friend; it takes the debilitated, the elderly, and babies. We don't expect to see a twenty-eight-year-old woman die from it. Next, the attending physician was Mark Davidoff, who, let me tell you, has a rep as one hell of an internist. His dad is Abe Davidoff, head of internal medicine at Columbia P. and S., for years. Next, we have the death took place in a private residence, not a hospital. And finally, the date of death was this past September 21. Davidoff signed the death certificate on September 21. Interesting, no?"

"No. Murray, I'm not following you. What's so special about the day?"

"What's so . . . ? *Oy vey*, what a Jew! Schlemiel! It was Rosh Hashonah. So I'm asking myself, Why is a Jew, one of the biggest internists in the city, attending a woman with viral pneumonia in a private house on Rosh Hashonah? Believe me, Mark Davidoff don't make house calls."

"She was a friend. He was doing a favor."

"Uh-uh, Butch. If it was a friend, and she was developing complications, he would've had her in a hospital before you could turn around. And he would have seen the complications in time. This is a young, healthy woman. There are no contributing factors on the certificate either—no fibrosis, no asthma, no staph."

"So he made a mistake. I know you think doctors are perfect, Murray—"

"Mistake? Butch, listen, if you saw Larry Bird pass to the other team six times in one game, what would you say? He made a mistake? No, you'd say something was fishy. The Mark Davidoffs of this world do not lose young, healthy viral pneumonia patients in private houses."

"So what happened, Murray?"

"Hey, you're the investigator. I'm just passing it on. But I'd like to cut that lady up."

"I bet. Okay, Murray, thanks for the tip. I'll look into it and let you know."

Karp hung up and turned back to his meeting, focusing his gaze on a nervous young man standing at the foot of the long table whose head was occupied by Karp himself.

"Okay, Gerry," said Karp, "take it from the witnesses again."

Gerald Nolan, the young man, resumed his explanation of the evidence in a homicide case called *People* v. *Morella*, one of the thousand or so ordinary killings that ran through the New York County D.A.'s homicide bureau in the course of an ordinary year. This particular one was: felon gets out of prison, finds his wife shacked up with another man, kills both. That was the People's story. The defendant Morella's was different, hence the forthcoming trial. The purpose of the exercise, and of the withering criticism that Karp and his senior assistant D.A.'s would shortly apply to the young man's case, was to bring home to the people in the room, and the criminal justice system, and to the city at large, that murder was never ordinary, that it retained its unique status among crimes.

Watching the young man do his spiel, Karp reflected, not for the first time, on the peculiar historicism of the scene. Fourteen years ago, more or less, the infant Karp had been standing down at the end of this very table, presenting his first homicide case to a group of men (men only then, of course) who were accounted the best criminal prosecutors in the nation, and the current D.A., Jack Keegan, had been sitting in the chair, the actual chair, that Karp now occupied as head of the Homicide Bureau. One of Keegan's first acts on assuming the position on a gubernatorial appointment had been to track down the chair and the table. The office was the same old bureau office too, a much better office than Karp had occupied the last time he had run the Homicide Bureau. Keegan wanted to send a message too about the unique status of homicide and that a new day had dawned at the D.A.'s, or rather a reprise of the old days, when the legendary Francis P. Garrahy had reigned as district attorney.

This public presentation of homicide cases had been part of the tradition then, and Karp was trying to reestablish it in all its brutal splendor. He looked down the row of faces to see how they were reacting to the young man's presentation. Doubtful but still polite expressions adorned most of the faces. A rather more various bunch of faces nowadays, of course. When Karp had started in the late sixties, the bureau had been staffed with the gentlemen who had started in the Depression, when a steady job at the D.A. had been among the best places a young Jewish or Irish lawyer out of Fordham or N.Y.U. could find. Under Tom Dewey and Garrahy they had faced down and broken Murder Incorporated, and challenged the Mob, when the Mob ran New York. These old bulls had all left when Garrahy died, left or been driven off by his successor, the exiguous and unlamented Sanford Bloom. Karp thought that this Nolan kid was lucky not to have been up there back then; by this time the old bulls would have been hooting and throwing balled-up papers at him.

Karp still had a couple of people on his staff who remembered the golden age. Ray Guma, sitting just to his left, was one of them; Roland Hrcany, Karp's deputy bureau chief, sitting halfway down the table, was another. Most of the other A.D.A.'s were young, eager, bright, and, in Karp's opinion, almost completely unprepared to try homicide cases. Training had not been a big priority of the previous management; for that matter, neither had homicide trials. This was changing, but slowly, painfully, and in the nature of things, it was these people who were going to bear most of the pain. Fortunately, Karp had a willing sadist in Roland, whose current twitchings, subvocalized profanities, and nostril flarings informed Karp that the bomb was about to go off.

Roland Hrcany brought his massive knuckles down on the table twice, like the crack of doom. Hrcany had the physique and mien of a television wrestler, with white-blond hair worn long to the collar and a face like a slab of raw steak. Nolan froze in midsentence.

"Ah, Gerry," said Roland, "this Mrs. Rodriguez, the neighbor, seems to be your chief witness. In fact, she's your only decent witness, am I right?"

"There's Fuentes," offered Nolan.

"Oh, *fuck* Fuentes!" snarled Roland. "Fuentes is the vic's sister. Morella used to beat the shit out of the wife before he went upstate. Fuentes'd say he was Hitler. No witness. So, you going to trial with Rodriguez, Gerry? Is that what you're telling us? With no gun? Where's the fucking gun, Jerry?"

"He had a gun," said Nolan. "We had a witness who saw him with it . . ." He started leafing frantically through his papers, seeking the name of the witness who had seen the D. with a gun.

"Hey, he had a gun? Nolan, *I* had a gun once too. Maybe *I* killed Carmen Morella and what's-his-face, the boyfriend, Claudio Bona," said Roland. "Anyway, what's Ms. Rodriguez's story? Did she get along with Carmen okay? Did she ever fuck Claudio? Did she ever fuck Morella? What about her kids? They selling any dope up there on East 119th Street?"

Guma said, "Yo, and I hear old Claudio was pretty tight with the Colombians." Everyone looked at him. Guma had a reputation as a man from whom organized crime in the City held no secrets. Nolan's face was blotched red where it was not cheese-like.

"I . . . um, there was no evidence of drug, um, involvement," he stammered.

"No evidence?" said Roland. "Did you check? Did you check with Narco? With Organized Crime? No, you didn't. You don't know shit about Mrs. Rodriguez either, just her statement. You know what you got? You're on your knees saying, 'Believe the Rodriguez woman and not the D.'s witness, the cousin, Morella's cousin, who says he wasn't anywhere near the place when the shooting went down.' "

"There's the forensics. He was there."

Roland hooted. "The forensics! My sweet white ass, the forensics! Schmuck! It was his *apartment* before he went upstate. The vic was his *wife*! *Of course* there're fucking prints and fibers. There's going to be his prints and fiber on her *snatch*! No, look: let me tell you what you did, sonny. You didn't build a case with your own hands. You just bought what the cops dragged in, and what the cops did was they caught this case, a couple uptown spics get whacked, no biggie, they check out the husband did time, got a violent sheet on him, and case closed. Well, fuck them, that's their *job*. *Your* job, which you didn't do, was to construct a case that would stand the test of no reasonable doubt. What we got instead is something any little pisher in Legal Aid with two weeks' experience could drive a tank through."

And more of the same, with Guma joining in, and a couple of the more confident of the group picking like vultures on the bones of the case. Nolan grew paler and quieter; he stopped making objections, and scribbled notes, nodding like a mechanical toy. Karp ended his misery by suggesting that he needed some more time to prepare, and after that the meeting dissolved. Everyone filed out with unusual rapidity, as if fleeing one afflicted with a purulent disease. Nolan was silently gathering up his papers when Karp said, "Gerry, the reason why we do this is that we figure it's better you get it here than in court, in front of a judge."

Nolan looked up, his lips tight, his chest heaving with suppressed rage. "I got twenty-eight convictions," he said. "I don't like being treated like a kid out of law school."

Karp had heard this before. "It doesn't matter what you did in Felony, Gerry. This is the Show, the majors. It doesn't matter you could hit the Triple-A fastballs. Homicide is different, which is the point of all this."

"Morella did it."

"I'm sure," said Karp. "But like I've said, more than once, it's irrelevant that he did it. The only question is, Do you have a case of the quality necessary to convict? And you don't. So get one and come back with it."

Nolan gave him a bleak look, stuck his file folders under his arm, and walked out.

Karp was sure that Nolan would be back, and with a better case too, because Karp had picked him as being the kind of skinny Irishman who never gives up. Nolan was an athlete. He had been a J.V. quarterback at Fordham, although someone as small as Nolan should never have gone anywhere near a football field. In fact, all the people Karp hired were athletes of one kind or another. It was a tradition. Roland was a wrestler and running back. Guma was a shortstop who, before he got fat, had been offered a tryout with the Yankees. Karp himself was a high-school All-American and a PAC-10 star before an injury to his knee ended his career. The other twenty-two attorneys on Karp's staff included enough football and basketball and baseball players to field complete teams, and good teams, in each of those sports. The three women on the staff included a UConn power forward, a sprinter, and an AAU champion diver. The one wheelchair guy played basketball. A jock sort of place, the Homicide Bureau; Karp believed, on some evidence, that no one who did not have the murderously competitive instincts of a serious athlete could handle the rigors of homicide prosecution, or the sort of coaching delivered by people like Roland Hrcany. The sports credential impressed the cops too, which didn't hurt.

The phone rang. Karp picked up, listened for a moment, said, "I'll be by in a minute," and hung up. He stood, and from long habit tested his left knee before he allowed it to take weight. It would undoubtedly hold, being made of stainless steel and other stuff he did not particularly want to think about. Karp was six feet five, with long legs and very long arms, and the ends of which were wide, spider-fingered hands. His face was wide too, and bony, with high cheekbones and a nose lumpy from more than one break. He still had his hair at thirty-seven, and he kept it shorter than was fashionable then, at the start of the eighties. The two surprising features were the mouth, which was mobile and sensual, and the eyes, which had a nearly oriental cast and which were gray with gold flecks: hard eyes to meet in a stare, hard eyes to lie into. Karp walked out of his office, told his secretary where he was going, and (a daily masochism) took the stairs two flights up to the eighth floor, where the D.A. had his office.

The man behind the D.A.'s desk was an older version of the sort of man Karp was, although of the Irish rather than the Jewish model. Jack Keegan's skin was bright pink rather than sallow like Karp's, and his hair was thinner and silver. The eyes were blue, but they had the same expression: bullshit me, laddie, at your extreme peril.

Without preamble, when Karp walked into his office, Jack Keegan roared, "Rohbling, Rohbling, Rohbling, bless his tiny evil heart!"

Karp came in and sat in a leather chair across from his boss's desk. The furniture was as close a match as possible to the decrepit City-issued suites favored by the late Garrahy, and as far as possible in style from the slick modern stuff with which the awful Bloom had surrounded himself. "What now?" Karp asked.

"Ah, nothing, I just wanted to blow steam at someone," said Keegan. "Political crap. I just received a call from our esteemed Manhattan borough president, a credit to his race, as we used to say, who informed me that he would take it very much amiss if we agreed to a change of venue."

"And you informed him . . ."

"I informed him, politely, that we had just nailed the little shit and his lawyer had not yet asked for one, but if he did there was no way we would go for it; nor was there a conceivable reason for any judge to grant it, this being New fucking York, and if you couldn't pick a fair jury from that pool, good night, Irene."

"This is the race thing."

"This is. The black community is concerned. They see this nice rich white boy from the North Shore with a funny hobby that involves killing elderly black ladies. It makes them irate. They're worried about what the esteemed gentleman called 'legal tomfoolery.' They want this guy dangling from a lamp post, and failing that, they want his white butt upstate forever." Keegan took a Bering cigar from his desk drawer, pulled it from its silver tube, and stuck it in his mouth, unlit. "So. Anything new?"

"Not much," said Karp. "We ordered a psychiatric evaluation and Bellevue says he's competent. Grand jury should start next week sometime. I think we want to expedite this—"

"No joke. Red ball on this one."

"Okay, it's the beginning of November. Five counts of murder are going to take some time to present, so let's say we arraign on the indictment before the end of the month, and then motions— say forty-five days?"

"Say ninety days, if you're lucky. This is Lionel Waley you got here on defense, the Duke of Delay."

"Okay, that rolls us well into next year. So we'll figure jury selection to start up in March."

"Yeah, that'll be a delightful experience too. It took a full month to select a jury for Bobby Seale. Count on at least that. Roland is going to do it, I presume. The actual trial."

Karp had been waiting for this. He met Keegan's gaze and answered, "No. I'm going to take it."

Keegan's eyes narrowed, and they stared at each other for an unlikely length of time. Then Keegan pursed his lips and examined the pale green wrapper of his cigar. He said, "You know, Butch, when I got to be D.A., I fondly imagined that my subordinates would do what I told them to do. I was mistaken, although I recall that when Phil Garrahy was in this chair, we all tried to do pretty much what he told us. Now, I think I've mentioned a time or two that as a bureau chief you can't take trials—"

"You used to take trials."

"May I finish? Thank you. And especially you can't take a horrendous long trial like Rohbling is going to be, and rebuild the Homicide Bureau, and run it, and keep on top of everything else you have to do. And have a life. You've got three kids."

"You had four kids and you did it."

Keegan's face dropped a shade into the red zone. "Yes, damn it, back in the sixties, when we had half as many homicides, and a dozen men in the bureau with twenty, twenty-five years' experience, who didn't need their noses wiped like your people do, and, frankly, before Warren and the Supremes got into the act, when we could do things to move cases through that we can't do now. There's no comparison." He held up a meaty hand to check the expostulation he could see forming on Karp's face. "Look, there's no point in discussing it. I think I've made myself clear on this. On the other hand, you're the bureau chief; I don't intend to second-guess you. But here's something to think about: if this case goes sour, there will be a shit storm of uncontrollable fury directed at both you and me. I have to face an election in a year's time in a city where nearly half the electorate is non-white. So all the things we're trying to do to bring this office back from perdition will be at risk. You need to understand that aspect."

"I do," said Karp. "I can handle it."

Keegan replaced the cigar in his mouth and stared at Karp down its length, as along a gun barrel. "You ever go up against Lionel T. Waley?" he asked.

"No. You?"

"I did. In 1963. This is before he became the nation's greatest criminal lawyer, as I believe he actually calls himself."

"Is he?"

Keegan grinned. "Well, he wins a lot of cases. He's up there with Lee Bailey and Nizer. You know what they say: if you can't get Bailey, get Waley. Of course, Lionel says it's the other way around."

"Did you win?"

"I did not. He whipped my young ass. This was the Sutton case, a classic society killing. Is that a blank look? Babs Sutton, department store heiress? No? How soon they forget. Jesus, that whole world is gone. Café society, so called. In any case, Babs, or as the society columns used to say, the Princess Radetsky, was married to this playboy, Prince Ladislas Radetsky, and of course the prince continued to play, and Babs found him in their suite at the Waldorf, on top of a sixteen-year-old whore. She took out, if you can believe it, her pearl-handled .32 and gave him five through the chest."

"She *walked* on this?"

"Oh, yeah. Waley gave them the defending the sanctity of the home horseshit. Driven to madness by the violation of the nuptial bed was how he put it. Had a jury full of decent Catholic women too, and he dressed the defendant like an understudy for the Little Flower. Oh, it was rare! My mistake was thinking that the facts spoke for themselves. Wrong, at least with Waley. You're sure you don't want to think it over?" He shot Karp another gunsight look over the cigar.

"No, and this is going to be a team thing too. I don't intend to do it all myself."

"Oh, well, *that's* a relief," said Keegan and laughed. "Jesus! Well, I knew you were a stubborn Jew son of a bitch when I hired you. I have only myself to blame. What I should do is call Marlene and get her to bang on your head. How is she, by the way?"

"Fine, I guess. We tend to pass in the night."

"I presume she's still . . . you know." He made a shooting gesture with his hand.

"Uh-huh. Apparently the business is flourishing."

Keegan shook his head. "What a world! And her a mother with three children!"

"What can I say, Jack? It's important to her. I'm married to her. I love her. Case closed."

"Well, yes," said Keegan. "I didn't mean to pry. Except, if there's any mercy left in the world, the next time she shoots someone, it'll be in Brooklyn. Outside the fucking County of New York."

"It's my daily prayer," said Karp.

TWO

Marlene Ciampi, wife of Karp, was at that moment standing in a shop in Chinatown buying a dozen pork kidneys for her dog, with any thoughts of shooting, in Manhattan or elsewhere, far from her mind. The dog, a Neapolitan mastiff only somewhat smaller than a Shetland pony, was outside on the sidewalk, slavering. Marlene's daughter, Lucy, aged eight, was wandering through the rear of the store, where the butcher shop faded into a dusty sundries emporium. Marlene watched the counterman wrap her dog food, feeling, as ever, the pang of guilt that came from purchasing for this purpose meat meant for Chinese humans. And she knew the counterman knew it, although the hostile glare with which he greeted her was no different from the same expression worn by nearly all of the merchants in the little Mott Street shops when they had to deal with the *guai lo*, the white ghosts.

"Can I have this, Ma?"

Her daughter was holding up a bag of dried lichees wrapped in the peculiar stiff cellophane, never seen anywhere else, that was used to package much of what was sold in Chinatown. Marlene assented to the treat, paid the surly cashier, and they left the shop. As they did so, there was a burst of nasty laughter from a group of young men loitering outside. Leaning against the wall and sitting on plastic milk crates, they were the type of young men often to be seen lounging in Chinatown, almost always dressed in black, their trousers loose and pleated, and silky, their hair worn long and artfully swept back, the fingernails on their little fingers at least an inch long. They were laughing because they were discussing, in Cantonese, the sexual uses to which Marlene might be put. While Marlene was untying Sweety, the mastiff, from a sign pole, Lucy turned to the young men and said, calmly and without heat, in reasonably fluent Cantonese, "Dead things! Impotent turtles! Your grandfathers disown you."

After a moment of stunned silence the young men howled in rage and came off the wall and up from the milk crates. Lucy stood by Marlene and stuck her tongue out at them. Two elderly women passing in the street, who had heard the exchange, giggled and hid their mouths with their hands.

"What's going on, Lucy?" asked her mother, giving the young men the eye.

"Oh, nothing, Mom, we were just talking," said Lucy, with the confidence of one who has a 220-pound attack-trained dog standing by as well as a literal pistol-packing mom.

The Chinese youths mumbled and glowered and pretended nothing had happened, like embarrassed cats. Lucy and Marlene moved on, Lucy cracking lichees and sucking on the intense sweetness of the fruit, and the slick, heavy seed within, crunching the fragile shells into fine sandy grains and scattering them as she walked. It was the best hour of her day, the only time she had her mother to herself, as in the blessed past, before the advent of Them. Lucy went to P.S. 1, where the Chinatown kids went, along with a handful of gringo children from SoHo, whose parents liked the idea of their offspring inhaling solid Confucian values with their lessons. The advantage of being able to speak with her friends a language that her mother did not understand had early appealed to her, and, discovering in herself a remarkable gift for tongues, she had avidly learned Cantonese from her little gang of bilingual schoolmates.

They were walking north on Mott, toward Canal.

"Are we going to Tranh's now?" Lucy asked.

"Uh-huh. What was all that back there, Lucy? With those punks?"

"They're gangsters, Mom."

"I know, honey, that's why you shouldn't talk to them."

"They were talking bad about you. Sex stuff."

"Yeah, I figured. Nevertheless . . ."

"If they give us any heat, you could shoot them."

"*You* shoot them, Luce. I'm through with shooting people," said Marlene, and changed the subject to the events of the past school day.

Chatting amiably, they came out onto Canal. Here Chinatown had flowed past its historic barriers, pushed by the new immigration attendant upon the partial collapse of the Bamboo Curtain and the oriental misadventures of the American government. Much of this immigration was not, strictly speaking, Chinese, for it included Thais, Filipinos, and Vietnamese, of which Tranh, of the eponymous noodle shop, was one. It was a tiny, narrow place, with steamed windows, rich garlicky smells, a counter and four shaky tables.

"Oh, here you are," said Tranh from behind the Formica barrier, when Lucy ran in. "Usual?" asked Tranh.

They agreed that it would be. Marlene had been bringing Lucy here for her after-school *goûter*, as they used to call it at Sacred Heart, for a little over a year, or just after the twins had arrived and Marlene had thought her daughter in need of a special daily treat. The place was nearly always empty at this hour, and unlike many of the proprietors of hole-in-the-wall Asian joints, Tranh did not treat them like lepers. He was grave, correct, and polite, although his English seemed limited to the two phrases he had just used plus "everything okay?", "thank you," and "good-bye."

Marlene liked the place because it wasn't cheeseburgers, because Lucy liked it, and because Tranh, through some odd telepathy had, on her first visit, while she watched Lucy gobble hot noodles with bits of pork and onion, placed before her a huge cup of the sort of milky, hot, very powerful coffee that Parisians call a *grande crème*. It was such an unlikely gesture from an oriental man on Canal Street that Marlene, stupefied, had simply thanked him and drunk the coffee gratefully. He had done the same on each subsequent visit, no comment passing between them beyond polite thanks on her part, a stiff little bow on his.

Tranh was thus one of her small urban secrets: an odd bird entirely. She reckoned he was in his late forties, although he could have been anywhere from thirty-five to sixty. His face was lean and hard looking, with a long, pensive upper lip and tufted black brows, topped by the typical, dreadful, Asian-guy haircut—nothing on the sides and a black crest above, like Woody the Woodpecker. His face's chief distinguishing mark was a circular indentation at the temple, as if someone had tried to shove the butt of a pool cue through his skull. His arms were thin and sinewy, finished by long-fingered, nicotine-stained hands badly scarred across their backs. His motions at the stove were crisp and economical. He smoked constantly, unfiltered Pall Malls, and read dusty-looking Vietnamese newspapers when business was slow.

The woman, Tranh thought, looked worried today. Usually she took one cigarette with her coffee, but now she had smoked two already, and the girl was barely half through with the noodles. Perhaps he should offer her another coffee. No, it was best to leave everything the same. He was well practiced in looking at things out the corner of his eye while pretending to read a newspaper. She was not like the other American women who occasionally came in to pick up a coffee or a take-out meal. She reminded him more of the women he had known in Paris before the war, the intense, shiny girls interested in politics or literature. One girl in particular—he could not recall her name, but she had that small grace, finely boned but strong, the dark curly hair, the ivory skin, still smooth, although she was no longer in the first flush of youth. Not a woman who had gone down the ordinary paths. She had only one eye too; the right one was glass. He had noticed that the first day. Also the left hand was missing fingers. Tranh was something of a connoisseur of mutilations. It could have been an auto accident, of course, but he suspected something rather more interesting had happened to her. And she carried a gun, a small automatic tucked in a plain nylon holster on her belt, on the left side, although she was right-handed. He had spotted that the first day too, although she always wore some sort of jacket to conceal it. There were, of course, many police in the neighborhood, because of the nearness of the courts and police headquarters, but he very much doubted that she was a police officer. He had a lot of experience spotting those too. In memory of Paris, he had made her the first *grande crème*. And she had accepted it with grace, and had not tried to use the offering as an occasion to chatter, for which he was in turn grateful. He would have liked to converse with her. He could not remember the last time he had spoken at any length to a woman. But he was stupid in English, and he would not have wanted to be stupid to this woman.

And there was the girl too, clearly her mother's daughter, the same delicate bone structure, the heart-shaped face, the black curls. The eyes were from the father, obviously, gray with lighter flecks. Sometimes when he looked at her, just a covert glance as she ate, he felt the ache of loss so strongly that his knees wobbled and he had to look away and concentrate on his breathing. He left the counter and walked over to their table, smiling.

"Everything okay?"

Their eyes met his, three smiling eyes and one glass one. Everything was okay. It was the peak of his day.

Karp's habit, when getting ready to leave work, was to hunt through the several yellow pads he had used during the day, and empty his pockets and wallet of the rags of paper he had used to jot down things that must not be forgotten. These he interpreted and converted into a Dictaphone tape containing instructions to his people and memos to the administrative powers, which tape he would hand to Connie Trask, the Secretary of Steel, with the confident expectation that she would cause the paper to fly in the right directions, and see that all was done that ought to be done. The junior attorneys were more afraid of Trask than they were of Karp, which was as it should be.

Karp dictated a memo holding off the trial in *Morella* until young Nolan had a chance to correct his errors, and was about to turn the page when his eye was caught by some notes that did not seem to fit the case at hand:

Selig/Longren/nurse/28/pneum./?? Davidoff doc/poss. hom./Fulton

He rubbed his face. The details were what got you, the necessity of keeping hundreds of names and dates in your head, the details of a dozen ongoing trials and a hundred or so active homicide cases, so that when someone came up to you on the fly and asked, "Hey, on the Ishkabibble case, should we do A or B?" you could give him a sensible answer. Karp knew himself well enough to understand that he had no natural talent for administration and required expert help to prevent the bureau from collapsing into chaos. In this, at least, he was superior to most of the world's bureaucrats.

The meaning of the cryptic message burst into his mind. Just as quickly he got rid of it. He clicked the button. "Connie, remind me to call Clay Fulton tomorrow and get him on a possible homicide. The deceased is named L-O-N-G-R-E-N. Murray Selig has the details, so send someone over there and get his file on it."

On to other items, most of which were covered by a "so-and-so is bugging me about X; take care of it!" and, done at last with the agony of command, Karp slipped the belt out of the machine, got into his coat, gathered his evening's reading, and went out. The outer office was deserted, except for Trask, who looked meaningfully at the clock.

"Sorry, Connie," said Karp, dropping the Dictaphone record on her desk.

"Some of us got a life," she remarked.

"Busy day, Connie, what can I say?"

"Not a thing. I hear you're going to do Rohbling yourself."

"Yeah, I am. You going to give me heat about it too?"

Trask put a phony big-toothed smile on her shiny brown face. "Gosh, no, boss, I'm just a dumb secretary, just like you're Superman. I'll sing 'Amazing Grace' at your funeral."

"I can handle it. I did it before."

"Uh-huh. And we were both a lot younger then. Meanwhile, you got a date with your wife five minutes ago. Speaking of funerals."

"Ah, shit!" cried Karp, and dashed out of the office.

"And a pleasant evening to you too," said Connie Trask to the slamming door.

The offices of Bello & Ciampi Security occupied the second floor of a loft building on Walker Street off Broadway. When Karp arrived there after the ten-minute walk from the Criminals Courts building (which had taken him seven and a half minutes), the office was closed. A sign on the white-painted steel door indicated what the office hours were and gave an emergency telephone to call after hours. In fact, the office never closed. Karp knocked on the door. No answer. He pounded, feeling the familiar irritation, attempting to suppress it.

"We're closed. Call the number," shouted a voice.

"It's me. Open up!"

The door opened a crack. A thin, foxy-faced, brown-skinned girl with a frizzy crew cut regarded him unsympathetically. She was wearing a black jumpsuit adorned with a remarkable number of zippers and pull rings. Seeing that it was her boss's husband, she stood aside and Karp entered the reception area, a small white room containing two vinyl couches, a table, a magazine rack, with neatly stacked magazines in it, a lamp, several well-tended potted plants, and a desk. On one wall hung framed movie posters, all featuring women in trouble: the original *King Kong*, *Sorry, Wrong Number*, *Psycho*. The other wall held Marlene's Yale Law School diploma, the private investigator licenses of Marlene and her partner, Harry Bello, and several laminated newspaper and magazine stories featuring Marlene's excursions into public violence.

"How's it going, Sym?" Karp said. Sym the receptionist, one of Marlene's foundlings. Karp always thought of her as the Rejectionist.

The girl scowled and mumbled something, and went behind

her desk, leaning over to press a button. A buzzer sounded and a door on the room's opposite side clicked.

Karp went through it and entered a large, high-ceilinged room nearly forty feet long. Light came in from a single huge arch-topped window to the right, opening on Walker Street. The office furniture was Canal Street Moderne, wooden stuff from the fifties, scarred but serviceable. The floors were wide, polished oak planks, covered in the center by a threadbare, but good, red oriental rug. In the center of that sprawled Karp's daughter.

"Hi, Daddy," she said when she saw him. She was surrounded by school books and notepaper.

"Hello, Luce," said Karp. This was their new grown-up relationship. Only a year or so before, Lucy would have greeted Karp's return home with a yell of joy, a dash, and a leap into his arms. He had still not become used to this ever underestimated tragedy of fatherhood.

"How was school?"

"Boring. I have a million math problems. Mrs. Lawrence sucks."

"I'd keep that opinion under your hat, if I were you. And keep that kind of language to yourself. Where's Mom?"

Lucy motioned with her head to the rear. "Back in the playroom, with Posie. And Them."

Karp placed his briefcase on Harry Bello's vacant desk and walked past Lucy to the right rear corner of the office. The partners had done a good deal of work on the loft since the birth of the twins last year. Despite himself, Karp had to admit it had been neatly done. Marlene had a little semi-private office behind a partition in the corner. There was a full bathroom next to that, and they had drawn a drywall wall across the full width of the loft, behind which were found a playroom-nursery, a small kitchen, and a sort of dormitory partitioned into a half dozen tiny private rooms supplied with junk shop beds and other necessary furniture, repaired and shiny with bright new paint. Sym, the receptionist and general factotum, slept there, as did Posie the nursemaid, and the occasional "guests," who were generally women on the run and their kids. It was all illegal as hell, which only added to Karp's low-level irritation.

Karp went through the door to the nursery. Marlene and Posie were lying on the bright shag rug that occupied the center of the room with Lucy's Them, the twin boys, constructing towers out of large, colorful foam blocks. The great black dog snored in a corner.

"Can I play too?" asked Karp.

"Cancel the 911, he's here," said Marlene, standing and giving her husband a peck.

"Hi, Butch!" said Posie, flashing at him her usual gapped-toothed idiot grin.

"Dah," said Isaac, lifting up his arms. Karp stooped and picked up the baby, enjoying the solid heft and talcumy smell.

"How about you?" This question was directed to the other twin, whose name was Giancarlo, but who was called Zik, to go with Zak, the nickname of his two-minutes-older sibling. Karp thought the dual nicknames excessively cute, but could hardly object since he had himself started the practice of calling the twins, during that early period when they had been indistinguishable larvae, such things as Mutt and Jeff, Hekyl and Jekyl, Abbott and Costello. They were plenty distinguishable now. Zik looked up at his father and then away, and carefully placed a block on top of a tower. Somewhat cool and methodical was Zik, at one year. Karp knelt and put Zak down, emotional and aggressive Zak, who promptly knocked over Zik's tower. Wails.

"That sounds like my cue, dear," said Marlene brightly. "Posie?"

Posie laughed and gathered the two infants to her mighty breasts, jiggling them, rocking them, crooning to them, until they calmed down. She was a seventeen-year-old from rural Pennsylvania with a disturbing chemical and sexual history and a remarkable touch for infant care. Marlene had rescued her from life on the street and a particularly violent boyfriend.

"Hey, have a good time, you guys," said Posie, her rubbery face grinning, as they slipped from the nursery. They had still to escape from Lucy.

Who whined, "Why can't I come?"

"Honey, you know we all go out together on Saturday. Your daddy and I need some time for just us. Posie is going to order pizza for all of you. We'll be home early. Did you finish your math?"

In answer Lucy sent her pencil skittering across the oak floor, and assembled on her face an expression of hollow-eyed despair suitable to a refugee from the Nazis. This expression touched Karp's heart, as it was designed to do, but he knew better than to suggest that just this once the three of them might go out, as they often had before the twins came. Marlene would not have stood for it.

She said severely, "Pick up that pencil and finish your work! I want to look it over before school tomorrow."

Lucy snarled something sotto voce that Marlene chose not to hear, and the two adults left the office.

"That child!" said Marlene when they were out in the street. "I swear, sometimes I want to throttle her. She was terrific this afternoon when we took our walk, and as soon as she got back to the office, she turned into a spoiled brat. She is *not* doing well in school either."

"Marlene, it's third grade," said Karp. "Give her a break. She'll still get into Smith."

"She won't get into *fourth grade* if she keeps on the way she's going. You don't get the notes from her teacher. She's acting out, as they say."

"The twins."

"I can't think of anything else," Marlene said. "It's too early for puberty."

"I'll try to spend more time with her."

"That'd help. Poor little kid! Here she is, doted on by two parents, and bango, all of a sudden she's an extra. We didn't figure two babies would take so much energy."

No, we did not, thought Karp as they walked slowly up Broadway. Nor did we calculate that one of us would be starting a heavy new job while the other of us would be up to her neck in a business that required night work, weekend work, and continual crisis. Guns in the house. Karp made a mental effort to stop this line of thought, which he knew from experience led to irritability, argument, and pain. As Marlene never tired of saying, he knew what she was before he married her. True enough, as far as it went. He had married a graduate of Smith and Yale Law, a rising prosecutor. He had long ceased to pine consciously for what still dwelt deep within his reptile brain, of a house in a leafy suburb, or a condo in a good building, himself coming home, she being there, wooden spoon in hand, smiles, the children taken care of, displayed for the paternal cuddle. No, Marlene was going to have a career, which was fine, but Karp had counted on a woman with Marlene's talent pursuing something more regular, at the D.A.'s, or a slot at some big firm, or even teaching at a law school. Marlene was smart; she could write; her intelligence was wide-ranging. A short fantasy played out on the video of his mind: Marlene teaching at Columbia, regular hours, long summer vacations, tenure, a nice salary to add to his, a settled life in the upper bourgeoisie of Manhattan, the children in good schools, perhaps an au pair, an au pair from Sweden, to help with the kids, rather than a pudgy, not-too-clean street girl with no front teeth, a smaller dog . . .

"Are you listening?" said Marlene, breaking in on these thoughts, of which, to give him credit, Karp was slightly ashamed.

"Sorry," said Karp. "I was drifting. What did you say?"

"Oh, nothing," said Marlene. "Just bitching and moaning. I was saying Harry and I had a little argument today."

"What about?"

"He wants to move into regular security. Events, rent-a-cops. Like that." She laughed. "Good old Harry. Four years ago he was a drunk thinking about eating his gun; now he's talking business plans, cash flow."

"Maybe he's right."

"Oh, I'm sure he *is* right, technically. It's just not right for me. Why're you giving me that look? Hey: I went in to this business to deal with a social problem that nobody else was dealing with, and also make some money, and, to be frank, because I liked the work. The point of starting B and C was that there are men who fixate on women and won't let go, and stalk them and, most times, either hurt or kill them. Call me crazy, but I think there should be at least one business in town that exists to prevent that."

"There is, Marlene. It's called the cops."

Marlene rolled her eyes. "I can't believe we're having this discussion *again*. Of course the cops! Don't we work with the cops? With the courts? I spend a good chunk of my personal time getting orders of protection, and making sure these guys get stung when they violate. On the other hand, there're guys who're like guided missiles. It doesn't matter what you do to them; they're going to home in on the woman, and if the choice is between letting an innocent woman get killed and taking out the guy, I have no problem deciding which. Every citizen has a right to use deadly force to prevent death or serious injury to themselves or others."

"I already heard the commercial, Marlene."

She wrinkled her nose and shook her head, as if shaking out unpleasant thoughts. "Yeah, right, sorry. We're supposed to be relaxing tonight, I'm giving you the lecture. My point was, and I said it to Harry too, that we have a decent business doing what I like doing and what no one else does. We have enough celebrity clients to pay the freight for the poor ones—oh, did I tell you? Speaking of the rich and famous, we got a call from Trude Speyr today. Her agent, I mean. They want us to handle personal security."

"She's being stalked?"

"Isn't everyone? Apparently she's been getting weird letters since she won at Wimbledon this year. She'll be here for the circuit next spring, and of course she's going to go with the most famous name in feminist security, *moi-meme*." Marlene did a little mock curtsy. "We're talking major bucks here, by the way."

"I'm glad to hear it. Harry isn't objecting to the money, I take it."

"No. He has no problem guarding celebrities."

With this, Marlene left the conversation hanging. They had reached Grand Street. A short block up was their destination,

Paoletti's, a small dark restaurant that was, along with the Ferrara
Bakery and Umberto's Clam House, one of the few remnants of
the original Little Italy.

Freddy the owner, a remnant likewise, a man shaped like a
fine brown egg, got up from his stool behind the cigar counter
and came out and shook their hands formally. Marlene had been
eating at Paoletti's for nearly twenty years, first with her parents
and then as a regular since she had moved to her loft on Crosby
Street in 1971. Freddy led them to their table and stood there
chatting for a while. The subjects were always the same: weather
(getting nippy; hot enough for you?); children (Marlene's and
Freddy's own); family (ditto); and the decline of the neighborhood, attributable, in Freddy's opinion, to the two-pronged in-
vasion of weirdos (by which he meant the artists and the vastly
larger number of artoids that had colonized lower Manhattan
since the seventies) and of Those People, by which he meant the
masses formerly of Asia, whose outposts now flowed up Mulberry
and lapped at Grand Street itself. Freddy usually supplied an
anecdote about the latest weirdo who had tried to obtain service
in Paoletti's and been turned away. The Asians, of course, knew
better than to try. Paoletti's clientele therefore consisted exclusively of Italians, both real and honorary. The real Italians included the locals, and their descendants, like Marlene. Honorary
Italians included all police officers, of whatever eth, people
friendly with real Italians or police officers (a double score for
Karp), and those few in the neighborhood that Freddy identified
as regular people. Regular people did not wear vicious leather,
had hair of a length and color appropriate to their sex and species,
and, if wearing earrings, were women.

Freddy finished his routine, and told them what they were
going to eat that evening. No menus at Freddy's for regulars. He
went back to his guard post, and Millie, his daughter, brought
bread sticks and wine, the wine in an unlabeled bottle. Marlene
drank off a glass of the potent red and felt herself relax. She
looked around. Paoletti's was neither a cop hangout nor a mob
hangout, but a place where denizens of either subculture could
enjoy civilized dining. No one had ever been shot or arrested in

Paoletti's. This evening two gangsters were entertaining their families at the next table, and beyond that one, by the wall, a couple of senior cops from the nearby police headquarters were finishing a meal.

Her eyes returned to her own table, where she found her husband looking at her and smiling.

"Back on earth?" he asked.

She smiled back. "Yeah. I was a little wound."

"Like a cheap watch. You know, that's what Harry's getting at, Marlene. He doesn't give a rat's ass about money or business plans. He doesn't want you killing yourself. Or getting killed."

Marlene poured another glass of wine. "I'm okay," she said.

No, you're not, thought Karp. You're living the life of a cop without the social and legal underpinning that cops have. You're doing stuff that's barely within the compass of the law, and some things that I don't want to know about because they're frankly criminal, and I'm an officer of the court and I can't know about them and it's a darkness between us, and it's going to wreck us. This, and similar thoughts, were Karp's version of those speeches that people long married play out in their heads but do not say to the other, or say, and then the marriage collapses, or is put on a different and better footing. Karp was not ready to take the risk. What he ventured at this time was, "Your name came up today. Keegan asked about you. He wishes you not to shoot anyone in New York County."

"Tell him I try to keep my blood lust under control. How is he?"

"Flourishing. He likes being the D.A., and he's good at it. He thinks I'm working too hard, though."

"Are you?"

"I will be. I'm going to try Rohbling myself."

Marlene's wineglass paused halfway to her lips. Her eyes narrowed. "You have to be joking."

"No. No joke."

"*Why* are you doing this? A major trial? Now?"

"Because I think I'm the best person for the job," said Karp, conscious of the pomposity of the phrase, but too tired to think of another. Besides which, it was true. He went on, "It'll be a team effort, needless to say, but I want to run it."

"This is because of his lawyer, isn't it? What's-his-face—"

"Waley," said Karp. "No, it's not—"

"Yes, it is. It's yet another of your dick-measuring contests."

"That's nuts, Marlene. You know I'd always planned to take a couple of important cases a year. This is the one."

Millie placed an immense plate of antipasto on the table, smiled at them, heard their usual comments about the impossibility of consuming so much antipasto, and left. The interruption was timed just right. Marlene did not utter the vicious one-liner that had poised itself on her tongue's tip, but ate a stuffed mushroom, sighed deeply, and said, "I must be getting more mature. In former times, had you dropped one like that on me, darling, I would have accused you of planning this so as to put more pressure on me, knowing that I would pull time away from *my* work so that Lucy wouldn't go down the tubes, even though I seem to recall that *you* just volunteered to spend more time with her."

"Marlene, I—"

She stopped the attempt at rejoinder by holding up a hand in which flopped a round slice of provolone. "No, no, that's what I *would* have said, when I still thought life made sense. What I *am* saying is as follows. I intend to eat this marvelous meal, drugging my higher faculties with food. I intend to get mildly drunk as well, which I recommend to you also. I intend further to drag you up to our luxurious *SoHo* loft, where I will attempt to get my monthly or maybe it's my *quarterly* lay, after which I will recline in a hot, perfumed tub while *you*, my dear, get dressed and drive over to the office to get the kids."

"Sounds good," said Karp, deadpan. "What's the catch?"

THREE

Marlene's morning meditation: a thundering speed bag, her flying gloves maintaining the rhythm independent of her conscious mind, which floated in what the Zen people call *mushin*, a no-thought realm supposedly good for the soul. A final slam, and the squeaking rattle of the punching bag shackle as the bag precessed into stillness. She stripped off her speed gloves and picked up the rope and skipped fast, snapping hard, both feet, alternate feet, five minutes with the sweat flying off her forehead in the air and blackening her gray T-shirt under the arms. By the time she hung it up, she could hear the twins burbling to each other in the nursery next door, and she let herself drift back into real life.

Boxing training was no affectation for Marlene: her father had briefly been a welterweight contender in the forties and had taught all six of his children to box. Marlene was the only one of the three girls who had taken to it, and she had kept it up over the years. Not a Jazzercise girl, Marlene.

She stripped off her sodden shorts and T-shirt, pulled a ragged terrycloth robe over her bare skin, and went into the nursery next door. It had once been Lucy's playroom, another deeply felt injustice, but what could they do? The loft was large but not infinite, and Lucy was a little old now to need a separate playroom.

In the nursery she moved with dispatch. First, Zak out of the crib (because if she did Zik first, Zak would go crazy, whereas Zik would watch placidly as she tended Zak) and onto the changing table, crooning (Zak, did you sleep well? Yes, you did, yes, you *did*, didn't wake up screaming even one little time, what a good-looking beautiful baby, what a yucky monster ugly baby, yes, you *are*, and so on) whipping the sodden Pamper off and into the waiting plastic bag, quick check for diaper rash, a blown raspberry on the hot little belly, squeals of delight, wipe-off with pre-moistened towelettes, dust with baby powder, new Pamper out, swick-swick, strip off p.j.'s, toss into hamper, into baby T-shirt, back into crib. Next!

Identical twins, Marlene had always thought, were among the most interesting things that could happen to a family, fascinating for the parents, but often a disaster to any other children. Who could compete for attention with such a show? Looking down at Zik as she serviced him (but in a slightly different way, with a different patter than she had used with his brother), she was struck by how differently he had played out the same genetic cards Zak had been dealt. His eyes: the same lovely mahogany, completely different expression. Zak's eyes said, "Yumm-yumm! Gimme!" Zik's said, "What's *your* story?" Zak was violent motion, quick moods; Zik was a gentle prober, and placid. Now he was touching her lower lip as she taped his Pamper. Zak never did that; punch and slap, yes, but not this delicate palpation.

However, no time to dawdle in naughty maternal eroticism! One babe on each hip, she marched into the kitchen, punched up the lights and placed each boy in his own high chair. She could hear the roar of water from where her husband was up and taking his shower. Briefly, she considered slipping under the steaming spray with him, to renew the stolen passion of the night before, stolen, because the twins absolutely refused to allow them any sexual space. Since the evening they were brought home from the hospital, their subtle oedipal radar had detected even the most careful insinuation of moist organs, at which time both sirens would go off full blast, banishing romance and wakening Lucy. It was uncanny. On the other hand, on the occasions when they did manage a date, their sex had the furtive urgency of an illicit affair. Still reasonably good sex too, for a wonder, after nearly eleven years, Marlene thought, not like it was at first, when they had screwed themselves sore every night, but comfortable, pleasing, married, a checkpoint. (Is it still *you*? Yes, it's still *me*.)

The water stopped; too late, Marlene. In any case, as she well understood, there was no time for anything that might upset the precise and scientific scheduling of the Karp & Ciampi Every Morning Railroad. Two bottles filled and warmed in the microwave (oh, blessed technology!), stuck into two little gobs, and then it was time for Lucy's first wake-up kick.

"I'm not going to school today," said a faint voice from beneath the Italian-flag-colored quilt. "I'm sick."

"You are? Let me feel you."

"No, I'm too sick to have a fever. I'm past the fever part."

Marlene reached under the quilt and grabbed a skinny limb, which was warm but not abnormally so, and heaved.

"Ow! Child abuse!"

"It'll be assault one unless I hear water running and dressing noises in two minutes."

Marlene left her daughter's room and walked down the long main hallway of her loft, as always experiencing a thrill of satisfaction with her home. She'd lived here over a dozen years, starting back in the illegal days, and for most of that time the place had been a barely habitable former wire factory. Two years of the big bucks had changed that; Karp's career with a firm of downtown tortmeisters and a couple of immense wins had sufficed to convert the vast space into a civilized apartment with real walls and doors, central heating and A/C, Swedish-finish oak floors, two bathrooms, and a kitchen out of *Architectural Digest* with a Vulcan stove and a stainless steel reefer. The building had gone condo in the great SoHoization of lower Manhattan, and Marlene now owned the place outright. She intended never to leave.

She passed the kitchen in time to see her husband, in his lawyer blue suit trousers, shirt, and boring dark tie, putting on a yellow rubberized apron with PROP. BELLEVUE MORGUE stenciled on the bib. Zak flung his bottle at her and yelled some happy gibberish. She fielded it neatly, wiped the nipple on her robe, and replaced it in its wet, pink hole. Karp extended one of his long arms and snagged the opening of her robe.

"Excuse me," he said, "but I wonder if you've seen the woman who gave me that really incredibly great piece of ass last night."

"Oh, Estelle? She's with a customer," said Marlene as a remarkably long finger whipped out to tickle her crotch. She giggled and pulled away. Zak's bottle flew again, and this time Karp caught it on the fly, and settled down to feed his two sons a jar of baby food each, in precisely alternating spoonfuls.

Showering under the antique brass shower head, nearly the size of a dinner plate, Marlene let the water beat against her face and soaped her body with patchouli soap, allowing herself her usual private ninety seconds for illicit sensual thoughts, making a short list of the men she knew who might serve if the opportunity ever arose, and imagining what it would be—no, time's up. Off with the water, a quick dry, hair and face slapped together, then dressing in her court uniform: low-heeled boots, a tan calf-length full skirt with leather belt, a maroon silk blouse, a short, loose tweedy jacket. She plumped the pillows, threw a duvet over the marital bed, and left the boudoir, now in full high gear.

To Lucy's second wake-up, a brief screaming match, while Karp swabbed down the twins and dressed them in determinedly non-matching outfits. Whip some food into Lucy, make her bag lunch. Feed the dog, walk the dog, scoop the dog, run up the stairs with the dog.

Then, the last thing, while her family clumped down the stairs, a walk to the gun safe under the desk in the office that occupied the opposite end of the loft from the master bedroom, and the extraction and donning of her Colt Mustang Pocket-Lite pistol in its black nylon sheath. She clipped it to her belt, reversed, on the left side. Marlene had a horror of someone sneaking up behind her and yanking out the weapon, and preferred to cross-draw if need be. The Pocket-Lite is an alloy .380 semi-automatic pistol that weighs twelve and a half ounces, which in Marlene's opinion was twelve and a half ounces too much, but Harry Bello insisted that she go armed, given her habit of insisting to enraged men that they could no longer pound on their women. One last check in the mirror to make sure her fashionable silhouette was free of unsightly armament bulges, and then she clicked on the security system, told the dog to guard, and cleared the door, twenty-two minutes after her alarm had gone off.

Marlene's car, a bright yellow VW square-back of a certain age, was parked in a nearby alley. Her family was waiting around it as she approached, Karp carrying a kid on each hip, a briefcase dangling from a hooked finger, Lucy hunched and sullen. First a little peek at the telltale tiny magnets she'd left on the hood and all the doors, to make sure some naughty person had not left an explosive device. This done, they strapped the twins into their tiny astronaut seats, and Marlene said the little prayer she always said that the car would once again start. Answered. She drove Karp to the courthouse and Lucy to school, and then herself to Walker Street and work. She unbuckled the twins and hauled them out of the car, using the convenient handles of their carapace-like car seats. They were both snoozing, simultaneously for a wonder; they usually alternated naps, to make sure that nothing important escaped their joint eye. She staggered up the stairs to her office with one in each arm and her purse draped fetchingly around her neck, reflecting for the millionth time that rearing twins was not twice, but four times, as hard as rearing one child.

Marlene had now been up for over forty-five minutes without either coffee or a cigarette, and so it was with gratitude that she beheld the face of Sym, who ordinarily supplied her with the morning's first hit of both.

"Coffee's ready," said Sym when Marlene came in, which is what she always said, and pushed forward her pack of Marlboro Lights so that her boss could take one. In the office Marlene pretended not to have cigarettes of her own, as she had officially stopped smoking.

Marlene plopped the car seats on the floor and poured herself a mug of dripped Medaglia D'Oro, tarry black, drank a grateful dose, and lit up.

"You got messages," said Sym. "Tamara says she don't want to go to court today. And some lady want us to whack her old man."

Marlene laughed. "What, she just called up, like L.L. Bean, I want to order a hit, size XL? Did you get her VISA?"

"I told her we didn't do like that," said Sym primly. "Also this lady name Edith Wooten called again. I wrote it down."

Marlene took the message slip and looked closely at the girl. Sym tended to be morose, which many visitors interpreted as hostility, but today she looked as if she was holding something in, or rather, that she was holding in even more than you might expect to be held in by a girl raped at age twelve and turned out as a whore by her daddy.

"Anything wrong, Sym? He hasn't been bothering you again?"

"Nah. It ain't, it *isn't* me."

"Who, then? Posie?"

A tiny shrug, which would have to do in place of a deposition. It was Posie, but Sym was not going to rat her roommate out.

"Okay, Sym, I'll take care of it." Marlene picked up the twins and headed for the door, which buzzed and clicked. In a low voice, to the closing door, Sym said, "You look real nice today, Marlene." She was in love, something Marlene would never see and Sym would never reveal.

Marlene took the twins to the playroom and placed them on the rug. Posie came in from the kitchen, barefoot, in ragged jeans and an old sweatshirt of Marlene's. She beamed at Marlene and the twins.

"They're sleeping!" she said, as if it were a scientific discovery.

Marlene's answering smile was stiff. "Yes, lucky you. Look, Posie, we need to talk about you running men in here at night."

"Oh, no, Marlene, I wouldn't do that," replied Posie, lying with crystalline transparency.

"Yeah, you did. Look, kiddo, I don't mind what you do on your off time, which is nearly every night and most weekends.

Go ahead, knock yourself out, get laid, whatever. But not here. Who was it? Luke again?"

Posie had, as far as Marlene was able to observe, only two emotional states: beaming, all-encompassing love and mulish withdrawal. She now flicked into the latter. "Uh-huh, no," she replied, hanging her head so that her long, lank black hair partially hid her face.

"Posie, listen to me. Our job is to protect women from men who want to get at them, just like when Luke was pounding on you—we protected you, we gave you a job and a place to stay. You pick up guys on the street, they could be anybody. They could get into our records, copy keys, burn the place down. It's a breach of security."

Ah, a third state: confused alarm. "Aw, Marlene, Luke wouldn't do nothing like that!" Posie protested, and then blushed and stammered, "I mean—I mean, if he was here. Not that I saw him or anything."

"Posie, not only did you see him, but you smoked dope with him."

"Uh-*uh*!"

"Oh, for crying out loud, Posie, I can smell it on your clothes. No, just be quiet and listen to me. I told you, I don't care what you do on the outside, although I can't believe you're seeing that little shit again—"

"He was nice to me, Marlene. No kidding! He's really changed. He got a job and all—"

". . . that *little shit* again, unless you want to give him a shot at knocking the rest of your teeth out, but not here. Never again, Posie, I mean it! And no dope here either."

The twins started to wake, whining. Marlene walked out as Posie's pathetic excuses and apologies blended with their more appropriately infantile wails. She looked into Harry Bello's office and found him on the phone. Waving a greeting, she went into her own cubicle, took off her coat, sat down, lusted for another cigarette, regretted yelling at Posie, yearned for a child-care worker who was not a street person, felt guilty about this, briefly considered the alternatives (sullen third-world types, day-care centers with restrictive hours), dismissed these, thought about how marvelous Posie was ninety-nine percent of the time, sighed, and dialed the number Sym had written down.

The voice that answered was light and youthful sounding, decked with the long, multi-toned vowels favored by the New York upper crust and made famous by the late FDR and his Mrs. (Yea-es? How gooo-od of you to cah-all!)

Marlene inquired as to why Ms. Wooten required the services of a security firm.

"Well. As to that, Ms. Ciampi, I would rather not discuss it on the phone. But, briefly, I have been getting disturbing letters. And other tokens."

"This is someone you know?"

"No. It's, um, I suppose one could call him a fan."

"You're a performer?" asked Marlene, and then mentally kicked herself for not finding out who Edith Wooten was before calling. There was a pause on the line, and then the voice, which now was tinged with amusement.

"Yes, I am. Do you suppose you could visit me at my home. I have quite a busy schedule and—"

"No problem, Ms. Wooten," said Marlene quickly. She got an address on Park in the seventies and ended the call.

She immediately punched in a familiar number, one that, if answered, would connect her with the only person in her acquaintance who might conceivably know someone with that sort of voice at that sort of address.

"V.T.? Marlene."

"Hello, Marlene," said Vernon Talcott Newbury. "This is remarkable. I am abandoned by the Karp clan for weeks on end, and now I get calls from both of the principals in one day. I have a message from Butch. Is this about the same thing?"

"I doubt it, V.T. This is a private thing. I was wondering if you knew the name Edith Wooten."

A laugh. "You need to get out more, dear. This is the cultural capital of the world, you know."

"I know. I took Lucy to see *The Great Muppet Caper* just last week. Who is she?"

"Ah, well, where to begin? She's a Wooten, of course, of the Wooten Island Wootens. Only two privately owned islands in the Sound, the Gardiners have one and they have the other. Her mother's a Temple, of the Sag Harbor Temples. Her brother, who I think is named Rad or Had, went to Harvard with Foley Maynard, who—"

Marlene interrupted. V.T. could go on. "She's a friend of yours?"

"Not a friend, exactly. She went to Brearley with my cousin Sniff, though, I think for a couple of years, and then switched to Juilliard; she was probably about twelve or thirteen. You really don't know who she is?"

"A musician obviously. I doubt it's rock and roll."

"Quite. Well, I'm no expert, but Mother, who is on the Philharmonic board, says she's another Jacqueline Du Pré, potentially in a class with Rostropovich. I'm sorry, maybe those don't ring any bells either?"

"Don't be snide, V.T., I'm just a dumb guinea from Ozone Park. So she's a cellist, huh?"

"Yes. Why the interest?"

"Oh, just checking something. Anything else about her? She married?"

"No, but she's not more than, say, twenty-four. She's Ginnie Wooten's sister, of course."

"Of course. V.T., who the fuck is Ginnie Wooten?"

"You do need to get out more, Marlene. She was on *Life* once. The Avedon shot, buried in sand, tits sticking out, with the sweat?"

A vague memory tugged. Like most native working New Yorkers, Marlene did not pay much attention to the antics of celebrities, most of whom were out-of-towners who came to the City to get famous, got famous, and then disappeared like the dirty snow on its streets.

"That's it? She's a model?"

"Not quite. A professional naughty, Ginnie, like what's her name in the sixties—Edie Sedgwick. Screws artists and rock stars, a major supporter of the pharmaceutical industry, like that. So, my curiosity is boiling over. What's going on?"

"It will have to turn into steam, then, dear. Thanks a million for the info. I owe you a Coke."

Marlene put the phone down and went into Harry's office. "You still mad at me?"

Harry looked at her and shook his head, a millimetric negative. Harry Bello was fifty-seven going on ninety, a solid, cylindrical Italian-American man with a tan, wrinkled face like a grocery bag left out for a month in the sun and rain. His eyes, deeply socketed, were still, black, holding no hope, void of compassion. A hard case, Harry. He didn't drink anymore, but on the other hand, as far as Marlene knew, he had not done any of the Twelve Steps either. Harry had until recently been a detective with the N.Y.P.D. There are around four thousand of these, of whom somewhat over a hundred occupy the highest rank, detective first grade. Harry Bello had been one of them, elite of the elite, for which reason, when Harry's wife had contracted a particularly miserable form of cancer, and Harry had started to drink heavily, and been drunk when his partner of fifteen years had gone into a building alone on a routine canvass and been killed, and Harry had drunkenly hunted down and executed a kid who may or may not have been the murderer, the Department had pulled a cloak over the affair and assigned Harry to a meaningless job and waited for him to drink himself to death or eat his gun. At that point, however, Marlene had casually extended a hand, which Harry, for reasons Marlene had never quite understood, had gripped with a dead man's grip. Harry was Lucy's godfather, a role he took with sometimes frightening seriousness, as if this antique commitment represented his sole remaining link with the human community, a reason for not becoming in actuality what he often resembled around the eyes, a corpse. During the period when he had worked for Marlene at the D.A.'s Rape Bureau, they had called him the Doberman. Before that, when he was still a cop, he was known as Dead Harry.

Meanwhile, there was that remarkable brain at Marlene's disposal, and a protective will that, while focused mainly on Lucy, spread its penumbra also over the mother, in a way that often pinched, as now.

She said, "I don't see why we should change anything, Harry. Honestly, you worry too much. We're doing okay."

"Marlene, I went over this," said Harry in his tired voice. "Domestics are poison. Either you got some guys want to whack out their women decide to punch your ticket while they're at it, or you keep on trying to reason with the same kind of guys, and things heat up, and you whack *them* out, which puts you up in Bedford on a felony."

"None of that has happened, Harry."

"You don't have cancer either, but I notice you're trying to quit smoking. I'm thinking of the kid here, Marlene. Leave that kind of shit to the cops, is what I'm saying. That's what they get paid for."

"God, between you and my husband!" Marlene cried. "Okay, you want out? You're getting nervous in your old age? Good! I'll work it by myself."

Harry held up a mollifying hand. "Marlene, I didn't say that. Look, this is getting to be a broken record. I got no problem with the protection program. Tennis players, the loonies and the celebrities, fine, okay. The others, help with protection orders, moving them into apartments, the shelters. You want to keep doing that, we can handle it. It's a business. But . . ." Here he paused.

"But, *what*, Harry?"

"No more setups. That's out. And no more Polaroids on the assholes."

Marlene took a deep breath. Another. "Okay, fine, Harry, you made your point. I won't involve you."

Harry stared at her for a moment and then nodded once. He *had* made his point, and Marlene would do what she was going to do. She might keep doing setups, which was where she used a stalked woman as bait and when the stalker came after her, armed, performed the justifiable homicide, which was the only way to make sure some (admittedly, a small fraction) of men engaged in this activity would never do it again. Or she might still get some other people she knew to pay visits to guys who pounded their wives, and show the guys Polaroids of what the women looked like at the emergency room and then work them over so that they looked just exactly like the Polaroids. But he thought it would slow her down, at least. He was thinking of Lucy.

Karp had expected Roland Hrcany to blow up when he told him that he, not Roland, would do the Rohbling case, and he was not disappointed. Crying, "Why!" Roland sprang from his chair and slammed his hands down on Karp's desk, beetling his brows, rolling his mighty shoulders, bulging his seventeen-inch neck, tightening his jaw, exhibiting, in fact, the full repertoire of anthropoid male aggression, and causing him to resemble a blond gorilla even more than he normally did.

"Sit down, Roland," said Karp in a calming voice. He had seen the display before.

"What, did I screw something up? What?"

"You did fine, Roland. Sit down and I'll explain."

Roland glared and then flung himself back into his seat, making it creak dangerously.

Karp said, "The reason is, this is the biggest and most politically important case we'll get this year. I planned to take at least one, and this one is going to be it."

"Oh, it's too important for *me*, is what you're saying," said Roland in a tone that approached petulance.

"And since I'm taking the case," continued Karp, ignoring the comment, "I need someone to watch the bureau, which has to be you. You're the most experienced guy on the staff, and the best."

"Next to you," Roland growled.

Roland glared when he said this and rolled his jaw. Something must have happened to my testosterone, thought Karp, reflecting that a couple of years ago he would've snarled right back and the two of them would have been screaming and throwing things at each other. Now, however, Roland just looked silly, like Zak when he wanted a toy. Maybe, he thought, it was the result of having two male babies in the house. The real thing spoiled you for the imitations.

Pitching his voice low, he said, "Actually, Roland, to be frank, yes, *in this case*, which is what we're talking about. And I'll give you two reasons: one, an insanity defense is highly likely here, a serious insanity defense, and as it happens, I've tried three major cases where that defense was offered and you haven't tried any. Okay, they're rare, but there it is. I'm familiar, you're not, and going against Waley we need all the edge we can get."

"I'm not afraid of Waley," snapped Roland.

"You're not? *Mazeltov*, Roland. But he scares Jack Keegan, and anyone who scares Jack Keegan scares the shit out of *me*. You want the second reason? This case is dripping with racial politics, white defendant, black vics. I don't like it, but I have to deal with it. Jack has to deal with it. You are not the first person I would pick for a situation like that."

"What, now I'm a fucking *racist*?" Roland's neck grew dangerously crimson.

"No, Roland, of course you aren't, but the prosecutor in this case is going to be under a microscope, and you got a mouth on you. You are free with racial expletives—"

"What, you mean *nigger*?"

". . . and you spend much of your time with white cops, cracking the kind of jokes that if a black juror heard about them, they would be less than well disposed toward the People—"

"For crying out loud, Butch, you been down the jail recently? The fucking *niggers* call each other *nigger*."

"I rest my case," said Karp.

Roland opened his mouth; it stayed open for a couple of beats, and then he let out most of his air and said, "This is fucked, you know that? I was pumped for this case."

"Great, then I'm sure your prep and notes are in terrific order. We'll do the grand jury together and then you'll phase out. Could you let me have them as soon as possible?"

Roland stood, snarling. "Yeah, boss, and fuck you very much!"

"Thank you for your support," said Karp genially as Roland slammed out.

The phone rang. It was V. T. Newbury returning Karp's call.

"I need a friend," said Karp. "Everyone hates me."

"With some justification, I might say. You're really going to take on Rohbling?"

"You heard already? What is it, on TV?"

"No, Keegan was unloading to Zepelli and some of the other bureau chiefs about your loose cannon-hood, and Z. mentioned it to me at a Fraud Bureau staff meeting."

"He was really pissed, was he?"

"Mmm, not as such. I gathered he was irritated but ruefully admiring of your chospeh."

"*Chutzpah*, V.T. You have to try to generate more phlegm with the Yiddishisms: *chhhhhutz-pah*."

"I'll try, but as you know, my people are phlegm-impaired."

"True. Look, why I called, let's have lunch, soon."

They made a date for the following day. Unlikely as it might appear from their respective backgrounds, V. T. Newbury was one of Karp's best friends and probably the smartest person Karp knew. Just now he badly needed both friendship and smarts.

A knock on the door and Connie Trask came in pushing one of the wire-basket carts used to transport case files around the halls. It was stacked with red cardboard folders, one for each of the murders for which Jonathan Rohbling stood accused, plus additional files Roland had assembled since the arrest.

"That was fast," said Karp.

"Yeah, he seemed upset," said the secretary. "He said he peed on them. You might want to check that out before you take them home. Oh, Lieutenant Fulton called. I told him you were in there with Roland giving him bad news. He laughed and said you could call him back."

"Thanks, Connie," said Karp, reaching for the phone.

Lucy Karp sat in spelling, morosely waiting for her turn to come around again. *Resemble* had been her word last time. Briefly, it had flashed through her mind to say, when using it in a sentence, "Mrs. Lawrence's face *resembles* a snotty kleenex," but had chickened out. Spelling was not a problem. Math was the problem. Math and Mrs. Lawrence, what she did in math class.

At the next desk, Robert Liu stood up and misspelled *surrender*, and sat down blushing. Lucy stood and spelled it right and said, "The general promised he would never surrender," looking

Mrs. Lawrence in the eye as she did so. The teacher gave her that phony smile and called on the next kid, and Lucy knew she was plotting her revenge when math class came along.

As it would, inevitably. There would be a recess at ten-thirty. They would stream out to the schoolyard, and Lucy's friends would set up the long ropes to dance double Dutch, chanting, and Lucy would leap among the strands, best of all of them, having learned to jump rope from her mother so far in the past that she could barely remember acquiring the skill. But then they would have to return to the orange-peel–smelling, hot-paint–smelling school building and have math, and Mrs. Lawrence would return the homework, Lucy's marked with shameful red crosses, which she folded quickly and hid away in her backpack. None of her friends, not Janet Chen, or Franny Lee, or Martha Kan, who could barely speak English, had the slightest problem with long division, with problems that made Lucy's brain freeze up and sweat start from her forehead. Then after the passing out of the homework, Mrs. Lawrence would chalk four problems up on the board, and *of course* she would pick Lucy for the hardest one, and Lucy would march up to the board, her face blazing, her stomach roiling, with three other kids, and the others would all do their problems right away and sit down, and Lucy would be up there trying to remember seven into sixty-four and what over, and the whole class would be silent, waiting, and then Mrs. Lawrence would say sweetly, "Lucy needs some help," and then she would talk Lucy through the whole problem as if she were a tiny little moron, with many a sarcastic aside about "somebody didn't pay attention when we were learning how to carry the number into the next column," and the sweat would run down her sides, and her vision would go gray from loss of face, and no, she could not stand it, not even one more time.

So, when recess came, Lucy put her coat on with the others and lagged behind with the fat kids who didn't like recess and, when she saw that the teachers weren't looking, dashed through the open gate, slipped between two parked cars, and was gone, a fugitive from long division, running up Catherine Street toward the Bowery, her mind as blank as a washed blackboard.

FOUR

"What's up?" said Karp into the phone.

"You asked me to check out your Jewish doctor," said Detective Lieutenant Clay Fulton.

Karp's mind had been so immersed in *People* v. *Rohbling* that the statement made no sense to him. Was Fulton sick? Had Karp recommended someone?

"Um . . . Jewish doctor?" he ventured.

"I don't believe it! I've been running around all day on this. For crying out loud, Butch! Davidoff?"

"Oh, yeah! Davidoff. The dead nurse. Murray's case. Okay, I got it. So what went down? He's kosher or not?"

"Not. The opposite. Tayfe."

"*Trefe*, Clay. What did he do?"

"I'm not sure yet, but one, he didn't attend this Longren woman at all as far as I can find out. Also, the apartment where the woman died is owned by a guy named Robinson, Vincent F., also an M.D., apparently a friend, or acquaintance, of Dr. D. Want to hear the kicker? Longren was insured, a private policy via Prudential with her parents as beneficiaries, plus another policy where she worked, through Mutual New York, beneficiary her boss, guess who, Vincent Robinson, M.D."

"Longren worked for Robinson, he's a doc, she gets sick, she dies in his apartment, and then he brings *another* doc in to do the death cert. Smells."

"Stinks. I talked to the insurance investigator from Mutual. He went by Robinson's place to check out the death scene and the beneficiary. While he was there, he used the john and noticed pills. Little white pills and caps, caught in the shag rug around the toilet, like someone wanted to flush a lot of stuff and didn't notice a few extras. He scooped them up and they turned out to be phenobarbs and Dalmane, sleeping pills."

"Oh-ho," said Karp.

"Oh fucking ho is right, son. We need to dig this lady up."

"I'll get on it," said Karp. "Meanwhile, why don't you ask Dr. Davidoff to drop by for a chat? And have him bring along his treatment records for the deceased."

Marlene spent a fairly unpleasant morning with Tamara Morno, the Tamara who did not want to go to court, standing in the hallway of her Chelsea apartment and yelling until the woman relented, and dressed and came with her, trembling and looking over her shoulder out the back window of the cab, to the courthouse on Centre Street, where Marlene arranged for an order of protection against Tamara's boyfriend. Then she had to sit with the weeping woman, and buy her coffee and pastries and calm her down enough so that she could go home. Tamara Morno was a small, round-faced woman with a dramatically sensual figure and a mouse-like disposition, a good combo if you were looking for trouble with men. Marlene made a note to have a talk with the guy, Arnie Nobili, the lover, yet another of the very many men who thought it the peak of attractiveness to swear that if they couldn't have her, nobody could. Having her in Mr. Nobili's case included partial strangulation and cigarette burns, plus hocking Tamara's stuff when he needed to pay off his gambling debts. Not lowlifes, either of them, though: she was a secretary, he was an electrician, both in work, both demonstrably sane except for a touch of impairment in the romantic zone.

Marlene checked her watch as Tamara's cab pulled away. A little early, but she would go uptown anyway and soak up some class. It was a dull day and chilly, and a long, slow ride in a warm cab would have a calming effect. She stuck two fingers in her mouth and let out a blast that lifted a thousand pigeons from the courthouse plaza and brought a yellow cab across two lanes of traffic to the curb.

Edith Wooten's building was one of the old dowagers that line Park Avenue between the Fifties and the Eighties, tan, ornate, brass-bound, and well-doormanned. Marlene was asked her name by one of these, white gloved and red faced, and made to wait while he rang up. After speaking a moment into the intercom, he beckoned to Marlene and handed her the instrument.

"Ms. Ciampi?" said Edith Wooten's voice. "I didn't expect you so soon, and . . . oh, I'm devastated, but, you see, I'm in the middle of a rehearsal, and . . . would it completely destroy your day if I had you just wait up here for say, a tiny half hour?"

"A tiny half hour's fine, Ms. Wooten."

"Oh, grand! You see, Anton came over from Amsterdam for just this concert, and his wretched plane was late. And, you know"—here she lowered her voice as if offering a confidential explanation—"it's the Shostakovich, the E minor trio, you see, so . . ."

"Oh, of course," agreed Marlene blankly, "the E minor, so . . ."

"Yes. Well, I'll tell Francis to send you up."

Sent up, and greeted at the door by a uniformed maid, Marlene entered the kind of dwelling rarely encountered in hypertransient Manhattan, for the Wootens had been in possession of it since the building was constructed in 1923. The maid parked her in a white paneled room with a nice view of Park Avenue through the champagne silk drapes. The furniture was old, of course, not the kind of old you get from antique stores, but the kind you get when you buy new from Tom Chippendale in 1804 and hang on to it: two elegant armchairs upholstered in rose silk, a small sofa in the same material, and a low Sheraton–design table with worn brass fittings. The rug was a silk Tabriz, Marlene thought, early nineteenth century, much worn. She walked across it to check out the paintings. Two nice watercolors, one a park scene by Prendergast, the other a portrait sketch by Sargent. There were tuning-up sounds coming through the door to her right, and shortly this door opened and there entered a solidly built, pink-faced blond young woman with pale, dreamy, gentle eyes. She wore a simple black wool dress reaching a dowdy length below the knee.

"Ms. Ciampi!" said this person, shaking Marlene's hand with a solid, warm grip. "I'm Edie Wooten. How good of you! I'm terribly sorry about this mess. Honestly, if you can bear to wait, I'd be so grateful."

Marlene estimated the woman's age at about twenty-five, although she also might have been eighteen, so fresh was her face, so mild and untroubled were her green eyes. Someone to whom nothing really bad had ever happened, was Marlene's instant thought, followed by a pang of envy, covered by a recoil of shame: nothing until now, or else she would not have called.

"It's no problem. You said half an hour?"

"Yes, thereabouts. One run-through. You can wait here or use the phone, whatever you like. I could have Audrey bring you some coffee? A magazine?"

"No, don't bother."

"I could close the door while we play, if you absolutely *hate* chamber music," said Wooten, in what Marlene thought a positive surfeit of good manners.

"Not at all," said Marlene quickly; although she was no fan, she thought this would come under the heading of "know the client."

The young woman smiled, showing the perfect teeth of the rich, and returned the way she had come. Her shoulder-length fine hair bounced fetchingly. Through the open door Marlene could see that the room it led into was large, floored in polished oak, and held nothing but a grand piano, music stands, and two straight chairs, one occupied by a thin, angular-faced young man with long, fair hair and a violin, and the other occupied by a leaning cello. Wooten sat on this chair and took up her instrument. From her seat on the sofa Marlene could not see who was at the piano.

They began. The cello voiced the weird, unbearably pathetic harmonics of the Andante of Shostakovich's *Trio in E Minor*. Marlene listened, at first repelled, then captivated, at last devastated. She was still dabbing her eyes when Edie Wooten came back into the room. The other two musicians were talking. Real Life had resumed. Wooten shut the door, sat down across from Marlene, and sighed, wiping the dampness from her face with a handkerchief. She looked as if she had just run a mile.

"That was incredible!" Marlene exclaimed. "Is that on a record?"

"Yes, but not by us," said Wooten, smiling. "You liked it?"

"*Like* is not the word. I'm dog food."

"Yes, it *is* a remarkable piece, isn't it? Shostakovich wrote it during the war. Music to stack frozen corpses by. It's what you write when most of your friends have been murdered, and the up side of your life is you work for Stalin, who killed them. The odd thing is, this . . . person, it's one of his favorites. He wants me to play it. Actually, he, well, he *demanded* it in his last letter."

"And you're obliging him?"

"Oh, no! We'd planned to do the piece anyway. We're at Juilliard next week as part of the New York Chamber Society festival. It was just a coincidence."

Marlene took a steno pad out of her bag. "So. When did this guy start to write to you?"

A smile. "It could be a woman, you know."

"Yes, and with a little practice I could play the cello like you. It's a guy, Ms. Wooten."

"Please . . . Edie."

"Okay. I'm Marlene. About when was it?"

"Let me see. It must have started this summer, after we got back from Edinburgh. There are lots of letters, of course, from fans. I have a secretary, but I try to answer as many as I can. Most just ask for photographs. Then there are the critics, we call them 'music lovers,' people who have something to say about the actual performances. Praise mostly, in rare cases nasty—you're not as good as . . . whoever. But this one was different."

"How so?"

"Oh, it was personal." A blush darkened the pink of her cheeks. "You know."

"I don't know. You have to tell me."

"Well, like, 'I could play your body like you play the cello. I feel your legs around me when you play.' Like that." She let out an embarrassed laugh. "It's the position when we play. Women, that is. There's that old joke, the conductor yells at the lady cellist, 'Madam, don't you realize you have one of the world's greatest treasures between your thighs?' And musical things too. He knows the cello literature. He writes lists of what he wants me to play at each concert, and of course, as here with the Shostakovich trio, sometimes he gets it right, and then in the next letter he praises me for playing the piece. He thinks I'm doing it for him. He says things like, 'When you played the scherzo in the Beethoven *Sonata in A*, I knew you were playing only for me, my darling, our eyes met,' and nonsense like that. And when I don't play what he wants, he gets angry. Crude. He doesn't want me to travel either. It's like having a jealous lover."

"I'll need every physical object he's sent you."

"Oh, God, I didn't *keep* any of it!"

"Well, please do in the future and hand it over. We need it if we ever get to build a harassment case."

"He spies on me too," said the cellist. She had twisted her handkerchief into a tight rope. "That's why I called you. The letters are one thing, but the idea that he's following me . . ." She shuddered delicately.

Marlene looked up from her notebook. "How do you know he's following you?"

"He leaves things. A rose in my cello case at a recital. Notes in rehearsal rooms. I get phone calls and no one answers when I pick up. In one letter he said he liked my nightgown, so somehow he can see in my window, even though it's sixteen stories up. And now I keep the curtains closed." She made a helpless gesture. "I'm starting to be quite frightened, John Lennon and all that. Should I be? Frightened?"

"Concerned, I think," said Marlene judiciously. "It would depend, of course, on several things. We have to determine if this guy is a genuine stranger or someone who has actual access, someone you know."

"Oh, no, it can't be anyone I know," said Wooten with blithe confidence. "I mean, I *know* them, don't I? I don't know anyone who would do something like this."

"Well, Edie," said Marlene, in a tone usually reserved for explaining the ontology of the tooth fairy, "I didn't actually mean your most intimate friends. Nevertheless, you have contacts who can get at you. The people who work in the building? The people who move you around and take care of you when you're on tour? The musicians, the orchestra players, your accompanists? You say this guy knows music; it might be the place to look."

"What, you mean people like . . ." She gestured toward the door to the music room, frank disbelief on her face. "I'm sorry, that's ridiculous."

"Well, I hope so," said Marlene. "But you know, people do have secret lives, sometimes really nasty secret lives. You would be surprised at the number of quite distinguished citizens, many of them happily married, who every once in a while like to pay some lady to tie them up and urinate on their face. Or get a transvestite whore to give them a blow job. Or worse."

Wooten was looking at her with a peculiar expression, which Marlene thought represented a war between her good nature and primal disgust. (*Get out of my life, you horrible woman!*) Marlene kept her own expression bland and professional, continuing, "On the other hand, you're what's generally referred to as a low-risk individual."

"That's nice to know," said Wooten, her smile showing faintly again. "What would a high-risk individual be like?"

"They would be like the ladies and gentlemen who render oral sex to guys around the bridge plazas downtown. Prostitutes in general. Barmaids. Cocktail waitresses. Drug users and pushers. Promiscuous people. Party people. We expect these folks to get hit on by wackos. My assumption going in is that you don't indulge in that sort of behavior."

Marlene paused, raising an eyebrow, open to a confession, not that she expected one at this stage. Yet something had passed across Edie Wooten's face as she recounted this list. A vagrant fear? Sadness? Marlene was about to ask a sharper question when the door to the music room opened. It was the Dutch violinist.

"Felix and I are off, Edie," he announced in a mild, faintly accented voice. Wooten rose and offered a formal European embrace, linked arms with him and carried him into the other room, where she presumably said farewell to the other member of the trio, whom Marlene had not yet seen. In a few minutes she was back. She seemed to be having difficulty switching between her world, the realm of delight, art, and comfort, and the dreadful city Marlene had begun to sketch for her. Marlene had seen this reaction before. In fact, she could predict what the woman was about to say next.

"I suppose I'm having a hard time dealing with all this, Marlene. I mean, why me?"

"Yes, everyone says that," said Marlene. "Why cancer, why car crashes? It happened, it's happening. To you. The only question is, do you want to do something about it?"

Wooten sat on the sofa and rubbed her face. "What would you suggest?" she asked.

"Well, the first thing is, as I mentioned, you have to keep anything he gives you and give it to me. I'll need a list of people who have access to your personal space—building workers, stagehands, record people, musicians, friends and relatives."

"Will you have to *bother* my family?"

"Not at all. I just need a sense of who's around you, who can get to you. They'll need to be eliminated, and if they are, we'll know we're dealing with a true stranger. If so, I can work up a security plan. The point, by the way, is not to have you live your life under guard. The point is to find this guy and get him to stop."

"However will you do that?" Wooten asked with interest.

Marlene grinned. "We have our methods," she said in a German accent.

Edie Wooten returned the grin. She really had, Marlene thought, the most marvelous disposition. "No, really," Wooten said, "how do you?"

"Really?" said Marlene. She shrugged. "It depends. Usually I talk to them. I reason with them."

"And it works?"

"Oh, yes," said Marlene confidently. "I have a very forceful personality."

Lucy Karp wandered through the edges of Chinatown, growing colder, hungrier, and more miserable with each passing hour. Twice she started back to school, and twice she stopped, unwilling to contemplate the uproar that would be made over her defection: Mrs. Lawrence would have her piece of skin and then the chief gorgon, Ms. Lee, the principal, and then, worst of all, her mother would be called and come to school and all three of them would stare at her, and of course, she would have missed math and fallen even further behind.

Illness was her only hope, she concluded, a long, lingering debility that would baffle medical science—and excuse her permanently from long division. A stomach ailment would be best, she thought. Her stomach actually did ache, for it was now past her lunchtime, and her lunch was still in its box in her cubby back at school, and all she had in her parka pocket was a nickel and two pennies. She would have to upchuck, naturally, to make it convincing; then she could run back to school red faced, weeping, with vomit all over her, and say she had wandered away under the influence of a strange disease that had affected her brains and . . .

However, if there was one thing she couldn't bear to do, it was puke, so she would have to really work at it. What was needed was some actual vomit to serve as an exemplar—the sight and smell would work their magic on her gut. Fortunately, finding street messes was rarely a problem in lower Manhattan.

So Lucy trod the crowded streets, looking in the gutters and in doorways, finding a good array of nauseating venues, including one bloated, stinking rat. She was gagging, well sickened, but still unable to bring up the necessary evidence. By this time she was on Canal Street, a familiar stretch. She caught sight of Tranh's noodle shop, and at this sight, redolent of those precious after-noons with her mother, Lucy experienced the first sympathetic mental pang. As a result of her mother's profession, there must have been few children of her age in New York as thoroughly indoctrinated as Lucy was in the dangers of kidnapping and as vividly aware of what losing a child meant. Her eyes stung with tears; she ran in desperate little circles, moaning. At last she sat on the curb and wept.

All this Tranh observed through the window of his shop. He came out and squatted down next to Lucy and said in rusty Can-tonese, "Little Sister, what is the matter? Why are you crying?"

"Because—because," answered the child in the same lan-guage, amidst the blubbering, "I ran away from school."

"*Wah!* You ran away? Did they mean to beat you?"

"No," answered Lucy. "I was afraid I could not do my lesson. I am a very stupid girl, and I feared to lose face in front of my friends. Now I am disgraced forever."

Tranh pulled free the white towel that he habitually kept stuck in his waistband and gave it to Lucy. "It may not be as bad as that," he said. "Forever is a long time. Wipe your face and come inside. First I will give you some soup with winter melon, noo-dles, and ham. Then we will think together about your diffi-culty."

"I have no money," said Lucy, rising, her stomach rumbling at the mention of food.

"That does not matter," said Tranh. "You are a good cus-tomer."

The school called Marlene's office shortly before noon, and the answering service forwarded the call to her beeper. Edie Woo-ten showed her to a phone and went into the music room to play some Mozart to improve her mood. She had entered only a min-ute or so into that sunlit, ordered world when she heard Marlene shrieking from the other room. She put down her bow and went to see what the commotion was about. She found Marlene in the act of slamming down the phone. Her face was dead white, including the lips, which had formed a rigid line beneath flaring nostrils. Bolts shot from her eyes. She looked like a Medusa on a Renaissance medallion.

"Is something wrong?" Edie asked.

Marlene seemed to look through her. Then she took a long breath and said, "No. Actually, yes. A domestic thing. In any case, I have to go. I'll be in touch. Work on that list of contacts. And don't worry!"

Then she was gone.

Outside the building, Marlene did not wait for the doorman to whistle down a cab, but ran out into Park and waylaid one in full motion. It screamed off, with Marlene flapping twenties in the driver's face.

From his vantage across the broad avenue, the Music Lover watched Marlene leave. He knew who she was and what she was doing in Edith Wooten's building. He was much vexed. Whistling the opening theme from Boccherini's Cello Concerto in B-flat, *he got into his car and drove off to the south.*

Lucy finished her soup and brought the empty bowl to the counter. She sat on a stool while several customers came and picked up cartoned take-out orders of noodles. When the place was empty again, Tranh lit a cigarette and regarded his guest solemnly. He said, "Now we must decide what to do. The school must by now have found you are missing. They will call your mother. Can you imagine what she will think?"

"Oh, don't remind me!" Lucy cried in English, and then explained, "Tranh *sinsàang*, my mother is a—I can't think of the word in *Gwóngdùngwá*—she is a guard against evil people, so perhaps one of these may try to hurt her, or me. So she warns me to be careful. She will think that one of these has taken me." Tears began again, and Tranh handed her a clean wipe rag. Then he placed a quarter before her on the counter and indicated the pay phone on the wall.

"Take this and call your mother right away, and let her know you are safe."

Lucy hesitated. "Oh, but she'll be so angry."

"Yes, afterward, but first she will be very happy. There is nothing worse than losing a child. What made you do this wicked thing?"

"I told you, sir. I failed at my lesson and was afraid of disgrace."

"You failed? So? Did this not make you work all the harder so that you would *not* fail?"

Lucy hung her head. Tranh said, "Listen to me. You are a clever girl, and things come easy for you. Therefore, when you need to work hard, you don't know how. Thus you disgrace your family by failing, and disgrace your teacher by running away. But you owe everything to your family. Without a family you are a ghost person, nothing! Understand? Rather than disgrace them you must study until blood pours from your eyes. Go, call your mother, now!"

Marlene's knees gave way when she burst into her office and Sym said, "Lucy called."

"Oh, Jesus, thank you!" Marlene gasped and flopped onto the couch. "Where is she?"

Sym told her. Five minutes later, Marlene was walking through the door of the noodle shop, thunder breaking around her brow. Lucy was sitting at a table sipping a Coke. Marlene nodded to Tranh and then sat down opposite her daughter.

"Well?"

"Guilty," said Lucy, "with an explanation."

"I'll hear it."

Lucy explained about long division and Mrs. Lawrence and the shame and what followed. Marlene lit a cigarette. Tranh brought her a *grande crème*. "Well," she said, "guilty with an explanation is a plea on a misdemeanor, like not doing homework. This is a felony. This is *felony stupid*, Lucy! You realize what could have happened to you?"

"Yes. I said I was sorry. I'll never, ever do it again."

"You bet your—you bet you won't, my girl! Now, this is

what's going to happen. This weekend, instead of you going ice skating with Janet and Marie, and instead of having a sleep-over—"

"Mom-mm!"

"Don't you *dare* 'Mom-mm' me! Don't you dare! Instead of doing those nice things, I was saying, you and I are going to be locked in a room together working on this math business, and we will not come out until you are on top of long division."

"What about your *clients*? What about the *twins*?" asked Lucy in a snotty tone that made Marlene want to wring her neck. She gritted her teeth and glared at her daughter. The child looked away in shame, for Lucy was aware of Mr. Tranh watching them and sending rays of Confucian disapproval, which for some reason had a more powerful effect on her than her mother's ire.

"I will take care of that," said Marlene tightly. "Daddy can handle the twins with Posie, and the clients will just have to look out for themselves. You are *not* going to fail in school. I may have to kill you, but you are *not* going to fail. Now, put on your coat. I'm going to take you back to school."

Marlene got up, her heart pounding, her mind grappling with a confusing mix of anger, fading fear, and burgeoning guilt. She shuddered and went over to the counter.

"Thank you, I . . . am glad you helped my daughter," she said to Tranh, speaking slowly and distinctly.

Tranh smiled and nodded. "Is okay. I like . . . I like her . . . and I foud . . . feeled . . ." He shrugged and threw his hands wide in a gesture of frustration. This gesture, however, attracted Marlene's attention to what was in one of his hands, which was a worn paperback book with a dirty white cover and red lettering on the spine. Marlene had a similarly worn copy of just that book on her bookshelf at home, had owned it for over twenty years. She gestured at it and said, in French, "Monsieur, I observe you are reading Baudelaire. Is it also the case that you speak French?"

Tranh's face was at first blank with amazement and then curiously transformed: a wiry intelligence appeared to flow into it, as from a pump. "But of course I speak French, Madame. I am a Vietnamese, am I not? And I was five years a student in Paris.

But I am astonished to find that you do as well. Although it is less remarkable, one supposes, than that your daughter speaks Cantonese. I have heard her speak it on the street. This was how we communicated, you see."

"Of course," said Marlene. "As for me, I was four years with the Mesdames of the Sacred Heart, who insist on accomplishment in French."

"So I have always understood," said Tranh, smiling broadly. "But surely they did not insist on *Les Fleurs du Mal*. Surely you proper young ladies did not read, let us say, *Métamorphoses du Vampire* under the watchful gaze of a nun."

"I am afraid we proper young ladies did much worse than that, monsieur; at least I did. My four hundred blows were unusually vigorous, I fear. And you may regard my daughter to prove it to yourself: we are two of a kind. It is the wages of sin."

"Come, Madame, it is not as bad as that. She is a brave girl, if overly proud. But you have warmed her ears, and I doubt she will repeat the offense."

"One hopes," said Marlene. She looked at her watch. "A pity, but we must go."

Tranh inclined his head and intoned, *"Horloge! dieu sinistre! effrayant, impassible, dont le doight nous menace et nous dit, Souviens-toi!"*

Marlene laughed, "You have it, my friend. Oh! I have forgotten to pay you for the child's soup, and for the phone call."

She reached into her purse, but Tranh held up his hand and said, "Dear Madame: I had not had a real conversation in five years; I had not had a conversation in French for ten years; and I had not had a conversation in French with a beautiful woman for thirty years. This brief moment has been worth a cauldron of soup, and a phone call to Tibet."

"Then, Monsieur," said Marlene with a slight bow of her head, "you have my most profound gratitude."

Outside, in the car, Lucy said, "I like Mr. Tranh, although he's sort of hard to understand. He's not a *Guóngdùngyàhn*—I mean, he's not Cantonese, is he?"

"No, he's a Vietnamese, educated in France—probably an official of some kind. The commies must have given him a hard time when they took over—he looks like he's been through it. Uh-oh, what's this?"

Lucy looked out the car window and said, "Those are those gangsters from the other day, I think."

Four oriental youths had just jumped from a Mercedes sedan and entered Tranh's shop. They leaned across the counter, and one of them started gesturing violently and yelling at the older man. Another unscrewed the top of a sugar dispenser and poured its contents on the floor. A third kicked over chairs and upset tables.

"Shouldn't we help him?" asked Lucy.

"Yeah, if he needs it. But I have a feeling that he may not."

In fact, Tranh was speaking calmly to the youth who appeared to be the leader of the gang. Marlene could not see very clearly through the steamed window, but it was obvious that whatever Tranh had said was not something to be lightly borne. The gang leader pulled out a butterfly knife, snapped it open, and leaped over the counter. He grabbed Tranh by the front of his shirt, waving the butterfly knife under Tranh's nose. Marlene could not see what happened after that: there was a sudden movement, a brief struggle, and the young man was somehow turned around, with his thick hair grasped in Tranh's left fist. Tranh was holding a thin boning knife in his right hand, the point of which vanished into the kid's ear. Everyone else was frozen. The kid dropped his butterfly knife. Tranh said something; the kid said something. The other three players began to pick up the upset chairs and tables. Then they backed out, stumbling against one another in the narrow doorway.

Tranh followed, still gripping the little thug, his thin blade held rigid, an improbable length of steel vanishing into the kid's ear, the kid's face twisted into a rictus of pain. Tranh was talking to the kid in a low voice. Suddenly he stopped, withdrew the knife. Blood oozed down the kid's neck. Tranh delivered a mighty kick against the base of the kid's spine. The kid went sprawling on the pavement. His friends picked him up, and without another word they got back in their car and drove away, tires squealing.

Tranh watched them go, nodded to Marlene and Lucy, and then went back into his shop.

"Wow!" said Lucy.

"Wow, indeed," said Marlene, starting her car. "Very impressive. You know, Luce, I think that whatever Mr. Tranh did in the war, it probably didn't involve a desk job."

"Or noodles either," said Lucy.

FIVE

D r. Davidoff came in to Karp's office later that day, accompanied by Clay Fulton and, somewhat to Karp's surprise, a man named Aaron Weinstein, who was introduced as Davidoff's lawyer. Karp and Fulton exchanged a brief look. The detective's eyebrows rose a quarter of an inch, his broad shoulders somewhat more: I didn't tell him anything, boss.

The three men settled themselves in chairs around Karp's desk. Weinstein, a portly, balding man somewhat older than Karp, projected an air of bonhomie, focusing charm on Karp, noting mutual friends, claiming acquaintanceship with the powerful. He told a small joke. The message: we're all friends here aiming at straightening out this little difficulty, but on the other hand, we are not pushovers. He did it well; that was what Davidoff was paying him for.

After the usual five minutes of smiles, Karp opened the real bidding with, "So, Doctor, how did you come to be the attending physician at the death of Ms. Longren?"

Davidoff paused, flicked a glance at his lawyer, and answered, "I was asked to as a professional courtesy by Dr. Vincent Robinson."

"I see. And was it usual for Dr. Robinson to call you in for consultation?"

"No. I mean, yes, it was unusual."

"Very unusual? Maybe unique?" Karp pressed.

Here Weinstein stepped in, asking genially, "Um, could we slow down here a little, Mr. Karp? Maybe we could answer your questions better if we had some idea where they were going. Surely, there's no implication or suggestion that Dr. Davidoff did anything untoward or wrong. So, what are we . . . ?"

"Well, actually, we don't know that, do we?" Karp responded. "What we see is a young woman dead under circumstances that we might call suspicious."

"Suspicious!" Weinstein exclaimed. "How 'suspicious'? Good Lord, there were *two* physicians in attendance."

"Yeah, that's the point, Mr. Weinstein. An overabundance of docs and an insufficiency of records pertaining to the deceased. There is no record of Ms. Longren ever having been a patient of Dr. Davidoff's. Moreover, Ms. Longren was an employee of Dr. Robinson, and Dr. Robinson was a beneficiary of her insurance policy. And drugs were involved; there is evidence of a hasty attempt to dispose of barbiturates and other drugs at Dr. Robinson's apartment."

The geniality had flown from Weinstein's face. He whispered something into Davidoff's ear. Karp caught the word "records." Davidoff nodded and licked his lips nervously. Weinstein said, "Actually, Dr. Davidoff does have records of his treatment in this case. Show him, Mark."

Whereupon Dr. Davidoff drew from a leather folder a manila records jacket that, when opened, proved to contain only an incomplete cover sheet and three pages of lined loose-leaf paper covered with hurried, scribbled writing. Weinstein sighed gently. Detective Fulton cleared his throat. Mark Davidoff flushed and jiggled his leg. Karp stared at him and said, "Doctor, you have a big decision to make right now. We have an exhumation order in on the body of Evelyn Longren. I think that whatever else we learn from it, we'll find that she did not die from viral pneumonia. So, pretty soon you're going to have to decide whether you want to be a witness in a homicide case or one of the defendants."

Karp's tone was polite, dry, firm, designed by years of experience to pierce the composure of middle-class, heavily lawyered culprits.

More murmured conversation between doctor and lawyer, at the end of which Weinstein said, "Without any admission of wrongdoing, we are perfectly willing to be completely frank and open as to Dr. Davidoff's part in this affair."

Karp nodded and picked up the phone to call for a steno.

Harry Bello was back in the office when Marlene returned from re-depositing Lucy at P.S. 1.

"What's with Lucy?" he asked, using a tone and wearing an expression designed to promote guilt. (Marlene's mothering had never been up to Harry's standards; even Harry's mother might have fallen short with respect to caring for Lucy.) Although she was prepared to cut Harry some slack, he having been a detective for thirty years and therefore incapable of asking a question that did not assume some vicious secret, she was not having any of it today.

"Nothing, Harry," she said shortly. "It's all straightened out."

A doubtful look, a 138-grain magnum doubtful look.

"She is *fine*, Harry!"

Tiny shrug, change of subject. "How did it go with your uptown fiddle player?"

"Cellist. I like her. It's some fan, a nut. He's started to follow her."

"Are we taking it?"

"Yeah, it feels like it could go sour. And she's got the money for it."

Harry's eyes flicked up to the large board pinned over his desk. He said, "Umnh."

Marlene looked at the board, at the names of clients and commitments, at the names of their largely part-time staff written in with black grease pencil on a plastic overlay, and saw what the grunt meant. Bello & Ciampi handled three kinds of jobs. The first was conventional security for celebrities, which entailed bodyguard services when the women (nearly all their clients were women) were out and about, performing, modeling, having lunch, being vulnerable. This was the cash cow, but also required the most time and the most rigid scheduling. The second was a kind of pest control: finding men who were stalking or abusing women and getting them to stop, either through writs and prosecution or through what Marlene called reason and persuasion. Finally, there was the pro bono work, which usually involved desperate women, often with children, who were fleeing dangerous relationships, passing through shelters, needing to be set up with new lives. This was by far the work most likely to lead to actual violence, and Marlene had always done most of it herself. Now, looking over the manning chart, Marlene had to admit they were overextended, especially if Marlene wanted to continue the time-consuming pro bono tasks. Which she did.

"We need at least another guy, full-time," she suggested.

"Two," said Harry. "Dane called, said he's bringing over a guy who might be okay."

"Checked out?"

Harry lifted a noncommittal eyebrow. "Ask him. He's supposed to be coming in today. Meanwhile, I'll look around."

"For one guy, Harry."

"Two, Marlene, you want to spend a night at home, tuck in your kids—"

"Okay, already, Harry!" Marlene snapped, and went back to her own office, her brow knotted. Harry was perfectly correct, but she resented being told that her fantasy of a cozy little crusade was fading. The little firm had grown perhaps too rapidly. Starting with just Harry and herself two years ago, it now employed the equivalent of twenty full-time people, but because many of their employees were part-time cops, they actually had over thirty people on their payroll. This was a serious problem: neither she nor Harry were famous for their management skills. Sym was bright and willing, and Marlene had started to load her with routine duties, but even Marlene hesitated at giving any independent responsibility to a nineteen-year-old ex-streetwalker.

So they muddled on; as yet no disaster had occurred. In order to do what Marlene wanted done, Bello & Ciampi needed cash flow, and cash flow came from frightened rich people, who, Marlene did not require a Chicago economist to verify, had all the cash. All businesses have natural scales: auto factories do not employ twenty people, nor do florist shops employ twenty thousand. The firm's natural size was going to plateau at about fifty full-time slots in the field, Marlene estimated. Of course, she could can the whole thing and go back to running what amounted to a risky hobby, turning down ninety-five percent of the women she might have helped. That, or give up her personal life in the cause of muscular feminism.

And it was not going to be so easy to get the people. Checking out potential staff was a tedious but necessary task, since security work was one of the favorite occupations of serial sex murderers, and Marlene would have preferred not to inadvertently bring one of these aboard.

At her desk, she saw the phone message slip Sym had marked URGENT in red letters and taped to the desk lamp. It bore a familiar name, Carrie Lanin, a name that, together with the red message, made her think, oh, marvelous, this is all I need today. The woman was by way of being Marlene's first customer: in a sense, the founding victim. An attractive single mother, a fabric designer, she had run afoul of a true obsessive, a man who had known her in high school and apparently had thought of little else since. He had arranged a meeting with her, and had instantly become jealous, aggressive, obdurate in his attentions. Marlene had once run a domestic-violence unit in the D.A.'s office, and had a good sense of what sort of man was likely to pose a physical danger. She had sensed that this man, Rob Pruitt, was the type that sang death is better than being without you, darling, and you go first. Marlene had therefore done a little preemptive striking, goading Pruitt into attacking her and then nailing him. He had gotten two to five for first-degree assault.

Marlene made a quick calculation of the usual time spent in prison for that crime, and concluded that Pruitt must have been sprung, unless Carrie Lanin had turned up yet another unsuitable swain. She dialed the number.

"Marlene!" cried Lanin in a shrill voice. "Oh, Jesus, thank

God you called. I've been locked in here crouched by the phone all day. He's back!"

"Pruitt."

"The scumbag called me like nothing ever happened. He still loves me. At work yet. I had to go home."

"Did you call the cops? The protection order's still valid."

"Oh, of course I called the cops, Marlene. They agreed to stop the war on crime to find this guy who wants to send me flowers and candy. An arrest is fucking imminent!" Her voice teetered close to hysteria.

Keeping her own tone calm, Marlene said, "Okay, Carrie. What exactly did he say to you?"

"Who, the scumbag? Oh, the usual shit. How he only wanted to be with me, take care of me—oh, and he had some choice words about you. You're the bitch who came between us. He's going to get you out of the way too." A pause. Then, sobbing. "Marlene, I'm really freaked. His voice. It was like a fucking zombie, like he was dead already. What should I d-d-do?" Blubbering.

Marlene waited until the crying had subsided, reflecting the while that she spent a good deal of her time, probably as much as some vacationing psychiatrists, listening to people cry over the phone. Then she said, "Carrie, listen to me. I'm going to put a man on your place. I'm going to call in some chips with the cops. We will get him and we will prosecute the violation. He's on parole, he'll go back to jail. Stay calm, let the machine answer. If it's me, I'll ring once, hang up, and call again. Got that?"

More protests, but the weeping phase seemed to be over for now. In a few minutes Marlene was able to hang up and start worrying about where she was going to find the guy she had promised Carrie Lanin.

"What did you think of that?" said Karp to Fulton, when Dr. Davidoff and his lawyer had left.

"He sounds on the level," the detective answered after a moment's consideration. "I don't think he'll be inviting Robinson over for drinks anytime soon—you could see he was really pissed off."

"Right, the guy set him up. He had a corpse on his hands and he wanted his buddy to carry the can, and it would have washed if not for Murray Selig. So, we dig the girl up and go from there."

Fulton nodded, and they moved easily into the various other cases the detective was handling for the Homicide Bureau. These were not many. Fulton was coming to the close of his career with the NYPD, a career so plump with glory—the Department's first black college-educated detective lieutenant, and holder of innumerable awards, including the Medal of Valor, was how he was usually introduced—that he could write his own ticket, and what he chose to write was a vague assignment that allowed him to function as the private cop of the head of the New York D.A.'s Homicide Bureau.

The two men had been close for years, since, in fact, Fulton had been a detective third and Karp a damply fresh assistant D.A. Fulton was a dozen years older than Karp in regular time, and about a century older in street experience, and something in Karp had attracted Fulton from the first day. He had barged in and became Karp's mentor, a post he still endeavored to fill.

"I hear you're going to take over this granny-killer thing, Rohbling," he observed casually, flicking a speck from the lapel of his beautifully cut blue suit. Something of a dude, Fulton. He wore custom shoes too, but since his wife was well off, an executive with a restaurant chain, he did not take bribes.

"Can't keep anything from a big-time dick like you," said Karp lightly. And then, noting Fulton's dour expression, added, "You don't approve?"

"Approve ain't the point, son. You're going to get creamed on this one."

"Why? It's a solid case."

"Case ain't the point neither. Unless you got a jury from a Black Muslim mosque, which you are definitely not going to get, this fucker going to fly away on an NGI."

"Race isn't going to be an issue here," said Karp stiffly, thinking in passing of his conversation with Roland.

Fulton gaped theatrically and wiggled his finger vigorously in an ear. "Sorry, son, I must be getting deaf. I thought I heard you say race don't count in this one."

"It doesn't."

Fulton's face broke into a broad smile, and he started to laugh, short bursts of low chuckle that went on for some time, an infectious merriment in which Karp was hard pressed not to join.

"What?" he exclaimed at last.

"Son, listen good here," Fulton said. "Look at it the other way. What if a black boy'd whacked five white grannies? They put him *under* the fuckin' jail, man. They put him so deep under, he be *oil*. You want to talk to that boy, you got to drive into the Texaco, say, gimme a quart of thirty-weight. Hey, how you doin', Leroy? Leroy say, glug, glug, glug . . ."

Karp, laughing, said, "That was a good imitation of a Negro, Clay. You're getting better at it."

"Yeah, well, I get a lot of practice."

"No, but seriously, what's your point? The system's so racist we nail a black kid for the same crime we give a pass to a white kid on?"

"This is a surprise to you?"

"It's a surprise you think I'd let it go down like that," said Karp sharply.

"It ain't you, son," replied Fulton, turning sober. "It's just the *fact* that nine times out of ten, your crazy nigger goes to the slams, and a rich white kid with a good voodoo head shrinker is going to walk. Now, if he happen to have killed a quinella of cute little blondie girls, that's one thing. Jury might say, he's crazy, but hang his white ass anyway. Now, a bunch of old black ladies, all but one of them on welfare?" He shook his head. "You might win it, 'cause you're that good, but it's going to be uphill, son. Way uphill. Steep."

Karp was shaking his head doggedly. "Say what you want," he said, "if the case is presented right, the jury will do the right thing. Meanwhile, what about this guy Featherstone? You know him?"

"Uh-huh," said Fulton, happy to change the subject. One of

the reasons he liked Karp was that he had rarely met a person of either race so devoid of race prejudice. On the other hand, that may have made it hard for him to understand how deeply that particular poison was etched into the bone of the society. "Gordy Featherstone. He just got his gold tin when I was in the Two-Eight, in '76 or so. Wasn't on my squad, but I heard he was a pretty good cop. Smart. Didn't take. Didn't kick ass that much. The collar on Rohbling was a nice piece of work too."

"Yeah, it was. I need to talk to him about it in the next couple days. But as far as you know, there's nothing in there that might come up to his disadvantage?"

Fulton grinned again. "Well, he's black. That's usually enough."

They finished their conversation, Fulton promising to look into the affairs of Dr. Vincent Robinson, and then the detective left, leaving Karp with the burden of Rohbling lying embodied in the thick files on his desk and on the wire cart nearby. He had already gone through it all once, enough to follow the case's presentation to the grand jury. That was coming up in a few days, and Roland Hrcany would bear the brunt of that task. Karp had no doubt that an indictment would be secured on all five homicide counts; grand juries almost always did what the prosecutor asked of them. Then they would arraign on the indictments, a judge would be selected, and the trial date would be set. The trial before a petit jury was, of course, something else again.

He picked up the file on the murder of Jane Hughes and resumed reading. This was the crime for which Jonathan Rohbling had been arrested, and was for that reason the key to the prosecution. The other four women had not even been classed as homicides until Rohbling had confessed to killing them. Mrs. Hughes had been sixty-eight, the widow of a mechanic, the mother of five, the grandmother of seven. On Saturday, April 20 of the current year, at around eleven in the evening, neighbors in her respectable St. Nicholas Avenue building had heard shouts and crashing sounds from her apartment. Shortly thereafter, witnesses had seen a young black man carrying a soft-sided dark suitcase leaving the building. He was unknown to these witnesses. The following day Mrs. Hughes's son had arrived early to take his mother to church. There being no answer to his ring, he had the superintendent open the door, and found his mother dead on the kitchen floor, amid signs of a violent struggle. The medical examiner had declared smothering to be the cause of death. Karp read through the M.E.'s report. There had been no sexual assault. Gordon Featherstone had caught the homicide case.

Karp read through the sheaf of DD-5's generated by the detective's investigation. With allowances for the stilted language required by the NYPD, these were good, clear reports, a separate form for every action carried out in pursuit of the unknown killer. What was missing was the contemplation, the thinking, the instinct, that had led Featherstone along his successful path. Karp had to piece this together from hints. Son reports nothing of value missing from the apartment. Son reports mother did not own a dark soft-sided suitcase. Coffee set out for two persons on coffee table in living room of victim's apartment. No sign of forced entry. Now the interpretation: Mrs. Hughes had known her assailant, had been entertaining him, in fact. The assailant was not a thief, nor was he a rapist. That let out the local bad boys. The family and friends all had alibis; there was no sign of murderous rancor there either. Confirmed: Featherstone's witnesses did not find the picture of the killer in the zone book at the Two-Eight. There were fingerprints (Karp read the forensics reports), but they did not match any stored in the files of the Bureau of Criminal Investigation. A request was sent out, without much hope behind it, to the FBI. Of more immediate interest were the fibers found under Mrs. Hughes's nails and, curiously, between her teeth and caught deep in her respiratory tract. They were navy blue cotton canvas fibers. A mystery.

Karp loved this part. He loved reading the DD-5's and the arrest reports, the crime-scene unit reports, the forensic and M.E. reports. He loved seeing how the little tendrils of information curled into cords, and then ropes, and then stout cables, winding around a particular person, tying him tightly, dragging him, with Karp's help, of course, to justice. Ultimately, he would have to re-create Featherstone's process for the jury, to show them that the cable had coiled itself inevitably around the throat of one man and one man alone, the D., Jonathan Rohbling.

And as he thought this, he could not help thinking a more disconcerting thought. In general, despite the importance accorded motive in the fictive universe of films and books, Karp thought motive irrelevant. If the facts showed the guy did it, who cared why he did it? Naturally, since juries read books and saw movies, motive inevitably made an appearance. Still, you never wanted the prosecution to rest on purported mental states—did the defendant hate, or love, or fear, or desire—because it was a place for the defense to introduce doubt, and of course, there was *inherently* doubt in any objectification of an inner state. So Karp never based his presentation on motive; he wanted to convince the jury only that the defendant was at a certain place and did a certain thing to the victim, which caused the victim's death.

Here, however, the nature of the crime cried out for some explanation. Why would a young white man from a wealthy Long Island suburb travel to Harlem, disguise himself as a black man, and murder elderly black women? The jury would want to know. *Karp* wanted to know. He read on, although he doubted he would find the answer among the DD5's.

"Hey, Marlene," said Marlon Dane at the door to her office, "this is the guy. Wolfe, this is Marlene Ciampi, the boss."

"Glad to meet you," said Wolfe, stepping forward and holding out his hand.

Marlene shook it and sized him up. A muscle guy, first of all. The hand was big, hard, and warm, and attached to a considerable arm and shoulder. Six-three, two-ten, Marlene's experienced eye estimated, a jock, a bodybuilder. The face was pleasant enough in an all-American way, sandy hair, cropped closer than was fashionable, odd sandy eyebrows that stood out sharply against what must have been a tanning-parlor tan. He wore a tweed jacket over a white sweater over a shirt and tie, with dark wool pants and shined shoes. The eyes were tan too, the nose undistinguished, the expression—what was it? Not quite mensch-like. An astronaut, but one of the ones who never got to go on a moon mission. Well, she thought as she gestured him to a seat, that's what you generally got when you hired security. The best you could expect was just enough of the almost right stuff to get by.

They sat down. A little small talk. He'd spent time down South and in New England, wanted to try his luck in New York. He reached into his jacket pocket and brought out a folded résumé. Marlene read it. Clean, neatly typed, not too many misspellings. Jackson Wolfe, age thirty-one, unmarried. It was a usual sort of history. High school (letters in football, track), one year of college, military service with an M.P. unit in Korea, honorable discharge, black belt in tae kwan do. The job history was a scatter of security work in several big East Coast cities, no longer than two years in each place. Also not untypical. Security was America's fastest-growing business and nearly the only one in which a strong, quick, presentable, unskilled man who didn't much care for the classroom could freely move from job to job and earn a modest living. It was the modern equivalent of being a cowboy or a seaman a century before, a drifter's job.

Marlene looked up from the résumé. "It says here you're working for Macy's now. How come you want to leave?"

"I don't much like working retail."

"Why not?"

Wolfe shrugged and said, hesitantly and with what seemed embarrassment, "Well, you know. It's all shoplifting, pilferage. I don't like . . . I mean, the people we pick up, most of them, they're pathetic. Some skinny teenager, they got to have the sixty-dollar bag with the logo, the right sneakers they saw on the TV. We bust 'em, they sit in the office crying, you know, what'll my dad say, and stuff. Even the pros, you know, miserable junkies, most of them. And the—what d'you call 'em—the guys who think they're girls—"

"Transvestites?"

". . . yeah, them: I couldn't believe it, a PR kid, a boy, trying to walk out with an eight-hundred-dollar gown. Pathetic! Anyway, I figure I'd rather, you know, protect people from, like, terrorists, wackos, and like that. And when Dane—Lonny—told me you might be looking—"

"Right. Well, as a matter of fact, we are looking for some people." Marlene looked at Wolfe. He met her gaze, his eyes mild, neutral, a reflecting lake, willing to be liked.

"You have any problems with working for a woman, Mr. Wolfe?" she asked.

Shrug. "No. A boss is a boss, as long as they're not, you know . . ."

"What?"

"A jerk. Let me do my job, and stuff." Wolfe allowed himself a shy smile.

Marlene smiled back. One advantage of hiring cops part-time was that your backgrounders were all done for you. The chances of getting a bum or a weirdo were much reduced. On the other hand, cops already had a job, a job that always came first, and it was becoming increasingly difficult to generate the coverage Bello & Ciampi needed for their clients out of the constantly changing patterns of their part-time availability. Also, when some dignitary visited, or some disaster happened, they might have the bulk of their coverage yanked away without much notice.

"Okay, Mr. Wolfe, let me check these references and run your name for record, and I'll get back to you."

"Okay, well, ah, thanks for the interview. I, ah, hope I can work here."

Marlene smiled and shook the proffered hand again, and Wolfe walked out. She took the résumé into Harry's office, where she found Marlon Dane waving around a Heckler & Koch MP5 submachine gun.

"No," said Marlene.

"Marlene, would you just listen?" said Dane, cradling the hideous thing like a puppy.

She glared, cocking her head to fix him with the full force of her good eye. Dane was a former cop, discharged on one of those odd NYPD disability pensions that paid people half their pay forever for extremely subtle injuries. Dane had been pushed down a flight of stairs by a fugitive, producing a stiffness in his right elbow such that were he to be involved in a furious gunfight, he might not be able to outdraw the desperado. Besides that he was fine: more than that, was bursting with energy. He was a stocky man with dense brown hair, dark eyes, and a curiously lush thick-lipped mouth. Today he was dressed in his undercover outfit, a red hooded sweatshirt stained with plaster dust, faded jeans, and yellow construction boots. He looked like he was about to set a rivet with the gun.

"I don't have to listen, Lonny," said Marlene. "This is not open to argument. I thought I made myself clear the first time you brought it up, and also the second through fifth times, but let me restate it in simpler terms. Ready? No machine guns. None. Not one. Negatory on the machine guns. We are eighty-six as far as machine guns go. Do I have to go on, or do you get it yet?"

"Marlene, I got to say, you're making a mistake here," Dane persisted, ignoring this last. "All the big security firms use these. The clients expect it, especially the big shots. It looks cool too, the client gets out of the limo, we're standing there with these babies slung under our coats . . ."

Marlene sighed. "But, Lonny," she said in a controlled manner, "you know, we have very few clients who are heads of state or oil ministers. The people who try to get to *our* clients are jerky boyfriends and lone nuts, not gangs of international terrorists. I get nervous with some of the guys we hire carrying *revolvers*. They start carrying something like that, I might as well check into a psycho ward."

"But . . ."

"Lonny? Please? End of discussion."

Which it was. Dane put the weapon away in his duffel bag, and conversation turned to a report on the man Dane was watching, Donald Monto, the rejected swain of one Mary Kay Miller. Monto had been spending his evenings drinking and cruising past Ms. Miller's Brooklyn home. Before long, Marlene had every confidence, he would be drunk enough to break down her door, as he had on two past occasions, and try to beat Ms. Miller into jelly in order to demonstrate his affection. On the next occasion, however, Dane would be there, would identify himself, and should the man fail to retreat (a reasonable expectation), Dane would, in the presence of Ms. Miller, render Monto incapable of doing anything anti-door for a good long time, perhaps indefinitely.

"That *stronzo!*" snapped Marlene when Dane had gone. "Fucking machine guns!"

"Muscle," said Harry. "He does okay, though, he don't have to do much heavy thinking. How was his friend?"

"Looks all right," she said, tossing the résumé on the desk. "More muscle. You'll check him out. If he's okay, let's give him a shot. He sounds like he's got a sympathetic heart, and he looks like he can take care of himself. This is not an everyday combo."

"He probably likes bazookas, your luck," said Harry. Marlene had her first serious laugh of the day.

Outside the building, the Music Lover looked up from across the street at the wide semicircular window. He could see Marlene and Harry. If she turned her head, he thought, she could look right at me. And then she would turn her head away. He was so full of delicious pleasure at the thought that he quivered, and his groin grew hot.

SIX

"You look beat," Karp said.

"I'm totally ruined," Marlene said. "I have to pee, and I can't bear the thought of moving my body out of bed to the bathroom. Could you, like, do it for me?"

"I would, but I'm too tired."

"Your trial, huh?"

Both of them were talking like zombies, lying corpse-like in bed, staring up at the ceiling with glazed eyes; it would have been amusing if either of them could have spared the energy to laugh. It was Sunday night after a weekend with no rest.

"Right," sighed Karp. "I have to see Waley tomorrow. I thought I should know the case and the relevant law before I met him. *He* probably does. But I had to spend all Friday with this silly woman who screwed up a perfectly simple case, where the witnesses weren't—"

"I don't want to hear it," groaned Marlene, putting her hands over her ears.

"Right, why bother? The bureau is going to go down the tubes."

"Uh-huh. Explain to me again why it was so important for you to take this case, even though everyone told you not to."

"It was important because I am an arrogant schmuck, and as

an arrogant schmuck I naturally believe I can do things that no one else can do, like managing a major case against the best defense lawyer in the country while running a homicide bureau that handles a thousand cases a year. How's Lucy doing?"

"Terrible. She went to bed in tears again. I feel like I'm tearing pieces of flesh from her body. She's so ashamed of herself she can't think straight, and I lose my temper. I am many things, but apparently a math teacher is not one of them. Why can't she learn this shit? I'm thinking. It's easy! And of course, it's *not* easy for her for some reason, and then I think she needs to go into some kind of counseling, so she can tell someone what a bad mother I am. Anyway, it's clear that something else is going on—it's not intellectual deficit. I mean, for Christ's sake, the kid speaks Chinese, she reads at the ninth-grade level . . . Fuck! I can't think about it anymore. Look, could you, like, stroke my head?"

"Like this?"

"Yes. Kind of ease the toxic thoughts out of there. Would you mind terribly if I wet the bed?"

"Not at all. On the other hand . . ." He paused, listening. "I think we are both going to have to get up anyway." A thin, cranky wail drifted through the loft, which was soon followed by a second, almost identical cry, and then both gained volume until they had reached the precise pitch and intensity that evolution had found to be the most irritating to the human adult—but doubled.

"Teething," said Karp unnecessarily, and swung his feet out of bed.

Marlene clenched her own teeth, distorted her face into a Medusa-like rictus, balled her fists, and thrashed her legs violently about, emitting a hideous sound somewhere between a muffled shriek and a sob. The spasm lasted for a good half minute, leaving Marlene limper even than before. Karp ignored the display, having grown used to it since the twins arrived. Marlene had assured him that the release it afforded helped prevent her from dashing their tiny brains out.

"I'll get Zak," said Karp nobly, the senior twin being notoriously the harder to calm.

Marlene grunted, cursed, stiffened her jaw, got out of bed, and clumped into the bathroom. This can't go on, she thought. I have to do something to make this stop.

Karp was not ready to meet with Lionel T. Waley the next morning. The regular meeting of the bureau to review cases had gone badly, although young Nolan had much improved his case against Morella and had received a nice round of applause. Karp was not as up on the cases as he usually was and was compelled to fake it, a habit he deplored in others and despised in himself. Roland Hrcany made sure that Karp knew he knew that Karp was screwing up, and Karp was certain that many of the others did too. While he could depend on Roland's native sadism to prevent any truly wretched cases from going forward, the meeting simply added to his feeling that things were slipping out of control.

Lionel Waley's presence made him feel it even more, through invidious comparison, for if anyone was ever in complete control, it was Waley. Karp had taken as much care with his appearance as he could manage, but he had slept only three out of the last twenty-four hours and it showed. He had definitely remembered to shave, because there was a prominent gash smarting under his chin, and he was dressed, although he realized just after he had risen to shake Waley's hand that the shirt button over his belt was undone, allowing a charming view of his undershirt.

Waley was, in contrast, as perfect as an oil portrait of a nineteenth-century alderman, and like one of these, he seemed to glow softly. He was a slight, well-proportioned man in his early sixties. His hair was white and curly, like that of a show poodle, or Santa, and this lent a softness to what otherwise would have been too severe a face. His eyes, large and canny under thick white brows, were gray-blue, and he wore a beautifully tailored, conservatively cut suit of a similar shade, the sort of ineffably custom color that never appears on pipe racks at even the best department stores. He spoke in deep, mellow tones, like an oboe in low register, and he had the perfectly neutral accent of a newscaster.

After a somewhat briefer than usual bout of pleasantries, Karp said, "Your meeting, Mr. Waley. What can I do for you?"

"Well, I believe we can do something for each other, Mr. Karp, and put this dreadful tragedy behind us in a way mutually credible to our respective causes."

This was not the sort of language that dripped from the mouths of lawyers much in evidence at 100 Centre Street. The stately period was not often heard in those precincts, and when it was, Karp was frequently the source. He enjoyed a certain formality of language, as befitting the dignity of the law (assuming it still retained any in Centre Street) and tending both to suppress the passion that could lead to legal errors and to allay the hostility of the lowlifes. Now, however, Karp found it irritating, perhaps because he sensed that Waley considered *him* one of the lowlifes.

Bluntly, therefore, he snapped, "You want to make a deal?"

"Any arrangement that would avoid the spectacle of a trial would, I think, be an act of mercy, for my client, for his parents, and, given the case's peculiar circumstances, for the community at large."

"What about the families of the murdered women? You think it would be a mercy for them too?"

Karp's tone was harsh, but Waley seemed not to notice. In the same mild voice he answered, "Frankly? Yes, I believe so, unless you still imagine that it would be purgative or healing for them to sit in a courtroom day after day, pecked at by the vulture press, while experts jabber on about precisely how their beloved mother, or sister, or grandmother died. You don't believe that, do you?"

In fact, Karp did not; nevertheless, and paradoxically, that he agreed only served to heighten his irritation. He said, "Okay, Mr. Waley, you made your point. If Jonathan says he's really, truly sorry, he can go home, no hard feelings."

A tiny pause, as if something faintly disgusting had occurred. Then Waley said, "Really, Mr. Karp, I did not expect cheap sarcasm from you, someone with your reputation among the criminal bar of this city as a decent and honorable man."

Karp's neck grew warm; he could hardly believe it. Embarrassed? By a *lawyer*? He cleared his throat and snapped, "What's your plan, counselor?"

Waley replied, "My only aim here, Mr. Karp, is to obtain for Jonathan Rohbling the psychiatric treatment he very badly needs, in a setting where he has some chance of recovery. We would therefore offer a guilty plea to manslaughter in the second degree on the homicide of Jane Hughes, the sentence not to exceed five years. All other charges would be dismissed. We would make application to the court that sentence be served in an appropriate facility, and we would expect the People to concur."

"You're serious?"

"Perfectly."

"So, essentially, we would give your client a free pass for four murders and around three years in a psychiatric country club for the fifth? I'm curious, sir, why you would imagine there to be any advantage to the People in such an arrangement."

"The advantage is avoiding a racially divisive circus trial, which cannot but lead to the same result."

"That's breathtaking confidence, even for you, Mr. Waley. We have a confession for all five murders. We have solid forensic evidence linking Rohbling to the murder of Jane Hughes—"

Waley waved his hand dismissively. "Mr. Karp, the murder of Hughes is neither here nor there. We concede Hughes died as a result of my client's actions. But the boy is *insane*, a palpable and obvious lunatic. Your confession, so-called, is therefore meaningless and without legal effect, as I'm certain any judge will confirm. And any jury confronted with the evidence will bring in a verdict of not guilty by reason of insanity."

"He was found capable of assisting with his defense."

"Oh, yes," said Waley irritably, "so he is. He can also tie his shoes and go to the toilet by himself. You know very well that has nothing to do with what we're discussing. He is, in fact, insane."

"That is your opinion. I disagree."

Waley stared at him for what seemed a long while. "You disagree? Tell me, Mr. Karp, have you met my client? Have you spoken at any length with Jonathan Rohbling?"

"No, of course not. Why should I? I know what he did, which is the only issue here."

"Is it? Yes, I suppose it must be, to you." Waley's face took on a look that was nearly wistful, with little flarings of the nostrils. "You know, Mr. Karp, as much as I respect our adversary system, it is at times like these I wish that we could simply sit down like civilized men and just do the decent thing, to do what we would want done if our own families or loved ones were involved in this dreadful affair. Instead we will lend our considerable talents to making each other look foolish or evil, we will bring out what the British charmingly call trick cyclists to pontificate upon whether this pathetic boy is mad or sane, and in the end the jury will either commit him for treatment, which is what we ought to have done during this interview, or else condemn him to certain, miserable death in some prison."

"Death?"

"Of course, death! I don't mean the formal penalty. But what do you suppose the fate will be in Attica or Dannemora of a slight, pale boy accused of murdering five black grandmothers?" Waley coughed and stiffened his face, as if the air in Karp's office had somehow congealed or turned noisome. Then, in one dramatic motion, he rose to his feet and slipped his fawn cashmere topcoat over his shoulders. He smiled sadly, extending his hand, which Karp shook. "A pleasure, Mr. Karp. Regrettably, it seems we will be much in each other's way in the coming months."

Waley paused at the door. "They tell me you have never lost a homicide case, Mr. Karp. A string of over one hundred now, isn't it?"

"Something like that."

Waley smiled. It was a warm, delighted smile, and Karp felt his face twitching to return it.

"Well, well," said Waley, and left.

"It was the most uncanny thing, V.T.," said Karp that afternoon over a mediocre Chinese lunch. "I mean, it's not like I'm a blushing virgin. I've been around the block with the defense bar, good ones, sleaze balls, the usual range, but this guy was a piece of work. You know, for an instant I actually felt myself wanting to accept his offer. He seemed so reasonable, so decent . . ."

"Perhaps he is," said V. T. Newbury. He was a small, fair, handsome, elegant man whose most common facial expression was one of ironic surprise. He wore it now.

"Oh, right!" Karp snorted. "V.T., he's a *lawyer*. Be real! No, but, Jesus, I tell you, man, I haven't had a warm douche like that in years. Some kind of weird rays coming off that guy."

"Probably has demonic powers."

"I'd believe it. Three sixes tattooed on his ass, the whole thing. What a technique, though! Fucker'll go through a jury like a dose of salts."

"Aren't you worried?"

"I'm pissing in my pants, V.T. You know, I'll tell you something strange. When he was sitting there, I swear I was flashing on Garrahy. Not because he looked like him, or he sounded like him, because he didn't, but there was a *presence* there, like the guy was the best and he knew it and it didn't affect him—there was no arrogance. You remember Garrahy—there wasn't an arrogant bone in his body. Well, this guy is the same thing, like God reached down and touched him and said, Hey, Lionel, somebody got to be the best fucking defense lawyer in the universe and I picked you."

"You sound like you're in love," said V.T.

Karp laughed. "I don't know, man, but I'm definitely going to have to bring my lunch to this trial. The thing of it is, whatever you do in life, there comes a moment—I mean, let's face it, I won a lot of cases, but seventy-five percent of them were mutts with a dumb alibi and a court-appointed good Democrat out of Brooklyn Law night school. This is going to be something completely different."

"As they say on the Monty Python show. So, you feel like backing out?"

"What I *feel* like is getting into my jammies, pulling the quilt over my head, and putting my thumb in my mouth. You want the last shrimp? Another thing I flashed on when I was coming over here. It happened back in '61. Summer after my sophomore year. I was a hot ball player, I'd just burned up the PAC-Ten, set a single-game scoring record, and set a couple of Cal records too. I had triple doubles in a dozen games. Okay, it's the summer, I'm playing ball in the Rucker Summer League, up in the Rucker playground on 155th Street. This, you should know, is like the killer playground of the world. There's guys playing there, that's all they do, street guys. If they could read and write, they'd've been All-Americans, first-round draft choices. So it's a tough game, but I'm hot, I'm like one of four white guys playing in the whole place. I could still move back then, and jump, not too embarrassingly, and shoot, of course. Okay, so at Rucker, in those days, the thing was, you never knew who'd turn up. Chamberlain would come by, Richie Guerin, Oscar Robertson, and the thing was, you weren't supposed to notice them as anything special, they would just jump in and run around with the playground guys. Now, of course, there would be TV cameras and the whole entourage, but back then it was still a game. Anyway, it's after the regular competitions, pick-up playground games, it's getting dark, that kind of blue twilight you get in the summers here when you think it's never going to be night, and you can play forever, the lights are on, and the game I'm in ends and some guys leave and others drift in. This is done on automatic pilot, five guys strip off their shirts, five guys keep them on, and you're playing, twenty-one points, deuce rule, make it, take it. Okay, so seven seconds into the game I notice the guy I'm playing against is something special, and I look, and I think to myself, holy shit, it's Elgin Baylor. This was the year he averaged thirty-eight points a game in the NBA. So, in the next fifteen minutes I learned the difference between a hot sophomore college ball player and one of the best basketball players in history.''

"How did you do?"

"He pounded me into the ground like a tent peg—what do you think?"

"And your point is . . . ?"

"I'm not sure," said Karp, his forehead wrinkling. "Obviously, I want to win, but maybe even more I want to be in the game with this guy. He gets my juices flowing. You know, we win cases all the time because we only go in there, to court, when we think we have an overwhelming case, and when the mutt hasn't got the sense to cop a plea. But the fact is, the system is skewed to let the guy off unless the prosecutor's really sharp. We should get beat a lot more, and we would if we faced more people like Waley."

"Lucky us," said V.T. "What am I hearing, you think you'll get creamed?"

Karp shrugged. "I'm not sure I'd bet my next three paychecks on me to win. He'll go with NGI, so it's going to be dueling shrinks, which is always a toss-up. Also, with him in there, I make one mistake it's all over. But that's the job: they let the bull in, you got to wave the cape. Otherwise, you walk up the aisles selling enchiladas. So what're you up to?"

What V.T. was up to was the undermining of a complex Medicaid–fraud scheme. He described the convolutions of this with verve and humor, while Karp, not really following the details, was content to relax and listen in the dim booth, occasionally dropping a piece of Mongolian beef into his mouth and nodding appropriately.

Suddenly, however, he grew alert. "What was that doc's name again?" he asked.

"Which doc? Robinson?"

"Yeah, Vincent Robinson. What do you have on him?"

"Oh, Vince! Old Vincent is a rare bird. He runs a string of clinics, three in Harlem, one in Washington Heights, two in the South Bronx. A social benefactor, Dr. Robinson. He does well by doing good."

"These are Medicaid mills?"

"We think so. Medicaid and Medicare."

"What's the difference?"

"You haven't been listening. I'm hurt. To review, Medicaid is the federally funded program for people on welfare. Medicare is for the old, regardless of income. The federal government sets rates for particular payments for medical procedures and drugs in both cases, but with Medicaid the money is run through the state, and through city agencies with the state making a contribution. The paperwork is extremely complex. For example, you can have a health-service provider bill another provider for services, only some of which are Medicaid–eligible under Part Two—"

"Snore," said Karp. "Just the story on Robinson, please. What's he up to?"

"But all the fun is in the details!"

"No, really, V.T. Tell me about Robinson."

"Well, since you insist, about a month ago the Southern District U.S. Attorney's Office got an anonymous tip that Robinson's clinics were dirty. They have a hotline for stuff like that. They did some preliminary screening and found discrepancies. Okay, no surprise there, the regs are so complicated that practically everyone in the program is in some kind of irregularity, but Robinson's operation was big enough and funny enough to flash on the screen. Paul Menotti caught the case. You know him?"

"By rep. A hard charger."

"To be sure. Anyway, Paul called me in, because of the state law violation, of course, but also because, though I blush to say it, if you want to find out where naughty money is flowing, I am The Man."

"And was there naughty money flowing?"

"Mmm, that's what we're trying to determine. There're a couple of different ways to defraud these programs. Most fraudulent docs just add on treatments they haven't done and bill for them. An old lady comes in, they have some lackey slip her the happy pills, and then they bill for a full examination, with lab work. A little upscale from that is where they invent patients, which has the advantage that they don't even have to have a real clinic, just a bunch of government patient numbers and a vivid medical imagination."

"Where do they get the numbers?"

"Oh, from actual people, alive or dead. Mrs. Jones dies and they keep using her number for billing. Or Mrs. Jones wanders off to another provider, but she's still, quote, getting her pills every week, unquote, and the feds're paying. And then, finally, we have the whole lab and drug business, kickbacks to and from labs and pharmacies—the labs pad their billings and the clinics get a schmear off it. Or the clinic generates scrip for drugs, but the pharmacy doesn't really supply them, and they get a cut of the billings. Or the pharmacy really does supply drugs, which the feds pay for, and then the drugs get sold on the street. The only limit is the human imagination."

"This is big money?"

"Immense. A bonanza. Fifteen *billion* in Medicare-Medicaid money goes through New York City every year. Robinson's clinics alone have over thirty million bucks' worth of the pie. How much of that is skim, God only knows."

"Assuming God is an accountant."

"*Of course* God is an accountant. It's the basis of all morality."

"You can't get to him? Robinson, not God."

"Not yet. As I said, he's a rare bird. Very smart, very smooth."

"You've met him?"

"Yes, we've had several dates. It's all a big misunderstanding. Dr. Robinson is a Park Avenue specialist. He maintains an interest in St. Nicholas Medical Centers, Inc., which is the holding company for the clinics, out of noblesse oblige: he has an investment in the corporation, and he gets a modest return in exchange for his medical advice and his Harvard degree. The board of the corporation and the management of the clinics are full of local fronts, of the correct ethnicity. We find any fraud, in other words, his tame Negroes and Hispanics take the fall."

"So what happened to the money he's supposed to be skimming here?" Karp asked.

"Ah, that's the question," said V.T., beaming. "And the answer? The answer is, we don't know yet. We have to move somewhat gingerly with Robinson. He is heavily accoutered with legal counsel. What we do know is, one, he set up St. Nicholas, and two, St. Nicholas is dirty. It follows that he has his fingers in the money stream somehow, but . . ." V.T. shrugged elegantly. "What's your interest in the doctor? Prostate acting up again?"

Karp laughed. "Au contraire. If anything, it is I who will be jamming large irregular objects up Doctor Robinson's rectum.

Tell me, does Dr. R. strike you as the sort of man who might remove a close associate if that associate grew troublesome?"

" 'Remove'? You mean the Big M?"

Karp nodded. "Could be. His nurse slash girlfriend turned up dead this past September, in his bedroom, and Robinson went through a lot of trouble to distance himself from the death. The death itself is suspicious."

"Oh-ho," said V.T. and was silent for a moment, playing with his lip. Then he said, "Well, since you ask, I'd have to give that a qualified yes. There is a shitload of money floating free here, and if someone was, say, threatening to tell us where it is, or trying to grab a piece of it, then, yes, I'd say Robinson could do the deed. As a moral being, Dr. Robinson is easily distinguishable from Dr. Schweitzer."

"It sounds like it," said Karp. "We're digging up the nurse for a full postmortem. If it shows anything nasty, we'll get the doc in for a frank exchange of views."

"Speaking of which, why don't you sit in with me and Menotti before that? It might give you some sense of a possible motive, or maybe you'll pick up something we missed."

Motive again, thought Karp, his mind drifting involuntarily back to Rohbling. Greed seemed so simple compared to whatever impelled young Jonathan. He made a mental note: if Waley pleaded NGI, he would have the defendant examined by somebody he trusted more than the usual Bellevue hacks.

He realized V.T. was staring at him. "Oh, sorry," he said. "Had a thought. Yeah, good idea. I'd like to meet Menotti."

"Then come with me," said V.T. "There's a meeting to talk about warrants at one-thirty today."

Still strained with each other, but holding hands nevertheless, Marlene and her daughter walked with the big dog down Canal Street toward Tranh's noodle shop.

"Oh, no!" cried Lucy when they had come near enough to see the debris on the pavement, the police sawhorses set up as barriers, the yellow crime-scene tape. Tranh's was a black vacancy in the row of shops, stinking of char and dripping with dirty water, from out of which presently emerged a stocky middle-aged man in a firefighter's coat and helmet. He paused at the barrier to write on a clipboard. Marlene approached him.

"Excuse me, I'm a friend of the man who ran this place. Do you know . . . did anything happen to him?"

"Not as far as I know," said the man. "Somebody lived back there behind the restaurant, but he must've got out."

"This was an arson, wasn't it?"

The officer's face grew blank. "It's a case under investigation."

"Yeah, right. Look, I used to be with the D.A. Here's my card. I saw a serious altercation the other day between the owner and a bunch of punks who were trying to extort him. I can ID them anytime you want."

The investigator took the card and expressed his thanks. Then Lucy shouted, "Mr. Tranh!" and pointed across Canal Street, where, indeed, Mr. Tranh was emerging from the all-night Chinese movie theater. He was dressed in an army blanket, black trousers, and flip-flops, and carried a cheap Day-glo orange vinyl duffel bag. Marlene and Lucy dashed across the wide thoroughfare to him and deluged him with a babble of questions in Cantonese and French, while the dog sniffed suspiciously at Tranh's blanket.

Tranh responded to Marlene in the latter tongue. "Madame, I beg you, relieve yourself of any concern. I am perfectly well."

"But what happened, M. Tranh?"

"I was visited in the early morning by arsonists. Interesting, because I had just made up my mind to purchase a grille for the window. This demonstrates the necessity of acting swiftly upon one's instincts, does it not? In any case, they threw a stone through the glass, followed by a gasoline bomb. I am not a heavy sleeper, and so I was warned and was able to escape through the back door."

"My God! I didn't realize you lived behind the restaurant. You must have lost everything."

"Yes. Everything, save for these trifles." Tranh indicated the duffel bag with his toe. "I regret only my little library, some items of which had sentimental value. This is now the third time I have lost everything. One grows accustomed to it, I find: to having nothing."

"But where will you stay?" Marlene asked. "And you can't go wandering around in a blanket. It is the autumn already. Have you got any cash?"

"A little, thank you. And I am given to understand that there are facilities for the destitute—"

"Ah, your compatriots of the Vietnamese community will provide for you?"

"I fear not. The Vietnamese community and I are not in communion. No, I refer to the establishment of the city itself."

"The men's hostels? Never! They are, you comprehend, a species of hell, full of robbers and those of degenerate tastes. I will not allow it. No, I have a suite of small rooms connected with my business. You will stay there until we can devise a better solution."

"Madame, I could not possibly impose upon you . . ."

"Nonsense!" cried Marlene. "I insist. Are you not my friend?" she said. "And it is no imposition. In return, you can perform a valuable service for me perhaps. I operate a security business. I detect that you are not altogether lacking in useful skills associated with such work. Therefore, let us walk!" She took the man's arm, whereupon he nodded in assent and lifted his bag.

"Mom! What're you talking about?" demanded Lucy, who was unused to being the one who was missing the story, at least in Chinatown.

"Mr. Tranh is going to live behind my office," said Marlene.

"With Sym and Posie?" Lucy began to giggle.

"We'll work something out," said Marlene, an interesting idea beginning to form in her mind.

SEVEN

Paul Menotti was a short, stocky, energetic man: a fireplug was the usual expression, which denoted not only his approximate shape but also carried the notion that in the event of a conflagration, he would be a good source of the wherewithal to extinguish it. Karp sat in a comfortable chair in Menotti's office in the federal building off Foley Square reflecting, not for the first time, that the offices of those who pursued the violators of federal law were more stately than those occupied by mere state prosecutors. Menotti's mahogany was bright, his brass shone, and his leather was thick and soft. He had a rug of some generalized colonial pattern on the floor and federally supplied artwork on the walls. He also had two windows opening on Foley Square.

With Karp and Menotti in the room were V. T. Newbury and a slim young woman with light blue eyes and nice cheekbones. Her dark blond hair was neck-long and held back by a tortoise-shell clip, but it fell forward as she wrote on the pad she had on her lap, hiding her face. She had been introduced as Cynthia Doland, Menotti's special assistant, with no indication of what was special about her and what she assisted in. Apparently, she was there to take meeting notes, since after the introductions she had kept mum.

Menotti and V.T. were now engaged in a technical argument, clearly one of long standing, about how to draft a warrant against St. Nicholas Health Care so as to extract enough information to nail Dr. Robinson without at the same time putting him wise to the extent of their suspicions and (possibly) prompting him to crank up his shredder. V.T. was holding out for the incremental approach, the Death of a Thousand Cuts, as he called it—a small demand, followed by another and another, until there was enough cause to justify a major raid. Menotti wanted to seize everything at once.

With no direct role in this argument, Karp was free to muse, and to examine the delightful line of Ms. Doland's neck. She was wearing a scoop-necked dress, and as she bent over recording the ever changing proposed language of the warrant in question, Karp had a nice view of her small, pointed breasts, enclosed in a pale rose bra. Karp was as faithful as a chow, but he had no objection to observing what was in plain view, as allowed by the Fourth Amendment.

Karp became aware that the discussion had ceased, that Menotti was looking at him, that Menotti knew where he had lately cast his eyes. A brief cloud crossed Menotti's face; Karp sensed that his relationship with the tasty Ms. Doland was not entirely professional. Or perhaps it was; Karp had never been very great shakes at ferreting out the intimacies of the people he met in a business way. In any case, Menotti had asked him a question.

"Well, it's not my area," Karp responded, "but if I had to choose, I'd go with V.T.'s slow and steady. I don't want this guy spooked."

"Why not?"

"Because your boy could be a killer as well as a fraud." V.T. had briefly mentioned the affair of the dead nurse at the start of the meeting, and Menotti grunted in acknowledgment. Karp went on, "The point here is that if in fact he went to that extreme, he's not going to cavil at trashing some records. Or somebody else."

They all thought about that for a while.

Then V.T. said, "Just an idea. Is it at all possible that our anonymous tipster was this nurse?"

Karp said, "Anything's possible, but how the hell would we ever find out?"

"They record all the calls on the hotline," said Ms. Doland. They all looked at her. She blushed faintly and batted long-lashed eyes.

"Check it out, would you, Cynthia?" said Menotti.

The woman made a note on her pad.

"I meant now, Cynthia."

She nodded and left the room. Since clearly no federal business could transpire without a note taker, the three men talked sports and politics in a desultory fashion until Cynthia Doland returned, about twenty minutes later, the time being punctuated by Menotti accepting several calls, during which he did a good deal of snarling and did not spare the obscenities.

When Doland came back, she was carrying a Sony portable tape recorder.

"You got it," said Menotti. It was not a question.

"They played it over the phone," she said. "It's fuzzy, but you can make out the type of voice." She sat down and pushed the Play button.

A voice said: "St. Nick's is ripping you all off big time. That Dr. Robinson got his hand in deep. They got phony patients, they got phony treatments, and there's something bad going on with the pharmacy, I don't know what."

"Sounds black. Middle-aged, I'd say," offered Menotti.

Doland clicked off the recorder and seemed about to say something. They all looked at her, but she shook her head and blushed again.

Then they all looked at Karp, who frowned and said, "Evelyn Longren was a twenty-eight-year-old white woman, so unless she was a pretty good mimic, that's someone else."

"In any case, are you going to pursue this as a homicide?" Menotti asked.

"Providing it's a homicide I will," said Karp. "They're doing the full autopsy now. I'll let you know when I know."

"I thought we weren't going to do this," said Karp, discontented in the bosom of his family. The twins had been efficiently bedded down by Posie, who was now watching the *Mary Tyler Moore Show* in the kitchen with Lucy, Lucy having done her homework with less row than usual. Butch and Marlene were in the living room of the loft discussing the new domestic arrangements.

"Yes, that's what I thought too," said Marlene. "No live-in nannies for me. No, I was going to run a business, and take care of Lucy, and a set of twins, and continue to be married and have a relationship with a man, you. Did I leave anything out? Oh, yeah, prepare meals, and not just meals but good ones, with home-made sauces and noodles, and baking once a week. And go to church. And go to the bathroom. Well, here's a flash: I can't do it. I give up. I have to be able to sleep, and I can't, and I have to be able to set my own hours and come and go more or less at will, and I can't. And I need more time with Lucy. So that's why Posie has to live in. We can leave the twins here in the morning now. We don't have to schlep them down the stairs and then up the stairs to my office. We can work on weekends without having to break off every ten minutes."

"I said I was going to watch them on weekends when you were out," objected Karp.

"You said, yeah, but that was before you started this trial. And after this trial there'll be another one, or some other crisis. Face it, *you* don't have any time either."

"And Posie is the best solution to this we can find? Jesus, Marlene, we don't know a damn thing about her. She's just somebody you picked up off the street."

"Who's been looking after the babies perfectly since they were twelve weeks old," Marlene replied with some heat. It was an old argument. "You want someone from an agency, with references? Well, let me tell you, bub, someone from an agency with references is not going to put up with us, or our hours, or what we can afford to pay, or walking up five floors, or pushing the stroller through this neighborhood, not when they can take care of little Tiffany and Lance on Central Park West. Be real!''

Karp grunted, fantasies of a Swedish au pair and a place on Central Park West, or Park Slope, at least, going glimmering. He did not have the energy for the seven millionth rep of this particular unwinnable argument, based as it was on his unshakable belief that a SoHo walk-up loft, however luxuriously appointed, was no place to raise a family. Nor did he think it the right time to raise the other possible solution, that Marlene stop running a half-assed security agency and take a respectable job with a law firm or a D.A. On the other hand, the less petulant part of him said, if she were someone who wanted such a job, she wouldn't be Marlene, and you wouldn't love her, so there! This set of thoughts flashed through his mind like a reflex, a kind of mental cramp. He wondered whether they would ever go away, or if he would continue to think them as long as he was with Marlene.

"This has to do with another of your waifs, I understand," he said, to change the subject. "Lucy said you've got the noodle man living in Posie's old room."

"He's not a waif and he's not a noodle man," said Marlene. "I think he was a policeman, or something like that, in Vietnam. I saw him face down four fairly nasty punks without breaking a sweat. He's educated, he speaks a couple of languages—"

"Not including English, I gather."

"So he'll learn. Anyway, I'm going to feel a lot better with him in the place at night, especially when we're taking care of runaway women. And I guarantee we're both going to feel better with Posie here." She poked him in the ribs. "Admit it! Don't you feel better already? The twins are fed and p.j.'d and nestling in their cribs, in clouds of baby powder. We're lounging at our ease." To demonstrate ease of lounging, she moved closer to him on the sofa and nuzzled his neck. "And if, God forbid, we should want to fool around in the marital bed some night and the yelling starts, Posie will leap out and do her thing."

"This, ah, you imagine is the clinching argument?" he asked, pulling her closer.

"It better be," said Marlene.

The following morning, feeling better than she had in weeks by reason of a luxurious eight hours in the rack, Marlene skipped lightly off to work. Posie had indeed done her thing with the night screams, so Marlene was also enjoying that oily-jointed relaxation that follows upon uninterrupted conjugal delights. Lucy was markedly calmer during the morning's preparation and ride to school; Marlene, observing this with satisfaction, reflected that the child's equilibrium had been as much affected as her own by the nonnegotiable demands of the twins. Things would now improve; she even had hopes for long division.

"How do you like your new roommate?" she asked Sym as the girl handed over the steaming cup.

"He's okay for a old guy," said Sym. "He cook better—he cooks better than Posie, anyway. He ain't got much to say, though."

"That's because he doesn't speak much English. Try to talk to him and he'll learn. You got your TV back there—watch shows, explain what's going on. Any messages?"

"Dane called last night. Said he ran off that Monto guy from in front of Miller's house."

"Any trouble?"

"He didn't say none. Guy drove by is all, saw Dane and got small."

"Um. Be hard to get him on a violation for that. But he'll be back. Harry in?"

"Yeah. He looked pissed off too."

"Oh?"

"Yeah. I don't think he features the old guy."

Harry's emotional range was a narrow one, covering only a few degrees on either side of what in a normal person would have been suicidal depression, but Marlene had learned to read the subtle arrangement of the ridges on his stony face and was able to confirm Sym's assessment.

"What's wrong, Harry?"

A movement of the head in the direction of the living quarters.

"What's the problem, Harry? He's a good guy. He needs a place to stay and I need Posie at home. Besides, he'll be security at night."

Harry frowned more deeply and with his eyes and head indicated an easterly direction, where lay Chinatown. "What about . . . ?"

"Not a problem. They put him out of business, which was what they wanted. They're not going to pursue him all the way to regular New York."

Harry grunted and turned to the window. The conversation was over. It would never have occurred to Marlene that Harry was jealous, that he considered himself the waif-in-chief, and wished not to share Marlene's rescuing talents with other desperate males. After a few moments of studying the Walker Street traffic, he said, "I checked on Wolfe. He's clean. He'll be by today, later."

Good, thought Marlene as she walked to the living quarters. That meant Harry had not been able to find any obvious lies or distortions in Jack Wolfe's work history, or any criminal record in any of the states he had worked, which meant she had her extra full-time man. She found Tranh washing dishes in the little kitchen.

Tranh looked up and smiled. "Good morning. How you are?" he said in English.

"Good morning, and I'm fine, thank you," replied Marlene in the same tongue, and then, in French, "I am impressed, sir, at your progress in our language. Recitations from Shakespeare cannot be far off. Meanwhile, I observe you have accomplished wonders of sanitation."

The kitchen was indeed gleaming, the floor and surfaces still damp and bleach-scented, while on the small stove a pot bubbled, releasing a spicy, meaty aroma.

"It is only a little thing, Madame," replied Tranh in French. "I am obliged to you."

"There is no obligation, for I intend to take advantage of you, if you are willing. As I said the other day, I suspect you have talents beyond the kitchen, which I will liked to have employed —no, pardon, which I *would like* to employ. Is that correct? The subjunctive mode—"

"Perfectly correct, Madame. You are offering me employment, then?"

"Yes, surely."

"Of what sort?"

"It would be in the nature of security. Often women and children, fleeing from violent men, must stay here. They require protection. Also, there is work of a similar sort outside, investigations and security . . ."

"But I am merely a cook," said Tranh. He was no longer smiling.

"With respect, M. Tranh, you were not always a cook."

Tranh dropped his eyes and scrubbed dry a spot on the already shining plate he was holding. "No, that is true. I was not always a cook. When I was younger, I was a teacher."

"Nor always a teacher," said Marlene. "You were, I suspect, a policeman or—"

"No, never! Not a *flic*!" Tranh replied curtly.

"Calm yourself, M. Tranh. I do not mean to pry. A soldier, then."

"Yes, a soldier. Of a type," Tranh agreed. "But you know, I do not believe I can accept your kind offer, Madame. My status in this country is . . . irregular. I would not wish for you to get into trouble with the authorities for employing me."

"That does not concern me," said Marlene. "Half or more of the waiters in Chinatown are in a similar position. I will pay you out of—how does one say—'petty cash'—you understand, the money we use to purchase stamps and so on. You will live here and take from the box I will show you whatever you need. For example, you will require clothing and other necessaries. I will place, let us say, five hundred dollars in the box today, and each week two hundred more. Well, what do you say?"

Tranh paused for thought and then sighed. "What can I say but thank you, Madame? I accept your kind offer. I can only hope that you have not purchased a cat in a pocket."

"Marvelous!" exclaimed Marlene, and shook Tranh's hand. It was like grasping a skein of cables. "And you must call me Marlene. 'Madame' makes me feel like a piano teacher, or the keeper of a brothel, or a nun of the Sacred Heart."

Tranh smiled broadly, and Marlene could see that he was missing several teeth on the scarred side of his face. He said, "Marlene? That is an American name?"

"I suppose. It is a contraction of Maria Elena."

"Ah! In that case, I will call you Marie-Hélène, if I may. I am Tranh Do Vinh. Vinh." He made a stiff little bow.

"Vinh it is," said Marlene. "Tell me, Vinh, is it possible that you can read English?"

"Oh, surely, and well too. I have read Jack London and Mark Twain. And Shakespeare. And I can understand the spoken words if the speech is not too rapid. Why, have you something you wish me to read?"

"Yes, wait here a moment."

Marlene went out to the office, picked up a thick file from her desk, went back to the kitchen, and handed it to Tranh.

"This is the file on a client I believe you can help. Would you look through it please, Vinh?"

He wiped his hands on a dish towel, and seating himself at the table, he flipped through the pages. Marlene suspected that whatever he said about not being a *flic*, it was not the first time he had examined such a dossier.

He looked up. "Interesting. This man is now free from prison?"

"Yes. And he is evidently still obsessed with Carrie Lanin."

"You fear that he will now do her an injury?"

"I'm certain of it. And since he knows, from before, that I will stop him, he may also try to eliminate me."

"I see," said Tranh. "Well, this we must prevent, no?"

He held up a photograph of Rob Pruitt that Marlene had taken when she first became involved with the stalking of Carrie Lanin. "They are a kind of vampire, these men, are they not? As in the poem: 'It is in my blood, the black poison; I am the sinister glass in which the fury sees itself.' " He tapped the face. "This one— a nasty sparrow, I think."

"Extremely nasty."

They smiled at each other. He said, "But of course, we can do nothing until he makes the first attempt. That is the law, I comprehend?"

"You comprehend exactly, my friend," replied Marlene. "He must make the first move."

"And I am to make the second, yes? In an anonymous fashion."

"You have seized upon the situation accurately," said Marlene. "Please keep the file. The information we possess is all there. And inform me as to your actions."

Marlene walked out of the kitchen feeling curiously light-headed. She reckoned that no other member of the Smith College class of 1969 was hiring a Vietnamese hit man in stilted schoolgirl French. Perhaps "hit man" was a trifle strong: hiring "Vietnamese noodle cook with presumptive quasi-military background and frightening martial arts skills" might have been more accurate— same difference. Once again that feeling of stepping off the little platform onto the rope, no net below, a feeling that terrified her, but one that (as she had realized for some time now) she could not live without.

After his meeting with Menotti, Karp walked the few blocks back to 100 Centre Street, where for the rest of the afternoon he watched Roland Hrcany complete the presentation of *People* v. *Rohbling* to the grand jury. Hrcany was coldly efficient at this. The witnesses were well drilled, and the whole affair proceeded with the smooth, nearly meaningless aplomb of a masque at Versailles. Hrcany did not speak to Karp either during the event or afterward, when the two of them waited in the little anteroom for the grand jury to signal the bringing in of a true bill. When the little light went on that indicated this legal milestone, Hrcany turned to Karp, made a little mock bow and a waving "it's all yours" gesture with his hand, and went back into the jury room.

Karp wheeled the wire cart containing the Rohbling case files to the bureau law library, hoping for a few hours of uninterrupted study, but Connie Trask, who well knew all his wiles, found him before he had made much progress.

"He wants to know where you been all day," she said, giving the pronoun the special intonation that designated the district attorney himself.

"Jesus, Connie, I was with the grand jury. He knows that," Karp said.

"I think he meant before that, when you were hiding somewhere, where you didn't tell me like you're supposed to."

"What does he want?"

"Well, you know, he don't discuss the legal niceties with me, although the fact is I've been running your bureau for you recently. You might want to have a little chat with Roland too, because he's fairly pissed off about things in general and he's started to take it out on me, in the absence of you, which shit, boss, I don't get paid for taking."

"Sorry, Connie," said Karp, genuinely ashamed. "It's this . . . I get caught up." He gestured to the stacks of files.

"Yeah, well, nobody asked you to take that on. In fact, they said not to."

"They did and I didn't listen and there's no help for it now. Is my spanking over? Thank you. Okay, I'll see Keegan and I'll fix it with Roland. Anything else?"

"Yeah, the M.E. called. They got that autopsy done on that exhumation order. Longren."

Karp ripped a sheet of yellow paper off his pad and wrote on it "DO NOT TOUCH THIS STUFF!!! KARP." He placed it on the Rohbling material and then went back to his office and called the district attorney.

"Where the hell were you?" asked that official when he picked up.

Karp explained. Keegan said, "Let me understand this. You don't have enough on your plate. You're *looking* for a homicide where two docs swore it was a natural death?"

"It was fishy, Jack. Robinson is a bad guy."

"Give me strength, Lord! Okay, buddy, it's your funeral, and that's not a figure of speech. What's new with the case of the year? I assume you got the indictment."

"We did. Also, I met Waley."

"What did you think?"

"A handful."

Keegan laughed, a full-throated noise. "Yeah, he's that. He make an offer?"

"Uh-huh. It amounted to we walk his boy with our sincere apologies."

"Expected. You'll arraign on the murder indictments tomorrow."

"Right. We'll go with murder on all five homicides he confessed to."

"Confession going to hold up?"

"If the judge likes it, it'll hold up," said Karp, verging toward the snappish, "same as always. You have some sort of problem, Jack? They revoke my law degree or what?"

"You have my full and utter confidence, Butch, you know that, until you fuck up and I throw you to the wolves."

They both laughed, releasing tension.

"Seriously, though," Keegan resumed, "if you lose the confession, all you have is Jane Hughes. Are we good on that?"

"We can show he did it, all right. What the jury will make of it is something else. As you're aware."

"Yeah, dueling shrinks. My fucking favorite. Who's our guy in the event of?"

"I was going to go with Emanuel Perlsteiner."

"Perlsteiner? Jesus, Butch, the guy's a hundred eight years old and he talks like Dr. Strangelove. Can't you get a more impressive mouthpiece for the horseshit?"

"He's seventy-four, he's convincing, he's extremely impressive, in my opinion, and I trust him."

"The Jews stick together, right? Speaking of ethnic matters, who do you have second seating on this?"

"Well, Roland can't do it, obviously, because he has to watch the bureau," Karp replied, and then, suddenly suspicious, asked, "Why, do you have a suggestion?"

"Yeah. What about Terrell Collins?"

Karp answered in a controlled voice, "Collins is a good lawyer. He's one of several that might be right for it."

"Come on, Butch," said Keegan, "a black face on the prosecution bench is not going to do you any harm. Not in this case. It also wouldn't hurt to let him examine some witnesses."

"Excuse me, there must be something wrong with the connection. I thought I was talking to Jack Keegan, the guy who taught me that one prosecutor has to work the whole case because otherwise the jury's going to get the idea that the case is too hard for one guy to understand, and therefore too hard for *them* to understand."

"Be nice, Butch," said Keegan.

"Nice is my middle name, Jack," said Karp. "And I want to stay nice, which is why I am going to forget that you just told me to put a guy in second seat because he is brown in color."

"Oh, for crying out loud, Butch! You just said he was a good attorney."

"He is. And I intend to give his skills due consideration when I make my selection."

A pause on the line. Karp could imagine the red creeping up Keegan's neck. "You do that," said Keegan tightly, and broke the connection.

Karp took a few deep breaths, put the conversation out of his mind, and called the chief medical examiner. He got a secretary, who put him on hold. He placed the phone on his desk and began going through the stack of paperwork that Connie Trask had marked with stapled-on notes, heavily underlined in red, as requiring his immediate and personal attention. About fifteen minutes passed in this way.

At last dim noises from the phone's earpiece informed him that the C.M.E. was on the line.

"You know, Murray," he remarked, "there are probably high public officials in this city who would resent being put on hold for a quarter of an hour."

"I was cutting," said Selig. "So, what can I do for you?"

"I'm returning your call, Murray. The Longren death?"

"Oh, yeah! Interesting case. Let me get a hold of it, just a sec."

Clunk of phone hitting desk, squeak of swivel chair, rustling papers. Minutes passed.

"Okay. She wasn't choked or strangled. Drug analysis shows phenobarbital, flurazepam, and ciretidine."

"Which are what? I know what phenobarb is."

"Well, flurazepam is a common tranquilizer; it's Dalmane, the sleeping pill. Ciretidine is an anti-ulcer drug."

"She had ulcers?"

"Uh-huh. But she shouldn't have been taking sedatives in those dosages if she was taking ciretidine, since ciretidine potentiates the effect of sedatives."

"So cause of death was . . . ?"

"She had the flu, she doped herself up, or was doped up, there was some fluid in the lungs, as there usually is with flu, but her breathing reflexes were so suppressed that she couldn't clear it. Essentially she just stopped breathing."

"You're ruling natural causes?" said Karp, his voice rising.

"Well, Butch, what the hell else is it? She might have recovered without the dope, sure, but the dope didn't actually kill her. I'm not saying there couldn't be a winnable civil suit against the doctor who treated her, a malpractice thing, but homicide? I don't think so."

"But, damn it, Murray! Why the hell did Robinson go through that charade with Davidoff if there wasn't something fishy going on?"

"Oh, fishy I'll grant you. Robinson screwed up, and he wanted the signature of the well-respected internist Dr. Davidoff on the death cert: cause of death viral pneumonia. It'll be useful in case of an inquiry, and Davidoff's insurance will participate in any defense and settlement. Fishy, yes. Slimy and unprincipled, yes. Murder? Can't show it."

"Oh, hell, Murray, first we have four homicides that you guys list as natural causes, and now you cry homicide and get me all worked up and it really *is* natural causes. I mean, what the fuck, Murray!"

"Hey, what do you want from my life? We messed up on Rohbling's victims, I admit it. Now we're being extra careful with anomalous cases, like this one. You don't want that?"

Karp let out a quantity of air. "Oh, shit, Murray, I'm just pissed off in general. Look, thanks for the quick turnaround on this. It's one thing off my plate at least."

Back in the law library, Karp found it hard to plunge back into the details of *Rohbling*. He was uncharacteristically confused as to what to do about filling the second seat in the coming trial. In fact, he had actually been thinking about picking Collins, a calm, serious man who had won a couple of nice convictions in small-time gang shootings, but had never worked on a major, high-profile case. He was certainly ambitious enough, and he was at the point in his career that he was ready to join the dozen or so senior people in the bureau, like Hrcany and Guma, who could be trusted to handle their cases with minimum supervision from Karp. Collins's race had pressed itself on Karp's consciousness to the same degree that Hrcany's Hungarianess or Guma's Italianess had; that it might be a factor in the man's employment had simply never occurred to him. Karp felt a bit of a schmuck about this, as he occasionally did when an office adultery was revealed, which every single person in the office except him had known about, including the janitors. Now, of course, he *couldn't* use Collins, because it would look to Keegan that he was acceding to a cynical manipulation. On the other hand, cutting Collins out of a chance he deserved because of that was . . . what? Double-English reverse nondiscrimination prejudice? With a curse he got up and stomped off down the hallway to Collins's cubicle, where he found the man, as expected, working late.

Collins looked up from his work and smiled. He was a

chocolate-colored, broad-shouldered man who retained the lithe grace he had exhibited playing football for Lafayette.

Karp said, "Look, Terry . . . ah, shit, this sucks!"

"What did I do?" said Collins, alarmed.

"Nothing. I want you to second-seat me on *Rohbling*."

"Jesus! *That's* what sucks?"

"No." Karp felt the sweat of embarrassment on his forehead. "But. Okay, here it is: the D.A. just told me I should use you because of the politics of this particular trial."

"Because I'm black? That does suck, if you want to know. So this would be like, a . . . decorative assignment?"

"Oh, fuck, no! I'll work your ass off. As a matter of fact, I told him to get stuffed, but I was thinking of using you anyway, so you can if you want to, I mean, I do want you, but not because of that."

Collins thought for a moment and played with his thin mustache. In the tangled racial politics of the time and place, it was a situation with which he was familiar enough, and he was mildly amused by his boss's discomfort. He grinned and said, "Okay, boss. In that case you got yourself a boy. So to speak."

EIGHT

"Harry, can you pick up Luce at school?" Marlene asked as the afternoon grew hectic. Wolfe had arrived and waited patiently, like a well-trained dog (he had donned a cheap sports jacket and polyester slacks and obtained a new, and even more unfortunate, haircut) for Marlene to take him to Edie Wooten's place, an appointment for which they were surely going to be late, because Marlene had taken longer than she had planned to instruct Sym in the intricacies of filling out quarterly withholding forms (Harry could have done that, but he didn't have time, since he had to deal with the agent of the German tennis star; the Germans liked to have endless meetings about Fraulein Speyr's tour, parodically thorough, them, and as far as *Harry* doing the teaching, Harry could not teach a cat to lap cream); and Marlene had to spend a half hour on the phone with the landlord negotiating the new office lease, and Posie had called saying Zak had swallowed a pin, but she wasn't sure, and could they have hot dogs for lunch, and there was *another* panicked call from Carrie Lanin (one more love offering/threat from Pruitt), and Marlene had to spend another half hour calling in favors from cops she knew from the old days to put the word out that the warrant on Pruitt was serious and not just some domestic horseshit.

"No problem, Marlene," said Harry, which is what he always

said, and what he would have said had she asked him to load the building on his back and dump it off Pier Twenty-eight.

"I'm forgetting something important," she said out loud to no one as she gathered up her bag and coat and beckoned to Wolfe. "It was something about you—have you got a gun?"

Wolfe shook his head. Marlene sighed. "Well, you'll need one. Can you shoot? Yes, of course you can shoot. I'll get Dane to give you one of his—he has about fifty of them. Sym! Concealed-carry application for Wolfe, okay? Don't forget! Okay, let's go!"

They breezed by Sym, muttering over government forms, and were out the door before Marlene braked sharply and called back inside. "Sym! I just remembered. Wolfe isn't bonded. Get the paperwork from Allied and fill it out and make sure he signs it and notarize it and get it back to them."

Sym rolled her eyes and grunted in acquiescence.

Marlene pushed the yellow VW (which for a wonder started right up and purred) through the uptown traffic as only a one-eyed, heavily armed woman was likely to push, endangering herself and others but escaping injury, and arrived at Edie Wooten's building only ten minutes past the appointed time. The doorman gave them what seemed like an extra fish eye as he rang upstairs and handed Marlene the handset. Edie Wooten sounded nervous and distraught.

"Oh, God, I forgot you were coming, *again*!" she wailed. "Look, I know this is an imposition, but could you come back another time? We're having some difficulty, a family thing—"

Marlene, however, was not having any of this. "No, Edie, we actually have to do this now. I have your bodyguard here, and he's on the clock, and I have to start going through your list of possibles with you, *before* the concert, which is the day after tomorrow—"

"Oh, God! Yes, all right, you'd better come up."

This time Edie herself came to the door to let them in. She was dressed in a navy skirt and sweater, and her face was flushed. There was music booming in the apartment, not the music of the cello but heavy, raucous, metallic rock. Marlene looked inquiringly at the woman as they stepped into the hall.

"My sister," said Edie, as if that explained everything.

Marlene made the introductions, and Edie shook Jack Wolfe's hand. Then she led them through a hallway lined with paintings to a small room set up as an office, equipped with a Sheraton desk, upholstered straight chairs, an Empire sofa in blue silk, and three oak filing cabinets. There was a marble fireplace, with some Meissen musicians on the mantel. The walls held framed concert posters showing Edie looking serene, wrapped around her cello. She closed the door against the din.

Wolfe was looking around like a mooncalf. Marlene noticed that he was staring at everything but the client.

"The list?" said Marlene, getting down to business.

Edie riffled through papers at the desk, apologizing. She was clearly under some tension; her face was drawn and lacked the beatific glow Marlene had observed during their previous meeting.

"Here it is," said Edie, handing over several sheets.

It was a list of names only, and so Marlene, suppressing her irritation, had to go through them one by one with Edie, to identify the people and find out where they could be reached. This took some time. Edie offered refreshments; Marlene declined. Edie got up and paced around the room. She was extremely nervous, and Marlene wondered why.

Marlene said, "Well, we'll check all these out. If your guy isn't on the list himself, maybe one of these people saw something or knows something. Meanwhile, have you had any more contact?"

"What? Oh, with the Music Lover?" said Edie vaguely. "Just a note. Wait, I'll get it." She walked out of the room. Marlene exchanged a glance with Wolfe. In Marlene's experience, being stalked tended to concentrate the mind of the stalkee to the exclusion of nearly everything else, but Edie seemed oddly distracted.

They heard voices off, angry ones, and an increase in the volume of the trashy rock music. The door opened, and Edie came in. She was even more flushed, with a desperate expression in her eyes. Following close behind her was a woman wearing a thin silvery spaghetti-strap mini-dress over pink thigh-length stockings and platform shoes. She was extremely thin, her face all sharp bones around bright, heavily mascaraed blue eyes, her neck stringy and taut, her collarbones staring through pale skin that seemed too fragile to hold in her vital organs. She pushed past Edie into the room and looked at Marlene and Wolfe with sharp interest, like a predatory bird examining a fallen nestling.

"Oooh," she said, "are these the bodyguards?"

"Ginnie, please . . ." said Edie Wooten. The thin woman ignored her. She looked Wolfe up and down, swaying slightly on her heels, and, apparently finding nothing to detain her, turned her gaze on Marlene. Marlene stood up and said, "Hello, I'm Marlene Ciampi."

Edie said, "Oh, excuse me, Marlene, this is my sister, Virginia Wooten."

Marlene was about to extend her hand but decided not to. The woman was on something, clearly. She combined the hyperactive movements of the speed freak with the slurred diction of the sedative aficionado. That suggested she was taking setups —Dexamils and Qualuudes together—or speedballs, injecting heroin and cocaine simultaneously.

"Marlene? Mah-leeeene! Mah-leen fum da Bronx? Oh, Jesus, Edie, you have no fucking class at all, do you? Where did you find this, in the yellow pages?" She laughed, a soundless giggle that contorted what was actually the (presumably) last years of an extraordinarily pretty face. The giggles died down. No one else made a sound. Edie was rending her usual tissue. Ginnie was staring intently at Marlene's face. "My God, this is rich!" she said, snorting. "What is that, *Mah-leen*, a glass eye? Oh, marvelous, a one-eye private eye! You're inimitable, Edie darling. She imagines someone is pursuing her, and then she hires a half-blind detective to stop him." A spate of laughter that ended with a racking cough. "Get me a fucking drink, goddammit," she snarled at her sister. Edie, her face white, dashed away.

Ginnie strode with the unnaturally careful stride of the drugged to the sofa and arranged herself on it, showing her thin white thighs nearly up to the crotch and the garters that held up her pink stockings. No tracks on the thighs, Marlene observed. She probably takes it in the veins on the tops of her feet.

Ginnie said in a mock confidential voice, "My dear little sister, you understand, *Mah-leen* darling, is a pather—a pathological liar. What'd she tell you? Some man was chasing her? Some *bad* man? Who was going to put his big weenie into her? Well, darling, *I* can tell you that—that the *only* thing that's been between her thighs is that fucking *costly* Stradivarius, that absolutely *no one* was ever allowed to touch. Now, I, on the other hand, am the one who really *needs* a bodyguard." She turned her attention to Wolfe. "How about it, Silent Sam? Would you like to guard my *body*?" She wriggled her hips and ran a long pink tongue around her mouth and giggled again.

Neither Marlene nor Wolfe responded to this, although Marlene noticed that Wolfe's ears went red. Edie came back into the room bearing a tumbler full of clear liquid and ice cubes. She handed it to her sister, who took a swallow, coughed, and sprayed out what was in her mouth. She came off the sofa like a cheap toy, her face reddening, the cords of her neck rigid. "You moron! I wanted a *drink*! Don't you know what a drink is, fuckface!"

She reached back to throw the heavy tumbler at her cringing sister, but Marlene was there with a neat wrist lock, on which she applied a hair more pressure than was strictly necessary. The tumbler fell to the carpet.

"Oww! You're *hurting* me!" the woman cried. She had to bend her knees to relieve the pain.

"Sorry, but that's a no-no. *Darling*," said Marlene. "Now, are we going to be good and let the grown-ups get on with their business?"

A burst of hysterical cursing, quite remarkable in its fluency and rage.

"Oh, don't hurt her," Edie wailed. Tears gushed from her eyes. Marlene shrugged and let the lock go, and Virginia Wooten fell down on all fours, still cursing. A loud buzzer sounded from elsewhere in the apartment.

"That's for me, that's for me!" Ginnie cried, and scrabbling to her feet, without a backward look or another word, she left the room, taking care to slam the door so hard behind her that the figurines shook on the mantel and the posters slid askew.

Edie collapsed in tears on the sofa. Marlene handed Edie a package of tissues from her bag.

When the weeping had lapsed into sniffles, she said, "I'm *so* sorry you had to go through that, Marlene. Oh, God, I don't know what to say. I'm so *mortified!*"

"Well, don't be. This is not nearly the worst thing that someone has said to me in this business. I have an *extremely* thick skin. But I'm a little concerned about you. Does she, ah, come here often?"

"Oh, she makes a *descent* three or four times a year, I guess, usually when she's having problems with her current man." This was said with sighing resignation.

"Why do you let her?"

"Why?" Edie seemed surprised by this question. "She's my *sister.* My parents gave up on her, oh, years ago, and I'm all she has. She was raised in this apartment. The idea of barring the door to her—I couldn't ever do that. I keep thinking that some day she'll . . . I don't know . . . *burn out,* if that's the expression. She . . . what she's like now, she wasn't always like that. She was beautiful and—we can't say *gay* anymore, can we—but spirited, and fun. The house was always full of her friends. My parents are rather solemn people, and of course the girl genius ha-ha was always sawing away, sawing away. Oh, I just *worshipped* her, my big sister . . ." She began to cry again, softly, a slow drip of tears.

"Yes, well, Edie," Marlene said, "the point from my perspective is, do you recall at our first interview, we talked about people with a disordered lifestyle and how vulnerable they were?"

"You mean prostitutes?"

"Yeah, them and drug addicts. And that also applies to the people they're in intimate contact with. A junkie is a doorway to some fairly nasty people. Your sister is a—"

"Ginnie isn't a drug addict!"

"Well, actually, she is, my dear. And one of the things we're going to explore is her possible connection to whoever is bothering you."

Edie shook her head metronomically during this last exchange as if by that motion she could order her sister's life. "No, no, that's just not possible, that's not—"

"As well as," Marlene continued, "the possibility that *she* is the one that's actually producing this harassment."

Edie Wooten just stared, struck dumb.

"While you were out of the room just now, she told me that you were making the whole thing up, that you were a pathological liar hallucinating out of sexual deprivation."

"I am not sexually deprived," Edie blurted, and then blushed, and then the two women burst into laughter. Wolfe looked confused and arranged his face in a bland smile.

"I'm glad to hear it," said Marlene. "We'll need his name too, or theirs. While we're at it, you said something about receiving another note from the guy?"

She had, and produced it, wrapped in a plastic bag.

The note was handwritten on expensive, creamy stationary.

"Good taste. Classy guy," said Marlene, handling the note by its edges. "Were all the notes written on this kind of paper?"

"No, just the ones in, oh, I guess the last four months or so. Before that they were on cheap stationery or lined paper."

"Could I see that?" asked Wolfe. They both stared at him; it was as if a chair had spoken. Marlene handed it to him. "Careful! Don't touch it like that. We may have to get prints off it."

"Sorry," Wolfe muttered and looked closely at the note, which read:

> You don't need anyone else to protect you my darling one. Get rid of them or I will be very displesed. I will be there. Play the E minor Shostakovich Mendelssohn D minor and the Schubert Rosamunde quartet. Remember I am watching you always. Be faiuthful.
> your only true love
> A Music Lover

"What do you make of it?" Marlene asked him. He shrugged and seemed surprised at being asked.

"I don't know. He printed. The *O*'s are funny. They look more like, you know, parentheses. *Faithful* spelled with a U; that's not right, is it?"

"No. And displeased spelled wrong too. Well, maybe it will help." She put the note back in its plastic and stood up. "Okay, Edie, we'll start checking this list. I'll run the names through the cops, see if anyone's got a weird streak. And we'll check with the security people at Juilliard about precautions at the concert itself. By the way, are you going to play the pieces he mentioned?"

"Just the Shostakovich, as I told you before. The other two are a Mozart quintet and the Schumann piano and strings quartet."

"Hm. What's he done before when you haven't played his favorites?"

"Nothing much. He writes an angry note and puts it someplace where I'll be shocked to find it. Under the pillow, in the underwear drawer . . ."

"Yeah, well, that's his mistake; it narrows it down because of the access he needs." Marlene secured the note and made ready to leave. She shook Edie's hand, as did Wolfe. The woman had recovered her composure; aside from a redness about the eyes there was no sign of the recent upheavals. Metal music blared as they left the apartment.

The elevator was opening as they entered the short hallway. A tall man stepped out, handsome, with straight blond hair, dressed in black clothing that included a tight leather motocross jacket studded with chrome rivets. He nodded politely to them and pushed the bell on the Wooten apartment.

"And let's find out who that one is too," said Marlene as they descended.

Part 56 of the Supreme Court of the State of New York was, despite its noble-sounding name, a calendar court, which is a sort of legal valve or appliance. Its grimy, crowded, noisy precincts provided a place for pleas to be entered or changed, plea bargains to be accepted or refused, trials to be scheduled or rescheduled, and for those who delighted in delay for reasons of legal strategy to obtain however much of this precious substance they required. In short, Part 56 could have been replaced by the sort of electronics now used to order pizzas or reserve a place on an airplane, if efficiency were all that were required of it, but such was not the case. Part 56 and its numerous siblings existed (and exist still) because the criminal law ultimately is not about numbers or efficiency. It is about our mortal flesh. And therefore there must be rooms like this one, high-ceilinged, echoing, unornamented, graceless, with peeling paint, tattered window shades over dusty windows, battered furniture, smelling of steam heat, old paint, and frightened, harried people, so that particular human bodies can be brought into physical propinquity for even a fleeting moment (it is usually fleeting enough), these bodies being the judge, the accused, the counsel for the accused, and the representative of the People.

Groups comprising the last three of this necessary quartet crowded the well of the court and moved before the bench as their case numbers were called off by the court officer. The well was in constant motion, a clumsy dance, which for music had a low tumult of many voices, with the time beaten out by the crack of the gavel. No case was distinguished from any other case—all received nearly the same time and attention—a few minutes, no more—from the harried gray-haired woman on the presidium.

Until the officer called out a number and then "*People* versus *Jonathan A. Rohbling*"; then there was a stir and a passing hush. Everyone knew who Rohbling was: the Granny Killer, and everyone, even the junkies, who ordinarily had no interest in anything whatever except their One True Love, paused a moment to cop a glance.

Karp was just as fascinated. He had never seen Rohbling in the flesh, and had been observing him closely from the moment he had been led into the room. The man was small and remarkably slight. Karp knew he was nearly twenty-two, but he could have passed for fourteen, for he was not five foot seven and weighed perhaps a hundred and thirty pounds, dripping. Waley, who stood by his side, was by no means a physically imposing man, but he towered over his client; as a couple they looked like a dad taking his unpromising son to his first day of high school. Rohbling's dull brown hair was cut very short (he had apparently worn a wig imitating short Negroid hair while committing his crimes), and he stared blankly out at the confusion through thick, smudged glasses. His eyes were greenish brown, unfocused and wandering. He had a peculiar mouth, whose thick, soft lips were the first things any schoolyard bully would have seized upon; "girl's lips" the bully would have called them. They had a dried whitish crust on them.

Karp tried to imagine this person wandering Harlem in blackface. More to the point, he tried to imagine the jury imagining it. It was plausible, yes. With dyed skin and the wig, Rohbling would have been able to pass as a frail, scholarly African-American youth. Did he look crazy? No, he was completely passive, and Karp supposed he had been sedated in Bellevue. Was that an error on Waley's part? An agitated client would have looked better, assuming Waley was going to go with the insanity plea. But Waley was a civilized man. He would not have subjected his client to distress if the man was really insane, if Waley really believed he was insane. But maybe not, maybe Waley *wanted* Karp to think that Waley really thought . . . Here Karp put a check on his line of thought. The man had gotten to him, and he was starting to do what he had lectured scores of young prosecutors not to do, which was to get caught up in strategy. Just present the facts of your case as well as you can and let the defense worry about strategy, about motives, about psychology; he had said that a thousand times.

They read out the charges, and the judge asked for Rohbling's plea. Rohbling said he was not guilty. That was a mild surprise; Waley had decided to wait on the insanity plea. There was nothing unusual about Rohbling's voice, and he seemed to understand what was going on around him. The judge sent the case for trial in Part 46, Supreme Court of the State of New York. The choice was at random, based on the current state of the various trial part calendars. Karp thought for a second, connecting part numbers with faces and names. Judge Marvin Peoples would be trial judge in *People* v. *Rohbling*. That would be interesting. Karp glanced over at Waley to get his reaction to the designation of their judge, but could detect nothing but a slight pursing of the lips.

Waley approached a step closer to the bench and said, "Your Honor, on the matter of the disposition of my client's pending trial. My client stands in need of psychiatric care not available in the prison ward at Bellevue. The North Shore Psychiatric Institute at Cold Spring Harbor would be able to provide such treatment and is a secure facility. My client comes from a distinguished family with strong community ties, who would be willing to offer any reasonable bail."

The judge looked at Karp. "Do the People have an objection?"

"Yes, Your Honor. The defendant is accused of multiple murders. There is no precedent for bail in such cases. And I believe that there are still a number of psychiatrists working at Bellevue who would be amazed to hear that they are incompetent to provide any treatment the defendant requires."

The court smiled thinly and said, "A good point, Mr. Karp. The prisoner is remanded to custody at Bellevue until trial."

The guard led Rohbling away. The court officer called the next case number, and the calendar court resumed its grinding.

Karp walked up the aisle with Waley close behind him.

"That was uncharitable and unnecessary, Mr. Karp," said Waley in a low voice.

Karp stopped and turned to face the lawyer. "Your boy gets treated like everyone else, Mr. Waley."

"Does he? Do you think the fact that our judge appears to be a black woman of grandmotherly age figured at all in her decision?"

"Why don't you ask her?" said Karp.

Waley said coldly, "How amusing. I only hope you have not precipitated a disaster." Then he brushed by Karp and left the courtroom.

Marlene spent an hour at Juilliard with Wolfe and the Lincoln Center security man, a grizzled ex-cop named McPhail, who thought they were making a big deal out of nothing, but who was willing to cooperate nevertheless to accommodate a star. He sounded like he'd done it before. She left Wolfe there to work out details and drove downtown to her loft.

There she was glad to find everything in cozy order, although the vast room smelled alarmingly of jasmine incense. She hoped Posie wasn't using it to cover the scent of marijuana, but she also knew that she probably would have done nothing more than rant had Posie come to the door with a bong stuck in her smile. The woman was just too valuable to dismiss.

They were in the living room, watching *Sesame Street*. Marlene plopped on the couch, kicked off her boots, and jiggled both her babies, who suffered the caresses of the near stranger with benign indifference. They were warm and dry and sweet-smelling, and if Marlene felt a sudden wrenching sense of loss, the twins clearly did not. She returned them to Posie, who was staring loose-jawed at the screen, seemingly astounded by what could be done with the letter M.

"How was school, Luce?" she asked her eldest, who was stretched belly down on the rug.

"Okay. I got an A on the math test."

Marlene raised her eyes to heaven and said dramatically, "Thank you, Jesus and St. Jude!"

Lucy laughed. "Tranh showed me some stuff when I was there the other day, and it just sort of clicked. Maybe it's easier in Cantonese. He's a good teacher."

Meaning I could use some work in that department, thank you so very much, my darling, thought Marlene. Then, starting to feel a hair *de trop* at her own hearthside, and already knowing as much as she wanted to know about M., she stood up, kissed all around, gave orders for dinner preparation, and announced, "I think I'll take the dog for a walk."

At the magic W word, there was a clatter and scrabbling in the kitchen, and the mastiff was at her side, pressing its nose into her midriff and slobbering down the front of her slacks.

She did take the dog for a walk, and then she loaded it into the rear of the VW and drove through a thin rain and the rush-hour traffic to a construction site at Madison and Sixty-third. There she waited, leaning against the car and smoking, while quitting time came and the construction workers streamed out of the half-finished condo. She had to turn down a half dozen lewd offers before the man she wanted came through the plywood door.

"Mr. Nobili!" she called. "Could I talk to you for a moment?"

The man, a shortish, swarthy fellow with a heavy Nixonian beard shadow on his jowls, wearing yellow oilskins and a red hard hat on backward, stopped and looked over at her.

"She wants you, Arnie," said one of his companions.

"Yo, Arnie, after you," said another. There were a number of whistles: good, clean construction-worker fun.

Arnie Nobili smiled and approached her. She smiled back, opened the passenger door of the VW, and gestured him in. More whistles and shouts. Marlene got in the driver's side and cranked the engine, which refused to start for a long minute and then came sulkily to life.

"Sounds like the alternator," said Nobili. "So what is this?"

She let the engine idle, producing heat for the blower, and handed him one of her cards.

"I'm Marlene Ciampi," she said. "Tamara Morno has retained us. I've helped her take out a protective order, which I understand you've already violated."

Nobili's smile vanished and was replaced by an unpleasant belligerent expression. "What, are you some kind of cop?" She noticed there was alcohol on his breath.

"No. I'm a lawyer and a private detective. I wanted to have a talk with you so that we'd understand each other."

"*She* hired you? *She* hired you to protect her from *me*?"

"That's correct, Mr. Nobili."

"Well, you can fucking unhire yourself, lady. Tamara don't need no protection." He gestured at her with a dirty finger the size of a center punch.

"You have to stop trying to see her, Mr. Nobili. You have to understand that the relationship is over."

Nobili moved his face closer to hers, jabbing with his finger. "Hey, it's over when *I* say it's over, understand? You fuckin' *tell* her that! No, *I'll* fuckin' tell her. She'll never fuckin' forget it, I get through with her." He jacked the door handle. "And fuck your order and fuck you!" he said, and, as an afterthought, "Bitch!"

Marlene called out, "Sweety, *l'affirati!*"

Nobili paused with the door open and looked at her. "What did you say?" he snarled.

The mastiff came out of the baggage space under the hatch-back in a black blur, grabbed a mouthful of Nobili's oilskin, and yanked him back into his seat. His hard hat came down over his face as he flailed and cried out. The car door swung closed with a slight click. Sweety, meanwhile, was doing its impression of the Hound of Hell, baring fangs, growling like distant lions, splashing hot slaver down the man's collar.

"This interview is over when *I* say it is, understand?" said Marlene.

Nobili's hat fell off in the shaking he was getting. "Make it stop! Make it stop!" he quavered.

"Sweety, *chiú gentilmenti,*" said Marlene. The dog stopped shaking Nobili, but retained its grip. "Yes, 'make it stop.' That's just what Ms. Morno said to me in reference to your attentions."

"You—you're not allowed to do this," said the man, gasping.

"No, I'm not, you're right. This is a sort of kidnap. It's a felony. I'm breaking the law, which I hate to do, but I don't think you'll complain, because a couple of nights ago you went by Tamara's place and pounded on her door for an hour, and when she wouldn't open up for you, you pulled the valves out of her tires. That's against the law too. Now, I tried to have a civilized conversation with you so that you'd understand that the situation has changed, and you insulted me and suggested that despite the protective order, you were going to see her and harm her. So here we are. Let me restate the case. If you go near Tamara Morno again, *you* will be the one that gets hurt, not her. Do you understand? Say you understand!" The dog caught Marlene's tone and snarled wetly.

Nobili shuddered and mumbled, "Yeah, yeah, I understand."

"Good. Now, if I were you, I'd do some work on that booze problem too."

"I don't got a problem," replied Nobili in a sullen voice.

"Yeah, you do. You start in brooding about why you're all alone, and that makes you sad and you drink, and when you got your load, you start feeling pretty good and you start thinking that you could fix things up with Tamara, and you go looking for her and when she doesn't want to see you, because you're drunk, you start thinking, hey, I put myself out, I'm willing to let by-gones be bygones, what the hell does this bitch want? You start feeling sorry for yourself. You blame her for things going wrong. Then you drink some more, and you start to break things and beat up on her. Then when you sober up, you forget what you did, and you can't figure out why she doesn't love you. And every time it's a little bit worse, isn't it? Yeah, it is. And you know, ordinarily something like this would end with her dead and you in jail, feeling real sorry about it. This time, however, you keep on with this horseshit, it's going to end with *you* dead, and her free, and not feeling sorry at all. Like they say in A.A., your life's out of control. Get some help, Arnold."

The man said nothing, but sat there cringing from the dog and glaring at Marlene. She sighed and said, "Sweety, *lu rilassi!*" The dog gave up its mouthful of jacket. To Nobili she said, "Okay, scram! For your sake, I hope I never have to see you again."

"What did you do today?" Karp asked at dinner that evening.

Marlene said, "I got screamed at by a rich junkie, and I terrorized a drunk. Those were the high points, I think."

"How did you terrorize him, Mom?" asked Lucy.

"I threatened to spank him on his bare heinie. It never fails." She cupped a hand to her ear. "Remind me again why I'm not a highly paid attorney at a white-shoe law firm."

"Because you're a self-destructive nutcase?" Karp ventured.

"Mmm. That doesn't sound quite right."

"I think it's because you're real brave, and you don't want women to get hurt," said Lucy, the literalist, the loyalist. Marlene's heart overflowed.

"Thank you, darling," she said, beaming. "First long division, now the inmost secrets of the psyche. Truly, there is no end to your excellence!"

NINE

Terrell Collins knocked twice on Karp's door and, hearing a vague grunt, walked in. He found his boss amid stacks of Xeroxed pages from law books, some actual law books, teetering in green- or red-and-ochre-bound piles, and a scatter of crumpled yellow legal bond. The two men looked at each other and smiled the smile of acknowledged exhaustion. They were working on responses to Waley's motions in *Rohbling*. It was not a trivial task.

"You get it?" asked Karp.

Collins deposited a short stack of Xeroxes on one of the desk's few bare zones. "White's dissent in *Massiah*, with commentaries on same. I don't see how it's relevant, though; it relates to counsel after indictment. The motion is to suppress a confession obtained in violation of *Miranda*. *Massiah* is about Sixth Amendment right to counsel being violated by the cops sticking a secret informant on a defendant out on bail *after* indictment."

"Yeah, I know that, but Waley mentions the dissent in his points and authorities, so we have to look at it. Why he mentioned it, I have no idea. It's a dissent, Whizzer White sticking up for the prosecution as usual, and getting creamed, but Waley uses it to make a general point about the use of interpersonal confidence to draw out a confession. It's all part of the weave here; he's spreading a net to catch the attention of the judge, tilt him his way." Karp tapped his teeth with a pencil, a habitual gesture. Then he looked up at Collins and said, "You ever read a pair of motions like this?" He indicated the actual motion documents, sitting alone on one side of his desk, festooned like barbaric brides with torn strips of yellow bond indicating legal references.

"They're pretty good," admitted Collins. "Dense argument, the guy knows the law."

"Pretty good? Terry, *you're* pretty good, I'm *very* good. This"—he tapped the motions—"is fucking *Mozart*. I'm reading this, and I'm thinking, yeah, he's right, we don't have much of a case. Peoples is eating this up, I know it. Do you know him at all well? Peoples, I mean."

"Just by rep," said Collins, settling himself on the edge of the desk. "He's real smart, a little arrogant maybe. No nonsense in the courtroom. Hates to be reversed on appeal. In general, a prosecutor's judge; I mean, you present a decent case, he'll support you, he'll resist the usual defense scams pretty well." He shrugged. "That's about all I know. All in all, I think it was a good break getting him for *Rohbling*."

"Maybe," said Karp. "I notice you left out the first thing an average person would mention about him."

Collins wrinkled his brow for a second or two. "You mean that he's black? Jesus, Butch, the guy's to the right of Reagan. He hates affirmative action, he never gives any credence to race-based exculpatory arguments . . ." He checked himself and then added, "Oh, I get it. The bend over backward to be fair to the white kid accused of killing black women. You think that's going to be important?"

"I don't know, but I would bet on Peoples taking the concept of fairness to its extreme limit. If we win one on the merits, it's going to take twice as much to win the next one, because Peoples is going to want to keep the score even. On the other hand, we won't get any freebies; we can forget the 'prosecutor's judge' business, especially with Waley in there. Not a cheap-trick guy, Waley."

Karp massaged his chest and took several deep breaths to relieve the tension he felt growing in his chest. Then he stretched and said, "My head's too full of details. I need to step back and see how it's fitting together. Why don't you tell me the case?"

"Tell you . . . ?"

"Yeah, tell me the case. Why do we have this mutt behind bars? Tell me a story. Amuse me."

Collins smiled and got to his feet. As he spoke, he paced back and forth, four feet in one direction, four in the other, as if he were in court.

"Okay. Saturday evening, April 20, a disturbance is heard by neighbors of Jane Hughes, age sixty-eight, of 1718 St. Nicholas Avenue. A witness sees a slightly built, short-haired, neatly dressed black man leaving that building at around ten-thirty. He's carrying a blue fabric suitcase. The following day Mrs. Hughes's son arrives to take his mother to church—"

"Right, cut to the evidence at the scene."

"Okay, Hughes is found lying in the wreckage of a coffee party—she was entertaining someone, two cups and so on. Stuff is smashed, she put up a struggle. She was a good-sized woman, by the way, a retired practical nurse. Gordon Featherstone catches the case, and right away he notices that Hughes has long nails and some of them are broken off, and he makes sure the hands get bagged. Autopsy shows she died from being smothered by an object made of heavy blue cotton canvas. She's got the fibers way up her tubes. No sexual assault, by the way, but forensics finds blue fibers, skin, blood, and body hairs under the nails. Skin is brown in color, but the hairs and the blood ID as Caucasian. They analyze the skin fragments, and they find commercial brown dye. So we have a white man disguised as a black man."

"Stop a minute. You talk to Featherstone yet?"

"On the phone, not face to face."

"You ask him was he surprised it was a white guy?"

Collins smiled and nodded. "As a matter of fact, I did. He was amazed. Never happened before." Collins seemed to share the detective's feeling.

"Okay, go ahead."

"Well, Featherstone does the usual canvass, the vic's friends and relatives. Turns out she was a church lady, her life tended to revolve around the Zion Baptist Church up there at 125th and Lenox, and Featherstone found people who had seen Hughes leave a social on Saturday night with a slight young black man carrying a suitcase. The guy said he was a stranger in the neighborhood. He offered to walk Mrs. Hughes home, which everyone thought was real nice of him. Nobody got his name. So, Featherstone smells a wacko—I mean, what else could he be?—and he figures wackos repeat; this guy is going to try to prey on older church ladies. Okay, lots of churches in Harlem, but he puts the word out to the ministers, we're looking for a white man in disguise, maybe with a suitcase, a stranger."

"But he didn't get a tip," said Karp. This was the crux of the problem.

"He did not. What happened was, this was around three weeks after the Hughes murder, Featherstone was cruising along 125th, late afternoon, when he saw this kid at the bus stop at 'twenty-fifth and Seventh. He just happened to stop for a light, and there the kid was, waiting on line there. And there was the suitcase, blue cloth. So the picture flashes in his mind: slight kid, suitcase. He checks the kid out—this is in the minute or so the light's red. The kid looks . . . wrong somehow."

"He didn't articulate how the kid was wrong."

"No. Just a feeling. He parks and walks over and studies the kid at close range, and he has to make a decision right away because here comes the bus and the kid's going to get on it and disappear. So he goes over to the kid and identifies himself as a police officer and asks him, 'Is that your suitcase?' And the kid says, 'No.' And then Featherstone asks a couple of people standing there on line if it was theirs and they all say no."

"And no one, of course, volunteers that they saw this kid walk up to the bus stop carrying the suitcase," said Karp.

"No, this being Harlem, no, they didn't. And here comes the bus and Featherstone says, quote, 'Sir, I would appreciate it if you didn't leave right now. I think you could help the police with an investigation.' And he grabs the suitcase."

"But not Rohbling physically?"

"He says not. Rohbling doesn't, in fact, get on the bus. That's the focus of their motion to suppress the physical evidence. The police had no reasonable suspicion to stop the suspect. There was no *Terry* v. *Ohio* activity on Rohbling's part—he wasn't acting in a suspicious manner, wasn't casing a jewelry store. He was just waiting for a bus."

"*Cortez*," said Karp, half to himself.

"Yeah, we would argue Featherstone met the *Cortez* test of a quote particularized and objective basis for suspecting. Anyway, the legal stop took place when Rohbling did not get on his bus. They say. He felt he could not leave. Under *Mendenhall* that's a stop. Featherstone takes the suitcase over to a bench and zips it open."

"We're, of course, saying this is a *McBain* situation here," Karp put in.

"Right, *U.S.* v. *McBain*: when a suspect when questioned about ownership denies ownership, he surrenders possessory interest in the property, and has no *Katz* privacy rights to be violated by police. Although, of course, they maintain that what Featherstone actually said was 'Can I take a look at that suitcase?' and when Rohbling said no, he meant 'No, you can't look in it.' Do you want me to cover the suppression-of-evidence case points here?"

"No, skip it for now," Karp replied. "Just run through what happened."

"Okay, in the suitcase Featherstone finds a number of fascinating items: an old blue baby blanket, a ceramic candy dish, a white orlon cardigan sweater, a doily, a glass tumbler with a picture of a steamboat on it, a plastic hair ornament, and a Mammy doll."

"I saw that. What the hell is a Mammy doll?"

"A cultural artifact. They don't make them anymore. It's a cloth doll about ten inches long. On one end it's a white lady with blond hair, and when you flick the skirt the other way, it's a black servant in a kerchief and apron. They used to be pretty popular. Not among black folks, of course."

"Okay, I got it. Go ahead."

"So Featherstone asks him for some ID, and Rohbling says he doesn't have any, and then he asks for his name and the guy says his real name, Jonathan Rohbling. And then Featherstone checks out his neck, and he sees it's the guy."

"The hairs there."

"Yeah. Black women call it the kitchen. Whatever you do to your hair, the first place it's going to go back to natural is the base of the neck. Rohbling should have had little kinky hairs back there, and what he had were dyed Caucasian hairs. So Featherstone arrests him, Mirandizes him, and takes him to the Two-Eight. Do you want me to go through the interrogation stuff?"

"I read the transcript," Karp said. "Smart guy, Featherstone, taping the whole thing. He figured this was going to be a tricky one, I wonder why. No, right now just give me your sense of how it all relates to the motion to suppress the confession."

"Okay. Rohbling got the Miranda warnings at the time of arrest, at the bus stop. At the precinct Featherstone asked him if he wanted to help out the police. Yes. Would he waive his right to silence? He hesitates. He wants his medicine. Featherstone tells him he'll get his medicine after they finish their chat. Rohbling signs the waiver. Featherstone confronts him with the candy dish. It's a handmade ceramic candy dish, and on the bottom it's inscribed, 'Happy Birthday, Grandma, from Serena.' Featherstone has already found that Hughes has a granddaughter named Serena and that the dish was a gift on the victim's sixty-fifth birthday. So how did you get the dish, Mr. Rohbling? She gave it to me. Back and forth. How did Mrs. Hughes die? I didn't hurt her, she was my friend. You pressed your suitcase over her face until she was dead, didn't you? Then he says, I'm confused. I want to see Erwin Bannock. Is Bannock your lawyer? Yes. They let him make a phone call. He calls Bannock. The interrogation stops, they feed Rohbling. But then Featherstone gets suspicious. He checks and there's no lawyer named Erwin Bannock. And then they find that Bannock is Rohbling's psychiatrist. Naughty boy, telling us he was your lawyer, they say—words to that effect. Then the interrogation resumes—still on tape—in the course of which he admits that he was trying to 'snuggle' with Mrs. Hughes and he's sorry she got sick and died. Featherstone gets an inspiration and shows him the other objects in the suitcase. He got these from other ladies he was snuggling with and they died, right? Right, he says, and he gives them the names and when he killed them. As you know, none of the others was listed as a homicide. They draw up a confession and he signs it; he's been in custody six hours. They book him for five homicides, and then Waley shows up with the parents. End of story."

"Legal points?" asked Karp.

"On the confession? All right, one: waiver of right to silence has to be voluntary, knowing, and intelligent, *Moran* v. *Burbine*. The case law is a little murky here. In *Colorado* v. *Connelly* the Supreme Court held that voluntariness under the Miranda doctrine pertained entirely and exclusively to the issue of police coercion. In the absence of coercion there was no flaw in the confession obtained, even though the suspect was mentally ill. Since *Connelly*, on the other hand, lower courts have held that mental incompetence voids a waiver—it can't be knowing and intelligent if the suspect is wacky. The motion claims that the waiver is void because of Rohbling's mental state, using *Smith* v. *Zant*."

"Asserting mental disease or defect at the time."

"Demonstrated by the reference to medication," said Collins. "They point out Rohbling was on a course of antipsychotics at the time. He asked for his pills and didn't get them. No pills, he's crazy."

"And, of course, they want to also define the deprivation of medication as coercion under *Connelly*," said Karp. "Good point, actually. Continue."

"Point two: he asked for a lawyer—"

"But he didn't," Karp interrupted. "He asked for a shrink. *Fare* v. *Michael*: request to see a third party is not an invocation of the right to counsel."

"No, but the cops *thought* he was asking for a lawyer and should have terminated the interrogation. The motion claims. Also, when he was on the phone with Bannock, Bannock said he was going to call a lawyer and Rohbling agreed, and Bannock did call Waley, so they're claiming *Fare* doesn't operate. Counsel was invoked through a third party and the interrogation should have stopped, especially if, as they're claiming, the suspect was mentally incompetent at the time."

"Yeah, but that third-party stuff is stretching it. I'm thinking that our best response is to lean on the resumption of questioning *after* right to counsel was invoked, using *Michigan* v. *Mosely.* The criterion is, did the cops, quote, scrupulously honor the right to silence. It's permissible for the cops to requestion the suspect on a crime different in nature and time and place from the crime they arrested him for. The other four murders—"

"Not different in nature," said Collins, "but different in time and place." He frowned. "But that kills the Hughes confession."

"We can afford to let it go if we have to," said Karp. "We don't need the confession on Hughes. We have solid forensics on Hughes. We have Happy Birthday Grandma on Hughes. But I'm not that worried about the black-letter law." He tapped Waley's thick memorandum brief. "No, what we got here is much denser than that. He's got appellate rulings for a dozen states, federal appeals cases, waiting for cert from the Supremes. He knows Peoples thinks of himself as a scholar, and this is a fat carrot he's dangling. Let's make some new Miranda law together, Your Honor."

Collins was still frowning. He had started to worry his little mustache too. "It's thin, Butch. *Mosely,* I mean."

"Yeah, maybe, but thin is what we got to work with. Look, we have to get started on drafting. I'll take the confession, you handle the suitcase."

Collins looked at him, surprised. "Solo? Just draft it?"

Karp grinned at him. "Sure. You're as good as Waley."

Collins smiled back. "I thought he was Mozart."

"So be Beethoven. Be Fats Waller. I'll do the Miranda stuff."

"Better you than me, boss," said Collins, standing up and flexing his knees. "A week, say?"

"Sounds good. Just watch yourself in traffic. By the way, you know the difference between Carmen Miranda and Ernesto Miranda?"

"No, what?"

"One is fruit; the other is nuts."

Collins snorted a laugh, waved and left.

Leaving Karp alone with the beautifully crafted motion to suppress a confession to five homicides. He got up, stretched, opened his office door, and looked into the bureau's outer office. Two of his junior people were there, and when the door opened they put on the eye and body language, hoping to catch his attention. Connie Trask glowered at him and wiggled a stack of yellow message slips. Karp put on a stone face, ignored the A.D.A.'s, and went back inside.

He pulled the motion brief into the center of his desk and began to scribble notes about the point raised in the first of the bookmarks he had inserted. The real world faded away.

Every prosecutor in the United States has good reason to wish that Ernesto Miranda had never been born, or that once born, he had not grown into a kidnapping, raping scumbag, or that having chosen that mode of life he might have avoided the attentions of the Phoenix police department, or that once arrested and justly convicted for his nasty crime, or, and especially, that the Supreme Court of the United States had been a mite more lucid when they ruled that the Fifth Amendment privilege against self-incrimination applied to custodial interrogation, and Ernesto got his long-sought walk.

Karp was personally a good friend of the Fifth, but he also knew, as all prosecutors knew, that the vast, vast majority of criminal cases are cleared not by the clever clues beloved of lady detective story writers but by confessions. Confession (with its less respectable brother, the plea bargain) made the horrible old system work. Because of this every cop and every prosecutor in the country pushed the limits of *Miranda* every day, and *Miranda*, naturally, pushed back, the result of this shoving being a mass of case law so tortuous and recondite that even academic legal scholars, with plenty of time on their hands, could barely master its intricacies. Karp, of course, had hardly any time at all, and Waley had insured that he would have to sweat blood to answer the motion without embarrassment. Nuts, indeed, thought Karp as he scratched away.

Marlene entered her office and passed Marlon Dane going out at a run.

"Where you running to?" she called after him.

"Miller," Dane said over his shoulder as he passed through the door.

Marlene looked inquiringly at Sym, who explained, "Mary Kay Miller called. Friend of a friend called her, says her loved one got a gun, got his load on, says he's going to whack her. She calls here, Dane happened to be here typing up his time sheets. He went to pick her up at work."

"Did he have his machine gun?"

"Not that I saw. We ever kill any of these bastards yet?"

Marlene hesitated. "Not as such. Not since we started the business. We haven't lost but one client and we haven't killed a loved one, and that's exactly how I'd like to keep it. Anything else going on?"

"Some messages on your desk. Harry's out. Tranh helped me with the IRS stuff."

Marlene's eyebrows shot north. "He did? He could read all that fine-print crap? In English?"

"Uh-huh. He real—*he's* real smart, you know? Like he was some kind of professor or something."

"You like him?"

A slow nod. It was hard for Sym to admit she liked any man. "He's okay. For an old guy."

The old guy was in his room. Marlene knocked and walked in. Tranh was on his narrow bunk, rummaging in his rubberized duffel bag. When Marlene entered, he seemed to freeze, his hand in the bag, as if some animal within had gripped it with its teeth. His face was unreadable.

She looked him over. He was dressed in a long-sleeve black wool shirt buttoned to the throat and black canvas pants. On his feet were cheap high-top sneakers, also black. Tranh had taken a surprisingly small amount of money out of the cash box and replaced his lost clothing. Black was apparently his color, for he had selected it in all the garments he had purchased in the surplus stores and the bargain going-out-of-business emporiums that lined Canal Street.

"What is going on, Vinh?" she asked in French. "How is Miss Lanin and her undesirable friend?"

He withdrew his hand from the duffel and rested it, with the other on his lap. "Not well, I am afraid. I have followed Pruitt to his apartment, which is located on Avenue B. There I observed him not two hours ago in conversation with a man of disreputable and malign appearance. I followed them to another apartment in the neighborhood, where they entered, and shortly afterward Pruitt emerged alone carrying a package wrapped in black plastic, like so." He held his hands about two feet apart. "I suspect it is a weapon, a firearm."

"Shit! What are you going to do?"

"I feel that now we must watch Miss Lanin continuously."

Marlene chewed her lip and considered this, working out coverage schedules in her head. Tranh interrupted her train of thought. "Marie-Hélène, I believe I can do this by myself, if you permit."

"What, you're going to move in with her?" said Marlene in English, forgetting herself in her surprise.

"On the contrary, I believe the correct strategy is to watch her dwelling and workplace at a distance until he should make an undoubted aggressive move."

"Vinh, allow me to remind you, it requires three agents to provide effective twenty-four-hour coverage."

"I know it; however, you have not two other agents to spare, I believe. No, Marie-Hélène, I will do it myself."

"You propose to watch her apartment from the outside all night? It is an absurdity!"

"I have done it before," Tranh replied quietly.

This stopped Marlene's next objection, because to pursue the point would certainly have brought up exactly how he had done

it before and where and when, and she was not sure that she
wanted to know. In any case, he was right. She could not mount
a twenty-four-hour watch on anyone just now.

He lit a cigarette and offered her one, which she took, and
they spent a few seconds on the business of mutually lighting up.
"All right," she said, "but if you spot him, I want you to call the
police."

Tranh raised an ironic eyebrow. "To be sure, the police," he
said. "They will arrest him, one supposes."

"Of course. He has violated his order of protection. Also, if
he is in fact armed, that is another offense."

"I see," said Tranh. "He will be imprisoned for several years,
and then released, and then?"

"Just call the cops, Vinh," said Marlene sharply, dispensing
with the French. "And don't let anything happen to her, okay?"

"Okay," said Tranh humbly, in English. "You the boss."

When Marlene left, Tranh took a small bundle covered in oily
rags out of his duffel, and unwrapped it on the bed, revealing a
large semiautomatic pistol gleaming dully with oil. Skillfully,
without thought, he began to take it apart. It was a very old pistol,
a Tokarev TT M 1930, manufactured in 1932 for the Red Army.
In 1959, along with a great mass of other obsolete Soviet equipment, it had been shipped to the People's Republic of Vietnam
as a token of fraternal concern with the liberation struggle against
the puppet regime to the south. It had come into Tranh's hands
that year, and he had kept it with him almost continuously since
then. He had not, of course, had it in prison. He had buried it,
heavily greased, when he learned they were coming to arrest him,
and he had dug it up after his reeducation, and taken it with him
when he left the country in 1978. He had used it to shoot five
Thai pirates who had attacked the crowded sailboat in which he
had made his escape to the Philippines. Since then he had not
required it.

After carefully cleaning and re-oiling the weapon, he assembled it, snapped a magazine of Mauser rounds into its handle,
put on a navy pea coat and a wool watch cap, and, with the pistol
snug in a pocket of his coat, left the office.

He took the subway uptown to Thirty-fourth Street and walked to the building at Thirty-sixth and Seventh in which Carrie Lanin was employed as a fabric designer. There he lounged among the garment district throngs until five-thirty, when Lanin emerged from the building. He followed her to the Sixth Avenue subway, getting off at Chambers Street, and then tailed her to her home, a loft on Duane Street. There he waited, crouched in a doorway. A car arrived, and he tensed, but it was only the daughter, Miranda, being dropped off after school by a car pool.

The sky became purple, then black. It was cold, but not too cold, and there was no wind. Tranh ate two Hershey bars. In a while he fell into the mental state, neither awake nor asleep, that he had developed during his military career and perfected in prison. In this state he could indulge himself in hynogogic dreams; he could imagine another life. In this life he was at the head of a classroom, teaching a class of bright youngsters in fresh school uniforms. Sometimes he taught mathematics, or it might have been French literature. After school was over, he would go home to his wife and daughter. His wife was a nurse; his daughter was nine years old.

Every time a car went down Duane Street, which was not often, he came out of the trance and was alert. Then he went back to the small house near the hospital in Ben Hoa in 1968. Thus the night passed.

In the morning it was the same in reverse. The car pool picked up Miranda, and then Carrie Lanin set off for work. Tranh followed. Carrie went into her office building. Tranh went into a coffee shop and bought coffee and a scrambled egg and bacon sandwich to go. He squatted against a wall across from the office building and ate; and waited. He thought that he had more patience than Rob Pruitt with his new gun, and that whatever was going to happen would happen soon.

He was correct. With a song in his heart and an M-1 carbine (the wire-stock model) under his coat, Rob Pruitt arrived in a stolen Chevy to pick up his sweetheart at work and begin a wonderful life of perfect romance. He parked at the fire hydrant in front of the building and went in.

Seven minutes later, he came out again, gripping Carrie Lanin by the arm. Nobody on the crowded street gave them any notice, except as another pair of objects to dodge: an ordinary-looking man with cropped brown hair and dark eyes set perhaps a little too close together and a blonde in her early thirties, with a classic American-pretty former cheerleader face, now unflatteringly frozen in the paralysis of terror. Pruitt had the carbine suspended by a strap around his neck, with his right hand under the coat gripping the stock and trigger and the muzzle peeping out between the buttons, pointing at his companion. Carrie hung from his grip, barely able to keep her knees working; she had just seen her supervisor and his secretary shot down.

Pruitt was extremely happy as he politely opened the car door for his bride. He had only had to shoot two people, which was less than he had figured on shooting. He hoped that they weren't hurt too badly. In any case what was done was done, and his plan was working well. He was positive Carrie would understand why it was necessary and would come to admire him for it.

He pulled into the crowded street, turned at the next corner onto Thirty-fifth, and headed west. As he drove, he explained his plan to Carrie. He had his own car parked on Eleventh. They would change to that car and drive through the Lincoln Tunnel. And they would keep driving until they reached Alaska, where they would start a new life. Nobody asked questions in Alaska about what you had done in the lower forty-eight. It was a frontier. He would get a good job maintaining the pipeline, and they would be happy.

"My—my daughter . . ." said Carrie. Her mouth was so dry that it was hard to speak. Her words sounded odd, as if they were being broadcast over a cheap speaker.

Pruitt frowned. "You're not understanding me, Carrie. This is a new life. We should've had this life before, see? We don't want any reminders of the old life, okay? Look, I got everything planned out. You'll see. It'll be great."

Carrie Lanin resumed her silence. She had already noted that the door handle had been removed from the passenger door. She closed her eyes; tears leaked out from between her lashes.

They turned south on Eleventh Avenue, drove for a few blocks, and then turned into a deserted side street near a ruined warehouse. Pruitt parked behind a blue 1977 Mercury.

"Here we are," he announced cheerily. "I got a great deal on this car, Carrie. Only six thousand—" Pruitt stopped. There were two eyes looking at him out of his rearview mirror. Instinctively, he swung his head around. Tranh smashed him across the face with his heavy Tokarev pistol, shattering his nose. Then Tranh leaned forward and cracked Pruitt across the face twice more, until the man lay still against the driver's door, blowing red bubbles. Carrie Lanin stared at him. He said to her, "Do not to be afraid, Madame. You are safe."

Then he unbuttoned Pruitt's coat and pulled out the carbine. He rested the muzzle against Pruitt's cheekbone and offered the other end of the weapon to Carrie Lanin.

"No . . . I can't," said Carrie in a whisper. She seemed to have no breath left.

Tranh nodded and gently lifted her right hand. He placed it on the pistol grip of the carbine. He worked her finger through the trigger guard, which was somewhat difficult because he was wearing gloves and her hand was entirely passive, like the hand of someone under hypnosis. She had her eyes closed.

He steadied the stock of the carbine with his left hand, and with his right hand he pressed the woman's finger against the trigger. He used five rounds.

Carrie Lanin still had her eyes closed. Her ears rang; she could not stop shaking. Tranh leaned forward, rolled down the passenger window, pushed Carrie against the dash, and snaked himself out onto the street. There was no one around. Into her ear he said, "You fight for the weapon. You shoot it. He is dead. I am not here. Do you understand? I am not here. Do you understand it is best?"

A slight nod. Tranh looked down at himself and brushed a few bits of brain and other tissue off his pea coat. The blood did not show except as a darker dampness against the navy blue wool. Then he went to a phone booth and placed an anonymous call to the police.

TEN

M arlene was backstage at Alice Tully Hall, in the Juilliard School of Music, standing outside the performers' dressing room, when her pager buzzed. She snarled an obscenity at the little box, choked it into silence, and stuck her head through the dressing room door. It was a small room, but just large enough for a small party, which was what it now contained. Edie Wooten was sitting with a glass of Evian water in her hand, flanked in the manner of Renaissance paintings by her mother and father, both of whom were drinking Krug from crystal flutes. In another little group stood the members of Wooten's quintet: Anton Ten Haar, the Dutch violinist whom Marlene had seen at Wooten's apartment, thin, long haired, pale, and dry looking; Felix Evarti, the pianist, squat, dark, curly headed, and damp looking, with a nervous manner; Norma Merriam, the second fiddle, a tall woman in her forties with a long gray ponytail; and Curtis Dumont, the violist, a portly dark brown man with a pointed white beard. They all paused and looked at Marlene when she appeared, as at a visitor from another, and more hostile, planet. Edie Wooten was the only one of the group who smiled.

"Come and have a drink, Marlene," she offered after a tiny uncomfortable pause.

Looking at the scene, Marlene flashed briefly on Degas, or some other painter of the bourgeois world in its theatrical manifestation. Black and white were the prevailing colors, the gowns of the three women, the white tie of the men, set off by the bright splashes of the bouquets, the glitter of the bottles and glasses, the exotic touch lent by the complexion of the single black. It looked so warm and cozy, so arranged, that Marlene briefly felt herself the wolf at the door. No, she thought, not the wolf, the sheepdog, but they still didn't want it in the house. She had felt this way before, in similar company, which was why she chose not to devote her life exclusively to the protection of celebrities and the rich.

Her eye cast once again around the room, a professional look. She had already checked out the bouquets—no contributions from the Music Lover—but the people were another matter. She caught an expression of active distaste on the face of the pianist, Evarti. Mr. and Mrs. Wooten showed the bland, tanned politesse of the wealthy. The others were neutral, uninterested. Marlene shook her head.

"No, thanks. I just wanted to tell you I've got to make a call. Wolfe is just backstage, if you need him."

"Is anything wrong?" asked Edie.

"No, this is something else."

She left and found a pay phone in the small foyer. People were already gathering there in numbers, heading for their seats. One of them had to be their guy. A face swam out of the crowd, a man, blond, well dressed, tall. Their eyes met and he passed on. It stirred a memory. It was the man they had passed in the elevator lobby at the Wootens'. Ginnie's boyfriend. Marlene made a mental note to ask Wolfe if he had checked him out yet. Then she stopped herself from examining the passing faces. An impossible security situation, of course, but Marlene thought that the man they wanted would move toward the performers' dressing room, as he had several times before. They had a chance of intercepting him there.

"What's up, Sym?" she said when the call went through.

"We're on the TV. Pruitt snatched Lanin from her office, and he drove away in a car. Then she got the gun away or something and shot him. Blew his head off."

A wave of adrenaline. Marlene's palms and forehead popped with sweat. "Where's Harry?"

"He's at the precinct. The One-Oh. With her."

"They're not *holding* her for it?"

"I don't know about that," said Sym. "He shot two people in her office. Maybe they going to give her a medal. Anyway, Harry said call, tell you what was going down."

"Okay, right. She'll probably call me from the precinct, and I want to be paged when she does. Where's Tranh?"

"In the back. Cooking something."

Cooking? "Put him on," she ordered, and when Tranh came on, she asked, "What happened, Vinh?"

"The man arrived at the office building," said Tranh in French, speaking staccato, a military report. "He came out of the office holding Madame Lanin. He took her into a car. I supposed he had a weapon under his coat, so I could do nothing. Then I followed them—"

"How? How did you follow them?"

"In a cab," said Tranh. "It was"—he seemed to search for a word—"*cinematique*, you know? Follow that car! So, they parked. I approached cautiously. There were shots. I ran and found them. He was dead. I went to a phone and called the police, without giving my name. This was correct, yes?"

"Yes. Then what?"

"The police, many cars. They took her in charge. I returned here. I am preparing noodles with scallions and cod, and hot peppers."

"How was she?"

"Frightened, of course, but well. And free now, naturally. Of him, I mean. I suppose it is a satisfactory denouement."

Marlene was about to press Tranh for more details, but decided she did not want to know any more details. No, definitely not.

She hung up and looked around the small, pretty space, feeling mildly disoriented. The bronze statue of Beethoven looked down at her, offering no inspiration. The crowd had thinned. She followed the last of the concertgoers through the doors of the little hall.

The stage was brightly lit, furnished with four straight chairs and a black Steinway for the first piece, the Mozart quintet. As she watched, a man in a dinner suit came out and made a pitch for the New York Chamber Music Society, and boosted the present concert, and then the lights dimmed and the quintet of musicians walked on, the string players holding their instruments. As they took their seats in the hushed hall, Marlene walked down the side aisle and through the door that led to backstage. Wolfe was standing at the entrance to the corridor that led from the stage to the dressing room.

"Anything up?" she asked him.

"No one who looks wrong so far," he said. "Not that we'd know."

"No. Okay, I'm going to hang out at the stairway end of this hall. I spotted that guy we saw in her building, the sister's boyfriend, the blond. You get anything on him yet?"

"Sorry, no. Working on it. He still wearing the leather jacket?"

"No, a suit and tie. Okay, we'll watch for him. Anyway, anyone who wants to get to the dressing room has to pass one of us." Wolfe nodded. He had his eyes fixed on the musicians, who were making tuning noises. Marlene went down the hall, and as she approached the dressing room door, she saw the stairwell door slowly swinging closed. Through the safety glass window she saw the shadow of a man.

She stopped, backtracked, and threw open the dressing room door. One look sufficed. She shouted over the Mozart, "Wolfe, he's here!" and took off toward the stairwell. There were sounds above her on the stairs, but they also seemed to come from below. She yelled, "Wolfe, check downstairs! I'm going up."

So she did and found herself on a floor of the music school, lined with practice rooms. The wide corridor stretched before her, quite empty. She ran to one of the glass-windowed soundproof doors. Empty. To another. A girl was sitting alone playing a French horn. All the rest of the practice rooms were empty, except for one in which a slender black youth was pounding away on a grand piano. Marlene had her hand on the door and was about to push through when she stopped herself. What would she say to him? She hadn't seen the intruder; thus, no identification was possible. It could have been the pianist or the horn player, but it could have as easily been someone else, who had slipped down some other corridor. The building was one of the most complex in Lincoln Center, containing not only Alice Tully but two theaters, dozens of studios, practice rooms, and offices, and a warren of hallways connecting these in odd ways, not to mention the unusually large number of exits such a facility naturally required. She thought again of the boyfriend, the blondie. He had seen her in the lobby; he had known she was out of position. He could have just lost himself in the crowd, gone out, entered again through the school proper, and approached the dressing room from the stairway side.

She sighed and walked back to the Tully. She wasn't a cop; she couldn't walk up to people and demand that they identify themselves; she couldn't call for squads of boys in blue to scour a building. She felt like a fool, and she was going to have to appear a fool before Edie Wooten and her family and colleagues. Sheepdog indeed!

"What did he do?" asked Karp later when she was telling the tale, lying in the crook of his arm on the red couch, with the television muted and a commercial making colored patterns designed to hypnotize and confuse.

"Oh, he neatly snipped the heads off all the flowers in the room, and left his own bouquet, with a note. Same fancy paper. Roses. They always leave roses, you know that? Nuts, I mean. I would expect mums, lilies, sometimes, but no, it's always roses. It's probably genetic."

"What did the note say?"

"It said, 'Darling, you're not listening. I may have to get angry with you.'"

"Sounds like my kind of guy," said Karp. "Ow!"

"It's not funny," said Marlene. "This guy is smart, and I'm starting to think that he could be dangerous."

"You like the sister's squeeze for it?"

"He was there, and not only there, I saw him again, after, and he gave me a look."

"A look?"

"Yeah, a look, a grin. He knew who I was. But what was I supposed to do, pat him down? See if he had scissors? Roses on his breath? Edie was wiped out when she came back at the intermission. It was incredible that she was able to finish the concert. I am not in good cess with her family and friends."

"That was quite a pinch, dear," said Karp, rubbing the inside of his thigh. "I think I'm bleeding."

"You *should* bleed, a crack like that! Oh, stop pouting! You look just like Zak. Here, I'll rub it and make it better."

"Maybe kissing would make it get better faster."

She gave him an appraising look. "I thought you had a big day tomorrow."

"I do, but the night is long," said Karp. He pulled her closer and began to knead the back of her neck.

"Wait," she said, attracted by a change in the light from the TV. "I want to watch the news first. Goose the sound."

The screen filled with the image of a dark car, the driver's door open, the driver's window shattered and covered with blood. Yellow crime-scene tape marked off the scene, and there was the usual crowd of cop cars and cops wandering about.

"What's this?" Karp asked.

"Sssh!" said Marlene as the camera focused on a well-groomed black man in a tan parka, holding a mike. He spoke for the required twenty seconds, explaining that after a daring daylight kidnapping in the garment district that had left one person dead and one gravely wounded, the victim, Carrie Lanin, had wrested his weapon away from Robert Pruitt, her abductor, and turned it on him, shooting him dead. The anchorman thanked the reporter. The scene shifted to the interior of an office, the camera dwelling lovingly on bloodstains on the wall and floor. A weeping Hispanic woman gave eight seconds about how quickly it had happened, how horrible. Then a still photograph of R. Pruitt from some official file, looking blank and ordinary— message: even guys who look like this can go nuts. Then, finally, a quick shot of Carrie Lanin, frail-seeming with that disaster- survivor stare on her face, being escorted into a building by a uniformed cop and a female detective.

Marlene zapped off the sound. Karp cleared his throat. He felt chilled.

"Well," he said, "you're not having much of a day."

"No," she said. "I sent Harry to straighten things out. Everybody was real nice to her, he said. I should have gone to see her, but I honestly didn't have the energy. I'll go see her tomorrow." Her tone was dull, as if she were talking to herself.

"Straight self-defense," Karp mused in a similar tone. "She got the gun away from him and shot him. That's not the way it usually goes down."

"No," she said. All the warmth seemed to be leaking from the room. His arm felt like a dead log across her shoulders.

"She must be a lot tougher than she looks," he said.

"Apparently."

"Yeah," he said. "I guess . . . I mean, it's probably not a good idea for me to be personally involved in this one. Because of your connection with her. I'll tell Roland to, ah, report directly to Jack on it. Not that I think there'll be much to report. If it went down the way it looks." A long pause. "Did it?"

"As far as I know," she said tightly. Neither of them cared to look at the other. Marlene stood up abruptly. "I'm going to bed," she said without invitation.

One of the advantages of the new live-in child-care arrangements *chez* Karp was that Karp could occasionally indulge his cowardice by slipping out of the house early. Normally the most uxorious and paternal of men, there were times when he did not want to engage in familial relationships, and this was one of them. For it was, in fact, a big day for Karp: in the morning Judge Marvin Peoples would entertain oral argument in re: the motions in *Rohbling* to suppress the confession and to suppress the critical evidence in Jonathan Rohbling's little blue suitcase, and after that he would rule. In all likelihood, of course, Peoples had already made his decision, or ninety-nine percent of it, but in a major case like this one, he would want both attorneys to stand up in front of him and whale away so that the issues would be apparent to the public. Or maybe he really did want explication of the arguments. God knew, they were tortuous enough. Karp had them packed into his head like a model made of bent Popsicle sticks. He felt as if his head was under tension from the inside, as if any emotional or mental shock would collapse the whole structure and leave him blithering before the bench.

Like, for example, the thought that his wife might have been involved in killing Rob Pruitt. He shook his head vigorously to bar the thought as he walked with characteristic long, stiff strides down Centre Street toward the courthouse. For this reason he had skulked from his home. He had not wanted to see Marlene, or to take the chance of seeing a lie written on her face.

Terrell Collins was there waiting in the bureau office, as tightly wound as his boss, dressed in his soberest suit and a faint cloud of Aramis. Karp smiled, invited him into his private office, and laid out the coffee and toasted bagels he had purchased for the two of them in the ground-floor snack bar.

They ate and drank, making desultory talk, listening to the outer office begin work. At five to nine, they walked to Part 46.

Ordinarily, motions are heard in nearly vacant courtrooms; oral argument is not a major spectator sport. With a case like *Rohbling* afoot, however, it was a different matter. The press was out in numbers, and Karp and Collins had to fight their way from the elevator to the door of the courtroom through a couple of TV crews and a crowd of journalists waving microphones and mini-recorders.

The courtroom itself was packed with people: the print press in rows, the families of the victims, their supporters from the black community, and the usual miscellany of legal geeks who showed up at every important trial.

Karp and Collins sat. Waley came in, looking like he had just spent a week at Gstaad; he nodded, they nodded back. In came

Rohbling with his guard; a murmur from the gallery, suppressed hisses. Karp noted that his glasses were still smudged, and that he retained the air of bemused helplessness he had borne at the arraignment. In came Judge Peoples; all rose, all sat.

Marvin Peoples had a head like a cannonball, one covered in smooth morocco leather. He had a wife and three children, and it is possible that he smiled in their presence, but no one had ever seen him crack a grin on the bench. His voice was a bass rumble.

"We will begin with the motion to invalidate the confession in this case. Mr. Waley?"

Waley rose and, in his remarkable voice, began his brilliant exegesis of the law as it related to the legality of confessions. Karp slouched in his seat and took notes. You could always learn something, he thought.

After the hearing, Karp went right up to see the district attorney.

"There's good news and bad news," he said.

"So I gather," said Keegan.

"You heard already?"

"I have sources, Butch. What happened?" Keegan was wearing his stone face.

Karp looked him in the eye. "You read the motions and the responses—what can I say? He bought Waley's argument out of *Moran* v. *Burbine*. Confession not voluntary, knowing, and intelligent. Especially the knowing part. The mutt was under treatment and on a course of antipsychotics, had stopped taking them, hence nuts, hence not 'knowing.' He went with *Smith* v. *Zant* too. I think the clincher was that Rohbling asked for the pills and the cops denied him. The foul breath of *Connelly* compulsion there, I think. I was nervous about that myself."

"And asking for the lawyer, that horseshit about the shrink?"

"Yeah, and that. Judge made a little law there—the operative fact is the understanding on the part of the police that the suspect is requesting counsel. That the person requested is not in fact counsel does not bear on the requirement to cease the interview. Then he bounced our point from *Mosely*—the resumption of questioning after the request for counsel was not about a crime different in time, place, and nature. 'Ingenious, but not compelling, Mr. Karp,' says His Honor. The critical word there is '*and*,' according to Judge Peoples. The guy has a legal mind on him, I'll give him that. Anyway, we lost the confessions."

"But you still have Hughes," said Keegan.

"Yeah, we still do. And we got the suitcase. The judge went down the line with the *McBain* argument. Suspect renounced the bag in front of the police and witnesses, therefore it was fair game."

"That kid you didn't want did a good job," said Keegan, smiling for the first time.

Karp smiled too. "You want me to take down my pants, give you a better shot? Yeah, he did real good on the motion to suppress evidence response—first-class. I told him he was a credit to his race. When Peoples rolled our way on it, he nearly broke his jaw to keep from grinning, especially since the great white hope here got sunk on *his* motion. On the other hand, the law is a lot more clear on the suppression of evidence side—"

"Oh, wah wah!" said Keegan, chuckling now.

"A *lot* more clear," said Karp with a straight face, "as well you know; Fourth Amendment is like Macy's window compared to the Fifth and the Miranda precedents, where we see but through a glass, darkly. That's why he did it."

Keegan looked confused. "Who did what?"

"The judge," said Karp. "Peoples. He had two motions. No way in hell was he going to give both of them to either side, not in *this* case. Guy's carving a statue—Mr. Fair, in fucking bronze. So he zinged us on the one with the most tortured law, and the one where we had the weakest line. He's saying, we're not going to play with confessions here, buddy. I'm giving you your physical evidence, now make a case! He wants this trial."

"As do we. And will you make the case?"

It was not a casual question, and Karp did not answer lightly. "As to the facts? Absolutely. The guy was there, ID'd going in and going out in lineups by stand-up citizens. We have the wig and the makeup, and both match evidence found at the crime

scene. His dyed skin was under her nails, for Christ's sake! The
suitcase fibers match the ones in the vic's throat. He left prints
on the tea things. On and on. And there's the ashtray. He was
there, he killed her. That's not the problem. The problem is that
after Peoples handed down on the suppression-of-evidence motion, Waley got up and changed his plea to NGI."

Keegan grunted. "This doesn't make me fall off my chair."

"No, me either. So it'll be dueling shrinks."

"Yes," said Keegan. A meaningful pause, and then the district
attorney said, "You're still going with the Ancient Mariner."

"Dr. Perlsteiner. Yes."

"This is an error, in my opinion. He's too old to make the
right impression."

Karp shrugged. "What can I do, Jack? I trust the guy. He's
done real good for us in the past. Meanwhile, if you don't like
the way I'm handling the case—"

"Oh, don't be an ass!" Keegan snapped. "Who the hell else
am I going to put in there? Superman's booked solid and Jesus
is dead. No, it's you, bucko, and as much as I'd like it if you
listened to me just once . . ." He stopped and picked up one of
his ever present Bering silvery cigar tubes and twirled it around
his fingers. "Let me say this," he resumed, "just so you understand. I am now bracing myself for calls from uptown, during
which I will express to what we used to call the colored community the highest confidence in Mr. Roger Karp and in his ability to win this case. This is not a lie. No, I take it back: it's only
a *little* lie, because I thought and I think that you were a damn
fool to take it on. Now I realize it's not your fault, but Rohbling
now has a free pass on the murders of four black women. If he
gets a walk to Happy Valley on the fifth . . ." Here he shook his
head and rolled his eyes. "There will be a typhoon of shit flying
around, and I will not be able to protect you, not without walking
away from this chair myself, which I don't intend to do. Now,
do we understand each other?"

"Yeah, we do. You really think I'm a jerk, don't you?"

"I do. But I also think you're the best murder prosecutor in
the city."

"Next to you."

The lights on the D.A.'s phone had begun to flash.

"No," said Keegan, "because I am the district attorney, and the district fucking attorney, like, as I once supposed, the chief of the Homicide Bureau, does not try gigantic murder cases. Now scram, and God bless you. I got to take these calls."

Marlene sat in her office wondering why, having devoted her life to helping people much in need of help, she did not have a friend in the world. She had just gotten off the phone with Carrie Lanin's sister, who was staying with her in the wake of her outing with Pruitt. The sister said that Carrie didn't want to speak to her, that she was devastated by what had happened. "Why didn't you protect her?" she had said. Why didn't *you*? was Marlene's thought, but she had said nothing, had just taken it and made soothing noises and had hung up the phone, depressed.

Her conversation with Harry had done nothing to improve the mood. Harry had gotten the buzz from the detectives who had caught the Pruitt case: much wrinkling of noses around the precinct. On the other hand, a great story—girl slays killer abductor—and the cops didn't see much of a percentage in spending a lot of time trying to break Lanin's story, if breakable, only to find out if she had received any help in whacking a guy who, all agreed, badly wanted whacking.

But Harry was mightily pissed, believing that somehow Marlene had set the whole thing up and, worse, set it up without consulting him. So Harry hated her too.

As did, naturally, La Wooten and her family and associates. Marlene fingered the copy of the *Times* on her desk, where it lay turned to the review of the recent concert. The reviewer had raved over the Shostakovich performance. It had "captured all the despair and agony inherent in the piece." No kidding, thought Marlene. Wooten and her group had gone back to play after seeing what the Music Lover had done in the dressing room, Wooten red faced and sniffling with her eyes streaming. It was just bad luck that the slimeball had gotten past *both* of them. She never should have left the hallway, never should have shown herself in the lobby, should never have answered her beeper, should have had another man . . . Meanwhile Marlene had started some of her people on an examination of Wooten's intimates and of the people known to be in the Juilliard buildings at the time. Not much hope there, just checking for criminal records and asking around. Any perverts among you musicians? Still, something could turn up, and then there was the boyfriend. Definitely she wanted to know more about the boyfriend.

Marlene threw the newspaper into the wastebasket and stomped out of her office. She could hear Tranh in the back of the office, rattling pots. Perhaps she should saunter over and sit down for a cup of excellent *filtre* and a discussion of Verlaine? *Non, merci.* For now Tranh was to be avoided, at least until she had arranged a suitably safe place for him in her mind.

She walked out of her cubicle to the open area. Lucy was lying in her accustomed after-school position, belly down on the oriental rug with her books and papers spread around her head end like a messy blossom. She was writing firmly and confidently on a worksheet. Marlene stood for a moment watching her daughter. She was certainly becoming a long drink of water: the pipe-stem legs were in constant motion, crossing and recrossing, flicking upward so that the heels nearly touched the barely swelling butt and then splaying outward in a demonstration of near-gymnastic limberness. Her head was thrust forward close to the paper so that her mass of black curls swung forward, obscuring the worksheet to all but their owner. Not an ergonomic position, but Marlene could remember doing her homework the same way at Lucy's age. Like her mother, Marlene thought: a precocious child, with a remarkable gift for languages. Unlike her mother, who had been a docile wimp at that age, Lucy was a wiseass who exhibited occasional flashes of adult-like perception and maturity. Eight going on eleven going on thirty.

She wondered if Lucy felt toward her as she had felt toward her own mother in those distant pre-adolescent days, when she had first understood that her own life was to be on a different course from the one her mother had followed. She was not going to marry a local and make a home in the womb of Italianate

Queens; nor was she going to get a "good job" as a schoolteacher while awaiting same. She remembered the sense of disappointed expectation in her mother's eyes as the woman waited in vain for Marlene to "settle down." She was still waiting, despite the marriage and the three grandchildren. A pang went through her, the mother's bane. Did Lucy feel the same way about *her*?

Something must have been communicated through the ether between them, for Lucy twisted and looked back at Marlene, startled.

"Spying on me again?"

"It's not spying. I'm your mother. I'm *required* to stare at you—it's a New York statute."

Lucy rolled her eyes and said something low and not in English.

"What was that?" asked Marlene.

Lucy giggled. "It means, 'they will believe it in Hunan.' "

"Yes, dear. Correct me if I'm wrong, but little Chinese girls don't talk that way to their devoted parents," said Marlene. She sat down next to Lucy, who closed her notebook, in a gesture of privacy.

"What're you working on?"

"Math. Factoring." Casually said.

Marlene put an impressed expression on her face. "My, my! Do you need any help with it?"

"No, it's easy. Tranh showed me how to do it."

Ah, Tranh, you indispensable monster!

"You're still getting on okay with him?"

"Uh-huh. He's neat. It's like having our own private restaurant here. He's learning more English too. He says, 'I watch much of TV.' " A pause. Lucy looked into her mother's face; Marlene looked into her husband's eyes. "Is Tranh, like, in trouble?" the girl asked.

"Not that I know of," said Marlene carefully. "Why?"

"Oh, nothing. Uncle Harry hates him. He was saying bad words to himself in his office. About Tranh. He was supposed to watch Miranda's mom, wasn't he? I mean, Tranh was."

A chill went through Marlene. "What gives you that idea, darling?"

"Because I was in Tranh's room and I saw the whatchama-callit, the folder with the pictures and stuff . . . ?"

"The case file?"

"Uh-huh. The case file about Ms. Lanin and that guy who was chasing her. He got killed, didn't he?"

"That's right, he did."

Lucy thought for a few seconds and then said, "Probably Tranh did it."

Marlene swallowed hard "What makes you say that?" she asked, managing with some effort to keep her face placid and her voice steady.

"He had a big spot of blood on his sneaker yesterday, the other pair. I saw it in his closet. But now it's not there. Also, he has a gun in his bag. A weird semi-auto. With Russian writing on it. It's not a nine or a forty-five, or—"

Marlene interrupted the gun talk, to which her daughter had become regrettably prone of late. "Yeah, but that's not what the police think, Luce. They think that Ms. Lanin got the gun away from the man who kidnapped her and shot him with it. He was shot with that gun, the bad guy's gun. That's the first thing. Second, it's not allowed to go poking around in other people's stuff. So don't do it anymore, okay? I mean it! And also, what you just said about Tranh? I don't want you to talk about it to anyone else, ever. Understand?"

Lucy nodded. "Sure, Mom. I would never say it to anyone but you anyway. I'm not a dope!"

"No, you're certainly not," said Marlene. "But, Lucy? Don't even say it to *me*."

"Okay." She held a forefinger to her temple. "Bzzzt! It's erased. Can we go shooting?"

Was this a quid pro quo? Amnesia in exchange for a treat? Marlene hoped not, although being taken to the range to bang away with a .22 was very nearly Lucy's favorite activity. She decided that math prowess, in any case, deserved a reward. Marlene looked at her watch. "Sure. After your homework's done," she said.

————

The Music Lover carefully pasted the review from the Times *into his scrapbook and took the opportunity to peruse the volume once again. He was in the room of his little apartment dedicated to Edith Wooten and her music. The walls and the ceiling were papered over with concert posters and programs, from the very first one to the one just passed. A white wooden shelf held more intimate souvenirs: a pair of white panties, a white brassiere, a toothbrush, a set of keys, a pink lipstick, a pair of tan leather gloves. Above these, pinned to the wall, was his private photo gallery, both standard publicity shots and his own compositions—Edie on the street, Edie shopping, Edie practicing, and several shot with a telephoto lens, of Edie in her bathrobe, Edie in a half slip, one small breast showing. His favorite.*

He placed the scrapbook back in its special trunk with the three others and lay down on the camp bed that was the room's only other furniture. The bed was made up with a white duvet covered with a white cotton duvet cover printed with tiny pink roses, the same as the one on Edie Wooten's bed up on Park Avenue. The pillow was a square one in oyster-colored silk that came from Edie's bedroom. That had been his biggest coup once; it still smelled of her Jean Naté. Now of course he could get anything he wanted. It was easy since he had learned how to make himself invisible.

Perhaps too easy? No, the thrill was still there. The Music Lover became excited, thinking about the treasures he would soon possess, thinking about control, about the power he had over her, over the music. He went to the closet and brought out a huge boom box. He really needed a good stereo system, but he moved so much, and so quickly too, that it was impossible. Into the slot he fed a tape of Edie playing Schubert's Quartet in A Major, *the* Rosamunde. *As the music swelled through the room, he lay back on the bed and fixed his eyes on the ceiling, where he had taped a poster-sized blowup of Edie playing her cello. It was an informal shot, taken during practice at a summer music festival. Edie was wearing a tank top and shorts, her head was back, and her face was full of joy. She was laughing, in fact. Exposing her throat. The Music Lover opened his bathrobe. He pressed the pillow against his cheek. Her naked thighs were pressing against the bare wood. The music swelled. He breathed in her fumes, her music, he stroked himself slowly, trying to make it last until the end of the first movement.*

ELEVEN

Sunday dawned, a dull day with yellowy-gray city clouds and a cold December wind. Karp the Infidel snored in bed, and Marlene got her daughter ready for church. Marlene and her husband had been walking on eggs since the shooting of Pruitt. Given the peculiarities of their respective personalities and professions, however, this did not bother them as much as it would have another couple. Shortly, Marlene knew, there would be the crisis—both of them would bellow, trample around like hippos, yolk-stained to the knees, and, still snarling, fall into bed.

Lucy was ready when Marlene came out of the bedroom, dressed in white tights and a deep purple velvet dress with a lace collar and little black buttons up the front. She had a round-brimmed hat in the same color held in her hands, and she had clearly tried hard with her hair. It shone, and the tangles were mainly at the back. Lucy liked church, as she liked all serious things, non-kid things—guns, for example. It was another aspect of her eight-going-on-thirty personality. Marlene sometimes feared that she was even a trifle too dour.

"Ow!" as Marlene plied her hairbrush.

"Be quiet, and think of the holy martyrs, as my mother used to say," said Marlene. Finishing, she stood back.

"There! Gorgeous! Ready for church. In fact, in that outfit, you look like a tiny monsignor."

Lucy was not amused by this remark. She put on her hat and her camel-hair coat, now somewhat too small, showing skinny wrist bones, and made for the door. They walked the dog, boarded the yellow car, which was nursed with many a prayer into fretful life, and drove to Old St. Patrick's Cathedral on Mulberry Street off Prince. In the car, Lucy asked, "Do you think they'll let girls be, like, priests while I'm alive?"

"I don't know, Luce. John Paul and I are trying to work it out, but we're still pretty far apart. Why? Feeling a vocation coming on?"

Shrug. "It would be neat to be, you know, holy."

"You could be a nun," suggested Marlene, shriveling.

"Yes," said Lucy. "I could be the kind that parachutes over the jungle and saves people from bad soldiers. But . . . I don't like the part where you can't"—a faint blush and a wriggle—"have babies."

Straight-faced, Marlene responded, "You want to have a family?"

"Only when I'm real old, like thirty-five or something. But maybe they'll let nuns have babies."

"Maybe," said Marlene. "In which case you could found your own order. The Little Sisters of the Fruitful Womb (Airborne)."

Lucy looked at her mother sideways, decided that she had been made fun of, sniffed, and fell silent for the rest of the drive. Marlene sighed. Their relationship seemed to be transforming itself into a wisecracking rivalry rather than the warmly supportive figment of Marlene's hopeful imagination.

That Marlene chose to go to Old St. Pat's instead of to St. Anthony of Padua, where every other Italian in lower Manhattan went, or Transfiguration, which was closer, was part of the same contrarian spirit that (aside from her vow to raise her daughter in the faith) kept her going to church in the first place. It was not expected that someone of her education, politics, and behavior —Jew-wed and all—would continue to be a regular communicant of the nasty old patriarchal racket, and so therefore she was. St. Pat's was also a venerable Gothic Revival pile, parts of it dating back to the War of 1812 (which antiquity she thought gave worship there an almost European style) and full of the ghosts of departed poor Irishmen and the present bodies of poor Latinos. For Marlene their déclassé presence took some of the sting out of doing something her mom approved.

They passed under the peculiar Gothic facade and into the echoing space, redolent of incense and damp stone. It was early, not much after seven, and they both joined the short waiting lines by the confessionals set out along a side aisle.

Lucy went in first. Marlene could not imagine what the child had to confess, not unless she *really* thought about it, and then she primly put the thought out of mind. In any case, Lucy had always been eager for that particular sacrament since she had taken first communion the previous year.

There were two boxes in operation. An old woman in shiny black emerged from the far one, and Marlene went in, wondering briefly whether it was manned by the pastor, Father Raymond, or one of his curates. In general, Marlene was not interested in the character of her priest, unlike many of her co-religionists, who were nearly Congregational in their concern with the style, character, and attitude of their pastors, and shopped around town for the one they considered most amenable to their own concept of Rome's doctrine. She did not particularly care for Raymond, a sheep-faced man of dull and conventional views, but, she believed, either it was magic or it was bullshit, and since she was here, she had opted for the magic, which could work via an asshole as well as via a Thomas Merton.

In the dim familiar box, after the ritual acknowledgments, Marlene began her tour through such of the Seven Deadlies as had afflicted her in the past week. Wrath, as usual, was top of the charts.

"In my work—I run a security firm that offers protection to women against stalkers and abusive men—I get so angry at them," she said, "the men, I mean. It frightens me. I want to hurt them and kill them. I sometimes do hurt them, in the line of duty, so to speak and . . . I get pleasure out of it."

The voice said, "Do you hurt them *for* the pleasure, or as a means to an end?"

Startled, Marlene stared at the grille. It had not been Father Raymond's voice, or that of any priest with whom she was familiar. The voice was low and husky, the diction precise with the flat accent of the outlands. New England? Not a New Yorker, at any rate. Marlene brought herself back to the question.

"I *think* it's as a means to an end," she replied hesitantly. "I want to frighten them away from the pattern of increasing violence. The law doesn't seem able to do that. I want them to know that if they continue there will be consequences, horrible consequences, for them personally."

"And does this work?"

"Sometimes. The shock works, I think. Like having blackouts works for a drunk sometimes. They have to choose between stopping drinking and losing their lives. But some drunks keep drinking and die, and some of these men keep after their women and kill them, and then they often kill themselves. Or I could kill them first."

"But in providing this shock, you feel pleasure. What sort of pleasure?"

"Not physical. More like . . . I don't know . . . moral satisfaction, the sense of meting out justice—now, you rat, you know what it feels like. Afterward, after one of these sessions, I feel depleted; sometimes, if it's bad enough, I feel nauseous."

A long pause. She could hear him breathing. She became aware of a growing interest in the priest, and a not entirely comfortable increase in that almost erotic feeling she always got in the confessional: sitting alone in the dark, telling your secrets to a man you knew, but who was professionally anonymous, a stranger, a stranger clothed in mystic powers, the best entertainment on earth, now closing in on its third millennium of continuous performance. Why all the churches were full of women.

"That's a very good sign," he said. "The sickness. I would be more concerned if you went out for a hearty meal afterward. It sounds as if you acted with good intention and when you caused pain it was to promote a greater good. This is slippery moral ground, as I'm sure you know, but it seems as if so far you are keeping your feet. The rage is another matter. Please go on."

She went on. Lust—stupid fantasies about men she'd met casually or seen on the street; sloth—a slight tendency toward *acedia*, the abandonment of hope; pride—yes, perhaps a serious problem there, more serious than Marlene was willing to recognize. Without quite knowing how she had started, Marlene found herself talking about her husband. This was another first, as the irregularity of the mixed marriage had always made her shy of bringing Karp and the church together in the same breath, and it came pouring. It was not complaint, precisely, but more like a spiritual confusion. Why did her life torment him? Why did his suspicions torment her? Where was the trust? Why did she feel stifled? Why did she feel compelled to lie to him—no, not exactly lie, as such; more a selective withholding of the truth?

"It sounds," said the priest, "as if your marriage is far from perfect, and that you yourself have fallen far short of the perfection you have every right to expect from yourself."

Marlene found herself nodding in agreement for a moment before it struck her that the priest's tone had been ironic. Irony is not much met with in the confessional.

"I don't understand," she said, although she did.

"I think you do," said the voice. It seemed to wait.

"You're talking about pride, spiritual pride," said Marlene.

"I'm not talking about anything. You're confessing your sins."

Who *was* this guy? Marlene took a deep breath. "Yes, right. I have been guilty of the sin of pride. I want to be perfect, and have a perfect marriage and perfect children and never make a mistake and save all the poor, poor women, every one of them. Yes, it's true. What can I do!"

Marlene had to struggle to keep from raising her voice. She could feel sweat rolling down her sides and clammy on her forehead.

"You can sincerely repent and make a good act of contrition.

For your penance, read the first four chapters of St. Teresa's *The Way of Perfection*. Do you have it?"

In fact, she did and said so.

"I thought you might," said the priest. "Now, is there anything more?"

There was not. Marlene said the ritual words with more fervor than was her wont—she *was* heartily sorry—received the absolution, and left the box.

"You were in there a long time, Mommy," said Lucy, who was waiting for her on a stone bench.

"Yes, well, I've been a very wicked woman lately."

"It doesn't matter how wicked you are. If you're really sorry, God will forgive you," intoned Lucy in her most sacerdotal voice.

"Yes," said Marlene, "that's the catch."

After church it was the tradition of the Catholic Karps to switch cultures and stop off at Samuel's on East Houston to buy fresh bagels, lox, cream cheese, whitefish, and carp, this last from an early age Lucy's special delight (That's *us*, right, Mommy?). When they arrived home with their aromatic burdens, Karp (the man) was, as usual, sitting at the kitchen table with the fat *Times*, in his frowzy blue plaid robe, unwashed and unshaven. She plunked her shopping bag down on the table and kissed his ear.

"Euueh! Take a shower," she said, and kissed him again, on the neck.

"How was church?" he asked, surprised at the attention. He pulled at the bagel bag.

"The usual. God loves us all, and the pope knows what's what. There's a new priest I'd like to get to know." Marlene continued her nuzzling and ran her hand inside his robe. Karp groped bagels.

"Would you rather have a bagel, or me?" she breathed into his ear.

"That depends on whether you're covered with crunchy little bits of onion," said Karp and held up an onion bagel to demonstrate. He got up and pulled a knife from the rack.

"It could be arranged," said Marlene, as Lauren Bacall.

"That must have been quite a sermon," said Karp dryly. "What was it on? Marital duty? The proper subjection of wife to husband?"

"The Immaculate Conception, if you must know. Jesus, Butch, how can you cut bagels like that!" It was an old argument.

"You mean, holding them in my hand against my chest with the razor-sharp knife cutting toward my heart? My mom always did it that way, and so did *her* mom. I always thought it bespoke an attractively cavalier disregard of death. Anyway, are we going back to being friends now?"

"I'm sorry," said Marlene, seeing the possibility of an egg-free reconciliation. "It was my fault, I take full responsibility. I should have talked it out with you when it happened. The thing is, I think Tranh either whacked, or helped Carrie whack, the guy."

"The noodle guy? He told you this?"

"He's not a noodle guy; he's a stone killer. And he didn't tell me, and there's no evidence—no, actually, Lucy saw some blood and a gun in his room. So he was probably involved, although I don't see how you'd ever prove it in court."

Karp took a deep breath. This was not the time to ask what the *fuck* his darling daughter was doing rummaging in the rooms of armed stone killers. He said, "Proving it in court is not the point."

"No, you're right. The point is, I need you to know I didn't set it up. I didn't hire a murder."

Karp sighed, a noise that represented the myriad frustrations of his life with this woman, as well as recognition that he had asked for it, and that he was not about to make any waves. He put down the bagel and the knife and hugged her. Lucy came in, changed out of her church clothes into jeans and a long-sleeve T-shirt. She said, "Yuck! Mushing *again*? Where's the food?"

Karp waited behind the prosecution table in Part 46 while the next panel of veniremen filed in. It was late in the eleventh day of what the *Post* had called in a big black headline, THE JURY SELECTION FROM HELL. Karp kept his expression neutral as he looked the new group over. They had gone through eighteen panels already and had agreed on but two jurors. Judge Peoples was being liberal with challenges for cause, and generous with the range of potentially disqualifying questions he allowed. Mr. Fair.

There are, generally speaking, two sorts of lawyers with respect to the voir dire: those who think that the selection of the right jury is tantamount to winning the case, and those who think that a properly constructed case will win with any but a blatantly prejudiced jury. Karp was of the latter persuasion; Lionel Waley was enthusiastically, famously, of the former: he had even written a little book on the subject, which Karp had, of course, read: *Choosing a Winning Jury*. It had not changed Karp's mind, but that didn't mean he couldn't play Waley's game, and right from the opening gun at that. It made him irritable, a mood he had to hide behind a mask of genial, bland interest ("Do you have any friends or relatives with emotional problems, Mrs., ah, Perkins? Your nephew? Could you tell us about him?"). That might, in fact, have been part of the reason why Waley did it.

In any event, the man's selection strategy was not hard to fathom. He wanted a jury composed of non-black people with crazy relatives whom they felt sorry for. This was somewhat unusual, since defense attorneys representing the average felon of whatever race typically wanted a "Bronx jury," that is, one composed of blacks and Hispanics inclined to take police testimony with enough salt grains to cause cardiac arrest. In *Rohbling*, however, the police were not the issue (although Waley would fling as much dirt at them too as he could); the issue was which psychiatrist you believed. Waley had made the not-surprising judgment that the people he wanted on the jury would have to combine low sympathy for the victims and high credulousness when it came to shrinks.

What Karp wanted was not as clear. He would have liked educated people, of course, people to whom an M.D. degree did not signify the shadow of God on earth, but he had scant chance of getting anyone brainy past Waley, whose attitude toward the well-schooled (on juries, at least) was similar to that of the Khmer Rouge. Waley was not going to allow any elderly women on there either, if he could help it, especially not elderly black women. What Karp had to look for, then, were bright undereducated people, skeptics about psychiatry and believers in justice, even for old black ladies. There were limits on Waley's design, of course; the judge was clearly determined to end up with a sexually and racially balanced jury, a little scale model of the people of New York that no one could challenge.

Within those limits, then, Waley and Karp were like a pair of poker players, each with the same number of chips, each chip a preemptory challenge that would scuttle one juror. The jurors were the cards they were betting on. Should Karp, for example, let this oyster-eyed white woman with the retarded kid on the jury? A dunce maybe, and doctors had helped her kid, hence a likely defendant's juror. If he challenged her, on the other hand, he might run out of chips and be unable later to bump someone worse. Karp passed her, in the event, and then, four hours later, they got another one, a pipe fitter, the first black on the panel. Karp hoped he had loved his mother.

Marlene finished reading Wolfe's report on Edith Wooten's associates and then looked up at the man himself. Today he was wearing a nubbly gray sports jacket over a gray and orange plaid shirt buttoned to the neck. His tan hair had been recently trimmed to maintain the hard edge of geekiness he seemed to favor.

She tapped the report. "This is good, Wolfe. Very complete." She smiled.

Wolfe, whose face had worn a look of apprehension while she read, now broke into one of his rare smiles, showing gum and a set of bad ochre teeth. Not a regular flosser, Wolfe.

"You put in some overtime on this, yes?"

Head bob. Worried look. Marlene wondered once again why a big guy who looked like he could walk through bricks should bear himself with so diffident a mien. Dane, and most of her other troops, all much smaller men, left damp trails of testosterone behind them. Of course, Wolfe had never been a street cop. . . .

The thought faded. She continued, "Well, you're supposed to get it authorized first."

"Sorry."

He seemed so. "But we'll let it slide this time," she said. "The client's loaded, and she wants closure on this real bad. I doubt she'll bitch about the extra." She leafed through the pages, all neatly typed and well organized. He wrote plain, grammatical English, with correct spelling, unusual in someone with his job history. As a rule, she had to rewrite the reports of her people. "This Felix Evarti looks interesting. The piano. What do you think?"

"Possible. He had that sheet. Sex offenses with a minor girl. And his sex life in general . . ." Wolfe pursed his lips and waggled his big hand from side to side.

"He likes getting the shit pounded out of him. Yeah, there's that, but it doesn't exactly connect with the kind of person who becomes a stalker."

"How do you mean?"

"Well, your average stalker is a regular person with an obsession about a particular woman. She left him, he can't stand it, so he chases her. Or he saw her in the bank and she's his heart's desire, but he can't get up the nerve to meet her, so he stalks."

"Like Pruitt."

Marlene nodded approvingly. "Sort of. Pruitt did get up the nerve to ask her out, originally, but he's that type. My point is that stalkers tend to be people with low social skills and outwardly *ordinary*. If they were born middle-class, they're downwardly mobile—like Mark David Chapman, the guy who did John Lennon."

"Ted Bundy had great social skills."

"He did, but serial-killing psychopaths like Bundy are not really stalkers in the sense we're dealing with here. I guess my point is we don't see successful, talented people like Evarti doing stranger stalking."

"He's not a stranger; he's a . . . you know, he works with her."

"A colleague. Okay, good point. He lusts after her, she doesn't know he's alive, except when he's tinkling those keys; he's like an appliance. So he gets pissed off, he tortures her with these notes and invasions. That could work. But I hate that he's a S-M freak. It seems somehow an . . . excess of weird, even for a musician."

Marlene thought about the last time she had seen Felix Evarti. He hadn't liked her, she recalled, and she had, in turn, been repelled by something vaguely wrong in his demeanor, a Peter Lorre–ish oiliness, a furtive quality. And he certainly had access to Edith Wooten, not to mention possessing the musical knowledge that the stalker had shown.

"Okay, let's put him on the short list. I'll ask Edie if he ever made a pass at her. We'll set up a watch on him, a little discreet shadowing, see if maybe we can catch him with the roses and the note." She shuffled through the pages of the report. "I see you found Edie's main squeeze."

"The violin, Ten Haar, yeah."

"He a possibility?"

"A long shot. He lives in Europe. He could be hiring it, though."

"Never happens," said Marlene confidently. "They love to do it themselves. It's the fun part. Forget him—I'm just glad she's getting laid, the poor little bitch. While we're on bitches, what about the sister?"

Wolfe rolled his eyes, a dramatic gesture on the usually impassive face. "The sister. Also into whips and chains. And drugs too. Strictly prescription, though, like I said in the report. Gets them from her boyfriend."

Marlene leafed through until she found the right page. "This is the doc?"

"Uh-huh. Very Park Avenue type too. Matter of fact, we ran into him the day I met Wooten, in the hallway outside her place. Big blond guy . . . ?"

"Yeah, I know. He was at the concert too."

"He was?" Wolfe seemed surprised.

"Yeah. And he knew me. And he had a shot at it while I was

making that phone call. What do you think about him and the sister for it?"

"Oh, she's mean enough. And he's not, you know, too tightly wrapped either. And Evarti could be in with them too, for the music part."

"Evarti knows Ginnie and what's his name, Vincent Robinson?"

"Uh-huh," said Wolfe. "They all go to the same club to get whipped. I got it down there somewhere. Cuff's."

Marlene looked at the page. "Yeah, I see it here—it's on First off the Bowery." She looked across at Wolfe, considering, trying to suppress a loony image—a faded socialite, a Romanian concert pianist, and a Park Avenue doctor with their white buttocks in a row, waving in the air, waiting for the lash. It was all she could do to suppress a guffaw.

"What?" said Wolfe, who was beginning to squirm under her gaze.

She snapped out of the reverie. "Oh, nothing, just thinking. Look, have you got a black T-shirt?"

"A black T-shirt?" Wolfe repeated.

"Yeah, and black jeans, a leather jacket . . . you know, swinging stud garments." A blank look from the man. "Don't get out much, eh, Wolfe? Okay, there's a place called Naughty Boys on East Eleventh. Go over there today and pick yourself up an outfit. We'll pay for it, or rather, Edie Wooten will. I'll meet you back here at, say, ten tonight."

"We're going there. Cuff's." Wolfe said it like "So the tumor is malignant."

"We are. Why so glum, Wolfe? There was a time when a young dude would've jumped at a chance for a night at the clubs with Marlene Ciampi. Tell me I haven't lost it all!"

Wolfe's face blossomed so with confusion that Marlene felt obliged to reach across and pat his arm. "Joke, Wolfe. We'll check the place out, get some background on our friends. We could get lucky and learn something useful. At worst, we'll have to watch them get whipped."

"Or whip," said Wolfe with a strange, cautious look. "What I hear, Robinson likes to whip."

When Wolfe had gone, Marlene called Lily Malkin, a sociology professor at NYU who specialized in the study of violence against women and who, like many among New York's *panzer-*feminists, was a big fan of Marlene's.

She was in but unavailable. Marlene left a message and then made a set of calls to a half-dozen of her clients, reminding them of court appearance, making referrals, and generally checking on how they were. All seemed quiet for a mercy, and she was pleased to learn from Tamara Morno that Marlene's dog interview with Arnie Nobili had borne fruit. Morno had heard from friends that he was going to meetings, had stopped drinking.

Marlene was thus feeling very much like a contributing member of society when the phone rang with Lily Malkin returning her call. Marlene told her what she was doing and what she wanted to know.

Malkin stayed silent for so long that Marlene thought something had gone wrong with the phone.

"Lily? Are you there?"

"Uh-huh. Just thinking. Exercising the great card catalog that is my mind. What you want to know is not quite in my field."

"But I thought sadomasochism would be right up your alley," said Marlene.

"So to speak," said Malkin, chuckling. "No, conventional S-M has nothing whatever to do with the kind of stuff I study. It's not violent. Or probably I should say it's 99.5 not violent."

"Wait a minute: you're saying sadomasochism isn't *violent*? Isn't that like saying water isn't wet?"

"Not at all. S-M is a sexual game. The people who play it are by and large solid citizens, high S.E.S.—sorry, socioeconomic status—by and large. They have code words that they use to stop themselves from actually getting hurt."

"That sounds like a joke, Lily," Marlene objected. "The masochist says 'hurt me!' and the sadist says 'no!' You're serious about this?"

"Yeah, it's all for fun. I've got a study here I could ship over to you, explains the whole dominance and submission scene. That sort of includes both straight sadomas and bondage and discipline. It's quite a read. There's another paper about professional mistresses—dominatrixes—that's a hoot and a half."

"My God, it shows you how sheltered I've been. I had no idea. Why do they do it?"

"Well, like I said, it's not my field, but, as with everything else, it's *the mother*—"

"What a surprise!" said Marlene, and they both laughed.

"I'll send those papers over."

"Okay, great," said Marlene, "but one thing—you said it was 99.5 percent harmless. What about the other half a percent?"

"Oh, well, in any communal activity you're going to see some deviance. For God's sake, look at marriage! The S-M community apparently does attract some actual psychopaths. You read the various S-M newsletters, you see photographs of guys with captions, 'This is John Jones, stay away from this stinker, he hurt me.' Like that. That's why it's actually unusual to find real what you'd call really violent sadists in S-M gatherings. It's like you wouldn't expect to find real professional killers at those fast-draw exhibitions where everybody dresses up like the Cisco Kid."

"Amazing! As a matter of fact, I'm going to one of those clubs tonight."

"Are you? Fascinating! Are you going to participate?"

Marlene hadn't thought that far ahead. "I'm not sure. It's never really attracted me. I guess I'll have to see what the scene looks like."

"Well, then," said Malkin, "if the opportunity arises for you to pee on some guy's face, I would encourage you to do so, if not for yourself, then for me."

After depositing Lucy back at the loft, Marlene spent the late afternoon doing some special shopping. Later, after the children were safely in bed, Marlene decided to push the New Openness by modeling her purchases for her husband in their living room.

"So? What do you think?" she asked.

Karp took his time replying. His wife, heavily made up with

scarlet lipstick, glittered eyeshadow, and thick mascara on her real eye and the other one covered by a thin wash-leather patch of the type favored by members of the Prussian general staff, was wearing lace-up knee boots with six-inch spike heels, a leather mini-skirt that barely covered her buttocks, black fish-net stockings held up with lace garters, and a black leather neck band with little chrome studs on it. Over this ensemble she had thrown her old black motorcycle jacket. To prompt his response, she threw open the jacket to reveal that on her upper body she wore only a skimpy black leather bra decorated with little spikes arranged in a spiral pattern.

"Jesus H. Christ!" said Karp.

"Impressive, no?"

"You could say that. I hadn't realized we were so short of money. Don't bring home any diseases."

"How dare you!" said Marlene in mock indignation.

As this juncture snorts and giggles were heard nearby. Marlene turned to see the faces of her daughter and her nursemaid peeking around the doorjamb.

"Far out, Marlene!" said Posie.

"Mommy, you look like Kiss," was Lucy's contribution.

"You! Bed!" said Marlene in her best dominatrix tone. To Karp she added, "And as for you, I resent the implication that I look like a . . ." and observing that her daughter had not budged, spelled the word.

"Mother! I can *spell*, you know," said Lucy indignantly. "And I know what a prostitute is, for your information."

"I bet you do. Scram! I mean it, girls."

They scurried off, giggling.

"So," said Karp. "What's with the outfit?"

"I got a date with Wolfe. We're going to visit a leather bar. We're checking out some characters who could be involved in the Edie Wooten stalking."

"I see. A plausible cover. Look, Marlene, I can see where you might be tired of me, you want to try some new things—"

"Oh, stop it!" cried Marlene, laughing and throwing herself down next to him on the couch.

"No, really, I understand. I get the ratty bathrobes, he gets the leather and lace . . . Ow!"

She had dug her knuckles painfully between his ribs.

"What is this, the home version? A little sadism before . . . no, don't touch me—I'll scream."

"You faker! This is turning you on, isn't it?"

"Me? I'm a public servant. I'm a pillar of the community."

"Yes, and I can see it right there in your pants."

He ran his hand slyly up her thigh. "What are you wearing under that . . ."

"None of your business, buster," she said, slipping away from him and slapping his hand. "You pervert!"

That left him speechless and laughing, and she skipped out of the room.

TWELVE

They drove north up the Bowery in Wolfe's old tan Caprice, a light rain spotting the windows, to the beat of the wipers and the radio, which was tuned to a soft rock station. Wolfe had his usual stolid expression on, one that went oddly with his outfit, which was black and moderately vicious. He had a well-studded leather vest on over a long-sleeve black turtleneck, engineer boots on his feet, and a chain belt around his waist with a clasp in the shape of a grinning demon. He seemed like an unusually dour farmer on the way to the milk barn rather than a stud primed for an evening of kinky fun. His car was well kept, remarkably well kept, and scented with artificial pine. Marlene, who had traveled in a large number of bachelor vehicles in her time, imagined he had cleaned it especially for her that evening, which she thought rather sweet. The car stereo, she noticed, was not the standard Delco crap but a pretty good Kenwood deck, with good Jensen speakers.

"Wolfe, got any tapes?" she asked.

"I keep most of them in the trunk, sorry," he answered. He slowed the car, rummaged under the seat, and pulled out a dusty cassette. "Conway Twitty?"

Marlene suppressed a snort. "Um, no, we're almost there

anyway. And we'll probably get more music than we need at this joint."

This was, as it turned out, the case. Marlene had not been to a real club since her spinster days, and while she was vaguely aware of the growth of the club scene in lower Manhattan, she had never felt the slightest desire to participate in it. In this she was like the majority of her fellow native New Yorkers, and unlike those who came to the city from elsewhere. Marlene did her drinking in working-class saloons, of which there were, thank God, still two surviving in Little Italy, and would occasionally, *very* occasionally, drag Karp out for an evening of jazz. She was prepared, however, for noise, mediocre performance, crowds, bad drinks, and discomfort, and was not disappointed.

Cuff's was located on the ground floor of a Bowery building that had once been a flophouse. The street windows of the floors above had been blanked with sheets of galvanized steel. The bouncer, an appropriately shaven-headed, pierced, and tattooed ogre, gave them the eye at the door and, apparently pleased with their equipage, passed them in.

It was immediately apparent to Marlene that you didn't go to Cuff's for the music. At the end of the black-painted room was a low stage, upon which a suitable leathered and painted quartet was doing a cover of a New Order song, the lyrics to which consisted largely of the words "baby" and "body," heavy on the feedback and writhing, at glass-cracking volume. When her eyes adjusted to the gloom, Marlene saw that they were in a large room that occupied the entire floor of the old flop, with a bar along one side, a dozen or so round tables in the center, and a dance floor in front of the stage. Everything that would take paint was painted matte black, of course, and the room's only light, aside from the glow behind the bar, came from red and blue mini-spots focused on the stage and on the obligatory spinning glitter ball, the great seal of the republic of fun. The walls were decorated with mock-ups of antique torture implements—at least Marlene hoped they were mock-ups—and a remarkable variety of dusty whips, chains, and manacles hung from the ceiling, like the webs of large, messy spiders. There were about fifty people in the room, all dressed to kill, or at least to harm, in the sort of outfits Marlene and Wolfe were wearing.

"Nice place," said Marlene to Wolfe. "See anyone we know?"

Wolfe made a noncommittal noise and cast his eyes around the crowd, as did Marlene. No Ginnie Wooten, no Evarti, unless, like many of the patrons, they were wearing masks. The two pushed their way to the bar and ordered a pair of five-dollar Schlitzes. Marlene paid with a twenty and asked the bartender, "Has Ginnie Wooten been in tonight?" The bartender was wearing a laced leather vest over a hairless chest. He was a skinny, hatchet-faced man with a badly pocked face, and to improve his appearance he had dressed his hair into three Velcro-like tufts with shaved furrows between them and driven a chromed twenty-penny nail through his nose, like a cannibal chieftain in a cartoon. It gave his voice a curious buzzing quality.

"You're new," he observed.

"Yeah, Ginnie said I should check out the scene." Here she gestured to the room. "It's pretty cool. So, have you seen her?"

"She's around. What about you? Top or bottom?"

"Oh, top, definitely," said Marlene. The bartender seemed to lose interest. She attempted to rekindle it by twitching one of her five-dollar bills. "I'd appreciate knowing where to find her."

The bartender took the bill and put it in a pocket of his vest. "You try upstairs yet?"

"No." Marlene had not been aware that the place had more than one floor.

"Private club," said the man, turning away. "See the guy, Melvin. On the stool there."

Back in the corner, to one side of the bandstand, nearly obscured by the huge speakers, was a door, lit by the red of an exit sign, and by the door they found the stool and on the stool was Melvin. This person weighed at least three hundred pounds and was naked to the waist except for several dozen chains around his neck, Mr. T fashion, and a black executioner's mask.

"Ten bucks lifetime membership," said Melvin when Marlene

and Wolfe made inquiries, and to Marlene, "I like your outfit."
He had a surprisingly light voice for such a large man.

"Thanks," said Marlene. "Membership in what?"

"The Asperians. We're an umbrella group, you know? Affiliations with the Til Eulenspiegels, Samois, Gemini, the S-M Church. We take anyone—male dominant, female dominant, gay, the whole nine yards. We rent the rooms upstairs."

They paid their money, and Melvin recorded their names and addresses in a ledger, and handed over a pair of membership cards.

"There's equipment for borrowing upstairs if you haven't brought your own. The only rule is have fun and don't get hurt," advised Melvin cheerfully, and nudged open the nearby door with his foot.

They ascended a narrow stairway lit by weak red bulbs, and at the top of it came to a room about half the size of the one below. It was carpeted in some industrial material, and its windows were covered with the metal sheeting they had seen from the street. There were perhaps a dozen people in the room, largely coupled off, most of the women in dominatrix gear and most of the men in a variety of costumes designed for ritual humiliation—petticoats, sheer negligees, diapers—or nude except for complicated-looking leather straps, both jock and restraining. Many were attached to their mistresses by chains or leashes. The room was lit by several photographic spots directed at its center, and in this pool of light a woman was shouting insults at her partner, a man dressed only in a diaper, who was cringing in ecstasy at her feet. She kicked him lightly with her pointed boot and called him a naughty, dirty little boy. It went on for quite a while. Some of the spectators watched with interest; others, the dominants, chatted. It was like being at a big dog show, Marlene thought, except that here the dogs were people. She looked at the faces in the group. Allowing for the peculiar qualities of the lighting and the odd makeup many of the women favored, they looked like quite ordinary people: supermarket rather than horror-movie faces, and Marlene concluded that Professor Malkin's assessment was correct, just plain folks having odd fun.

The diapered man was led off by his mistress, crawling, through a door Marlene had not noticed. Shortly, through the same door issued a woman dressed all in white, a startling sight in the circumstances, drawing an appreciative murmur from the group. She was clearly posing as a little girl going to first communion, in a white dress, tied with a sash, white stockings, a white patent leather purse, and white patent mary-janes on her feet. Her face was made up to look not made up, and she wore a white ribbon in her straw-colored hair. She walked into the spotlight and waited, twisting her toes girlishly.

Marlene looked around for Wolfe, who had, however, wandered away. "What's going on?" Marlene asked the man next to her, a beefy fellow wearing a dog collar, red corset, and panty hose. He started to answer reflexively, but the woman he was with cut him off violently by yanking on his collar.

"You dare to speak without my permission!" she hissed. "You dare! You filthy, disgusting worm! Get down! Lower!"

He groveled, his face in the carpet, while she put her booted foot on his neck and ground his face, while giving him a couple of good ones across the bottom with a little cat-o'-nine-tails she carried.

Marlene was about to apologize and then realized that the rules of courtesy were different here. She smiled at the woman, who was thin and pretty and younger than Marlene, and dressed in a formal black-silk suit, velvet hat, and veil, like Marlene's grandmother. She got a bland smile in return, of the sort you get in the laundromat when you've handed someone a quarter.

Another stir in the crowd. A man in a long raincoat had come out of the door and approached the faux little girl. He was dirty and unshaven and wore a slouch fedora that shadowed his face. He was breathing hard; the rasping noise he made seemed to drown out the faint throb of the music coming from the room below. In a violent motion he flung his raincoat open to reveal that the crotch had been cut out of his trousers and that his penis was rigidly erect. There was a moment of frozen silence. Then the girl-woman let out a piercing shriek and attacked the man, kicking him in the knees and shins and shouting, "Filthy, dirty old man!" over and over. She reached into her purse and brought out some kind of flail and swung it at the man's head. No, Marlene saw, not a flail, a heavy rosary, of the type borne by old-fashioned nuns. The man's hat flew off. He was Felix Evarti.

The white-clad woman kept up her frenzy of beating and kicking, shouting all the while ("Dirty! Filthy!"). Evarti made ineffective shielding motions, and went down on his knees and then his back. Marlene knew enough about serious fights to realize that for all her extravagant motion, Mary-Jane was pulling her blows. The others were closing around the scene in a circle, avid. With Evarti down, the woman could now concentrate her fury on the peccant member, which remained upright and twitching. She beat at it with the rosary, and Marlene wondered how she kept from doing him damage. The vituperation reached a crescendo. The woman leaped upon Evarti's naked belly and ground her white mary-janes into his genitals, grinding the penis underfoot as if squashing a cockroach. Evarti was making incomprehensible noises, groaning, thrashing from side to side. He arched his back and shouted something in another language, Romanian, Marlene supposed, and then came in a thick gush over the woman's white shoes.

"Euugh! You disgusting man!" cried the woman. "You dirtied me with your filth! Clean it up! Clean it up this minute." Evarti started to dab the shoes with the edge of his raincoat, but this was clearly not satisfactory. After a few especially vigorous lashes, the woman shouted, "Lick it! Get it all off, you foul man!" Evarti prostrated himself before the woman and licked the semen off her shoes. She made sure he got it all and then, straightening her dress and replacing her rosary in the little purse, she skipped off. She actually skipped. Evarti rose shakily, clutched his coat around him, picked up his hat, and shuffled away. There was a collective release of breath around the circle.

Marlene was again conscious of Wolfe standing close by. In a low voice she remarked, "Gosh, and I thought *I* had some weird relationships. What did you think of that, Wolfe?"

Wolfe shook his head. "Un-fucking-believable. I checked the place. He's here."

"Who?" said Marlene.

"Robinson. I think he must have been in one of the little rooms off the corridor there, behind the door. Now he's over in the corner under the windows." Marlene looked. There was a man standing in the corner, leaning against the wall. He was wearing a dark suit and tie and a white shirt, but Marlene could not make out his face.

The woman in the black grandma outfit was putting Mr. Panty Hose through his paces under the spot, but Mary-Jane was obviously a hard act to follow. The circle of watchers grew more diffuse. Marlene moved away from it, pulling Wolfe along.

She said, "Look, why don't you go and get a drink downstairs?" and at his doubtful grimace, added, "Wolfe, I can take care of myself, and besides, if you're not around I can try my flagging charms on the bozo. And you can look for the lovely Virginia Wooten."

Wolfe shrugged and walked off, a good soldier. Marlene removed her leather jacket and walked toward Robinson's corner, dragging the jacket behind her. She walked slowly, thrusting out her breasts in the leather bra and rolling her hips, although the spikes on her boots did most of the rolling for her.

She walked to the wall of covered windows, took a turn in front of Robinson, walked to the other end of the room, and then walked back, slowly. When she was a few paces away from him, she could see that he was looking at her. She turned and started to stroll away again when he spoke.

"Trailing your cloak?"

She stopped and faced him.

"Yes, as a matter of fact," she said.

"Do I know you?" Odd, Marlene thought. It was dim and she was heavily made up, so perhaps he really hadn't recognized her. Or maybe this was part of the game. She decided to play it out.

"I don't think so. But I always make it a point at any gathering to approach the most interesting-looking man in any room."

"And why am I that?" he asked, smiling now.

"Well, for one thing, you're not dressed up. How come, I wonder."

"But I *am* dressed up," he replied, spreading his arms and posing ironically. "This is a dominance and submission party, and I'm wearing the most dominant possible costume—a blue pinstripe, custom-made Savile Row suit, with accessories to match. This sort of suit rules the world."

"I take your point. But that's not very playful, is it? The leather, the little whips that don't do any damage, the domination skits over there—it's supposed to show it's all fantasy."

"I suppose so. Actually, all of that's not particularly interesting to me."

"Oh, no? Why not?"

"Because I take domination seriously," he said. He stopped smiling and stared hard into her eyes, in the manner of Mandrake the Magician.

Marlene burst out laughing, and as she did she saw something truly dangerous pass across his eyes, but only for an instant, before he remembered and turned the charm back on.

It was considerable charm, Marlene thought, or rather, felt: the man had a remarkably powerful sexual aura, of the type often possessed by extremely nasty men. It was one of God's little jokes, this, and Marlene had seen it played out innumerable times in her professional life. In fact, it might be said that it was nearly the *source* of her professional life. Not that she was immune to it herself; rather the opposite, to tell the truth. My, she thought, he is an attractive devil, and knows it too. She wanted to kick him in the groin. She wanted to bite that gorgeous mouth.

Smiling again (and the bastard knew just what she was thinking, he'd seen it before), he said, "So, there aren't any interesting men where you come from, and so you drive in from . . . where is it? . . . Forest Hills? Valley Stream?"

"Ozone Park," said Marlene coolly, naming her actual birthplace, a low-rent Queens district.

"Ozone Park!" repeated Robinson in a tone of mock amazement. "And what do we do out in Ozone Park? Help hubby run the brake shop?"

"Something like that."

"Then you should fit in quite well with the . . . Asperians.

Actually, it could involve some upward mobility for you. Play your cards right, and you might even get to urinate on an assistant bank manager. Would you like that, Queensie?"

Marlene regarded him with sick fascination. He didn't recognize her. Instead, he was being casually, effortlessly cruel in a way that would have been devastating to the woman he thought she was. Marlene had met any number of awful people in her life, including some that could have eaten Vincent Robinson as a canapé, but as an exemplar of that much misused category "sadist," this guy took the palm. And still the attraction was there.

She asked, "If this is such a low joint, why're you here?"

"Oh, one occasionally finds a rough diamond, a seeker after something a little more intense than those S-M sitcoms we just saw. And they make rooms available for more, ah, advanced practices. For a price." He reached out his finger slowly and flicked a leather lace that dangled from the center of her brassiere, where the two cups met.

"Actually, I'm about to rejoin my party," he said. "If you promise not to be shocked, you can come along."

"I'm not easily shocked," said Marlene, and thought, God, what a dumb thing to say! It's exactly what some girl from Ozone Park *would* say.

"How nice for you," Robinson said. He actually curled his lip when he said it. Then he walked rapidly away, leaving Marlene to hobble behind him on her ridiculous heels, feeling unbearably stupid. Which was the point, of course.

Robinson strode through the door from which the various "performers" had emerged, Marlene following, and then entered a dimly lit hallway lined with closed doors. He went into one of them, leaving the door open.

The man's face was the first thing Marlene saw, staring out of the darkness of the little room, hanging in space like a jack o'lantern. His mouth was stuffed with some sort of elaborate medieval-looking gag, a wooden apparatus with complicated straps that distorted his face, which otherwise was twisted in either pain or ecstasy or perhaps both combined. His short dark hair was sticking up, stiff with sweat, and a thin trickle of black blood depended from his lower lip. She entered the room, and someone behind her swung the door closed.

In a few moments her eyes had adjusted to the light, which came from four huge black candles stuck in their own grease onto the old, splintery floor. The man, she saw, was naked, and he was hanging facedown and spread-eagled from padded cuffs tied to his wrists and ankles and affixed to chains, rigid with tension, that extended up to the four corners of the ceiling. He was moving rhythmically in short swings, and at each swing he grunted. She could hear the breath whistling in his nostrils and another sound from farther back, to the same beat.

There was a woman standing behind him, between his legs. She had both hands sunk deep into the flesh of his buttocks, deep enough to draw blood, and she was using this grip to heave him onto the huge ivory phallus that was attached to her groin by a sculpted, thick black leather harness.

Remarkably, Marlene's first thought when she registered what was happening was that the woman had a much better outfit than she herself did. It was a leather corset, laced up the front, and elaborately layered with black and red panels, into which had been set little relief sculptures in ivory and polished metal—skulls, and swastikas, and gargoyles—and the part of it that covered her small breasts was cut away to reveal her nipples. These were pierced with silver rings, from which long red velvet tassels depended. The woman was wearing a half-mask too, also in laminated leather, decorated with the appropriate domination designs and bearing a crest of black plumes. Despite the mask, Marlene could see, from the staring collarbones, the tight-tendoned neck, the sharp, small chin and the tight scarlet-painted mouth, that the woman was Ginnie Wooten.

She looked deeper into the room. Robinson was sitting at ease in a wooden armchair with his legs crossed. Behind him were ranged several people, all standing, including, Marlene was interested to note, the Mary-Jane from before. Robinson looked at Marlene and raised a mocking eyebrow. She cleared her throat heavily and said, "Okay, I'm shocked."

At the sound of her voice, Ginnie Wooten stopped thrusting

and looked up. She peered at Marlene through the eye holes in her mask and did a slow-motion double-take. Pointing an accusing finger, she snarled, "What the fuck is *she* doing here?"

Robinson seemed mildly surprised at the reaction.

"She's a tourist, Ginnie. What's the problem?"

But Ginnie pulled back, staggering, the dildo coming free with a wet, disgusting noise, and stepped around the swinging man's legs. She was clearly drugged and seemed to have difficulty keeping her feet. The thing sticking out in front of her groin made eccentric little circles. Marlene felt a laugh bubbling up in her. With difficulty she suppressed it, until the suspended gentleman started trying to look over his shoulder while making inarticulate but puzzled noises through his gag. Then Marlene began to laugh, and once started, she couldn't stop.

This had an effect on the assembly. Robinson stood up, an annoyed look on his face. Ginnie screamed a curse and took a step toward Marlene. She shouted, "She's that fucking detective my sister hired. About the—about the—"

"Shut up, Ginnie!" Robinson snarled. For the first time his face showed something other than contemptuous disdain, a slight furrowing of the broad forehead.

Ginnie did not. "She's—she's . . . investigating . . . you don't understand . . . the fucking bitch is . . . my sister . . ."

Robinson backhanded her across the face, a solid, meaty blow that knocked her off her six-inch spikes. An interested noise issued from several of the observers. As she fell she grabbed vainly for one of the chains supporting the naked man and started him gyrating like a carnival ride out of control. His muffled cries grew louder and more frantic. Marlene had to lean against the wall to recover. Tears ran from her eyes, and when she wiped them, her hand came away with smeared mascara.

Ginnie was wailing on the floor. Robinson knelt over her and grasped one of her nipple rings. He was saying something in a hissing voice. Marlene could not make out what it was. He twisted the ring cruelly. Ginnie screamed and writhed, kicking her legs against the floor. The other members of the group gathered around, leaning close like a bunch of relatives around a new baby. Marlene chose that moment to slip away, blowing a kiss at the wildly grimacing face of the hanging man.

She found Wolfe in the bar.

"No sign of her," he said.

"You've been asking the wrong people. I found her."

"And?"

"Oh, I think it's definitely them. Robinson didn't make me, but she did. I must have made an impression. She was zonked on something, and she almost gave it up. Robinson had to practically knock her out to keep her quiet. Let's get out of here."

"Um, your, uh"—he gestured to her face—"is all smeared."

"I know. I was laughing so hard it ran."

He gave her an odd look but said nothing more as they left the club. The next thing he did say, as they approached his car, was "Oh, shit!"

Marlene looked up, startled, and saw that two youths had the door of Wolfe's car open. Wolfe yelled and ran toward them, Marlene following at a totter, cursing the over-long heels. One of the youths saw Wolfe coming and shouted, and the other one slid like an otter from under the dash, holding the stereo unit. They both took off, track shoes flashing under the streetlights, with Wolfe right after them. Marlene called out once and then gave up as they vanished down First Street, heading toward the Lower East Side. She sighed and lit a cigarette, leaning on Wolfe's car. She doubted he would catch them in his new engineer boots.

After a cigarette plus ten minutes worth of waiting, Marlene began to feel stiff and chilled. The rain had stopped, but it was damp and the air was misty, making rings around the streetlights and softening the neon of the signs. She thought of calling a cab, but it was not much more than a half mile to home and the weather was ideal for a brisk midnight walk through the city. And she was armed.

East Houston Street was still jumping, of course: cruising cars and cabs were hissing in numbers down the broad, wet street, and the sidewalks were thick with little knots of people, mostly young and looking for a good time. Dressed as she was, Marlene got numerous offers from carloads of young men from Jersey, but nobody gave her any trouble.

She turned south on Mulberry Street. Passing Old St. Patrick's, she paused at the steps to tighten and retie the laces of her boots, which, she had discovered, had been designed for walking on faces rather than sidewalks. Finished, her eye was attracted to something moving within the shadows of the Gothic archway. A man, in a long black coat: she could tell he was watching her. She tensed, and then relaxed when the man moved slightly and she saw the faint flash of white at his neck. A priest. But not Father Raymond—he was not the sort to be standing in the doorways of churches at midnight.

Intrigued, Marlene waved and called out, "Good evening, Father!"

The priest waved back and stepped forward into the light from the street lamp. He was a blocky man, not tall, about fifty, his dark hair in a vaguely European-looking brush cut. His face was an Irish one of the bony and beaky rather than the smooth, pug-nosed type, with the eyes shadowed under bushy eyebrows.

Marlene smiled up at him and he smiled back. She took a crumpled pack of Marlboros and lit one. There was something about strolling down a night street on a damp night that called out for ciggies, and she decided to invest one of her rationed daily half pack in the experience.

"Ah," said the priest, "here I was yearning for a cigarette and not wanting to go back to the rectory."

Marlene held out the pack and her Zippo. The priest walked down the steps and took them, lit up, inhaled gratefully. "A filthy habit," he said. He had pale blue eyes that seemed colorless under the orange sodium light. They were intelligent eyes, she thought, yet with a sliding-away quality that masked considerable pain.

"You're new at Old St. Pat's," Marlene observed. She recognized his voice, of course.

He gave her an appraising look, taking in her costume. "A parishioner, are you?"

"A regular communicant," said Marlene. She held out her hand. "Marlene Ciampi."

He took it. "Michael Dugan." He paused. "So. What brings you down Mulberry Street on a fine soft night like this?"

"It's a long story, Father. I'm just walking home from . . . I guess you could say work." She saw his expression change to one of pastoral concern and quickly added, "I'm a private detective, Father. I was at a sadomasochistic club as part of an investigation."

A grin flashed across his face that took twenty years off it. He chuckled. "Allow me to compliment you on your disguise. A sadomasochistic club, hm? I've always wondered what such places were like."

"Really?"

"Yes. You know, *homo sum: humani nil a me alienum puto*?"

They smiled and exchanged a little Catholic moment, dense with information about each other. Of course she would understand the tag, hence educated in a very good convent school; he could quote Terence with a perfect accent, hence almost certainly a Jesuit elaborately overeducated for a curacy in a poky city parish.

She said, "Believe me, Father, you wouldn't want to have anything to do with S-M clubs."

"No," he said reflectively, as if he had been seriously considering it. "No, I suppose you're right. Although some would say that I'm already in one."

They both laughed. He had a loud one, although it seemed out of use, rusty. Marlene asked, "And what about you, Father? What brings you here?"

"Here? It's a church. I'm a priest." Blandly.

"Right. But this is a church for priests like Father Raymond. Whom God protect, but you know what I mean. Dwindling parish, the only reason they don't get rid of it is because of the historical importance of the building and the parish and so on. Someone like you I'd expect to find a little higher up in the Church. On the provincial's staff. A dean at Fordham. Or running a mission. Or in Rome."

He examined the glowing tip of his cigarette and said, off-handedly, "Well, I *was* in Rome for a time. Some time ago."

"Really? What doing?"

His smile thinned, and when he answered his voice was flat. "You certainly are a detective, aren't you? Since you ask, I was at the Gesù."

Marlene raised her eyebrows. She thought, My, my, you must have been quite the boy to get busted all the way from the headquarters of the Society of Jesus back to here, and wondered what it was he had done, but forbore asking.

Yet the question hung in the air between them and made further conversation difficult. When their cigarettes were gone, they said good night. Marlene walked home thinking about why a Jesuit so clever as to have once been one of the dozen or so aides to the Black Pope himself should have ended up as a curate in Old St. Pat's, and then ran through a similar set of questions about herself: why a Sacred Heart, Smith, and Yale Law graduate was trotting along Mulberry, fresh from the kind of evening she had just had, with a gun in her pocket and her garters flapping in the chilly breeze, and had as little answer.

Karp was still awake when she let herself in, propped up in the bed with a scatter of papers and files around him, making notes on a legal pad.

He grinned at her when she came in. "So how did it go? Did you always hurt the one you love?"

She groaned and flopped crossways on the bed. "Don't ask! And if you were any kind of loving husband, you would help me get out of these fucking boots. Christ, my poor feet!"

"Gosh, I was hoping you'd walk all over me in them and show me all the tricks you learned."

She twisted herself around and looked at him. Yeah, she thought. What better way to get that place and that man out of her head. "All right, wiseass," she said, "you asked for it."

She went to her bureau, pulled out four scarves, grabbed a corner of the duvet, and yanked it off the bed, scattering legal papers. As usual, Karp was wearing only a T-shirt.

"Hey!" he protested. "What're you . . . ?"

Marlene got onto the bed and seized Karp's wrist.

"Marlene. What are you doing?" he asked. "I was just kidding, Marlene. Marlene? Marlene, come on . . ."

But he did not, however, resist physically as she tied all four of his limbs to the bedposts.

Then she went to his closet and got his black leather belt.

"Marlene," he said, giggling, "you touch me with that thing and you're history. I mean it, Marlene."

"Silence, disgusting worm!" cried Marlene, leaping up onto the bed and strutting around on it.

"Disgusting *what* . . . ? Marlene, cut it out!" They were both laughing and trying to stifle themselves at the same time, in the fashion of couples in bed who share a dwelling with minor children.

She dangled the belt over his groin. "Hm. See, he's pretending he doesn't like it, but the body never lies, does it? Does it?"

She fell to her knees and straddled his chest and slowly inched her way up until her crotch was nearly at his face.

"Take my panties off, slave!" she hissed nastily. "With your mouth."

Remarkably, Karp was able to stop laughing long enough to do it.

Some time later, Karp whispered into her ear, "Dear, could I say something? Could we *never* do this again?"

Marlene shifted so she could fix him with her real eye. Except for her underpants she was still fully dressed, boots and all.

"Gee, Butch, you could've fooled me. I thought that really turned you on. I was just thinking that we could get our money's worth out of the ten bucks I had to shell out for the membership card in that S-M club. You could borrow it, go down there, make a regular thing of it."

"Maybe in my next life."

"So . . . what? It's back to the biweekly three-minute special in the missionary position?"

"I guess so," said Karp. "I now find I'm really an old-fashioned girl. Although . . . I could maybe crank it up to four minutes. I hear there are dietary supplements . . . say, could you take off that dog collar? I'm getting spiked here. Jesus, I go to bed with my wife, it's like playing second base against Ty Cobb."

She laughed. "Oh, it's always *something* with you. The good thing about *real* masochists, I've found, is that they never complain." She removed the spiked collar and said, "Now. I am going to take a long, hot one and then return in my shapeless virginal white nightie. That should make you happy."

"It will," said Karp. "Oh, before you get too comfortable, you had a message from Bello on the private line. Some kind of emergency in Brooklyn."

She sat up with a start. "What! Why didn't you tell me?"

"I was tied up," he said with a grin. "There's a number by the phone."

Marlene found the slip of paper, dialed it, got an answer from a precinct house in Brooklyn, asked for Bello, and when her partner came on the line said, "Harry, it's me. What happened? What? How? Oh, shit! Harry, okay, I'm sitting down. Please, please, tell me he didn't use that fucking machine gun. Oh, thank you, Jesus! Where is he now? They haven't booked him through yet? Have you talked to the homicide A.D.A.? Okay, I'll meet you at the precinct in like half an hour. Okay. Okay. Bye." She slammed the phone down and glared at Karp.

"What happened?" he asked.

"Oh, Lonny Dane shot and killed Donald Monto over in Bensonhurst. He came after Mary Kay Miller with a .22 rifle, and Dane took him down. I got to go over there and straighten it out. Oh, *shit*! This had to happen tonight!"

She staggered to her feet and scooped her car keys off the dresser and her leather jacket off the floor. She blew Karp a kiss and said, "Sorry about this—it shouldn't take too long, but if I'm not home by the time you have to leave, *please* don't forget to walk Sweety. Posie'll handle the kids, except don't let Lucy wear jeans to school, okay?"

"Fine," said Karp, keeping a straight face. "You sure you haven't forgotten anything?"

She wrinkled her brow. "I don't think so. Why?"

Karp held up a scrap of lacy black. "Your panties, one, and two, you're going to make a better impression down at Brooklyn Homicide if you change out of that outfit."

After they stopped laughing, Marlene said, "I'm glad to see you're not all bent out of shape about this, at least."

Karp shrugged. "Hey, what can I say? As long as you guys shoot them in Brooklyn."

THIRTEEN

The third week in November and they still hadn't finished picking the jury in *Rohbling*. Judge Peoples had made it clear that he did not want to go into the holiday season without a completed panel, and neither Karp nor Waley thought it prudent to defy him in this. In truth, there was little choice, for the weeks of grinding had eaten away their initial thirty peremptory challenges until, on the last day, Karp had two left and Waley had none. Karp was not sure whether that was a victory or not. He had bitten his lip to keep from challenging some venirepersons who had ultimately been impaneled, and had used his challenges to knock off some people he thought should have been removed for cause, most of which had to do with attitudes toward psychiatry. Peoples, of course, had steered this process through his ability, which he was not loath to use, of ruling what was "cause" and what was not.

Nevertheless, they now had a jury—seven women and five men on the panel proper and two alternates, both male. Of the fourteen, five were black, two were Asian, four were Hispanic, and the rest non-minority white. No singletons that anyone could observe; Karp made it a rule never to have singletons on homicide juries, because having someone who felt isolated from his peers was asking for a holdout and a hung jury. Karp made an exception to the rule with respect to college educations, and there was but one on the panel who had a degree, a retired NYU professor (male) who had been the last one picked, after Waley had exhausted his challenges. Karp felt pretty good about that, although the man was just an alternate. The rest were your basic New York solid types—homemakers, small business owners, clerks, artisans, a bike-messenger manager, three housewives. Their average age was rather older than the city's average age, retired people being the only citizens who *want* to get picked for a jury. Five of them were, in fact, retirees.

Judge Peoples swore in the jury and announced that the trial would start on the day after the Thanksgiving weekend. He said that he had decided not to sequester the jury because of the season, and filled the air with blue smoke and rockets about not paying attention to media coverage of the trial and not discussing the proceedings with anyone outside the courtroom. Then he sent everyone home for the long, somnolent weekend.

Karp went back to his office and was delighted to find no one waiting for him and only two message slips, one from Dr. Emanuel Perlsteiner and one from V. T. Newbury. The staff of the Homicide Bureau had at last got the message and were now bothering Roland Hrcany. Karp hoped they were all enjoying it. He pocketed the one from V.T. and returned Perlsteiner's call, which led him to ring up his police driver and have himself driven to Bellevue Hospital.

There, in one of the oldest and shabbiest corridors of Bellevue's psychiatric hospital, he found Dr. Perlsteiner, in a tiny office hardly larger than a janitor's closet. This office resembled one of those apartments that the police have to break into after the neighbors complain of the smell. It held a metal desk, a desk chair, and a straight-backed visitor's chair. Its residual volume, save for narrow paths necessary to reach the two chairs, was almost entirely consumed by books and papers, stacked in teetering piles that reached nearly to the ceiling. Barely visible among this wrack was the proprietor.

Karp entered and stood by the desk. The visitor's chair was covered with files and journals.

"Dr. Perlsteiner?"

Perlsteiner smiled up at him. He was a seventy-four-year-old man who looked ninety. His head was a hairless dome covered with tight skin the color of faded burlap, adorned with large liver spots and (as almost always, and now) on the broad forehead a pair of heavy, thick tortoise-shell eyeglasses. His teeth as he smiled were startlingly false. His eyes were bright and dark, shining out from deep, ash-colored pouches on either side of a little falcon nose. This head sat precariously on a short, thin, wattled neck. The general impression was of an extremely ancient sparrow.

"Yes, how are you?" said Perlsteiner. "Sit, sit, move that trash away, please."

Karp cleared the chair and sat. Perlsteiner cocked his head and looked at his visitor, emphasizing the sparrow effect. "So," he said, "your name is, please?" His English was only slightly accented.

"Um, I'm Roger Karp, Dr. Perlsteiner. You called me, remember?"

Wrinkled brow, followed by delighted discovery. "Karp, yes! And how are you feeling today, Mr. Karp?"

Karp was at the moment not feeling well at all. The old guy's lost it, he thought. I sent a senile shrink to examine Jonathan Rohbling. He thinks I'm some patient. But he said, carefully, "I'm fine, Doctor. This isn't about me. I'm here about your examination of Jonathan Rohbling."

Dr. Perlsteiner's eyes narrowed. He slipped his glasses down into position, magnifying those eyes, which, Karp now saw, were far from gaga, were alert, even piercing. He said, "Yes, I know that, Mr. Karp. I asked out of courtesy, and because I detect you are ill at ease. I wondered why that is."

Karp felt sweat start beneath his arms and on his upper lip. It was true that he had felt somewhat odd since the sexual extravaganza of the previous night. Karp was not a prude in the sense that he took any minatory interest in the sexual behavior of others (except, professionally, when it included murder as a delight), but he had a strict sense of what was proper for *him*, a meat-and-two-vegetables sensuality, that is, and the funny business with Marlene had touched areas in his psyche that he wished had not been touched at all, that he did not wish even to think about. And he was at that moment subject to an absurd fear that *it showed*, was obvious to the searching eye of this shrink, who, in truth, was the canniest whom Karp had ever encountered. It also briefly crossed his mind that the doc had picked up on the now embarrassing thought he had entertained that Perlsteiner might be ready for the soft-brain ward, which clearly he was not, far from it. So Karp sat and blushed.

Perlsteiner, for his part, knew what guilt looked like from fifty years of practice and knew also that, Karp not being a patient, the thing to do was to drop his gaze and clean his glasses, which he did, and then he unerringly yanked his notes on Rohbling out from a stack of identical-seeming files. He paged through them briefly and then spoke, looking down at the pages of spidery writing.

"Yes, Rohbling. What have we here? No gross neurological defect. No systematic delusions. No paranoid ideation. Hm, hm. Actually, you know, an interesting case."

"Is he insane?"

Perlsteiner looked up sharply at the word, and slid his glasses back onto his forehead. "Well, as you should know very well by now, Mr. Karp, this is not a judgment I like to make."

"Yeah, right, Doc, it's a legal term. But in your opinion, I mean, give me a sense of what you can testify to with respect to the defendant's state of mind when he committed the crimes he's charged with."

Perlsteiner seemed to ignore this question. "Yes, an interesting case. Almost, one could say, the sort of case we might have seen in Vienna in the twenties. I review. This young man is raised, the only son, in a secure bourgeois family. The father is an engineer, very vigorous, very correct, quite wealthy. The mother is neurotic, naturally, by turns smothering and bored. She wishes little Jon to be a good boy, but, it seems, boys are not always good, and so she leaves much of his upbringing to Clarice, the servant. Who is a colored woman, of course."

"He told you all this?"

Perlsteiner smiled. "Oh, yes. He was the kind you wish they would shut up for one moment. But you know, it was all *material*. You understand, it is cheap—psychically, I mean—to utter material. It is not at all the same as working with the deeper feelings. He shows the signs of having spent much time with mediocre psychiatrists. Well trained to spout. Shall I continue? It is very interesting, I assure you."

"Please," said Karp.

"All right, so we find at an early age the boy begins to show signs of oddness. He will not play with other children, for example. He is slow to walk and speak. Perhaps retarded? No, they test him; he is normal, perhaps a bit above. But the behavior! Most significantly, he has, by the age of four, one habit that disturbs the parents: he rubs his face and hands with pigmented material, of preference brown or black in color. He uses for this paints, chocolate, ashes, earth, mud, whatever he can. Of course, the parents are concerned. They take him again to a specialist, this time a—you must pardon the expression—a child psychiatrist, who assures them that this is normal behavior of the anal period."

"Is it?"

Perlsteiner gave him a look both sharp and pitying. "It is not, and there is no such thing as an anal period. To resume, they wait, but it does not stop. They cannot take him anywhere for fear he will make an embarrassment. At last the poppa loses patience. He tells Clarice, who is, of course, in complete charge of disciplining the child, no more with the paint and mud! He must be scrubbed when he does it with the floor brush and the laundry soap on the face. So he is, and so the behavior stops, or at least it no longer appears where it can annoy the poppa. Now, at our remove, we can see what has happened. The father is a stranger, prone to violence; the mother is 'nervous' and cannot bear the ordinary conflicts of child rearing. All the love and discipline the child knows comes from the servant. Yet when the child looks at himself, he sees he is not like the maid in appearance: he is pale, she is dark. So he wishes to correct this and does."

"Wait a second, Doc," Karp objected. "Thousands of white kids have been raised just that way by black nannies. It's an American institution, or it was. But those kids didn't go around painting themselves."

"True, so far as we know. But also thousands of little boys were raised by authoritarian Austrian officials and sad mothers, and only one of them grew up to be Adolf Hitler. Did you know that Hitler's father was an avid beekeeper? Perhaps this, then, explains the pattern of Nazism and the führer principle, eh? No, we do not, we never *predict* from the material; it is impossible. But sometimes we can see an interesting pattern that may help us understand where the development has gone wrong. So, to continue, the servant Clarice is in charge of this punishment, and also the source of all rewards too. She had, by the way, four children of her own, who were being raised by her own mother while she stayed at the Rohblings' home and raised their little boy. A common situation, with emotional results that no one has ever bothered to discuss. Now, Clarice was a great believer in regular bowel movements. So who is not, eh? Especially at the time. But Clarice, it appears, was something of a fanatic on the subject. When the regularity was not such as she would wish, she resorted to enemas. As a rule, of course, children object to getting enemas, and so this also became part of the punishment regime. But because of certain aspects of the male anatomy, the enema is often sexually pleasurable. Also, Rohbling tells me, Clarice was in the habit of removing her uniform when she gave him this treatment, to avoid the wet and the mess spoiling her appearance, her white uniform. Or so she said. And so we must imagine the scene. The huge, half-naked colored woman in the bathroom. The boy is helpless, held down. Sometimes she would tie his arms with a towel. She inserts the nozzle. He is screaming in rage, but also he experiences these nice feelings. His penis erects." Perlsteiner shrugged, smiled bleakly. "A potent mix. Shame, helplessness, sexual pleasure, the surrogate mother, love and hatred. And she also touched him sexually."

"Jesus!"

"Oh, it is far from uncommon, you know. The nursemaids of

King Louis XIV used to entertain themselves by manually bringing the little prince to orgasm, and I don't doubt that such things
still go on and not just to princes. In any case, that is the background. By the way, these sessions lasted to the age of twelve. At
that time they stopped, and Clarice left the Rohblings' service."

"He ratted on her?"

"Far from it. He was devastated when she left. He says. No,
they felt that since he was going to boarding school, they had no
need of a permanent nursemaid."

"And this is connected to the murders."

"It is hard to think otherwise. The boy becomes obsessed with
elderly black women. Now that he is adult, he can indulge his
desire to become a Negro, and he does. He seeks these women
out, becomes friendly with them. And . . . here, significantly, he
is less forthcoming. What are the events leading to the actual
homicides? He doesn't recall. He meant them no harm."

"What do you think happened, Doctor?" Karp asked.

The old man rubbed the bridge of his nose and stuck his lower
lip out speculatively. "Well, one cannot say for certain, but given
the background, we may suppose that he requested that they provide the same service that Clarice did. A respectable colored
woman asked by a stranger for such a thing would be shocked
and outraged. There were altercations perhaps, and then perhaps
he panicked. The means he used are indicative of a panicked
reaction. He does not use a knife, or gun, or even a garrote. No,
he used a suitcase. If I were still a Freudian, I would say, a symbol
of that long-ago departure." He smiled. "Who can say, at last,
what goes on in here?" He tapped his skull. "But in any case,
after the first one we see the development of an obsessive pattern,
leading in each case to the death of the woman."

"Obsessive," said Karp, not liking the word. "Are you suggesting that he couldn't control himself?"

Perlsteiner snorted. "That is a meaningless tautology, my
friend. Clearly, he did *not* control himself in the event. Most of
us are obsessive about something. Observe this office! Is it not
the office of a man who is obsessive about throwing things away?
So, am I crazy? Maybe, but not a criminal, because my obsession

is not against the law. Rohbling's obsession was, which is why we are here."

"As simple as that, huh?"

Perlsteiner chuckled. "Yes, but the law complicates things, yes? Look, let me ask you—are you a collector?"

"You mean, like stamps?"

"Yes! Stamps, coins, art, books . . . anything."

"No, I'm not," said Karp. He wondered whether successful homicide prosecutions qualified as collectibles, but decided they did not.

"Ah, well, then it may be difficult for you to understand the obsessive mentality. I myself was for many years a book collector." As he said this, his eyes closed for a moment as if he were experiencing a different time and place. Then, suddenly, he fixed Karp with a look both intense and amused. "Let me give you an example," he said. "This was in Vienna, about 1930. I was just married and completing my studies, and I was an avid book collector, to the extent that I could afford it, which was not much. One day I entered Winkelmann's shop, on the Ring, which to me was Aladdin's cave, and suddenly, there in its case, I see it. A first edition, 1825, of Heine's *Lyrisches Intermezzo*, and not only a first edition, but Heine's own copy, with autographic annotations. In the poet's own hand, you understand. I was in rapture until I saw the price. Let me see . . . perhaps it was the same as twenty thousand dollars now, an impossible sum. Now, in the next moment I recalled that my dear wife possessed an emerald and diamond necklace, handed down in her family for generations. In an instant the scheme sprang full-blown into my mind. I would fake a theft. The necklace was insured. I would sell it, and with the money I would buy the book. I had to have it—the thought of not having it was unbearable, excruciating. As I say, all this sprang ready-formed into my mind, and seemed for the moment perfectly reasonable. This is obsession in its purest form."

Perlsteiner sighed and rubbed the underside of his wrist. His shirt rode up enough for Karp to see the blurred blue numbers tattooed there.

"Did you do it?" Karp asked after a silence.

"No, I did not. In me the social control was more powerful than the obsession. I shuddered at what I had been thinking and left the shop. Had I done this crime, however, I would have been doing what Rohbling is doing now. Denying to myself that I was to blame. That I meant any harm. And so forth."

"So the bottom line is, he knew what he was doing was wrong."

"Of course he did," said Perlsteiner. "And it afforded him the intensest pleasure, you can be sure, which is why he repeats it. Now, it is bizarre, no doubt, this behavior, and the behavior of people with mental illness is also bizarre, but we must be careful not to confuse the two. So, there it is: you will have my report in, say, two days. This is agreeable?"

It was. Karp took his leave feeling rather better than he had before. If Perlsteiner was willing to testify that Rohbling knew what he was doing and that it was wrong, then Karp had the basis for a prosecution. But only a basis; he would have to convince twelve ordinary people that a set of behaviors that every one of them would have classified as "crazy" was not evidence of insanity in the exculpatory legal sense.

Karp went back to his office and wandered through near-deserted halls until he came to the office of V. T. Newbury in the Fraud Bureau. Somewhat to his surprise, V. T. was still there, and Karp went in.

No institutional furniture for V.T. Karp sat himself in a leather sling chair that had never seen a procurement order and smiled across the mahogany banker's desk at his friend.

"Don't you have a family to go home to?" V.T. asked. "I thought it'd be Monday before you got back to me. In any case, I'm impressed."

"Thank you. What's up?"

"Well, I thought you might want to take a look at our dear and glorious physician in the flesh. We're having him in on Monday for a chat."

"You made your move."

"Yes, the impetuous Menotti has struck. The warrants were

issued today, and at this moment federal marshals are racking up overtime seizing records. Menotti's got a team assembled to dig into the stuff over the long weekend."

"What, he doesn't want his turkey?"

"I think he plans to feast on Dr. Robinson this year. So—you interested?"

"Fascinated, but I got this trial. I could come by afterward, though, late afternoon. You think he'll still be there?"

"Oh, he'll be there," V.T. replied confidently. "We have much to discuss. How's the trial? I hear you have your jury."

"Yeah. Also, Perlsteiner says he's not crazy."

"I'm glad to hear it. Just another sane average granny killer in blackface, hey?"

Karp rolled his eyes. "Bite your tongue, V.T.," he said.

Marlene sat on the living room couch with her daughter, reading and rubbing each other's feet. The twins were blessedly napping, simultaneously for a change, Posie was off for the weekend, and Karp was at the office, using the pre-Christmas lull to catch up on neglected duties. A rare moment of peace, this, or should have been. Marlene was looking forward to Christmas with her family, as she always did, and, despite herself, rolling over in her mind the most recent Thanksgiving dinner, which she had spent at Karp's father's place. After a dozen years of marriage to Karp she still had not grown used to the barbarism of his family. From the first year, the deal (and it *was* a deal) was that Thanksgiving would be spent with the Karps, and Christmas would be with the Ciampis. Karp's father, who had made a small fortune in corrugated boxes, and like most of the self-made rich was used to getting his way, had never entirely accepted that he was not to have *all* his grandchildren around him at Yuletide (which, as an elaborately assimilated Jew, he had made his very own) to squeal at his overexpensive presents and do him honor. Marlene had early made this a divorce-court issue, holding to the principle *Natale con i tuoi e Pasqua con chi vuoi*: you spent Christmas with your family and Easter, or Thanksgiving, with whom you pleased.

The event itself was always the same, and might have been

specifically designed (in her more paranoid moments Marlene thought it literally might have) to produce irritation on a grand scale. The gathering consisted of Karp's two older brothers, one a CPA and the other the president of daddy's firm, their lovely wives, the elder Karp's lovely wife, a former starlet not ten years older than her oldest stepson, six assorted children, ranging from three to twelve, plus, of course, Butch and Marlene and their three. After the meal, which was immense (prepared and served in sullen silence by Edna, the family retainer), it was the custom for the children to run screaming around the house, for the men to lock themselves in the "study" and watch the football games, and for the women to sit in the living room and talk, and referee the constant squabbles of the children. All three women were bores. The starlet stepmother had the grace to keep fairly mum and slip, as the afternoon progressed, into her accustomed boozy somnolence, but the sisters-in-law had strong opinions about everything and the sensitivity of tyrannosaurs. As they were upper West Side Jewish matrons, these opinions were (Israeli politics aside) all virulently liberal, and however the conversation began, Marlene always found herself forced into the position of defending both her husband (that persecutor of the downtrodden criminal classes) and her Church (that persecutor of everything else) from the abortion policies of the current pope to the excesses of the Spanish Inquisition.

Inevitably, around the third quarter of the game, Marlene, who by then was starting to think that the Inquisition was not an entirely bad idea, would storm into the men's retreat and give Karp a Look. Then, after a brief conversation in the hallway, conducted in harsh whispers, the Karps would make their excuses and leave, not, if the truth be told, much missed.

Although used to this misery, Marlene found that its effect on her had increased in recent years. Perhaps she was getting shorter-tempered in her old age, or her work was somehow lowering the barriers against violence. One day, she realized, she would lash out at the stupid women in some unforgivable way, and that would be the end of it all.

She glanced up from her book at Lucy, for whose sake, largely, she endured the torment; children, she believed, had the right to a complete family.

Lucy felt eyes on her and looked up from her own book, a Nancy Drew, and smiled. "What're you reading, Mom?" she asked.

"I'm reading *The Way of Perfection*, by Saint Teresa."

"The Little Flower?" said Lucy with interest. She was at the age when Thérèse of Lisieux was most appealing.

"No, Teresa of Avila."

"Is that her on the cover?"

They inspected the cover together. It was, inevitably, a photograph of the great Bernini statue.

"Hey, she looks like you, Mom," said Lucy.

"So I've been told. But that's just the imagination of the sculptor. Maybe she didn't look like that at all."

"What's it about? The book."

"Oh, you know—saintly stuff. Teresa founded a bunch of convents, and this is what she thought the nuns in them should do."

"Like what? Teaching school and stuff?"

"No, different kind of nuns. She wanted them to pray without ceasing."

"They had to pray all the time?" Astonishment.

"Uh-huh. Every minute."

"Even . . . even in the *bathroom*?" Giggles ensued.

"She thought," said Marlene sternly, "that if she did, God would talk to her."

"Did it work?" asked the infant pragmatist.

"Apparently so. That's why she's a saint."

A discreet pause, and the child studied the figure in ecstasy. "Do you ever try to do it?" she asked.

"Uh-huh."

A longer pause. "Did it work?"

"No," said Marlene in a tone discouraging further inquiry.

Yes, thought Marlene as they both returned to their reading and foot rubbing, she had been a little older than Lucy was now when she tried it. How many thousand Our Fathers on her aching knees, sweat and tears pouring off her, her parents looking askance, her brothers teasing, her friends abandoned and hurt, and then the realization, unappealable, devastating, that there would not be a rapture, that the arrow from high heaven would not pierce her heart, that she would not hear the Voice say, as it had to St. Teresa, "I would not have you hold conversation with men, but with angels."

From the distance of years, Marlene could be easier on herself. Queens in 1960 was not as congenial to the contemplative life as sixteenth-century Spain; Teresa had not had to contend with rock 'n' roll, makeup, James Dean movies, and greasy beautiful boys roaring down the street on chopped Harleys and stroked and channeled candy-flake Chevys. Marlene, thin and exhausted after this venture (the booby prize was that she became even more exquisite out of the travail), had thereafter begun in earnest to hold conversation with men, and put the ecclesiastical world on hold for over a decade.

Here she was again, however, with the same book, and a daughter who had the potential for being even wilder than her mother. How soon before Kermit the Frog comes down from her wall and AC-DC goes up, or the Sex Pistols? After that, how soon until the worthless boys started to hang out?

Before Marlene could think, she reached out in an almost convulsive motion and pulled Lucy to her, jamming the child's head tightly against her own.

"*Mah-ummm!* What're you *doing*!" complained Lucy.

"I'm trying to jam all my horrible experience into your head so you don't have to go through it all over again and break my heart," said her mother.

Lucy struggled from the head lock and gave her mother a sharp look. Marlene was about to explain (not that it *could* be explained) when Zak let out a cry from the nursery. In a moment Zik had joined the duet.

Marlene went down and chirped at them, changed them, tickled them, and, tucking one on each hip, walked back to the living room. They seemed solid and sturdy to her, indestructible. Boys. She had been surprised to find that although she loved them both dearly, she did not have the sort of terrified feelings for them that she had for Lucy, the sense that the child was clone of one's own soul. The boys would be all right. They were little men already at age one, dividing the vast male province amicably between them: to the one War (Zak), Culture to the other. And, of course, they had each other: they had recently started communicating in a secret twin language.

She plopped them on the living room carpet among a scatter of soft toys. They, of course, went straight for Lucy, who made a show of playing with them for five minutes and then flounced off to her room. Another family problem, but one that Marlene thought time would heal.

Unlike, for example, the Wooten family problem, which Marlene thought that time would only make worse.

Stop it, you're ruining my life! A spontaneous and irrational outburst from Edie when Marlene told her about what had happened upstairs at Cuff's, and she had even spared Edie some of the wetter details. Edie had actually put her hands over her ears to bar the knowledge that in all likelihood the Music Lover was a conspiracy of her sister, Vincent Robinson, and the pianist Evarti. Marlene had sent Wolfe off to tail Robinson, without much hope, to try to catch him in the act. Which meant that Marlene would have to go back on the street, since Dane was still recovering from the shooting, having found that gun-nuttery and actually killing a human at close range are rather different things. The grand jury inquiry into the death of Donald Monto would not take place for a month. While Marlene did not think there would be any problem with it, Dane was taking it very seriously indeed.

Marlene tried to get back into her book but quickly saw the wisdom of Teresa in keeping babies out of the convents of the Discalced Carmelites. Setting the book aside, she descended to the floor and spent the next two hours in squealing mindless play, lost in motherhood's Way of Imperfection, her lot.

FOURTEEN

Marlene came up from an unpleasant dream involving babies, whips, and priests to the furious shaking of her daughter.

"*Mah-om!* Get up! I'm going to be late for school, and they're screaming their stupid heads off!"

They certainly were.

Marlene sat up, rubbed her face, and shook her head. Clearly Karp was gone. No surprise on the first day of that miserable trial, but . . .

"What—where's Posie?" she asked around a thick tongue.

"*I* don't know. Anyway, she's not here," was the reply. Marlene groaned and slipped back into automatic mode: dress, no shower, babies cleaned and fed, dog walked, Lucy to school, Marlene to the office, with the little boys.

"Sym, did Posie call or anything?"

"No." The girl looked doubtfully at the pair of squirming rug rats. "Do I have to take care of them?"

"No, Sym, I'll do it myself," said Marlene, taking the proffered coffee and sticking the sheaf of message slips between her lips. "I'm sure they'll be fine playing out on the fire escape," she mumbled, and regretted it immediately when she saw Sym's expression. Sym would kill for Marlene, or take a bullet, but watching babies was out, at least for now.

Marlene gulped down her coffee, placed the babies in what used to be the nursery, and which had become something of a dumpster and storeroom, removed the poisonous and deadly materials and objects, dug out the few pathetic toys that had been left behind, set up the folding gate at the nursery door, and went to her cubicle to smoke and return calls, with the door open so that she could hear any wails.

The message sheaf was unusually fat. Like Macy's and Toys "Я" Us, Marlene's was a business that thrived amid the warmth of the holidays, reaching a crescendo around the twelve days of Christmas. It was then that the eggnog flowed and made rational such thoughts as, "Because you won't take me back and let me be a loving dad again, I will kill you and the kids and myself." Also, the merry season stimulated any number of women to let the guys come around, whereafter they almost always recalled just exactly why they had tossed them out in the first place, which no amount of tinsel and ho-ho-ho could disguise, and told the guys this, and got their lumps, again. It was not, for Marlene or for many of her clients, A Wonderful Life.

Three from Edie Wooten, one marked urgent. Marlene put these aside: it couldn't have been that urgent or Sym would have beeped her. A call-in from Wolfe. Six violations of protect orders, two serious, three phone harassments. Four cold calls, ladies having problems with their gentlemen. These first, some counseling, referrals, an appointment made. Some calls to friendly cops. Calls to men, at work, telling them to cut it out, that someone was watching. An hour, two hours, passed this way. Suddenly, Marlene leaped to her feet, heart in mouth, and slammed down a ringing phone. The silence had just struck her. The babies! She dashed out.

Tranh was sitting on the floor next to the playpen. He had made up a solution of dish-washing liquid in a pan, from which he was drawing bubbles with a piece of twisted wire. The twins were rapt and cooing, clinging to the playpen's bars, bouncing on their chubby legs and grabbing at the iridescent globes as they floated past. Tranh looked up and smiled.

"L'innocent paradis, plein de plaisirs furtifs/Est-il déjà plus loin de l'Inde ou que la Chine?" he said.

Marlene's heart went back into its place. A Vietnamese assassin who quotes Baudelaire is watching my kids, she thought briefly, then sighed and trotted back to work. Good, affordable child care is hard to find in New York.

Karp had blocked out his opening statement over the weekend, and that morning he had reviewed it carefully with Terrell Collins, even rehearsing it a couple of times, which was a thing he rarely did. The presentation of an opening statement is a peculiar art form that, like singing the blues, has many pretenders but few masters. Like the blues, the opening statement tells a story; like the blues, it is, or must seem, extemporaneous, natural. It must have a sort of artless grace to it, yet it must also penetrate deeply, so that all the evidence that appears during the course of a long trial will be slotted by the jurors' minds into the places that the prosecutor has prepared for each piece.

Karp was good at this, and liked doing it. On the other hand, this was not your usual liquor-store shooting. He was starting to feel . . . not precisely nervous, but that he was overtraining, that Waley had him spooked. Since he had arisen that morning at six, something had been nagging at his mind, and he couldn't bring it to the surface. It irritated him, like a ripped cuticle. A half hour before they were due in court he found himself walking back and forth down the length of his office, taking deep, slow breaths and trying not to think of anything.

"I'm taking notes," said Collins, watching him. "This is great, the secrets of trial prep revealed. By the master."

"No, the secret is, wear three pairs of underpants. Also, rub the Speedstick over your whole face, so they don't see you sweat."

"You're kidding," said Collins.

"Yes, I am." Karp looked at his watch, again. "Okay, last

minute: what did we forget? Witnesses all here, we're missing witnesses . . ."

"Yes," said Collins, "they were all here ten minutes ago, the last time you asked, but I sent them down to Coney, get some hot dogs, some beers, relax a little."

"Nobody likes a wiseass, Collins," said Karp, not unkindly. He had grown to like and admire the younger man. Without being asked, Collins had taken over all of the tedious tasks involved in trial preparation—the marshaling and scheduling of witnesses, sending the cops of the D.A.'s squad on necessary errands and ensuring these were accomplished, tracking down and securing physical evidence, and keeping in order the mass of paperwork associated with any major trial. As a result of having this work taken from his hands, Karp had arrived at the first day of trial tired but not utterly exhausted.

Collins replied, "Especially not a preternaturally handsome Negro wiseass. I know it. I try to deal with it."

"Try harder," said Karp. He shuffled through Collins's carefully done backgrounders on the defendant and the witnesses, reflexively, to do something with his twitching hands. He was reading through Rohbling's brief biography for the twentieth time when the thought finally emerged, like a bubble in thick soup. He snapped his fingers. "Oh, I know what I wanted to ask: did a nanny called Clarice ever show up as a subject in any of this?"

Collins thought for a few seconds. "Not that I recall. Where did you get the name?"

"Perlsteiner mentioned it. It could figure later, so why don't you dig a little—find out what happened to her. She apparently made our boy what he is today, or helped."

Collins scratched a note. Karp resumed his pacing and breathing. Collins said, "You think that between your opening and Waley's we'll take the whole morning?"

Karp stopped and turned. "Oh, Waley won't open now."

"He won't?"

"No, why should he? He doesn't have a theory of the case

that's different from ours. He's not out to show there's a reasonable doubt that Rohbling killed Jane Hughes. He'll let us go ahead and do that, and stress the bizarre aspects of the case on cross, and then when we conclude, he'll get up and say yes, yes, this terrible crime, but it could only have been committed by a madman."

Wolfe came in just before noon, looking haggard and worried. Marlene asked him what was wrong.

"You talk to Edie yet?"

"No, what happened?"

"The guy came in last night, into her bedroom."

"Oh, Jesus! Did he do anything?"

"No, just stayed there and stared at her. Sat on the bed. He had a stocking on his face. Didn't say anything."

"Was it Evarti?"

"She couldn't tell who it was, but it wasn't Evarti. I checked. He's in L.A., playing piano. Anyway, she didn't recognize the guy. She was pretty freaked out."

"You saw her? Last night?"

Wolfe did not answer immediately. He rubbed his face and cleared his throat. "Well, what it was . . . I was following Robinson. Guy left a club downtown, not Cuff's, another one on St. Mark's, about eleven. Got in a cab, going uptown. I followed him in the car. I think he made me. He must've, because he got off at Lex and Forty-first and ran into the subway. I parked and tried to chase him, but you know—it's a big station. I went up to the street again and I saw a guy go by in a cab that I thought was him and I followed that, but it turned out it wasn't. So then I went by her apartment to check, and he'd already been and gone. The doorman didn't see anyone. I feel real bad about it, Marlene."

"Don't. It takes three people to set up a real tail, which means twelve for a continuous job. We're not set up to do stuff like that. You did good, Wolfe. At least now we know for sure who it is."

"She called him," said Wolfe.

"Oh, crap, she shouldn't have done that!"

"Yeah, I said. She said he just laughed at her and told her to relax and enjoy it."

"That sounds like Robinson. I should call her."

She did. It was a brief conversation. When Marlene put down the phone, she said, "Well, well, that's interesting."

"What?"

"She wants somebody to sleep in, dog her steps. Doesn't care what it costs." She looked at Wolfe. "Interested?"

She saw his Adam's apple move as he gulped. "Um, yeah, I guess. If you think it wouldn't be, you know . . ."

"What, improper? For crying out loud, Wolfe, the sister is the town pump! High society isn't going to worry if Edie's got a live-in guard."

He shrugged and bobbed his head. "Then, okay, I guess. Sure."

She laughed. "Gosh, Wolfe, you sound like somebody was twisting your arm. You get a nice room on Park Avenue, get to mix with the culture vultures, travel to exotic places—" She stopped. His jaw was tightening. She said, "There's a problem here that I don't see. What?"

"Oh, nothing. Just, you know, being around classy people. It's, um, I keep thinking I'll do something dumb."

"Hey, ninety percent is don't drink from the finger bowls, don't fart too loud, and always flush. The rest you'll pick up. So, can I tell her you're the guy?"

He nodded.

"Great! One thing, though. If Robinson is serious about this, and he feels blocked, he could try to get through you. I need to know that you're ready for that. Whatever it takes."

"Oh, yeah. That part I got no problem with," said Wolfe with a ghostly smile, and then Tranh came in and announced that he had made lunch.

Karp was into his peroration, rolling, feeling good, feeling the jury was focused, attentive, with him. He had told them what the crime was, had told them Rohbling had done it, and now he was about to defuse, to the extent he could at this point, the only possible defense.

"This is an unusual crime, ladies and gentlemen, something you don't see every day. Some would even call it bizarre. But throughout this trial I would like you to keep one thing clear in your minds. We are not here to examine the inner workings of a human mind. The law does not trouble itself with reasons. We all have dark feelings, fears, rages, worries. I do. You do. But we are civilized, decent human beings. We don't let ourselves be carried away by our obsessions. And so we must try to concern ourselves exclusively with Jonathan Rohbling's actions. We will show in the course of the trial just exactly what the defendant *did* to Jane Hughes. We will show how he *planned* to disguise himself as a black man, so that he could walk freely around Harlem and insinuate himself into the confidence of Mrs. Hughes. We will show that, far from succumbing to any spontaneous mad rage, he brought into the apartment of the unsuspecting victim his murder weapon, a cloth suitcase, with which he *planned and intended* to smother her to death. We will show that after the crime, far from surrendering himself to the police, shocked at what he might have done in a moment of uncontrollable rage, or in the derangement of his mind, he stealthily and carefully made his escape. We will show that days later, when confronted by a police detective on the trail of Mrs. Hughes's murderer, as you will learn, he steadfastly *denied* that the suitcase he had used in the murder was even his. He was fully aware of the evil he had done, fully aware that it was wrong. He didn't want anything to do with that suitcase, because he *knew* that it connected him with the crime. He knew, as you will learn, that in that suitcase there was evidence that placed him in Jane Hughes's apartment, that announced him as the murderer. And so, ladies and gentlemen of the jury, when you have considered all the evidence we will present, we believe that you will find that the defendant, Jonathan Rohbling"—here Karp paused and looked for a scant three beats at the defendant. Out of the corner of his eye he saw the jury looking too, which was the point. Rohbling appeared scrawny in his nice gray suit. His glasses were still smudged, and his lips were still flecked with the white crust. In the moment that the eyes turned on him, the muscles on the side of his face gave a decided twitch. Karp twirled on his heel and faced the jury, selecting at random the eye of juror number four, Mrs. Ethel McNamara, to hold with his own, and continued—". . . *planned* to murder Jane Hughes, *did* murder Jane Hughes, and sought to *escape* from the consequences of a horrible crime that he *knew* he had done, that he *knew* was the worst crime one human being can perpetrate against another; and therefore, the People expect that you will find the defendant guilty of the crime for which he has been indicted, the crime of murder in the second degree."

Karp sat down at the prosecution table. Judge Peoples said, "Mr. Waley?"

Waley rose and declined to open until later. Karp caught from the jury box a tiny sigh of disappointment, a fainter version of the sort heard at the theater when they announce that the star is to be replaced by an understudy. Karp, oddly, felt disappointed himself. At the judge's direction he rose again and called city engineer Michael Constanzio to present a drawing of the crime scene.

"That went pretty good," said Terrell Collins.

"Yeah, well, there's not much you can do to screw up the obligatory witnesses," Karp replied. "He's not going to waste much time opposing the fact that a woman got killed in New York County." They were gathering up their materials, cleaning off the long prosecution table.

"I thought he'd object more. When we showed the crime-scene shots—"

"No, he's piling up treasure with Peoples," said Karp. "Peoples likes a smooth run. And like I told you, he doesn't need a different theory of the case. He's going to walk the little turd on insanity."

The hallway outside the courtroom was packed with the press and garishly lit by the lamps of the TV crews. Karp and Collins no-commented and body-checked their way through the throng to the elevators. Once in the car, Karp passed his folders to Collins and slipped out of the building via the D.A.'s back exit.

He trotted south through the chilly street to the Federal Building and went up to Menotti's office, where a secretary directed him to a conference room.

He slipped in and sat in a chair against the wall, meaning to be unobtrusive, for someone as large as Karp always a difficult goal. In fact, everyone in the room looked up at him. Paul Menotti, sitting at the head of the table, glowered. V. T. Newbury smiled and waved. Cynthia Doland, at her boss's right hand, regarded him with her usual neutral expression. Menotti paused and hastily introduced Karp to the three strangers at the table. The elderly black man in the dark jacket and clerical collar was Ephraim Coates, the chairman of the board of St. Nicholas Medical Centers, Inc. The thick middle-aged woman in the cerise suit and the gold jewelry was Dr. Sylvia Olivero, the director of the St. Nicholas clinic at 135th Street in East Harlem. The third stranger was Vincent Robinson.

The meeting continued. Karp was something of a connoisseur of interrogatory events, and before too many minutes had passed he realized that this one was not getting anywhere. It was, in the parlance of the prosecutorial bar, a mere circle jerk. Coates was clearly a respectable stooge who had no answers to the technical questions the federal prosecutor wanted answered. Olivero had the answers, but her performance seemed too pat, as if she had been rehearsed, and the answers she gave drove the meeting ever deeper into the bottomless morass of Medicaid regulations, an area in which the doctor had more experience than anyone else in the room. Robinson was polite and bored; they had nothing solid on him and he knew it.

Equally bored, and starting to feel the exhaustion of a day in court, Karp had started glancing at his watch and thinking about how he might gracefully retire when V.T. rose and walked out of the room, motioning Karp to follow him.

In the hallway, V.T. grinned and rolled his eyes. "Fascinating, isn't it? All the thrills and glamour of Broadway as it used to be."

"I'm uncharmed, V.T., and I'm beat. Like the old lady said, where's the beef?"

"This is the vegetarian part, I'm afraid," said V.T. "What do you think of Robinson?"

"He looks as bored as I felt. What've you got on him?"

"Between you and me? In the language of your people, bupkis. St. Nicholas is dirty, we know that, but welcome to the club. Whether they're dirty like every other poverty health operation, or dirty dirty, felony dirty, is something that it's going to take the usual eighteen months to determine. Meanwhile, my quasi-legal sources in the banking industry inform me that the doc has something like seventeen million dollars in accounts in various banks in Grand Cayman. The deposits started nine years ago when Robinson first got his Medicaid mills going, but approximately three-quarters of that total had been placed there over the last year—*cash* deposits. What does that suggest to you?"

Karp shrugged. "That he's found some new way to scam Medicaid?"

"Uh-uh. Medicaid pays in attractive green checks. Robinson's declared income is in the form of checks paid by private clients, and checks issued to him by St. Nick as a shareholder and medical adviser. He could conceivably have drawn cash off those, but we checked with his banks and he didn't. So wherefrom all this cash? Who that we know runs an all-cash business?"

"What, he's connected?" Karp laughed at the thought. "Robinson is a Mob guy? Come on, V.T., the guy may be slime, but he's Park Avenue slime."

"I'm glad you think it's funny," said V.T. huffily. "But it's hard to explain those deposits any other way."

"Okay, so what's your theory? He's moving coke to the upper crust?"

"No, not coke. He doesn't need coke. He's a doctor who runs a ton of drugs through a network of clinics. He's also got a multimillion-dollar accounting system. I'm thinking prescription drugs, or money laundering, or a little of both. He lays off some of the cost of his product on the public fisc, and then sells to the wise guys for cash on the barrel."

212 / *Robert K. Tanenbaum*

"Hm, put that way, it's not too funny anymore," said Karp. "It sure adds weight to the possibility that Robinson whacked that nurse. A white-collar fraud is one thing, assuming she was going to rat him on it, but now you're talking Rockefeller Law minimum sentences for dope. Look, V.T.: let's go back in there and you get Menotti to let me ask him a question."

They did so. Newbury whispered into Menotti's ear. He frowned, then nodded. After finishing the line of questioning he had under way, Menotti said, heavily, "The Homicide Bureau would like to ask Dr. Robinson a question. Mr. Karp?"

"Yes, thank you, Paul. Dr. Robinson, was Evelyn Longren ever involved in transferring payments of any kind for the St. Nicholas organization?"

Karp watched Robinson's face very carefully when he said the name and was rewarded by a fascinating display. First, the quick involuntary flicker of alarm, which was what Karp was looking for, then a brief moment of calculation, the eyes blank, then the feigned innocent recollection, the handsome brow knotted. (The other two St. Nicholas people were genuinely puzzled. It was clear that they had no idea who Evelyn Longren was.)

"No, Miss Longren was my private nurse at my private practice," Robinson said. "She had no contact at all with my work at the medical centers." Robinson was looking Karp right in the eye as he said this, and after he said it he smiled and kept the stare. Karp had been lied to by experts, and he knew the signs, and he also knew well the arrogant gaze of the malefactor who knows you have nothing on him, who knows he's going to get away with it, and loves rubbing the world's face in it. Why can't they ever resist showing off? Karp thought, and returned the smile. Deep in his prosecutorial heart, almost below the conscious level, he felt a familiar little sensation, a precise analogy to the beep that sounds in the cockpit of an F-15 when its missile has locked onto a target.

"Posie's back," said Sym over the intercom late that afternoon. "She already sneaked in the back there, but you ought to go see her."

Marlene found the young woman in the nursery with the twins, who were bubbling with glee to have their nurse back and, apparently, delighted with the new colors in her face. Tranh had vanished into his kitchen. Zak was on her lap, trying to tug off the fresh bandage that covered her left eye and ear. Zik was tapping like an osteopath on the cast on her right wrist, using a rubber Zimby.

"Christ in Heaven!" Marlene cried. "What happened to you?"

"I'm sorry, Marlene," said Posie in a whispery voice. "I should've called. I had to go to the emergency room and—"

"Oh, don't be silly! You're hurt. What happened?"

"I was, like, in a car wreck," said Posie, looking at Marlene and then quickly away.

"Oh, yeah? Whose car? When was this?"

"Um, last night. Some guy, I didn't know his name."

"Uh-huh. You went to St. Vee's?"

She had. Not wanting to waste time listening to more lies, Marlene went back to her office and called St. Vincent's emergency room. Identifying herself (illegally) as a police officer, she found, after a number of calls, the duty nurse who had treated Posie. The duty nurse, a woman for whom blunt trauma was as an open book, did not think Posie had been injured in a car accident. She thought Posie had been beaten, and had so reported it to the police, as required by law.

Marlene said nothing after she got off the phone, but went back to work. Harry came back, cursing equally the Germans and ladies' professional tennis. They shared news, and then Marlene took Posie and the boys and Lucy back to the loft. While Posie was giving the boys their bath and Lucy was settled with her homework, Marlene rifled the patched denim bag that served Posie as a purse, locating a ragged address book, from which she recorded one address. She changed into her black leather pants and engineer boots and put on her motorcycle jacket and a Yankees cap, into which she thrust her hair. Then she went to her tool closet, took an eighteen-inch pipe wrench from her plumber's chest, wrapped this object in several sheets of the *Times*, and walked out.

Twenty minutes later, Marlene was pounding on the door of a tenement apartment at Sixth Street off C. The door was painted the color of old dried blood, and little flakes of it bounced into the air as she struck it. The hallway stank of hot lard, it being largely a Latino building now, but the smell seemed to be mixed with the scorched chicken feather stink of the former Jews layered over the cabbage of the yet more former Irish.

After three minutes of banging a voice answered from the other side: a curse and an inquiry. Posie's Luke was a late, heavy sleeper.

"It's me, Luke. Open up, honey!" Marlene called out sweetly.

Heavy steps. The door rattled and swung open. Luke Last-name-unimportant stood blinking in the doorway, dressed in a pair of ragged blue jeans and nothing else, a thin man in his late twenties, with a stupid-handsome face and shoulder-length dirty dirty-blond hair.

"Yeah, what?" he asked and then, looking her over, "Who're you?" Marlene had her baseball cap pulled low over her forehead.

"Do you always come to the door with your fly wide open?" she inquired. Of course, he looked down, and when he did, Marlene whacked him over the head with the pipe wrench.

He staggered back into the apartment, his knees sagging. Marlene followed him in, slamming the door behind her, and hit him across the face with the wrench, a two-handed tennis serve swing. He went down, sprawling on his back, blood exploding from his nose. Marlene stood above him, adopted a woodchopper's stance, and brought the head of the tool down on his groin as hard as she could. He shrieked high and loud, and curled up on his side in a fetal position, breathing hoarse, bubbly cries. Marlene knelt beside him with her knee pressed into his neck.

"This is for Posie," she hissed into his ear. "You are not to see her again. You are not to talk to her on the phone. If you see her coming on the street, you are to run away. In fact, the best thing for you to do is to get out of town permanently. If I hear that you have seen her or talked to her, I will come back, with help, and then I will take you apart. You will not be able to walk or talk or move for *years* after that. Nod your head if you understand."

He nodded so hard he sprayed blood all around his head, like a flower.

Down in the street, Marlene had to lean against her car with her head down before the nausea passed. She stripped the bloody, shredded newspaper from the wrench and tossed it into a wastebasket. She used a tissue to wipe up blood drops. They came off easily from the oily leather.

Marlene drove slowly to Grand Street to buy her family dinner. She ordered two large pizzas at Lombardi's on Spring Street and, to kill time while they were baking, she walked down Mott to Grand and Ferrara's. There, at one of the tables in the back, she saw Father Dugan, dressed in a canvas jacket and a flannel shirt, sitting with a youth of about eighteen wearing a maroon parochial school blazer. The boy had the kind of Irish beauty that drew the eye, especially Marlene's eye: shiny red curls, that milky skin, eyes from heaven. She sat one table away from them. They were deep in conversation, speaking in low, confidential voices, and if the priest noticed her, he made no sign. The waitress came, and she ordered a double-shot americano and a napoleon pastry. After violence, sugar was Marlene's rule.

The two had stopped talking while the waitress was at Marlene's table. When she left, Father Dugan met Marlene's eye and nodded, smiling. "Join us?" he said.

Marlene moved her coffee and napoleon and sat in a chair at the other table. The boy stared at her, confused. He blushed, the red moving up his pale cheeks like spilled wine on a tablecloth.

"This is Kevin Mulcahey, Marlene. Marlene Ciampi, one of our parishioners," said the priest. The boy mumbled a greeting but did not offer to shake hands. He said, "Well, hum, thanks, Father. I'll see you later." He got up so abruptly he knocked his chair over, made an embarrassed noise, righted the chair, snatched up an ugly plastic, bulging briefcase and almost ran from the restaurant.

"Gosh, I'm sorry," said Marlene. "I didn't mean to scare your friend away."

"Oh, Kevin's all right. He's a little nervous. We were discussing his vocation."

"You're recruiting him?"

"Rather the reverse. I'm advising him to take some time."

"You don't think he'd make a good priest?"

Father Dugan sipped his cappuccino contemplatively. "I have no opinion either way, but the fact of it is, he lusts after women and it frightens him to death, and so he imagines that becoming a priest will solve the problem. I was trying to suggest to him, gently, that this is not necessarily the case."

"You're speaking from personal experience?" Marlene ventured lightly. He looked at her, his face calm but his eyes radiating the sort of soul-shriveling loving disappointment she recalled so well from Sacred Heart. They must have a special school that teaches them how to do that, Marlene thought as adolescent sweat broke out on her face.

He broke the gaze and said musingly, "Yes, sex. It's so difficult for secular people to comprehend that there are a certain number of men and women in the world who don't care for it, for whom it's rather an irritation. Like psoriasis, for example. Or they just don't like it, like some people just can't stand olives or peanut butter. Some of these people are naturally attracted to celibate institutions and are content in them. Others of them persist in sexual activity because the society seems to demand it and they don't wish to appear odd or unhealthy, and so they are unhappy and make their partners unhappy. Conversely, there are highly sexed people who have been taught that those feelings are shameful and so seek refuge in celibacy. They often get into trouble. As they say, when priests fail it's either Punch or Judy. But there are worse things too, sad to say. Choirboys, et cetera." He paused and looked at her closely before resuming. "A few of these, however, are able to convert their passion into spirituality, and these become the great saints in the world—Augustine, of course, Francis, Teresa of Avila, St. Ignatius Loyola—"

"Ignatius? I thought he was a misogynist."

"Well, he thought it best to steer clear of women, but that was because they couldn't get enough of him. A little, skinny, limping guy and they practically followed him around on the street, slavering. Fine ladies, princesses, even, and of course he wanted to avoid scandal, which would have torpedoed the Society. It did, of course, eventually, but that was much later." (Marlene knew the story, naturally, from school: the Sacred Heart has something of a grudge against the founder of the Jesuits because, by his fiat, the Society of Jesus is the only religious order that does not have a sister house of nuns, and Sacred Heart nuns are ordinarily just those whom nature has designed to be Jesuits. Marlene occasionally thought that this unfair exclusion, much alluded to by the mesdames, had something to do with her own choices in life.)

"What Kevin needs," said Father Dugan, steering the conversation again, "is a nice but not too nice girl, experienced but unthreatening."

"I'll keep my eyes peeled," said Marlene. "Would you like the rest of this pastry? My eyes were bigger than my stomach. Besides, I have to go pick up my pizzas."

"Bless you, no, thank you," said the priest, smiling again and patting his belly, which as far as Marlene could see was perfectly flat. "It's an indulgence I can't afford."

"Oh, come on! I won't tell—seal of the confessional."

The priest laughed. "Ah, Loyola, how wise you were to protect us from the temptations of charming penitents! No, really, dear, *quodcumque ostendis mihi sic, incredulus odi.*"

"Um, anything you thus press on me, I discredit and revolt at?" Marlene translated.

"Yes, Horace. Very good." He beamed at her, his eyes full of affection and pain, mixed well. She thought that he must be nearly as lonely as Tranh, or Harry. He stood up and dropped some coins on the table.

"Now, I have to go too," he said. "I have to fix the trap in the rectory sink. Oh, you would know where can I find some plumber's dope and a cheap used pipe wrench?"

"You plumb?"

"We Jesuits are advised to be all things to all men. To Father Raymond and Mrs. Finn, our housekeeper, I am a plumber."

"In that case, you can get the dope at Canal Hardware off

Lafayette," said Marlene. "I just happen to have an eighteen-inch pipe wrench in my car. You can borrow it." They walked out of the restaurant to Marlene's VW, where she handed over the tool.

"Ah, thank you. You were plumbing today too?"

"No," said Marlene, "I was using it to beat up a guy."

Father Dugan inclined his head inquiringly.

"Sunday, Father," said Marlene. "In the box."

"What happened to Posie?" asked Karp as he helped Marlene clear away the remains of the family's informal dinner.

"Some piece of shit pounded on her. Again. The worst part is, she went *looking* for it. Christ, Butch, she lives with *me*. She knows what I do. It's like . . . shit, I don't even know what it's like."

"A nun on the stroll?" suggested Karp.

"Thank you. You know, I may have to hand in my feminist card, but I'm starting to think that some women want to get pounded, just like some guys like to have women pee on them."

"It's the natural result of the contradictions caused by our corrupt patriarchal society," said Karp primly.

Marlene snorted. "God, and if you believed that, wouldn't you be the perfect man!"

FIFTEEN

Christmas fell on a Wednesday that year, and Judge Peoples decided to forgo trying to fit in any trial sessions in between the big day and the second of January. Karp thus had a week off to spend with his family, or rather with his children and their nursemaid, since his wife was heavily engaged with the violent discontents of other families. Karp did not mind this as much as he thought he would. He was, for one thing, a low-maintenance husband: neat, lacking noisy or time-consuming hobbies, not fussy about meals, of moderate libido. After the extraordinary tension of the Rohbling trial he was more than content to sink into slovenliness, rolling around with his two boys in piggy filth, unshaven, eating junk, watching holiday shows and soaps on TV, going to Macy's to see Santa (the boys shrieking in horror, Lucy blasé) and to shop for presents.

Lucy virtually took over the operation of the household, her natural bossiness now at last having full scope. She had been around kitchens, helping, since the age of five, and had no problem with simple meals of the heat 'em up plus salad variety, which was vital because Karp could not boil water, and Posie was not much better. Lucy incorporated this duty into her perpetual rivalry, and considered she had done well by it; *they* had mere cuteness, she had lasagna and minestrone. Daddy went shopping with her alone, and took her and her pals to Rockefeller Center to skate, and to downtown movies *in a cab*.

During this period Marlene would often be out half the night, or all of it, and come staggering in at dawn. They did not talk about what she was doing. He didn't want to know.

The actual holiday, naturally, remained literally sacred to Marlene, and she consigned her besieged ladies to the hands of God and Harry Bello, going out to her parents' house in Queens on Christmas Eve and eating the traditional dinner of twelve fish dishes (her aunt Celia explaining to Karp, as she did each Christmas without fail, that these represented the twelve apostles), attending midnight mass with the whole family (including Lucy, a glorious first for the child) at her girlhood church, St. Joseph's, driving home sleepily to Manhattan and returning Christmas day to exchange gifts and eat heroically.

Karp enjoyed this event. He had minimum social responsibilities and no horse in any Ciampi race. He was, in fact, often appealed to as a neutral party, a being so alien that he might be expected to bring a uniquely fresh judgment to the field of Italian-American family squabbles. These were marvelously colorful, brief and violent as summer squalls, full of operatic gestures and imprecations. Karp much preferred them to the quarrels of his own family, which were covered over by a poisonous geniality and lasted for decades.

Besides that, the Ciampis treated him as a guest, since it was clear that he could never be a *paisan*. John, the oldest, the orthodontist, a basketball fan, talked to him about teams and players, and checked the smiles of all the kids, of which there were fourteen; Patricia, the city planner, discussed politics with him, assuming that Karp, as a Jew, was more liberal than he actually was; Anna, the big sister, cooked and kept her five kids in line, and interacted with Karp only on the subject of food and children; Paul, the handsome one, the youngest boy and a chef, flirted unconvincingly with all the wives, and was not allowed in the kitchen; Dom, the middle boy, was supposed to have gone into his father's plumbing business but had gone instead to Vietnam, from whence he had returned minus a foot and something else, for which reason when he became as he always did, terribly drunk and abusive and violent, his brothers and brothers-in-law took him out in the backyard and restrained him, talking him down in shifts until he was fit for company again or stumped off yelling down the street. Karp, for some reason, although by far the largest person in the room, was excused from this duty by unspoken agreement, another aspect, he supposed, of his special outlander status. The true family attitude toward him was, he imagined, summed up by ancient Nona, Marlene's grandmother, tiny and nearly blind, who once remarked to him, "My grand-daughter, Marlene, the crazy one, married a (whispering) *Giudeu*, may God forgive her, but they say he doesn't look like one of them, and besides, the *pazza*, she could have brought home a black *niuru*, God forbid!" (crossing herself)

Both Butch and Marlene were to remember this particular Christmas in elegiac terms, as a calm before the storm. Indeed, it seemed in retrospect almost to live up to the seasonal hype. The Ciampis were less operatic than usual, the babies were charmingly cute, Lucy discovered that being the big sister of twins had certain advantages, in that she was included, as impresario, in their act (the cousins changing their clothes, amid giggles, and seeing whether anyone could tell), brother Dom went early into stupor, and Marlene could tell her mother that she had not missed a Sunday mass all year.

On the day after Christmas, the Karps usually held an open house for friends and neighbors, but this year the co-op association was putting in a real elevator. This labor had begun at a time of maximum inconvenience, mid-December. It meant that their loft, being on the top floor and the location of the original industrial lift engine, which had to be removed, was the site of considerable construction and strewn with immense pieces of apparatus.

They did, however, go to the annual New Year's Eve party thrown by V. T. Newbury at his Murray Hill brownstone. Although Taittinger poured like water, the affair was as decorous as a cotillion compared to what went on at the Ciampis', and made an interesting change. Butch and Marlene sipped, ate shrimp and pâté, conversed with numbers of V.T.'s astounding range of friends and relations. At V.T.'s party you could find an expert on slime molds, the CEO of a major bank, a defrocked orthodox priest, a diva, a man who lived alone on an island in the Queen Charlottes and only returned to civilization for this one event, the recipient of the Yale Poet's Prize for that year, a man who lived upstairs and was in ceiling tiles, a welterweight contender, a Hungarian diplomat, and, apparently, as Marlene saw, the world's premier female cellist.

"Edie!" Marlene cried, "you look great!" She glanced around. "Is Wolfe here?"

"I gave him the night off. It's New Year's Eve. Besides, I have Anton to protect me." She clutched the arm of the reedy violinist standing next to her.

Marlene smiled uncertainly at Anton, who looked as though he might need some protection himself, and said, "Well, I haven't heard anything from you, and Wolfe's reports are terse to the point of nonexistence. I presume—"

"Oh, that's all over," said Edie breezily. "He still sends those notes, which I dutifully turn over to Wolfe, but nothing else. My life has been completely transformed. Besides, after we're married, we'll be living in Europe most of the year."

"You're getting married?"

"In June." She hugged the violinist's arm tighter and beamed. "We're keeping it rather dark. The parents are inclined to make a fuss."

"Well, *I* won't tell," said Marlene. "In fact, I'll be glad to get Wolfe back. How come you're here, by the way? I didn't know you knew V.T."

Edie smiled. "Oh, everybody knows V.T. I was at school with his cousin." Suddenly she blushed, reached out awkwardly, and clutched Marlene's hand.

"Gosh, Marlene, I can't tell you how *ashamed* I am at the way I behaved after the concert! After how you tried to help me and—"

"Well, that's all right," said Marlene, patting her hand. "As I once said, I have a thick skin. At least we found out who the guy is."

"Oh, no, Marlene. It can't possibly be Vincent Robinson."

"Why not?"

But the reason why not was never pursued, because at that moment Karp, who was standing with his back to her, spun around and said, "Excuse me, did you say Vincent Robinson?"

Which was how they found out that Marlene's prime suspect for stalker-of-Edie was also Karp's prime suspect for killer-of-Evelyn Longren.

The trial resumed its weary pace in January, although that grim month was more to Karp's liking than the former gay season. The jurors had been distracted by family thoughts, thinking about what to get for Aunt Emma instead of concentrating on the evidence, and beyond that there had been the danger that, under the influence of the Yuletide spirit, they might be inclined to New Testament mercy rather than Old Testament justice.

As the prosecution's case unfolded, Waley remained passive, rising only for perfunctory cross-examination and hardly objecting at all. The press, which had maintained a strong interest in the case, commented on this. The TV stations had talking-head lawyers on at night to render their opinion of what Waley was up to. Wait, they admonished: he's biding his time, the fireworks will come.

Meanwhile, Karp constructed his typical careful case, a rising arc of evidence from the general to the most detailed testimony. First the crime scene, with photographs. Waley made the usual objection on the grounds that these were inflammatory and was overruled. The jurors got to see Jane dead. The cop who had found the body was brought forth to give his stilted testimony. He performed well on both direct and on cross, in which Waley merely brought out the position and condition of the body.

Next the medical examiner. Cause of death was defined in detail. Waley wanted to know if the medical examiner had found evidence of hypertension or atherosclerosis. He had. On redirect,

Karp had to establish that Mrs. Hughes's condition was not immediately life-threatening.

Then came a quartet of forensic specialists who talked about fibers, blood, flesh, and dyes for three days. Waley barely stirred during this time. He appeared more concerned with his client, as well he might have been, for young Rohbling seemed to be deteriorating as the trial progressed. Each day, as the officers brought him in, his step was slower, almost limping, his head hung lower, his face was more wan and blotchy, with what appeared to be yellowing bruises at the temples. His hair was even more unkempt, sticking out at all angles in the style of the late Stan Laurel. Karp wondered if this was a ruse to garner sympathy and thought briefly of going to the judge with a complaint, but what, after all, could he say? And he knew very well what Waley would say: that his client was fit for a rubber room and not much else. He looked crazy because he *was* crazy. So, stalemate in that corner. The witnesses who tied Rohbling to Hughes came next. Waley shined them on.

It was March before Karp had Detective Gordon Featherstone on the stand, his last witness, the prize witness. As on a TV show, the audience was now going to hear how the detective caught the bad guy. Featherstone looked the part too. He was a blocky, cordovan-colored man in his late forties with a brush mustache and close-cropped hair whitened on the sides. His voice was deep, strong, and confident. When the detective took the stand, Karp could sense the subtle vibration of renewed interest from the jury box.

Karp took him through the investigation from the beginning so that the jury could see how the evidence, which they had just heard certified by experts, appeared to the working detective, and how it led inexorably to the confrontation with the disguised Rohbling at the bus stop.

They came to the famous blue suitcase. Here it was: Karp raised it high, like a holy relic. The jury was allowed to paw it. Featherstone described the denial of ownership by Rohbling. No mistake about that. Karp had him repeat Rohbling's words so that they would stick in the jurors' minds. Now came the Opening of the Suitcase. The childish ceramic dish was displayed, entered as evidence, handled by the jurors, the affectionate message from the little girl read out in the detective's deep clear baritone, the unscheduled sob from the mother of that little girl, sitting in the courtroom to see justice done for her own slain mother, the jury rapt.

Karp, on a roll, thinking, no, he's not going to let me get away with this, but giving it a shot:

"Detective Featherstone, do you recognize this object?"

Karp held high a crocheted doily.

"Yes, I do. It was found in the suitcase."

"And did you determine who the original owner of this object was?"

"Objection!" Waley was on his feet. "Irrelevant and immaterial, and tending to the inflammatory, Your Honor."

Peoples frowned and motioned the two counsels to approach the bench.

"Where are we going with this, Mr. Karp?" asked the judge.

"Your Honor, we feel the jury should know that the defendant had in his possession four physical objects belonging to four other elderly black women found dead under unusual circumstances," said Karp.

"The circumstances were hardly unusual, Judge," said Waley. "The four women to which counsel adverts were ruled by the medical examiner to have died of natural causes. This is a purely inflammatory move with no relevance to the case at hand."

"Your Honor, you admitted the entire contents of the suitcase as evidence," replied Karp. "That the defendant was carrying the possessions of four other recently dead black women speaks to the character and habits of the defendant."

"Very well," said Peoples. "Mr. Karp, you may present your evidence. Mr. Waley may bring its relevance into question on cross if he desires. Proceed, Mr. Karp."

A nice little win, thought Karp as he went back to his place. He took Featherstone through the souvenirs Rohbling had taken from his victims, each time asking the detective to describe the woman and her current status, and receiving the answer, elderly, living alone, in Harlem, and dead. He did not pursue the issue of how they had died. Unless the judge instructed them otherwise, the jury would, without further prompting, easily deduce that Rohbling had a habit of visiting elderly black ladies, none of whom had survived his visits.

On cross-examination, Waley showed for the first time in this trial why he was considered one of the half dozen greatest masters of that art. To Karp's surprise, he ignored the four other dead women. Instead, he was doing an impression of an attorney who, confronted by an overwhelming case, was simply going through the motions of a defense. His demeanor subdued, his voice just loud enough for the jury to catch, Waley took Featherstone almost apologetically through some minor clarifications of his direct testimony. What time of day was it when you first saw the defendant? How far away? What was the weather like? How many people were at the bus stop? What was it about the defendant that caught your attention? Something not right about him? Pray elaborate. The detective elaborated. Waley was fascinated. With care and respect, he helped Featherstone elucidate what had enabled him, passing in a car by a crowded bus stop, to pick Rohbling out as the man they wanted. Unlike the average counsel on cross, Waley was building up rather than tearing down the credibility of the opposing side's witness. Karp understood what he was doing but still could not see the payoff, nor was there a legitimate way for him to object; the material was legitimate, and he was not harassing the witness. And Peoples was hell on frivolous objections.

"Now, Detective Featherstone," said Waley, "you've told us in impressive detail how you intuited that the defendant was not what he appeared to be. At that moment, how long had it been since you had learned from forensic evidence that the man you sought was a white man disguised as a black man?"

Featherstone paused judiciously. He was relaxed now, not on guard at all, and he answered, "Ten days."

"Very good. Tell me, Detective, had you ever had a case like this before, this sort of disguise on the part of a homicide suspect?"

"No, this was a first." A faint smile.

"Unique, in other words." Returning the smile. "Was it hard to believe at first, from your detective experience, I mean?"

"Oh, sure. But the evidence was pretty conclusive."

"Right. And what did you think of the man you were pursuing? What sort of person did you think you were after?"

Blithely, Featherstone swung at the breaking curve, the fabulous knuckleball that Waley had been winding up for since the trial had started. He said, "Oh, we thought he was a total nutcase, crazy as a b—"

"Objection!" cried Karp, but he also had waited too late to swing. "Calls for a conclusion."

"Your Honor," said Waley, "the witness is a senior police officer of vast experience. His opinion as to the mental state of the defendant was germane to the conduct of his investigation."

"The witness is not a forensic psychiatrist—" Karp put in heatedly, but Peoples forestalled him, saying, "I'll allow the testimony. Please go ahead, Mr. Waley."

Waley nodded, paused for three beats, turned to Featherstone. "You were saying, sir, crazy as a—?"

"Bedbug," said Featherstone, grimacing now.

"Crazy as a bedbug," repeated Waley slowly, with relish, now using the full power of his remarkable voice. "Thank you, Detective. I have no further questions." He walked back to his seat, seeming four inches taller than when he had started. The jury, Karp saw with a sour feeling in his stomach, was entranced, enchanted, by the transformation. And Karp was stymied; his big witness, whose expertise had been elaborately complimented by even the defense, had declared that the cops thought the defendant was crazy. And Karp could not clarify on redirect either— far from considering it, he wished that the bulk of Featherstone would resolve itself into a dew and vanish right now, taking with it from the jury's mind these last disastrous minutes.

Feeling lame, he dismissed the witness and said, "Your Honor, that concludes the prosecution's case." It then being close to four-thirty, the judge declared the court in recess until the following day, at which time they would resume with the case for the defense.

"That was worth a year of law school, my son," said Karp around a corned beef sandwich to Terrell Collins. They were in Karp's office, assessing the damage.

"You mean his cross?"

"I do. The way he softened Featherstone up? Jesus, Gordon's been a cop for eighteen years, he *knows* not to say stuff like that on the stand. Hell, he softened *us* up. He fed us that little win over the suitcase evidence, we get to show Jonathan's a serial killer, we're feeling good, here's our witness, our last witness, the case is on a clear arc, he's lying completely low, and so we forget. He wanted us to forget, the bastard."

"Forget what?"

"That he doesn't care how bad we make Rohbling look, or how guilty. He's going to walk him on insanity. And so instead of focusing our whole attention on *that*, we let him allow our major witness to say that he thought the defendant was nuts, just at the end of our case in chief. And of course, Peoples, the prince of fairness, allowed it when he really shouldn't have, because just a few minutes before, on direct, he gave us a big one, which was just how Waley played it to happen." Karp crushed his sandwich paper into a ball and flung it at the wastepaper basket he kept perched on a bookcase. It brushed the front rim and spun out, falling to the floor. They looked at each other. No one in the office had ever seen Karp miss a shot to his wastebasket; Karp himself could not remember ever having missed. He stood and retrieved the paper and dropped it in.

"Not much of an omen," he said lightly.

"Hey, we'll get 'em," said Collins. "Look, I've got their updated witness list here. There's something you ought to see."

"Yeah, what?" Karp took the list and ran his eye down it. Shrink one, shrink two, shrink three, and . . . he wrinkled his brow. "Who the hell is Jamal al-Barka?"

"An angry black man set on destroying the age-old hegemony of you ice people."

Karp shot him a look. "You'd like that, would you?"

"You bet! The day will come when we're in the big house and y'all're out there chopping cotton."

"Sounds good at this point," said Karp. "By the way, what *is* chopping cotton exactly?"

"Search me, Jack," said Collins. "I'm from Tarrytown, New York. But, meanwhile, it turns out that Mr. al-Barka is originally Cletis Brown, son of—ta-dah!—Clarice Brown."

"The nanny?"

"The nanny. I think we're being set up for a tale of child abuse as exculpation."

"Yeah, great. What do we have on this guy?"

"Not much, Butch, just the name and the association with his mother. Who's deceased, by the way. I got a request in for a full investigation, but they haven't got back to me yet. Maybe you could stir them up a little."

"I can do better than that," said Karp, reaching for the phone. After dialing and waiting for some minutes, Karp said, "Clay? What're you up to? Uh-huh. Well, bag that for now. We're dying here with this trial, and Waley has just slipped us a strange one. Guy name of Jamal al-Barka . . . Yes, he's a colored gentleman, which is why I thought of you. Same to you, asshole."

Karp read off the man's address and place of work from the paper Collins handed him, listened for a moment, and then said, "Yeah, actually I do want to impeach his black ass. Find something. Yeah, like tomorrow."

Karp was about to break the connection and send Clay Fulton about his business when a vagrant thought popped into his mind. "Oh, yeah, and Clay? After you get that, I got another little thing. Remember Dr. Vincent Robinson? Uh-huh, with the Jew doctor and the nurse, right. We need to take a look at him. No, nothing specific on the death, but the guy's seriously dirty. Yeah . . . no, no, not just the Medicaid. There's a possibility he's pushing pills big-time. Yeah, bulk. For millions. Talk to Narco, talk to Ray Guma, maybe he knows something. Oh, and make sure he knows you're poking. Right, harassing a private citizen without cause or evidence, that's just what we want."

"Ladies and gentlemen," said Lionel Waley, "you are participants in what I hope I can make you see is a great tragedy: a woman is dead, a woman has been murdered, and a young man, my client, Jonathan Rohbling, aged twenty-two, stands accused of that murder. Ordinarily, a jury such as yourselves is required to examine the facts of the case—the testimony of witnesses, their credibility, the importance of physical evidence and what experts say about what that evidence means—to examine and sift these facts and decide whether the defendant is guilty or innocent beyond a reasonable doubt, whether he did, in fact, do the crime for which he stands accused. But this trial is different. Our plea in this trial is not guilty by reason of insanity. That means you will be called on to decide not whether Jonathan Rohbling caused the death of Jane Hughes, but whether in causing that death he was guilty of the crime of murder."

Waley paused for a moment, and Karp saw him cast his look over the jury, selecting the next recipient of his gaze. Waley spoke to the jury one at a time, as did Karp. During the course of an opening statement he would have twelve intimate moments, one with each juror. Karp tried to see which one he was targeting, so he could judge the effect and focus his own intimate conversations on the ones that seemed most susceptible to his opponent's charm. He did this almost unconsciously, taking notes on Waley's pitch at the same time.

Waley continued, "Because the law says that in order to be convicted of a crime a person must be capable of making a moral choice. When we convict someone of a crime and punish that person, we are saying, as a society, you made the wrong moral choice and so you must suffer the penalty of the law. But the law recognizes that there are some unfortunate people for whom the capacity to make such a moral choice has been gravely diminished. The law, in fact, says a person is not responsible for criminal conduct if, at the time of such conduct, as a result of mental disease or defect he lacks substantial capacity either to appreciate the wrongfulness of his conduct or to conform his conduct to the requirements of law. In other words, if someone is insane, either we don't expect him to understand what he is doing or we don't expect him to be able to tell right from wrong and act accordingly. Now, ladies and gentlemen of the jury, my client, Jonathan Rohbling, is insane. He has been insane for some time. He was insane on April twentieth, when Jane Hughes met her death, and he is insane as he sits here in the courtroom today."

Waley paused and obligingly pointed. The jury looked, as did Karp. Yes, thought Karp, he did look, in the immortal words of Detective Featherstone, crazy as a bedbug. Waley picked up the rhythm again, outlining for the jury how he was going to demonstrate just how insane his boy was. He named his expert witnesses (three) and told the jury that they would additionally hear shocking evidence about the horrible childhood experiences that had contributed to little Jonathan's mind snapping, and to the peculiar form that his insanity had eventually taken. He closed with the usual flashing lights and gongs. As Karp's notes recorded: the great tragedy theme again, a tragedy without a villain, one victim of homicide, one victim of insanity—let us not victimize him once again by imposing—a disease killed Jane Hughes, a mental disease . . .

By the time he finished, it was near noon. The first of Waley's witnesses, a psychiatrist named Lewis Rosenbaum, was first on the schedule. Peoples looked at the clock and motioned the counsels forward.

"Mr. Waley, how long do you think on direct?"

"An hour, certainly, Your Honor."

"Mm-hm. And Mr. Karp, I assume you would prefer that your cross came immediately after the direct."

"Yes, sir," said Karp. "I think it's particularly important in this sort of case, when the issues are technical."

"Well, yes. Let's break for lunch early, then," said Peoples, and announced this to the jury, from whence issued an audible murmur of relief.

After a brief conversation with his client, Waley came back to the bench and addressed the judge, who listened and then called Karp over.

"Mr. Waley has something to say to us," said Peoples.

232 / *Robert K. Tanenbaum*

"Yes, Your Honor. I am extremely concerned about my client. His mental state appears to be deteriorating seriously. He has been self-abusive. You observed the bruises on his head. His parents are frantic. With all due respect for Bellevue as an institution, and despite the current suicide watch, it seems unreasonable for Mr. Rohbling to expect proper care for his disease from an entity that is a part of the same state apparatus that maintains that he *has* no disease. I would like to apply again for appropriate bail so that my client can be placed in a secure private facility where he can receive actual treatment."

"Mr. Karp?" inquired Peoples.

"Your Honor, the situation has not changed. We acknowledge that Mr. Rohbling is unhappy. He is a wealthy young man used to the best and most comfortable surroundings, and Bellevue is not in the class of what he's used to. Nevertheless, he has all the care he needs if he decided to avail himself of it—"

"He's not going to open up to a psychiatrist who works for the state," Waley interrupted angrily. "Have some sense!"

"If I may finish my remark, Mr. Waley? Thank you. The suggestion that the doctors at Bellevue are in some sense in league with the district attorney's office in slighting Mr. Rohbling's condition and denying him treatment is either slanderous or, frankly, delusional. If Mr. Rohbling finds himself for the first time in his life in a situation where his parents' money is of no avail, then he has my sympathy, but I would hardly call it a medical emergency requiring the upset of long-established custodial procedures. As for bail, Mr. Rohbling's father has a personal fortune of some three hundred and eighty million dollars—that we know about. He has connections all over the world and access to a private transcontinental jet plane. I think the risk of escape is enormous and unjustifiable, and therefore the People would oppose any bail."

"I believe I agree with the People in this case, Counselor," said Peoples.

Waley took a deep breath, and seemed to be struggling to retain his legendary control. No one had ever seen Waley lose it in a courtroom. He was white around the nostrils, however, and

Karp almost regretted the jab about delusions. But only almost.

"In that case, Your Honor, may I request that my client's personal psychiatrist, Dr. Erwin Bannock, be allowed free access to Mr. Rohbling, as free as if he were on the Bellevue staff?"

"No objection, Your Honor," said Karp charitably.

Karp returned to the prosecution table to help Collins gather up their material.

"Boss, that man don't like your ass one little bit," said Collins.

"Who, Peoples?"

"No, Waley. You should've seen the look he gave you when you walked away. I'm surprised you're still wearing a suit. What'd he want anyway?"

"Oh, he's still bitching his boy's got to bunk with the low-class homicidal maniacs at Bellevue. He wants him to stay in some private nuthouse. I told him no way, and the judge backed me."

"What's it matter to us?"

"Risk of flight. His folks could have him out of there and on a private jet to Switzerland in twenty-four hours, and walk away from a five-million-dollar bond without breathing hard. Besides . . ."

"What?"

Karp shrugged. "Besides, fuck them both. The little shit wanted some consideration, he shouldn't have killed five women."

Dr. Lewis Rosenbaum was one of the editors of the *Diagnostic and Statistical Manual of the American Psychiatric Association*, the famous *DSM III*, in which it is written how to tell the crazy from the sane. Rosenbaum was a hefty, gray-bearded man who wore his own sanity like a suit of mail. His speech was slow and judicious, and he took an unusually long time before replying to questions, as if he were generating scientific knowledge before your eyes.

Waley wanted to establish how psychiatry defined paranoid schizophrenia. This Rosenbaum was notably able to do, recounting in detail the four major symptoms of this disorder: blunted affect, that is, a lack of ordinary emotional arousal; retreat from reality, including delusions and hallucinations; depression, in-

cluding suicidal tendencies; and severe impairment of social function, including inability to hold a job or to establish normal social
relationships with peers. Rosenbaum had examined the defendant
and (no surprise here) had discovered that he evinced all the
symptoms.

In his cross, Karp was careful not to challenge Rosenbaum's
definition of psychosis. Instead, he focused on the specific acts
that Rohbling had done and asked the doctor to explain how
these accorded with the defendant's supposed insane state.
When the defendant was crushing the life out of Jane Hughes,
did he think she was a statue? A monkey? Did he know he was
killing a human being? Answer: it was part of his delusional pattern. What part? What was the nature of the delusion? The doctor
could not say. If he did not know that he had killed a human
being or that it was wrong, why did he flee? Why did he take care
not to be associated with the suitcase full of incriminating evidence? Rosenbaum's answers to these and similar questions
seemed like blather to Karp and, he hoped, to the jury as well.
Karp was attempting to use his cross-examination to paint a picture of what a real crazy person would have done—hung around
in Jane Hughes's apartment, say, talking to a corpse.

"Now, Doctor, you've testified that when the defendant killed
Jane Hughes, he was responding to the dictates of an inner world,
a world cut off from ordinary reality, is that correct?"

"Yes."

"And this inner reality also prompted him to carefully don
theatrical makeup and a wig, travel up to Harlem, pose as a man
of a completely different race and culture, and pose convincingly,
inveigle himself into Jane Hughes's good graces, extricate himself
from the scene of the crime, and, finally, to understand the consequences of the damning evidence of the blue suitcase and its
contents? Is that what this psychotic inner reality did, Doctor?"

The doctor took his usual time before responding. "Well, the
psychosis acts chiefly in the areas relevant to the delusionary system. In this case the delusionary system is focused on hostility to
elderly black women. We should not let ourselves believe in the

stereotype of the raving lunatic foaming at the mouth all the time."

"So, you're saying that Mr. Rohbling was competent, sane in his actions up until the moment when he killed Mrs. Hughes, when he became insane, and then he became sane again while he made his getaway. Is that a fair summary?"

A patronizing smile from Dr. Rosenbaum. "I think I would call it an oversimplification of what I said in my testimony. Often psychotics can be extremely clever and perform convincingly in the ordinary world. This, uh, says really nothing, really, about their inner mental states, which are disturbed."

"I see. Fascinating, Doctor. So you would say, would you not, that although Mr. Rohbling acted in every way as if he were sane—he disguises, he calculates, he escapes—he acts in every way like he knows what he is doing and that it's against the law, he's still insane because when he eventually talks to a psychiatrist, that psychiatrist finds the symptoms of psychosis laid out in *DSM III*?"

"Um, yes. In effect, that is the case."

Pause. Face the jury. "How terribly *convenient* for Mr. Rohbling that must be—"

"Objection!" from Waley. "Not a question."

"Sustained."

"Withdrawn. No further questions, Your Honor."

A draw, is what Karp thought. It was not hard to make psychiatrists seem like fools in court, which was one reason why insanity pleas failed nine out of ten times. On the other hand, a big-shot shrink, the "guy who wrote the book," as he had been presented, had testified that the kid was nuts. There was nothing he could do about that except keep the focus on Rohbling's actions and hope the jury was heavy on common sense and resistant to voodoo.

SIXTEEN

"Isn't *this* a pain in the neck!" said the district attorney.
"So to speak," said Karp. The D.A. scowled and sent over a black look. It was a Sunday, far too early on a Sunday, and the two men were sitting in a spare bedroom fitted out as a study in Jack Keegan's apartment, Keegan behind an oaken desk in a black leather judge's chair, Karp in a comfortably worn armchair opposite. This apartment was a large, high-ceilinged one on West End Avenue. The Keegans had been in it since the fifties, but Karp had never before visited there, which served as well as the unlikely date and hour to demonstrate just how remarkable a pain it was. Karp looked out the window. He could see the trees just beginning to leaf out, the palest fuzz of painfully delicate green. It was April 2; the previous night, appropriately, Jonathan Rohbling had tried to hang himself in his cell in Bellevue, and had very nearly succeeded.

"Waley's going to sue the city, you know," said Keegan, "and maybe me too."

"What the hell for?"

"I don't know. Failure to yield to the wealthy, maybe. He'll think of something. You talk to everybody already?"

"Uh-huh. Cops, Bellevue administration, the orderly who found him, the ER doctor who treated him yesterday—I mean, this morning—and the current attending doc. Also Rohbling's private guy."

"And how *is* the little piece of shit?"

"Not that great," said Karp. "He apparently found a burr of metal on his bunk and used it to tear his T-shirts into narrow strips, which he then braided into a thin, strong rope . . ."

"Wait a second, in a suicide-watch cell?"

"Yeah, with the windows up high and no sheets. What he did was he tied a pencil to the end of his rope and flung it up so that it caught on the window grille. Then he jiggled it until it passed through the steel grille and fell down again. So now he had a double thickness of rope. He made a noose, slipped it around his neck, grabbed the double rope and heaved himself up the wall like the commandos do in the movies. When he got to the grille, he hung on with one hand, made a clinch knot around the grille with the other, and just let go. He fell about three feet, not enough to break his neck, but he squashed the hell out of his larynx."

"Marvelous. You know what this whole thing'll look like if we have to go on with the trial?"

"It won't help," said Karp. "Most people think a sincere suicide attempt is a pretty good indication that the guy is deranged. On the other hand, Rohbling knows that. So does Waley."

Keegan raised an eyebrow. "Meaning . . . ?"

Karp shrugged and sipped coffee. "Meaning that Rohbling dropped just before the orderly reached his cell. He could have heard the guy moving down the hall. We should not rule out the possibility of a scam. Yeah, he hurt himself, maybe he miscalculated the damage . . ."

Keegan was silent and looked Karp over as if he were a used car of doubtful provenance. The look went on for an uncomfortable while. Finally Karp said, "*What?*"

"Oh, just trying to figure out where you're going with this, and how loose a cannon you really are. I get the feeling you don't want to quietly arrange for a plea here, send our boy off to the funny farm for an indefinite stay?"

"Do you?" Karp tossed back, and without waiting for a reply,

said, "There's a principle here. We spend ninety-five percent of
our time pleading out pathetic scumbags, generally of the black
and Hispanic variety, and when we do go to trial, we're up against
mostly Legal Aid kids who've spent a day prepping the case, and
of course we win almost all the time. Okay, that's what we get
paid for, putting asses in jail, but—we get to run this assembly
line because there's an assumption that the law functions the
same for everyone. It may be real dim sometimes, and it's real
easy to be cynical about it—hell, I'm cynical about it—but we
both know it's still there, ticking over, and it's the reason why
the communities that produce the big crops of criminals put up
with the system. We don't have a Casbah in this city, not yet: we
don't have a place the cops stay out of, where anything goes.
Because on the rare occasions when we get a bastard from the
ruling classes in our sights, we put the screws to him the same
way we do for the skinny black kids, and we go up against his
high-priced lawyer and his high-priced shrinks, and we do our
best to whip their ass. If we buckle on it, if we say, hey, white
boy, uh, too bad about killing those old ladies, not a good choice
for a hobby, there, Jonathan, but no hard feelings, here's a pass
to a country club for, say, five years, and when you've had a nice
rest we'll let you out to resume your rich boy life, and Jonathan?
In the future, think stamps, think coins, think trout fishing . . ."

Keegan snorted and clapped, heavily, slowly, four times.
"Very impressive. Did I teach you to do that?"

"Partly," said Karp, feeling a trace of shame at letting himself
go. "Some of it is my own work."

Keegan chuckled and said, "Besides the noble sentiments, it
might also have something to do with Waley, beating his *particular*
ass."

A slight acknowledging inclination of the head. "I'm a competitive fellow, what can I say?"

"Your case, your funeral," said Keegan, rapping his knuckles
gavel-like on his desk, as if formally closing off the issue. "When
do you figure you'll be back in business?"

"Hard to say. When the docs declare him fit to stand. Could
be a week, maybe more."

"So . . . we're talking late April?"

"At least," said Karp. "Assuming nothing else goes wrong."

An overly sanguine assumption, as events proved.

The suicide attempt of the rich-boy granny killer was widely reported. Karp assigned Terrell Collins to field questions, and learned that the New York and national press are a lot less disinclined to beat up a well-spoken black person than a white one, which discovery did not make him particularly proud of himself, but neither did it make him throw his own body into the breach. Waley also held press conferences, and hinted broadly that the tragedy largely resulted from Karp's personal intransigence in opposing bail when all evidence had pointed to his client's suicidal state. The black press, such as it was, supported Karp. There were a few spontaneous street celebrations in Harlem when the news about Rohbling got out and a transient fad for draping nooses over lamp posts. The cops tensed, but a spell of damp, cold weather suppressed whatever tendencies may have existed toward anything more violent.

By May 1, Rohbling could croak speech, and it appeared that his brain was not damaged, or not any more damaged than it was originally. Bannock, the private psychiatrist, issued a report claiming that his patient was in deep depression and could not aid in his own defense. Karp sent Perlsteiner to examine him, and, to Karp's surprise and disappointment, he concurred.

Thus was Karp reminded once again that although criminal justice is often dramatic, and is in fact the subject of an immense genre of fictional accounts, the actual thing more often than not violates the traditional dramatic unities, most especially that of time. What we like is to see the chilling crime, the sleuth in pursuit, the exciting chase, the final conflict, and justice done in the end, preferably without the boring legal details, all within a few hours, but that is not what we get. Karp too had allowed himself to be caught up in the drama of the case, like any spectator, and was now sadly deflated.

Running the Homicide Bureau, he found, now had less charm

than in the past, was even more like public sanitation than it had been; the training of young lawyers seemed somehow less urgent. The essential nastiness of its major work (the locking up of society's rejects for murdering other rejects), the fervid preparation against the always faint possibility that a harassed public defender would deflect by some legal brilliance the virtually certain conclusion, the constant and faintly sordid plea bargaining that greased the system, all these seemed increasingly unbearable. Going from *Rohbling* back to the stream of nearly identical *People* v. *Assholes* was like going from the sunny uplands of the law into its fetid outhouse. Roland Hrcany had taken over the bulk of the work of the bureau chief, and Karp made no serious effort to reclaim it. Roland *liked* the meat grinder. He enjoyed flogging the young A.D.A.'s so that they would flog the system's vicious-but-pathetic captives the harder. Karp withdrew his spirit from the work, supervised vaguely, came late, left early, and waited for winter to pass and his trial to start again.

On May 8, Rohbling was examined again and certified as fit to stand trial. Lionel Waley objected to this finding but was overruled by Judge Peoples. The trial was scheduled to resume on May 11, a Monday. Two days before that, however, a man named Amos Harder, a retired New York Central warehouse manager, stood up at the dais during a fraternal association dinner in Harlem and made a brief speech. Harder was a sober man, generally, but he had had a few that evening. In his remarks he noted that it was just a little over a year since Jane Hughes had been put to rest, and observed that, despite his tricky lawyer, Jonathan Rohbling would burn in hell, but before he did, he would spend the rest of his life in prison for murder, if Amos Harder had anything to do with it. Which he did, being one of the jurors.

There was a reporter for the *New Amsterdam News* in the room that evening, who wrote a story that included these comments, and the *Post* picked up the story and played it large ("BURN IN HELL!" ROHBLING JUROR SAYS). The next day Waley was in Judge Peoples' chambers with a motion for a mistrial and a repetition for a change of venue. Peoples assembled the jury and interviewed each member alone, after which he dismissed Harder, replacing him with an alternate, the retired professor, and, rather to Karp's surprise, denied both the mistrial motion and the change of venue. It appeared that the judge wanted this case nearly as much as Karp did. The trial would therefore take place in the county of New York, commencing on the fifth of June.

During this medico-legal katzenjammer the rest of the world moved along its merry way. In the Karp household, the twins became toddlers, establishing the usual reign of terror but doubled. Posie proved less able to cope with highly mobile and destructive beings than with cuddly lumps. The twins got into Lucy's room. After she calmed down, Lucy bought, with her own money, a lock for her door and installed it herself. It opened with a shiny key that she wore around her neck. Marlene realized that her nanny was over her head and, not wishing to risk fratricide, cut back the time she spent at the security firm to three days a week and no weekends. She took on more night work to make up for it. Increasingly, she handled the pro bono rather than the big-shot side of the business, which was what she liked anyway.

Lucy, now nine, began to attend Chinese school in the afternoons with her friends, occasioning a certain amount of expostulation from the organization that ran it, which Marlene quashed with veiled threats of legal action. Lucy took up brush and ink stone and attacked the 214 radicals, and learned some Mandarin. Third grade continued in good form, Lucy having conquered not only long division but fractions under the tutelage of Mr. Tranh.

Beyond even this Tranh made himself indispensable around Bello & Ciampi. He cooked, he cleaned, he guarded, he took over the accounts and payroll and got Sym through her GED. He learned enough English to man the phone; surprisingly, he spoke it with a French rather than a Vietnamese accent. On three occasions during this period, Marlene asked him to cover a case where deadly violence had been credibly threatened by a sweetheart, and in all three cases the woman was never bothered again.

Marlene did not ask how Tranh had accomplished this, nor did he volunteer the information. In any case, no bodies showed up, so Marlene told herself that he had used moral persuasion.

Harry was the only person in the firm who did not consider the Vietnamese an asset. Harry Bello was changing. He had successfully switched his addiction from alcohol to work. He met with the rich and celebrities. They treated him like a real person, and he found he liked that. He bought several expensive suits and good shoes. Dead Harry with a spit shine. New York is full of famous people who do not want to be the next John Lennon. The firm grew. Harry began making noises about getting a real office. It is often, sadly, the case that when we are rescued, no matter how much gratitude we feel toward our savior, the presence of that person necessarily reminds us of our former fallen state. So it was with Harry Bello. Marlene observed this happening and was both happy and sad.

Marlon Dane came back to work. He did not talk about machine guns anymore. The Heckler & Koch MP5 itself stayed in a plastic bag in the bottom drawer of a filing cabinet in Harry's office.

Wolfe continued as Edie Wooten's bodyguard.

Paul Menotti advanced his case against the St. Nicholas Medical Centers, Inc., by obtaining indictments on 167 counts of Medicare fraud from a federal grand jury. Dr. Vincent Robinson was also charged, but a federal judge dismissed these charges for lack of evidence. V. T. Newbury was unable to find any direct connection between Robinson and the sale of prescription drugs.

Clay Fulton observed Robinson for some weeks, off and on. He reported back to Karp that the man was a crazed rich sadist, whose medical practice consisted largely of shooting cocktails of dope and vitamins into the nicely toned buttocks of young society. This Karp already knew. Robinson seemed quite indifferent to being watched.

The Music Lover waited. He knew she was booked for a series of summer concerts at Tanglewood, Wolf Trap, and Westhampton. He assiduously clipped reviews and notices of her tour concerts and pasted them into his scrapbooks. He did not interfere in any way with the plans for her wedding. There would, of course, be no wedding. He had his own plans for Ms. Wooten's future.

June arrived. Karp oiled his sword and shield and began to review the proceedings in *Rohbling*, feeling tense and a little anxious, like a soldier long away who is about to meet once more the girl he left behind him.

On the weekend before the trial was to start, there opened the Festival of St. Anthony of Padua, which in Little Italy marks the beginning of summer. Sullivan Street is decked along much of its length with green, red, and white bunting, and arches lit with those colors are thrown across the street, which is lined with booths selling pizzas, drinks, sausage sandwiches, zeppole, games of chance, and other items suggesting Italy. Nowadays it is largely a tourist affair run by professional festival operators, but Marlene had been going since infancy and she intended to keep up the tradition.

The family set out at seven, on foot, Karp pushing the twins in their duplex stroller, hand in hand with Marlene, Lucy and Posie trailing behind with the mastiff, Sweety, on a leash. The evening was fair and warm, with the air just thickening into the blueness of twilight. It was shirtsleeve weather, and the family were all lightly dressed, except for Marlene, who wore a cotton madras jacket to conceal her pistol. They walked west on Broome and north on Sullivan into the heart of the old Italian West Village. They walked slowly, joining an ever thickening throng. Posie and Lucy sang together, amid much giggling, that summer's big song, the Diana Ross and Lionel Richie tune, "Endless Love."

They could see the lights glowing italianately in the distance, and then could hear the sounds, music, and laughter, and the many-voiced, echoing noise of a large crowd in narrow streets. Closer still, they could smell it, hot grease, frying meat, onions, peppers, the overpowering sweetness of cotton candy, ices, spilled sodas. A pair of mounted police had stationed themselves just outside the entrance to the street fair, and Lucy dashed forward to caress their horses. They were chatting with two Franciscan friars in brown robes, which Marlene thought an appropriately medieval vignette. There was another man standing by the group, and as she came closer she saw that it was Father Dugan. He was wearing a dark sports shirt, blue jeans, and Nikes.

She greeted him and indicated the Franciscans. "It's a religious festival, Father," she said amiably. "I thought you'd be wearing the full regalia."

"But the Jesuit tradition is to blend in. It's why everyone thinks we're sneaky. However, I still have a real soutane; perhaps I'll wear it for you one day." He looked at Karp, smiling.

She said, "Butch, this is Father Dugan. My confessor."

The two men shook hands. Karp said lightly, "The confessor, huh? You must have your hands full."

Father Dugan grinned and held his finger to his lips, and then knelt down and started goo-gooing Zik and Zak.

Lucy came back from the horses and demanded fair food, and Karp took this for an excuse to push off. He was always uncomfortable around priests, and especially so around one with whom his wife clearly had a special relationship.

"Nice family," said the priest when it had moved off. "How about yourself? How are you feeling?"

"All right, I guess," said Marlene with a harsh laugh. "About as well as the average unindicted violent felon."

"You laugh, but it's a serious matter. I've been doing some reading about your case."

"Oh?"

"Yes, although I hesitate to puff you up with any more pride than you're already afflicted with. 'My confessor!' How could you, with the poor man ready to bolt at the sight of a priest in the first place? In any case, it's a very interesting moral point, allowing me to plunge deep into the casuistry for which we Jesuits are justly famous, he says, reeking of pride himself. Did you know that Augustine wrote that war is justified as love's response to the plight of a neighbor threatened by force?"

"No kidding? Well, that goes a long way toward making up for a lot of the other stuff he says."

"The difficulty," Father Dugan continued, ignoring her remark, "is that you are doing things reserved to competent authority. You are not, after all, a prince. A better argument would be what we call the principle of double effect, when you are forced to do an evil in the course of performing a good act. There are four justifying conditions. First, the action from which evil arises must be good in itself. Second, the intention of the agent must be upright, that is, the evil must be unintended. Third, the evil effect must be coincident in time with the good effect—this is not an ends justifying the means argument. Finally, there must be a proportionately grave reason for allowing the evil to occur."

Marlene thought for a moment. "Hm. Absent the third condition, you could use that to justify anything. So, pounding a guy is wrong, but if I had acted just as he was about to hurt his girlfriend, it would've been justified. Not very practical, is it?"

"No, but practicality is not the point, is it? *Ut est aemulatio divinae rei et humanae.*"

"God's ways are at odds with the ways of humans," said Marlene. "Who said that, Augustine?"

"Tertullian."

"Oh, right. Mr. 'It is certain because it is impossible.' My kind of guy." She looked up and could not find her family in the crowd. "Father, I got to go. Take care."

"*You* take care, Marlene," said the priest. His eyes held hers for a few seconds. "I'm concerned for you. Once you step off the map, it's not a simple thing to find your way back again."

The crowd was dense in the center of the street, especially where the projecting stalls narrowed the way into choke points. She stepped up on a handy milk crate and was able to spot Karp's head bobbing above the throng, one great advantage of marriage to a giant. She cut between the stalls to the sidewalk, which presented an easier passage, and passed the monastery church, where she noted that the take this year was pretty good. There was a statue of the saint set up, surrounded by a fence of chicken wire, into which people had stuffed currency, lots of high-denomination currency. There were people passing all around, but no one in particular was guarding the cash, it being well known in the neighborhood what would happen to anyone who stole from the saint. It would be a fate requiring the intercession

---

of neither heaven nor the NYPD: extremely unpleasant and extremely Sicilian.

The thought of this brushed Marlene's mind, and she wondered what the principle of double effect would have to say about the (very) occasional good deeds performed by the Mob, and in what way she differed from its members. She shook her head in annoyance and chased the thoughts—what you got from hanging out with Jesuits.

The people who lived along Sullivan Street had set up aluminum lawn chairs for the old folks, now assembled in little groups to gossip and enjoy the evening. Passing around one of these, Marlene almost collided with a young woman whose face was familiar.

"Tamara?"

"Oh, hi," said the woman unenthusiastically.

"How're you doing?"

"Oh, you know, okay, I guess."

"Any more . . . you know . . . ?"

Marlene didn't like what she saw in the woman's eyes when she said this. The last she had heard, the lovely but unwise Ms. Morno was no longer receiving unwanted attentions from Arnie Nobili. She gave Morno a quick once-over. Hair clean and shiny, face unmarked, V-neck aqua sweater with the sleeves pushed up, skin-tight white jeans, heeled sandals. Apparently, a young Italian-American woman in fine shape.

Tamara said, "No, not since, you know, last year."

"Arnie's still off the sauce?"

Shrug, a worried look. "I don't know. Look, I got to go back. My grandmother lives here, I got the whole family . . ."

Marlene let her go with a smile and an indication that she should call whenever she felt the need. She walked a few yards down the sidewalk, cut between a pair of booths, and there was her family. Karp had bought zeppole all around. He handed her a warm bag of the little golden spheres of sweet dough sprinkled with powdered sugar.

Marlene accepted it and looked at her sons and laughed. The little fat faces were covered in grease and white powder. Each had a tiny paper bag of zeppole with which they were doing all the things that children of that age do with soft, edible items in bags. Lucy exhibited elaborate disgust and ate her own zeppole like a duchess. The dog hovered pantingly in front of the stroller, its massive head poised to catch any fragments, of which there were many dropped. Marlene linked arms with her husband and chewed her ancestral bread, thinking warm and satisfying thoughts.

Suddenly, the dog growled, a deep, alarming sound. Marlene startled, looked at her dog, looked at where the dog was looking. A man was pushing through the crowd. He passed them almost near enough to touch. He was dirty, unshaven, and even through the odors of the fair, Marlene could smell the chemical stench of the chronic boozer. The dog snarled and bared its teeth. Marlene saw that the man was Arnie Nobili. He was wearing a loose, orange-striped sports shirt over a grubby old-fashioned under-shirt, and filthy gray work pants. He vanished between two booths, heading for the sidewalk beyond.

Marlene felt ice form in her belly. She knew exactly where he was going. She pressed the bag of zeppole into Karp's hand and said, "I got to do something."

Karp saw the expression on her face and felt a stab of fear. "What's wrong?" he asked. "Marlene?"

She disappeared between the stalls. "Marlene!" he called again, louder, and then pushed the stroller after her, followed by Posie, Lucy, and the dog.

"Arnie!" Marlene called. "Arnie, wait up! Stop!"

Nobili stumbled, looked over his shoulder. His face, stupid with drink and mindless determination, twisted into a scowl as he recognized her. He skittered around clumsily to face her, reached behind his back, and pulled a large blue revolver out from his waistband. He pointed this at her menacingly, backed away a few steps, and then continued on his path.

There were shouts, a scream, but these were lost in the general noise of the fair. Marlene saw a woman run into a building. A man grabbed two young children and pressed them to the wall. She was ten feet from Nobili. Over his shoulder she saw a blur of aqua blue and white. He stopped and extended his arm, pointing the gun at Tamara Morno.

"MAR . . . !" Karp shouted.

Marlene cleared her pistol from its holster. Nobili's gun went off. Shrieks and screams.

Marlene could not see if the woman had been hit. She heard the sounds of the stroller's wheels approaching behind her.

". . . LEEE . . ." said Karp.

Marlene had the front sight of her pistol in the center of Nobili's back. She fired twice. Nobili stiffened, threw his arms wide, and dropped to his knees. Marlene saw Tamara Morno flattened against a wall, an overturned lawn chair at her feet. She saw Arnie Nobili lift his pistol again, slowly but steadily. He couldn't miss her.

". . . NNNN!" Karp finished.

She shot Nobili twice more, once in the back and then in the back of the head. He dropped the pistol and fell slowly forward until his face touched the sidewalk, so that for a moment he looked as if he were worshipping something only he could see. Then his body slumped sideways and was still. Tamara Morno was gone.

Marlene's ears were ringing from the shots. She turned slightly, and there was her whole family in a line on the sidewalk, looking at her, as in a dream. Her husband was shouting something at her, and there was an expression on his face that she did not recall ever seeing before. She had to sit down. She tottered on legs that had gone quivery over to a lawn chair and sat down on it. She put her hands on her knees and dropped her head down between her legs and fought to control the nausea. When she lifted her head back up, she saw two police officers pointing their pistols at her.

"Don't tell me Rohbling tried it again," said the district attorney over the phone.

"No," said Karp, "and I wouldn't have called you this late, but I got a real mess here and you need to know about it. Marlene just shot and killed a guy on Sullivan Street."

A pause and a whispered "Jesus Christ!" Then, "Where are you now?"

"At home. I had the kids to handle also . . . I didn't think it was smart for me to get involved down at the precinct."

"Right. She's being held at the Six?"

"Uh-huh. I called Joe Lerner. He's going to go over there."

"Good move. Okay, as of now I'm suspending you from supervisory tasks in the Homicide Bureau, except as they relate to *Rohbling*, until this case is resolved. You're out of the chain of command. I also officially tell you not to discuss this case with anyone in this office. Is that clear?"

"Perfectly."

"Good. Now, as friends, off the record, how bad is it?"

"Fairly bad. She shot the guy four times in the back. Name was Nobili. He was going after one of her clients with a pistol. The cops have the pistol, one shot fired, no injuries, also no client. The woman took off running. They're looking for her, but . . ."

"You were there, you saw all this?"

"Right, I did. But, Jack . . . God, I can't think straight anymore. It went down so fast! One second we're standing there eating fucking zeppole, the regular happy family at the fair scene, and the next she's off after this guy who went past us and the next, it's bang-bang-bang."

"Okay," said the district attorney, "try to put it out of your mind. You have *Rohbling* on Monday, focus on that. I'll take care of everything else. Oh, yeah: what's the situation with the press?"

"They're on it," said Karp tightly. "Drooling."

SEVENTEEN

K arp was not popular with the courthouse press, who among themselves referred to him as N.K.Two, which stood for No Komment Karp. He considered that he had absolutely no obligation to inform the press about the progress of anything whatever *sub judice*. Since, in the nature of things, Karp controlled access to some of the hottest items on the calendars of crime, and since the defense bar was generally loquacious, it was difficult to compose a decent war story with balancing quotes from either side, which is all that distinguishes journalism from P.R. and writing about Elvis sightings for the checkout counter press. This rankled, and so the press was more than delighted to learn that the wife of the chief of the Homicide Bureau, and the prosecutor of the biggest case of the year, had herself just been arrested for killing a man on the street.

There were reporters and a TV crew lying in wait for him on Crosby Street when he came down in the morning. He had expected this and had arranged for a car and driver. It was extremely unpleasant, especially since he had Lucy by the hand. Just as they were about to enter the car, a hard-faced blond woman stuck a tape recorder in Lucy's face and shouted, "How do you feel about your mom going to jail for murder?"

In a clear voice Lucy replied, in Cantonese, "Demons will

suck your brains out through your eyes, pestilential cockroach."

This ran taped on the CBS morning show (translated with some glee by a Chinese-American anchorperson), and for Karp this took some of the sting out of the succeeding shot of Marlene doing the perp walk out of a van toward her arraignment along with a string of whores.

In *Rohbling*, the morning was consumed by the next defense witness, Dr. Martin M. Morland, a child psychiatrist who had treated the young Rohbling. Karp objected to the witness on the grounds that Rohbling's mental condition as a child was irrelevant to the issue of his current sanity, but Peoples cut him off sharply.

"That was harsh," whispered Terrell Collins.

"Yeah," Karp replied, "the judge figures since he gave us the big ones on the mistrial and the change of venue, he owes Waley. Waley'll run wild for a couple of days."

Morland was a small, cheerful, avuncular man with a monastic fringe of silver hair around his bald head. Waley got him to paint Rohbling as the sickest little boy who ever lived. At present he harbored an all-encompassing obsession with elderly black women, the result of the childhood traumas imposed by Clarice, the nanny. The crazy little boy still lived in the young man and took control, hence the crimes.

At the lunch break, Karp pushed silently past the press gantlet and went to his office. He knew he needed something to eat, although his appetite was gone, and called down to a local deli. While waiting, he read the papers. The *Times* had given the shooting story page one below the fold, an unusually high status for a crime story in the *Times*, but it was an unusual shooting. The reporter referred to Marlene's colorful past, noted this was the third person she had killed, and quoted the D.A. as saying that the office would offer no special treatment and that Karp had recused himself from any involvement. The *News* devoted its front page to a big photograph of the dead man on the sidewalk and the headline VIGILANTE 'HIT' SHOCKS FAIR.

Karp was eating his pastrami sandwich when Roland Hrcany and Ray Guma walked in and sat down at Karp's conference table, carrying their own brown bags. They nodded to Karp, and Guma said, "So, Roland, what's the story with Marlene?"

Karp said, "Guys, I can't talk about this."

Guma put on an affronted expression. "Excuse me, I don't believe I was addressing you. I was talking to my pal Roland, here."

Roland said, "Yeah, you can't grab lunch in privacy anymore without somebody sticking their nose in. Anyway, Marlene got R.O.R. She's probably home by now."

"That is truly amazing!" exclaimed Guma. He spoke with exaggerated precision, like a rube reading a testimonial for a patent medicine. "She shoots some citizen in the back on a street full of people, and she gets to walk with no bail? What's the city coming to? Probably it was favoritism, she being a former D.A. and the wife of a big shot."

"It might look that way, but nothing could be further from the truth," said Hrcany in the same stilted tone. "First of all, the vic had a violence sheet on him. Second, he had a gun and fired it. Third, we found the vic's intended target, the lovely Miss Tamara Morno."

"Remarkable!" said Guma. "How was this feat accomplished?"

"It seems that Dead Harry dragged her into the complaint room this morning, and she wrote out a full statement before the acting bureau chief of the Homicide Bureau—"

"Yourself, that is."

"Myself. And from this it appeared that Miss M. was indeed threatened with death by the vic, who, even when shot twice by the aforesaid Mrs. Karp, still tried to point his weapon at her. The facts of the case support a finding of justifiable homicide, since Mrs. Karp acted to prevent a violent felony. Of course, the grand jury will still have to render a finding, but . . ."

"We can rest assured that the grand jurors, guided by yourself, will find likewise with no trouble?"

"I'm confident of it, Raymond," said Hrcany. "And you know what? It's such a nice sunny June day that I think we should take our lunches outside to the park."

"Good idea. If we stay here, we might be tempted to discuss the case with Butch Karp, and that would be a violation of official policy."

They got up and walked to the door. "Yes," added Guma, "poor Butch! He must really be worried about what's going on with his wife."

That afternoon Waley finished his direct examination of Dr. Morland, and Karp rose for the cross. A hard thing, cross-examination of a well-prepared, intelligent expert witness, and Karp was not at his peak, hardly even on the upper slopes. He had before him the background investigation of Morland himself, excerpts from Morland's professional articles, the case notes from Morland's examination of the child Jonathan, and his most recent examination of the defendant, and the notes he himself had made during Waley's direct. Out of this material he had to sculpt *ex tempore* a line of questioning that would convince the jury that however tortured Rohbling's mind had been back when, and however disturbed he might now be, he had not been legally insane at the time of the crime.

So, begin with the big question. At the time of the crime, in your opinion, Doctor, did defendant have substantial incapacity to conform his behavior to the requirements of the law? Morland had an opinion. Paranoid ideation. Lack of anchoring to reality. Long minutes of psychobabble drifted by. Karp hacked into it. Did the defendant know who he was? Yes. Did he know where he was? Yes. Did he know what he was doing? That depends on what we mean by "know." A patronizing smile, and more babble, this time of an epistemological nature. Karp was looking at the jury, saw the eyes glazing. In a minute they would be blaming *him* for making them go through this. So: break and reverse field. Morland had an article differentiating obsessional character defects from psychosis in children. Using that and the therapy notes, Karp got him to admit that he had never diagnosed Rohbling as psychotic back then. Let that line alone. Change field again. Get an admission that obsessional-character defect was not psychosis. Cut off the doctor when he tried to expand the answer.

Karp lost his place, repeated a question, got an objection. Sustained. He bore down. It was hard to keep focused on the mental image of the yellow sheet on which he had written his line of questions. He kept slipping away to night, the colored lights, the noise, gunshots, Marlene standing over the bleeding corpse, the sharp stink of burnt gunpowder wafting by, masking briefly the smell of the fair. Okay, recover. Breathe. His sense was that the cross was running out of steam. Fine. Fall back on the standard: are you being paid by the defendant, Doctor? How much? Then, close with a strong note. Karp asked, "Doctor, why, in your opinion, did the defendant refuse to acknowledge the suitcase?"

No sooner were these words out than Karp felt a chill roil through his belly. He couldn't believe he had asked the question in that form, but there it was, hanging in the air like a thick gas.

Morland smiled, shrugged, answered in so many words that the defendant was so divorced from reality that he really didn't understand that it was his suitcase. Try to recover—or was it that he knew the suitcase was full of incriminatory evidence? Pathetic! Objection, of course, witness has answered. Sustained, jury will disregard. A no-brainer. Karp attempted to obscure this disaster by picking at details, secondary stuff, but he had heard that deadly murmur, seen the faces in the jury box.

Sitting down, he caught Collins's eye. The kid looked stunned. Judge Peoples checked the clock, asked Waley if he had redirect. Of course Waley did not, he was quite satisfied to leave the witness with Karp having beat himself to death with the blue suitcase. Would Mr. W. like to call his next witness fresh the next morning? Mr. W. would, thank you, Your Honor.

The crowd of newspeople was thicker than ever outside the courtroom, heading toward the blood Karp had just spilled in the water, yelling and pushing against the court officers trying to keep a lane clear from the courtroom door to the parts of the building restricted to D.A. personnel. How does it feel? How does it feel? Karp wished he could tell them. He was still numb, although this feeling was being replaced by a dull anger, at Marlene, at himself, the two angers inextricably mixed and tangled. A small, neat black man with a cassette machine leaped in front of him.

"Butch! What happened in there today? Could you respond to the rumors in the black community that you're throwing the case?"

Ordinarily, Karp would have said "excuse me" and edged around the man, but there was no room and the lights were blinding and his adrenaline was pumping, and so his body took over as it had been trained to do. He faked a step, the reporter went with it, Karp gave him the hip and cruised by. But instead of merely staggering, the man caught his foot on a power cable and went flying against a sound man, who tripped too, bringing his boom around to catch a cameraman across the temple. The camera went loose, the cameraman lunged and tripped. The heavy camera went flying and landed on the head of the original reporter. Blood flowed. Strobes popped continuously, catching Karp in dozens of shots, looking over the chaos he had caused, the close of a perfect day.

He thought, but there was more. Back in his office there was an urgent message from the principal of Lucy's school—come at once. Karp arrived at P.S. 1 in an unmarked police car, lights flashing. He found his daughter slumped in the principal's office wearing a big shiner and a split lip. She had, it turned out, gone after a good-sized fifth-grade boy after a day of insults related to Marlene's arrest. Such behavior was not tolerated in P.S. 1, Karp learned, and Lucy and the boy were both suspended for three days.

Lucy was sullen and uncommunicative on the way home. The mob of newspeople in front of their door was much larger than it had been in the morning; the news had spread that Karp had viciously attacked one of their own. They were baying, foaming. Besides the questions they had been asking all along, about the trial, about Marlene, and newer questions about the vicious attack by the racist giant Karp on a small, tiny, harmless black reporter, the sight of Lucy's injured face prompted others. Hey,

Lucy, look over here! Did your mother do that? Did your father? Lucy started crying on the way up the stairs and went straight to her room without saying anything to Marlene.

Marlene was in the living room, watching *Jeopardy* with the sound off. She was in her bathrobe with her hair done up in a pink towel. She smelled of roses and red wine, a bottle of which was on the coffee table, two-thirds empty.

"So. You're back. How was jail?" said Karp, feeling inane, not knowing what else to say, resolved to control his anger.

"Jailish. What was with Lucy?"

"She got into a fight. Some kids were ragging her about you."

Marlene nodded, played with her lip, drank some more wine. Karp sat down next to her. "Marlene . . ."

She shook her head violently. "No. I don't want to hear it."

"What? What don't you want to hear?"

"How bad I am. How I'm screwing up your fucking trial of the decade and my daughter's life, not to mention my own life. Harry too. He laid down the law, you know. To me! My Frankenstein, Dead Harry Bello. He wants to get out of the crazy-boyfriend business. Completely. I got this after he brought in Tamara and saved my ass. He wants to move uptown and expand the celebrity security operation."

"Maybe that's a good idea, Marlene," said Karp carefully.

"It is!" Marlene cried. "It's a great idea. Fuck 'em all anyway, the stupid bitches! Let 'em all die." She poured her glass full again and drank half of it. Then she glared at him. "Look at you!" she said, her voice thick. "You think I'm disgusting, don't you? I can see it on your face."

"Don't be an idiot. I love you," said Karp in an unloving tone.

"Yeah, when I do what you want."

Karp stood up suddenly, shaking the coffee table. He took a deep breath. "Look," he said, not looking at her, "let's just clear some of this shit away. You killed a guy on the street. It was a justifiable homicide, legally. But . . . Jesus Christ, Marlene! You shot him in front of your own children. There could have been bullets flying all around. He could've turned around and shot back at you. What if Lucy or the babies had caught a round?

Didn't you think? Okay, you have some . . . *need* to go out and risk your ass on this crusade of yours, okay, you're an adult, but to put your own children at risk . . ."

She regarded him stonily. "So what's the moral calculus here, Butch? I should just stand by, let an innocent woman go down because there's a faint chance that one of my kids could get hurt?"

"*Yes!*" shouted Karp. "Yes! There were nine hundred and sixty killings in Manhattan last year, and there'll probably be more this year. You know what one or three or seven extra mean to me compared to the safety of my kids? Nothing! Zilch!"

"I see." Marlene spoke in the unnaturally even voice she used when she was angry beyond passion. "Well, it seems we have a difference of opinion. And it's nice of you to remind me of my deficiencies as a mother. Which you never fail to do when something like this happens."

"You obviously need reminding!" Karp snarled back.

Marlene looked at him and then back at the TV screen. "Uh-huh. Then in that case you'll be happy to learn that I will not be endangering them anymore in the near term. I'm leaving."

Karp felt an icy spear penetrate his vitals. "You're what?"

"Leaving. As in not being here. Oh, I don't mean *leaving* leaving. Edie Wooten just called. Her admirer dropped by yesterday evening and trashed her bedroom. Slashed her clothes up and generally wrecked things. She's moving out to her family's island in Gardiner's Bay out on the Island, and she wants me to come and guard her. Actually, she just wanted *a* guard, and I thought okay, Wolfe can go, but we'll be doing that tennis star and I think Wolfe is getting stale behind watching Edie, and I haven't got anyone I can spare, and fuck it anyway, I need to get out of here, away from the jackals down there, and I can help Harry guard his kraut tennis girl wonder out at Southampton too, and so it all works out. Lucky me."

"You'll be gone for what? The whole summer?" Karp asked uneasily, feeling things slipping out of control, wanting to hug her, wanting things to return to what he considered real life, but unable to make the necessary effort.

She shrugged and stared blankly at the screen. "I don't know," she said. The news started. The lead-off tape showed fifteen seconds of the scuffle in the courthouse hallway. Marlene watched without comment. Karp got up and went to the phone and ordered Chinese food delivered.

Marlene stayed in front of the set, drinking wine, while Karp ate and fed himself and his sons and Posie. Lucy would not come out of her room to eat. Marlene finished her bottle and opened another one and drank half of that. At eleven-forty or so, she switched the set off in the middle of Johnny's monologue and went into the kitchen, where she ate some white bean soup and bread. The loft was quiet, the only sounds the perpetual whir and dull rumble of the city outside, elevator sounds, refrigerator sounds.

And faint steps. Lucy came into the kitchen. She was wearing a green Notre Dame T-shirt that reached to her knees. She said, "Oh," when she saw her mother. Without a word Marlene ladled warm soup into a bowl, buttered some bread, and poured out a glass of chocolate milk. Lucy sat down and ate.

"You smell drunk," said Lucy.

"That's because I *am* drunk," said Marlene. "I think I am entitled to tie one on every time I kill somebody and spend a night in jail."

Lucy said, "How come Daddy's mad at you?"

"Well," said Marlene, "he thinks I shouldn't have gotten involved in shooting somebody when my family was around. He was worried that you or the babies would get hurt. Also, I think he thinks it's bad for you to see somebody get shot. He would rather I was in a different business. Also, I don't think his trial is going real well. This garbage outside, all those news guys hanging around, bothering us—it was the last straw."

Lucy thought about this. "Is why they call it the last straw because if there aren't enough straws, like, somebody has to drink out of the glass and the ice cubes clunk against their teeth?"

Marlene laughed and explained. Then she grew serious and

said, "I'm going to go away for a while, to help Uncle Harry guard somebody and guard some other lady too. It's a nice place, and when school is over next week, you can come out and visit me."

A long pause. Then, suspiciously, "You're not getting *divorced* or anything, are you?"

"No, we're not," said Marlene with a sigh. "Your father and I are tied to each other for all eternity. We may kill each other, but we're not breaking up." Marlene rose and lit a cigarette, a rare event in the loft, which she smoked standing in the corner of the kitchen, thus reducing her daughter's cancer risk to some extent.

"How's your eye?" Marlene asked.

"Okay, I guess. A little sore."

"What happened?"

"Nothing. This fifth-grader boy got in my face, talking bad about you, and I said something back and he pushed me—"

"This was a Chinese kid?" Marlene said in surprise.

"No, a *bokgwai*, an American kid, so he pushed me and I pushed him and then he hit me in the face and I punched his nose out. He was bleeding like crazy."

"Okay. I should thank you for sticking up for me, but you can't fight in school, babe. You should have walked away."

"*You* didn't."

"No, you're right. But that wasn't a schoolkid fight. A man was going to commit murder, he was going to kill a woman that relied on me to protect her, so I took him down. And you *can* make a case that it was a risk to you all. Your daddy's right. Anytime bullets start flying, you can never be sure where they'll end up. But I figured the risk was worth it because it was a sure thing that the woman was going to be dead, and I was between him and you all, and I thought I was a better shot too."

"What if a bullet hit me and killed me, what would you do?"

Marlene put out her smoke in the sink and sat down next to Lucy. She said, "I would cry for a year and a day, and tear all my hair out, and then I would have another little girl."

"Better than me?"

"Oh, far, far better than you. You have a smart mouth and you're much too skinny. Look at this! Ribs!" Tickling.

"And you're much too fat!" giggled Lucy, tickling back.

The next morning before dawn, Marlene wrote out notes for Karp, Lucy, and Posie and slipped out of the loft with a duffel bag over her shoulder and her dog at heel. By the time it was full day, she was tooling east on the Long Island Expressway, watching as the westbound lanes made their daily transformation into the world's longest parking lot, and feeling nearly herself again, whatever that was. Although she was going to work, it felt like a vacation, the first break from daily domesticity in nearly ten years. It was a nice day, warm, fleecy clouds overhead. The idiot light for the electrical system flickered on and stayed on; Marlene cared not for idiot lights. She turned the radio up high. The dog stuck its great head out the rear window and lolled its tongue, attracting startled looks from the drivers of the passing cars.

At Riverhead, she turned south and joined the Southern State Parkway, which she took into Southampton. She had no trouble finding the South Shore Club, a huge, glittering-white, over-architected, angular structure on a private road just northwest of Southampton village. The Meadow Club is the place where old money plays tennis in Southampton, and they don't let just anybody in, and those that they do let don't get to play tennis in anything but white. In contrast, anyone who has the $150,000 fee can play at South Shore, and they can hit the courts in Day-Glo knickers if they so desire. The management of this club had worked long to capture the women's professional tennis tour as a symbol that the arrivistes who made up their membership had indeed arrived and to give the snoots at Meadow one in the eye.

Marlene told the guard at the gate who she was, and he directed her to the employees parking lot, around the back. There she parked next to Wolfe's Chevy and Harry's Plymouth. A pimply youth in a pale blue blazer, holding a portable radio, gave her directions to the security meeting. She left Sweety in the car, the windows cracked.

They were holding the meeting in a basement room used for changing and breaks by the staff of the club: there were lockers along one wall and uniforms of various types stacked on shelves or hung in cleaner bags from the pipes that lined the ceiling. About twenty men were sitting on metal folding chairs or standing about in groups. These were the bodyguards of the tennis celebrities who would be playing in the tournament. Most of them had the serious, cynical faces you picked up in the cops. There was a stir when Marlene walked in, smiles, not entirely sympathetic ones. Marlene was famous in the bodyguard world.

She found Harry Bello and Wolfe and sat down next to them. Harry was wearing a blue Lacoste shirt, pressed gray slacks, and polished loafers. He was blending in again.

Some men entered the room: a short redhead wearing a blue blazer with a club crest on it, a man in the white-shirted uniform of the Southampton police, and a tall, crop-headed state trooper. The man introduced himself as Mort Griffin, the head of security for the club, and introduced the policemen who were to serve as security liaisons with their respective organizations. He began to speak about the security arrangements for the tournament, and the coordinations necessary to prevent large numbers of armed men from getting in one another's way. Marlene was soon bored, but she observed Harry taking detailed notes. He likes this, she thought, and he's good at it. It saddened her that their old relationship, like the old casual organization of Bello & Ciampi Security, was passing away. The fact was that Harry was a pro at this and she was not, nor did she especially want to be.

The meeting broke up after the security chief had pointed out a row of pale blue blazers, hanging from a pipe, each in bags marked with a name. All security personnel working the event were required to wear them.

They shrugged into their blazers. To Marlene's surprise, hers fit perfectly. Wolfe went off to a meeting about radio procedure. Harry handed Marlene a thick folder.

"This is what we got on our guy," he said.

She opened it and leafed through the pages. "Harry, this is all in German," she said.

"Yeah, but there's a couple of sheets there says he's in the country as of last Tuesday. Check out the picture."

Manfred Stolz, the stalker, had been arrested twice for harassing Trude Speyr, once in Bonn and once in Paris. The photos showed a wiry man with a bony face, a big Adam's apple, and frizzy reddish hair. He wanted to marry Trude Speyr, failing which he intended to kill her—the usual. What wasn't usual was that he had declared it quite openly, been jailed for it, and gone on declaring it.

"He looks easy to spot," said Marlene.

"Maybe. In Paris he wore a wig."

"Fiendish," said Marlene. "Okay, Harry, I got to go see Edie Wooten right now. I'll spend the night there, and I'll meet you back here tomorrow morning. Say seven-thirty? We'll have breakfast, providing the help is allowed to eat on site."

"She wants to meet you," said Harry.

Marlene rolled her eyes and protested, but then she recalled all those meetings Harry had gone to with the Germans, and she meekly followed him up a flight of stairs to the club dining room, where a reception for the tennis stars was under way. The room was large and white, with huge angled windows facing the ocean, and everyone in it who was not wearing a uniform was rich or famous or both or a worshiper of wealth and fame. Harry led her through the crowd and penetrated a knot of people surrounding what turned out to be a lithe blond teenager. Trude Speyr stopped talking to a short world-famous pop music star and cast an interested blue-eyed gaze at Marlene. Harry made the introductions. There was a startled murmur from the group. Marlene and the girl shook hands. Strobe lights flashed.

They exchanged some banal words, Speyr speaking halting, accented English while the sycophants beamed. Some manager-type in lime green slacks made a crack about the shooting at the fair, and all the famous people tittered. Marlene would have said something vicious had not Harry gently pinched the back of her arm.

"How can you stand it, Harry?" she asked when they were back outside. "Those people . . ."

"Beats chasing scumbags down stairways. Beats corpses with maggots in their eyes. Beats waking up covered by your own puke. And it pays the bills."

She was about to object that wearing a pissy blazer and dancing attendance on gilded assholes was not what she'd had in mind when she started the business, but bit it back. She looked at her friend in the clear afternoon light of a Long Island summer and saw that he looked good, not great, of course, but not a three-day corpse either. He was doing a man's job, and a difficult one, on his own, and Marlene could, almost for the first time, see the person he had been before his life came apart, a quiet, decent man with a wry sense of humor.

And who was she to talk, she who was just dashing off to care for her very own gilded asshole genius? So instead of having another fight, she hugged him and smiled and was rewarded by a flickering smile in return. She kissed his cheek and got into her car. Which did not start. Sweety whined.

"Won't start?"

"You're some detective, Harry," said Marlene peevishly. "What'll I do?"

"I'll get Wolfe to drive you. No problem," said new Harry, the exec.

Twenty minutes later, Wolfe pulled his Caprice around. Marlene and Sweety got in, and as they did, Wolfe pulled a tape out of his stereo and shoved it under his seat.

"What's the tape, Wolfe?" she asked.

"Um, nothing," he replied. They pulled out of the parking lot and onto the narrow road.

"Come on, Wolfe. What, you're ashamed of your musical taste? How bad could it be? Worse than Conway Twitty? Mantovani? Tiajuana Brass? Lawrence Welk?"

His face worked nervously. "It's, ah, not music. It's like, uh, a motivational tape. For, you know, dealing with people."

It was Marlene's turn to feel embarrassed. She had not thought Wolfe a striver; nor had it occurred to her that what she considered a throw-away muscle job could represent, for someone like Wolfe, the basis for a career. To cover she said brightly,

"So, do you have any music tapes to go with your fine stereo?"

"In the glove," he said.

In the glove compartment were two cassettes in new boxes, a *Greatest Hits of the 70's* collection and a *Best of the Eagles, Volume One*. Marlene slipped in the Eagles and turned up the sound, and they headed north with "Take It Easy" playing, Marlene singing along, Wolfe driving, stolid and silent.

They drove north to Sag Harbor, to the marina she had been told to look for, which they discovered to be a white-painted storefront with signs in front of it advertising charter boats (*Donna T., SeaWind*) and rental Lightnings and Whalers. There was a long gray dock and a small gray beach next to it where some kids were messing with Jet Skis. While Marlene searched out the proprietor, Wolfe took Sweety to throw sticks on the beach. The dog liked him and he was good with the dog. It occurred to Marlene that the firm could send Wolfe to guard dog school and get him a big dog of his own. A little staff development.

She found the manager, a thin old boy in greasy gray coveralls (*Ralph* embroidered on the breast) and arranged the ride. Edie Wooten had already called him, he said, and was that your big dog?

Wolfe left, saying that he would pick her up the next morning, and with her dog on a leash and her duffel bag slung, she boarded a shining, elderly mahogany launch. Twenty minutes later, after a passage over calm, boat-flecked Gardiners Bay, they disembarked at a little dock at Wooten's Island.

Marlene let Sweety off his chain and walked up a path dressed in tan gravel between thick fir hedges. This led to a wide lawn, shady under old maples and sycamores, and the house itself, a Tudor manse like a small Nonesuch, done in soft-looking carved stone the color of lips. Weathered garden chairs and a round table were arranged on the velvety lawn, and there was a walled rose garden off to the left of the house, with the bright blooms showing over the wall.

Music came floating out from an open leaded-glass casement, the same liquid phrase repeated several times, as they approached the front door. Marlene knocked on it with a massive iron knocker, feeling like a gothic novel heroine despite the fairness of the day. The music stopped.

Edie Wooten opened the door, smiled at Marlene, and gave a little yelp when she saw Sweety.

"What is *that*?"

"It's a Neapolitan mastiff. His name is Sweety. He's perfectly harmless, aren't you? Aren't you?"

Sweety shook his monstrous jowls and flung drool in all directions to demonstrate how harmless he was. The two women sat down on a pair of Adirondack chairs, and chatted about how each of them was getting on, avoiding such topics as getting your clothes slashed by a maniac and shooting someone in the middle of a carnival. A stout gray-haired woman in an apron came out, whom Edie introduced as Bridget Marney, the housekeeper. Bridget Marney looked suspiciously at Sweety, who had found a shady spot under a yew hedge, and Sweety returned the favor. Bridget brought out a sweating pitcher of iced tea and glasses on a tray, and departed.

"Is he a guard dog?" Edie asked, having observed how closely the dog had watched the servant.

"Yes, he is," said Marlene. "I'm going to have to be away working this tennis match for the next couple of days, and I want you watched. Sweety'll do the job, maybe better than I could."

"We have cats," said Edie. "Will he eat them?"

"No, but he'll eat anyone who comes into the house except you and me."

Edie's eyes widened. "Isn't that a bit extreme?"

Marlene sighed. Somehow she still didn't get it. Except for a couple of million dollars and a cello, she was just like Tamara Morno. "No, it isn't. Look, I am extremely worried about you. This guy was never into violence before. Something seems to have set him onto a different track. Now he's taken a knife and ripped up your possessions. He has to know you're here, and he's going to come after you. Luckily, this place is a lot more defensible than your apartment or a concert hall. When he does come, I want to nail him, physically. Now, is anyone else besides you

266 / *Robert K. Tanenbaum*

and Mrs. Marney on the island? I mean, for the next couple of days."

Edie seemed surprised by the question. "Well, yes, there's Bridget's husband. Jack takes care of the boats and the grounds. And Ginnie—"

"Ginnie's *here*?"

"Naturally she's here. She and some of her friends are in the east cottage."

"Jesus, Edie! How could you *do* that! Her friends? Tell me Robinson's not one of them!"

Edie's face stiffened. "It's her *house*, Marlene. I mean, she owns it. She can have anyone there she likes. Besides, I thought we had disposed of this notion of yours that she's the one who's been doing all these awful things. Or Vincent."

Blind as a bat, thought Marlene. Why do I even bother? She took a breath and said, as calmly as she was able, "Okay, she's a saint. Does she come in and out of *this* house much?"

A significant, embarrassed pause. "No, not at all. I have my life and she has hers. The island is fifteen acres, after all."

"Good. So, what we need to do now is introduce Sweety to your couple, and after that he won't let anyone else into the house. You might want to convey that message to your sister and her guests."

"He'll bark at them, you mean?"

"No, Sweety doesn't bark," said Marlene. "He'll just hold them until I come back, which might be an annoyance, especially if they need to go to the bathroom."

Edie coughed around her iced tea. "God! This is just for a day or so, yes?"

"Oh, yeah. I'll be back full-time, or I'll send Wolfe, day after tomorrow at the latest. Earlier if we can catch the guy who's stalking Trude Speyr." Marlene explained briefly about Manfred Stolz and his goal in life.

"Is he dangerous, do you think?" Edie asked.

"Fairly. No, I take that back. Very," said Marlene, and, to satisfy her irritation at this sweet, oblivious woman, added, "About like yours, I'd say."

EIGHTEEN

"Just do me one favor," said the district attorney. "Next time you beat up a reporter, could you try to make sure that he's not a member of one of our fine identifiable minorities? This strikes me as not too much to—"

"I didn't beat him up, Jack," Karp interrupted in an exhausted voice.

"*. . . too much to ask.* I know you didn't, but that's what it looked like. The phone's ringing off the hook. I got the borough president telling me to pull you off the trial."

Karp breathed into the phone. There didn't seem to be anything to say.

"Should I? You're not having much of a game, if yesterday was any evidence."

"I can do it, Jack."

"I hope," snapped Keegan, and then, after a pause, "How's Marlene?"

"She's fine. She's out of town for a while."

"Thank God for that!" Keegan exclaimed with fervor. A longer pause. "So, what you're saying is, the arm is okay? You can go the distance?"

Karp chuckled in spite of himself. It was just exactly that, top of the seventh, score tied, one out, two men on, he just gave up a couple of runs, and here was the manager out on the mound, having one of those conversations the fans never get to hear. Karp said, "You want to send the new kid in, throw a bunch of fast balls?"

Keegan laughed too. "I thought of it, Butch, believe me. Like I say, it's been suggested too, and not gently either. Could Collins do it?"

"Oh, yeah, he could," Karp replied flatly.

The seconds ticked. Karp wished that he was face to face, not sitting here listening to the blank hiss of the telephone. Then Keegan said, decisively, "Okay, Chief, I'm not going to change policy, I'm not going to change Francis Garrahy's policy at this late date. It's yours to win or lose. But, Butch? You blow this, there's going to be consequences. I got an election five months away . . . you comprehend what I'm saying?"

"You told me this already, Jack."

"I know I did. A lot of times I tell you once, you don't get it. Take care."

After Keegan hung up, Karp immediately put the conversation out of his mind and returned to his prep. He had no hard feelings against Keegan. The district attorney's job was a political office, although Keegan kept it as unpolitical as it could be in its daily operation. If *Rohbling* crashed, someone would have to be offered up to the voters, and Karp understood the justice of it being himself.

Terrell Collins knocked and walked in. He looked remarkably fresh, pressed and shiny in a nice dark suit.

"You get the last of the stuff from Fulton?" Karp asked.

"Yeah, right here," said Collins, placing a neat folder on Karp's desk. Karp looked through it. Lieutenant Fulton and his troops had spoken with anyone who had ever known Clarice Brown, the Rohblings' nanny, or her son, Cletis, now known as Jamal al-Barka. Collins had knocked this mass of data into a summary, with questions, to which the detective had now supplied the answers. Karp smiled and placed the new material on top of the thick folder he had assembled for this witness.

"Little Cletis was not that popular with the neighbors, it

seems," said Karp. "This is good stuff on his juvenile sheet, by the way." Juvenile records were sealed, but there were ways to find out what witnesses had done as kids that did not involve searching criminal records.

"Stole stuff from the Rohblings, and from Jonathan," Karp continued, reading. "Hm, set a fire too. One adult stretch for armed robbery, went with the Muslims in the joint, Elmira, been a good citizen since. I doubt we'll use any of this, but it's nice to know. You look like you have a question."

"Yeah," said Collins, "what's Waley doing with this guy, and why now?"

Karp leaned back in his chair and checked his watch for perhaps the fifth time in the past half hour. "The arc of the case. Waley's telling a story, same as us. The book says go from the general to the particular, the broad brush first and then plug in the holes. But there's also the performance aspects to it. He's just had two shrinks up there. The first one's an expert on what's crazy—he literally wrote the book on it, and he says Rohbling is. The next is the child psychiatrist. Rohbling was crazy then, he's crazy now: he wants them to draw the inference. But these guys are not exactly the Rolling Stones, the audience is a little snoozy, so Waley wants to wake them up. Therefore, next witness, a boyhood companion who understands the relationship that the shrinks will say forms the focus of the exculpatory insanity and explains the rage against elderly black women. It's meat. It's sex and child abuse. It'll wake them up for the clean-up hitter, who's Bannock, the current shrink. Also, to be frank, the guy's black, and not only that, but a race man too. Waley's got a race card here, and there's no reason for him not to play it, in his typical elegant fashion, of course."

"How do you figure he has a race card? I thought *we* had the race card. The victims—"

"Yeah, we do," said Karp, "but like all race cards it's double-sided. We want the jury to think, rich white boy racist killing poor black ladies for thrills and crying insanity when we catch him. The blacks vote race and the whites vote guilt to convict. Waley wants them to think, poor little white boy brutalized by a black woman, driven crazy, hence this tragedy. The whites vote race, the blacks vote guilt to acquit.''

"You really believe it works that way?" asked Collins. There was disappointment on his face.

Karp grinned. "No, I don't. I've tried dozens and dozens of cases with black D.'s and white vics, where black jurors stood up and played straight and convicted. Of course, I've never been a racist myself before, so that could make a difference." He put this one out lightly, watching the other man.

Collins didn't react. Instead he asked, "So what do you think his line with al-Barka is going to be?"

"Wait a second. *"Do* you think I'm a racist?"

"Sure, Butch. Everybody's a racist. I am. You are. This is America. It's our national religion. The question you want to ask is, do I think your racism affects how you're handling the trial, or how you behave toward me, and the answer to that is no, not so far." He was looking Karp directly in the eye as he said this, his gaze calm and implacable. He held it for a moment and then repeated, "So, what do you think his line'll be with al-Barka?"

Thwock. Thwock. Thwock-thwock-thwock-thwock. Ahhhh! Clap-clap-clap-clap. Tennis was not Marlene's favorite game, not to play and not to watch. The matches seemed much of a muchness to her, although from the behavior and conversation of the people sitting near her in the back of the stands, Trude Speyr was having a terrific day. Marlene was at the center rear row of the portable grandstand, positioned so she could sweep the crowd with the Leica mini-binoculars she carried. She had a button earphone in her ear and a lapel mike, both connected to the portable radio hung at her belt. Harry had splurged for the best stuff; when they elected a woman president, Bello & Ciampi could take over from the Secret Service.

Under her pale blue blazer she was wearing an ill-fitting, uncomfortable shoulder rig in which sat a Colt Lightweight Commander .45 pistol she had borrowed from Marlon Dane, since her own gun now resided in some NYPD evidence locker. She had a pair of handcuffs in a side pocket.

Although she was not where she wanted to be, or doing what she wanted to be doing, she was a good soldier. This job was important to Harry, and to the firm that supplied the cash that enabled her to pursue her real interests, and so she stood in the mild sunshine and scanned the crowd, looking for Manfred Stolz's red hair and bumpy neck.

"Marlene. Wolfe Post Two, come in," said a crackling voice in her ear button.

"Marlene here. What's up, Wolfe?"

"I think I spotted him."

"Where?"

"Section B. Four rows up from the court. Yellow shirt, white floppy hat."

Marlene trained the binoculars. It was hard to see the man's face under his hat, but as he moved to watch the action (Speyr was about to win her third straight set), she was able to see his neck and the fringe of pale hair over his ear.

Into her mike she said, "Okay, Wolfe, move into the aisle behind him. Bring up Dane and the others and place them on the cross aisles above and below. Don't do anything until I get there."

"Copy," said Wolfe. Marlene started to move down the aisle.

Jamal al-Barka was a tight-faced beige man, dressed in the characteristic bow tie and dark suit of his organization. He had a lot to say, and Waley gave him ample scope to say it. Karp threw a number of sidelong looks at Collins, to which he received eyebrow raises and shrugs. With only occasional direction by counsel, Mr. al-Barka spoke on and on. The jury learned about the long history of oppression of the black nation at the hands of whites. They learned about the child-rearing customs of slavery days, and how the slave children learned the differences between white and black people, and the traditions that underlay the use of black servants to raise white children. There was little that Karp could do about this, other than occasionally object to the relevance of the question asked, but since it had been established by experts that Rohbling's disorder, if any, was rooted in his childhood experiences with Clarice Brown, an exposition of the facts thereof was clearly allowable. There was no limit, other than the judge's patience, to how long and in what detail a witness was allowed to speak. And Peoples was a patient man.

From Waley's point of view, Karp thought, it was something of a bravura performance, bringing a black nationalist up as a defense witness for a white man accused of cross-racial murder. Once again he had to remind himself that Waley was trying to demonstrate insanity. The rules were different now. Karp began to work out a counter strategy for his cross.

As the day wore on, the witness's theme moved slowly from the old plantation to the Rohblings' house on Long Island some fifteen years ago. The questions became sharper now. Did your mother hate the Rohblings? Yes. Did you? Yes. Did she hate Jonathan? Yes. How do you know this? Descriptions of abuse, the pinchings, the twistings of arms, the famous enemas. Did Jonathan report these abuses to his parents? Never. Why not? They didn't care about him. They just wanted him out of sight. Was that the only reason? No. He loved her. She was the only one in the world who paid attention to him. That's what they were buying for their fifty dollars a week, a black woman's brutal love.

The jury was entranced, as they always were when soap opera played on the witness stand. Waley tried, in the form of a question, to slip in a little summation of what the witness's testimony meant in relation to the other testimony, but Karp objected and was sustained. An icy smile from Waley, a tiny nod. Your witness. It was four-twenty.

The judge said, "Mr. Karp, as it has become late, perhaps you would like to hold your cross-examination over for tomorrow?"

"Thank you, Your Honor, but no. My cross-examination will be quite brief."

Karp approached the witness, who glared at him and tightened his jaw.

"Mr. al-Barka, why are you here?"

The man seemed surprised by the question and suspicious of

its intent. "Mr. Waley asked me to come and testify," he answered.

"But you were not compelled in any way?"

"No."

"So it was a favor, then, was it?"

"I come to speak the truth in the interests of justice. Justice is dear to Allah."

"As is money, apparently. How much were you paid to testify, sir?"

"I didn't get nothing."

"But Mr. Waley made a substantial contribution to your mosque, did he not? A thousand dollars?"

"We are enjoined to give alms and be charitable. As this money is a tiny portion of the reparation due the—"

"Thank you, sir," Karp cut in. "So that's one reason why you're testifying for a man that ordinarily you would not lift a finger to help. But there's another reason, isn't there? You are a member of the Nation of Islam, are you not?"

"I am, yes."

"And you are therefore a reader of its newspaper, *The Messenger*, yes?"

"Yes, I read it." Uncertainly.

Karp went to his table and pulled from a folder a copy of that paper. "Did you read this past Thursday's edition, where the editor says that white justice will never convict a white man for murdering black women, and that when this happens the black vanguard will rise up and, I quote, 'Put the city to the torch'?"

"I may have. So what?"

Mr. al-Barka was looking confused. Karp said, "Well, I was just wondering sir, would you like to see what you call white justice fail in this case? Would you like to see the city put to the torch?"

"Objection!" from Waley. "Hypothetical and irrelevant."

"Sustained. Jury will disregard."

Karp changed step like a forward driving past a blocking guard. "Mr. al-Barka, you've testified that you spent considerable time in the defendant's company when you were boys. What, if any, peculiar or unusual behavior did you observe? No, don't look at Mr. Waley, look at me!"

"He was just a typical spoiled white brat."

"Typical, I see. Did he do anything strange?"

"Besides rubbing shi—stuff all over him?"

"Yes, besides that."

The man thought for a few moments. "He was really sneaky."

"How so?"

"Lying all the time. Breaking stuff and blaming it on the dogs. On me. Hiding. Driving everyone crazy looking for him."

"I see. Sneaky and secretive. Did he ever talk to people who weren't there?"

"No."

"Or say he heard voices?"

"No."

"Or think he was somebody other than Jonathan Rohbling?"

"No," said al-Barka, and then, remembering why he was there, hastily added, "But he was a crazy kid. I mean, he—"

Swish. Karp turned away. "No further questions, Your Honor."

Marlene sat with Jack Wolfe at the edge of the tennis court, near the umpire's stand, in the place reserved for security personnel. Wolfe was having some sort of tantrum, and Marlene didn't quite know what to do about it.

"Wolfe," she said consolingly, "it was an honest mistake. I thought the asshole looked good too."

"I should have waited," Wolfe said, pounding his fist on his knee. "You told me to wait. I should have waited."

"Wolfe, everybody makes mistakes. You thought he was going for a weapon, you reacted."

Wolfe had indeed reacted, throwing his hard-muscled body across two rows of spectators and flattening the man in the yellow shirt and white hat, who proved not to be the stalker but a lawyer from New Rochelle, who was going to sue Wolfe, Marlene, the firm, the club, the tournament, the town of Southampton, Suffolk

County, and the manufacturers of the camera he was reaching for when Wolfe had jumped him, which had negligently shattered, scratching his hand.

It was not these legal threats that had brought Wolfe to this state, Marlene thought, but his own exaggerated sense of responsibility and a kind of self-scarifying perfectionism that Marlene had often observed among members of the police, and which she believed was one of the side effects of the drug testosterone. So she counseled him, stroking his ego with her voice, while the *thwock-thwock* went on and Trude Speyr won set and match.

Cheers, the crowd rose, the rivals embraced at mid-court, hordes of press descended, clicking madly like giant insects. Marlene, Wolfe, Dane, several other security hirelings, and Speyr's personal entourage drew the girl athlete into their protective embrace and made for the showers. The VIP locker room at South Shore was a suite of nicely appointed cubicles on the ground floor of the main clubhouse, reachable from the courts via a breezeway. Marlene led the way, went into the women's section, checked that there were no lurkers, stole some courtesy miniatures of cologne and shampoo, and passed Speyr in.

Fifteen minutes later, dewy-fresh, dressed in a white linen ensemble, Speyr emerged from her cubicle and said, "Oh, Marlene, I have such a headache. Do you have aspirin maybe?"

Marlene did. Speyr took two, and began a complaint about how rude the press corps was in America, not like in Germany, except for the Italians, who were even than the Americans more rude, and, if it possible could they go by a way not the press to see?

Naturally, Marlene and Harry had scoped out all the possible ins and outs associated with the building. Marlene raised Harry on the comm. channel and had a brief discussion. They could take her out the front parking lot, reserved for members during the tournament, rather than the rear lot, where the press and fans had gathered. There was an inner stairway that led from the locker room to the dining room on what was, since the building was constructed on a slope, its second-floor rear but ground-floor front. They would take that stairway, pass through the dining

276 / Robert K. Tanenbaum

room, and go out the front of the building, where a limo would be waiting.

This they did. Marlene sent the two temp guys out to check the route. These radioed back the all-clear, and then Marlene, Speyr, Dane, and Wolfe went up, through the deserted dining room, through the lobby, and out into the dazzling, sun-washed parking lot. A long gray Caddie was parked at the curb, Harry standing by the door, talking to the tennis player's father and her manager. They were all smiling.

Walking rapidly with the little group, Marlene cast her eyes around, checking the people. Two uniformed valet parkers, a groundsman in a blue coverall and tan pith helmet, carrying a trash basket, a group of three women, staring, an elderly couple, the man raising his camera.

They were twenty feet from the car when the groundsman charged. His pith helmet fell off. Marlene could clearly see Manfred Stolz's red hair. He did not look much like the New Rochelle lawyer, after all, if anything somewhat less bloodthirsty. He had a sword in his hand. Sunlight flashed for an instant off its edge.

Marlene reached for her gun. Dane engulfed the tennis player in his arms. Stolz raised his weapon, which Marlene could now see was not a sword but a long machete-like brush knife. Her gun was not on her left hip where it usually was, and so her hand grasped futilely at air, until she recalled that she was wearing a different gun in a different place. By then it was too late. The man was right over her, his arm lifted for the killing blow. Marlene had time to note that his face was oddly calm, as if he were about to clip a rose.

Terrell Collins said, "Well, I think we got some back today." He was looking at Karp with more than the usual admiration. They were in Karp's office for their standard postmortem.

"Yeah, well, we were due some," said Karp. "I've been fucking up so badly lately . . ." He let the thought die. "Now that I look at it again, Waley was taking a chance there, but it could've paid off."

"How do you mean?"

"Focus on the psychology. What 'made' him do it. It's the sly way into the irresistible-impulse defense."

"But there *isn't* an irresistible-impulse defense, not in this state anyway," Collins objected.

"Not legally, but it's there, in the jury's mind. Look, what's his real game plan, Waley? The D. got a trauma so overwhelming that he couldn't help going after black old women. Hence the witness testifying to the specific trauma, an eyewitness to the supposedly exculpatory events. Now, this is horseshit legally. The law doesn't care what happened to Rohbling back then. It doesn't care what his mental state was back then or what it was at any moment aside from the moment when he committed the crime. But the jury does. It's like looking at clouds. Look, there's a horsy, there's a bunny! Juries like vivid stories, and irresistible impulse is the story Waley's selling, although he'll never use the phrase out loud. It's great too, because everyone's experienced a moment of blinding rage, a time when they thought about doing something really horrible. Waley's saying, imagine not being able to resist that. What we have to do, on the other hand, is focus on the crime—was he crazy at that moment? A hard sell, which is why the insanity defense is fucked. Ordinarily, I mean."

"Well, you took the starch out of al-Barka's part of it, anyway. You discredited him—he just came for a soapbox and for money. And the D. wasn't crazy as a kid."

"Yeah, but it was a nice-to-have for him and a had-to-win for us, as bad as we're doing. He's got the big mo right now." Karp sipped the dregs of cold coffee in his cup and made a face. "Well," he said, "I've got to go home."

"Me too," said Collins. "Good day, though."

"Fair day." Karp gave his colleague a sharp look and went on, "We're not going to win this one, I hope you're prepared for that."

With an uncertain look Collins said, "What do you mean, we're not going to win?"

"Just that. We're fighting for a hanger here and a rematch."

"You're joking! I mean, we're not doing *that* bad."

"No, just bad enough. I don't know how many times I've said

it in bureau meetings, and here's the practical demonstration. A murder prosecution has to be as perfect as human beings can make anything. And I wasn't. But you *will* be, ace."

"Me?"

"Uh-huh. When we retry this fucker, if we get the chance, it'll be all yours. Sit down, Terry, you're turning white."

Collins laughed explosively, a release of energy, but he did not appear to be amused.

"What did you think," said Karp benignly, "that I was going to repeat? You know the difference between a man and a rat? If you put a rat in a maze and every time he turns to the right you shock the shit out of him, after a while he starts turning left. I aspire to rathood in my old age. I learned my lesson: the bureau chief can't do major trials, or maybe *this* bureau chief with a wife and three kids can't. Yeah, Connie . . . what?"

The secretary had burst into the office without her usual brief knock, her face pulled into deep grooves by concern. She said, "Butch, is Marlene out on the Island, at some tennis tournament?"

Karp had to think. "Yeah, she is. Why? What happened?"

"Jerry O'Bannion from Part 41 just called and said he was watching TV in the court officers' coffee room and they had a news flash. Some maniac attacked a tennis player. They caught him, but they said he cut up some security people, and Jerry thought they said one of them was Marlene. He said he thought he saw her on the TV with—" She stopped, her voice breaking.

"What? With what?" Karp demanded.

"With blood all over her."

Marlene was covered with blood—her hair was matted with it on one side, and it had granulated in the creases of her neck. She had wiped her face with her hand so she could see, but her blue blazer and shirt and bra were soaked through with blood, heavy, sticky, congealing gore, pulling at her skin in the most disgusting manner. Her nose filled with the reek of it, that nasty butcher-shop stink.

Her head hurt too. When the blow hit her, she thought for a moment that it was Stolz's machete, and that her skull was split and that she was going to die. She fell into that dark, reverberating place where you go in the first seconds after a physical trauma, and she thought briefly, with sadness, of Lucy, and how she would grow up without a mother, and then she felt a weight crushing her into the pavement. She could hardly breathe, but this feeling itself gave her some confidence that she was not in fact lying on the ground with her brains indecently exposed.

Suddenly, the weight was off her. She raised her head, then went up on her elbow. There was grit in her eye, and she started to rub it out. She was aware of grunts and a heaving mass a few inches from her face, and the sound of screams and running footsteps, and someone was shouting, "Get her away! Get her away!"

And then she heard a peculiar bubbling, whistling sound that she had never heard before and never wanted to hear again, and instantly her face and the upper part of her body were covered in hot liquid. She was blind. A second or two later Harry was at her side. He had scooped her up, and before she could fully catch her breath, she was in the ambulance that had been parked in the lot for the tournament, and rolling at speed with its siren screaming.

Now she was in a little screened-off area of the emergency room of Southampton Community Hospital. A doctor had come in to see her, had found that there was nothing seriously wrong, had given her two Darvon and left her alone. Marlene's mind was more or less frozen solid. She would have sat in that cheap plastic chair until it was time for her to be moved to the geriatric ward, or so she thought.

Then Harry Bello came in carrying a Styrofoam cup. He handed it to her. She drank the warm liquid and found that it was a scant ounce of coffee on top of what tasted like John Jameson's.

"Oh, God, Harry, thank you!" she sighed. "This will earn you three hundred years' remission in purgatory."

"I need it. How do you feel?"

"Oh, I bet I feel a lot better than I look, and I feel like shit," she said. They both smiled. She drank some more and felt humanity flooding back into her. "How's Wolfe?"

"Cut. His arms're cut, his chest. Lots of stitches but nothing seriously wrong."

"That's terrific! And . . . I presume Herr Stolz is no longer with us?"

"Oh, yeah," said Harry. "I think you got the whole five quarts."

"Did you see it go down? It's still a blur to me."

"Yeah, more or less. The whole thing took five seconds. Stolz charged, waving that machete. By the way, he'd been working there three months. Phony name. He really was a groundskeeper, in Germany. Fucking Griffin—"

"Forget it, Harry. Then what?"

"Okay, as soon as he made his move, Dane picked up Speyr and started running with her toward the car. It was incredible. He practically tucked her under his arm, like he was going for a first down. Wolfe knocked you out of the way with his forearm and climbed all over you to get to Stolz. Fucker missed his first shot, and then came backhand and cut Wolfe up, and then Wolfe grabbed his arm and popped him one in the face, but he tripped over you and dragged the both of them down on top of you. Then they rolled off and wrestled for the thing, and Stolz got his throat cut. Wolfe can't remember doing it."

Marlene's beeper went off. "Oh, Christ, that's my husband," she moaned.

"The fucking blade was sharp enough to shave with," Harry finished.

Karp calmed down appreciably when he understood that she was not hurt. Then he got mad.

"I can't stand this, Marlene."

"I know."

"I *love* you!"

"I know. I love you too, but it's not enough."

"What do you *mean*, it's not enough? I don't love you enough?"

"No, I mean you hate what I do. And I want to keep doing it."

A long silence. Marlene disliked talking this way on the phone, and being covered with congealing blood did not help.

"How're Lucy and the babies?" she asked.

"They're fine, Marlene." Tightly.

"I need to go wash myself, Butch. And take a rest. I'll be at Edie's. Call me there."

"Is that guy still bothering her?"

"Not lately. But he's probably there."

"Who, Robinson? Where?"

"On the island. Her sister has a house there and she parties with her pals, and he's one of them."

"Oh, shit, Marlene!" A wail.

"I'll be fine, Butch. I have a gun and a big dog, and after tomorrow I'll have Wolfe."

Another silence. When Karp spoke again it sounded as if he was struggling for control. "Let me understand this. You're guarding her, he's there, and clearly, you don't expect him to hold off just because you *are* there, or else you wouldn't *be* there, right out front. So . . . you expect him to try to get to her right through you. Is that what's happening, Marlene?"

"Yeah. I think he loves getting through opposition. It's part of the thrill for him. He'll make a move."

"That's great," Karp said. "Terrific! The guy's a *killer*, Marlene."

"That's okay," she said, almost giddily, "so am I. Tell Lucy to call me at Edie's tonight, okay? Bye, Butch."

As she hung up she was reflecting about what she had just said about opposition whetting the thrill for Robinson. It certainly fit with what she already knew about his personality, if that was the word. She thought that if stalking had an NFL, the late Manfred Stolz would be a lot lower draft choice than the Music Lover.

NINETEEN

They let Marlene take a shower in the hospital. She spent three-quarters of an hour in it, and washed and rinsed her hair thrice. When she emerged, she found that her bloody clothes had been removed and replaced with a blue T-shirt printed with a picture of Montauk Light, white jeans, and a bra and panties. Everything fit. Harry clearly, and Marlene smiled at the idea of Dead Harry Bello buying undies in some tony Southampton shop. Her bag, a zip-up canvas number, was there too, with Dane's gun and holster in it. She picked it up and went to visit Wolfe.

He was lying in bed with an IV running into his arm, looking pale and younger than he had before. Dane was there with him, but clearly about to leave.

"Take care, Wolfie," said Dane. "Some stuff, huh, Marlene?"

"Some stuff is right," said Marlene.

"How's that piece working for you?" asked Dane.

"The gun? It's fine, Dane. I love it. I want to marry it," replied Marlene snappishly, and regretted her tone when she saw the man's boy-handsome face stiffen. She sighed and touched his arm. "No, really, Dane, I like it. It's real light for a .45, and I realize I should be carrying something with more stopping power anyway."

Dane smiled, and the gun-nut lights flicked on in his eyes. "Yeah, you got one-shot knockdown with that thing. I loaded 185 grain Silvertips in there. I like them better than the old 230 grain round. Better velocity, better expansion."

"I feel the same way, Dane," said Marlene with an utterly straight face. "Expansion is the key. I can't wait to try it out on the range."

Dane left, a happy man. Marlene pulled up a straight chair and sat down next to Wolfe's bed.

"How're you feeling?"

"Okay. They just have me in here for observation. I lost a lot of blood, they tell me."

"Not as much as Stolz," Marlene said, and then, when she saw the expression on his face, "Oh, shit! I'm sorry, Wolfe. I can't seem to control my mouth today."

"That's okay. I just never killed a guy before. I mean, in civilian life. 'Nam was different, you know?" She didn't, but nodded anyway. "I thought it would be, you know, like in the movies, you walk away kind of macho and say some cool shit. But . . ." He seemed sad to have learned that he was not the sort of person portrayed in the movies.

Marlene patted his arm. "Yeah, I know. Meanwhile, you saved my life. I wanted to thank you."

He looked her in the eye, and Marlene was surprised by what she saw in his: pain, confusion, some unbearable longing. She wondered briefly if he had a thing for her personally, or for what she represented. Then, in what appeared a conscious effort, he gathered up this potent mixture and stuffed it away behind his bland and phlegmatic daily mask.

"Well, you know, you're a nice person," he said with as much of a shrug as a prone person could manage. "You were decent to Dane just now. He's kind of boring about guns and all, and you kind of made it all right for him. Not many bosses give enough of a shit to do that."

They must have given him some dope, Marlene thought as she heard this uncharacteristically sensitive remark. There was clearly more depth in the man than she had imagined.

"And if I were a bitch, you would've let Stolz chop me up?"

"He wasn't after you. He was after the client," Wolfe said, and then, after a moment, "What do you think makes a guy like that tick? I mean, travel all that distance, twist his whole life into a knot, just to kill some tennis-playing girl."

"Oh, it's love, without a doubt," answered Marlene confidently. "In the wrong channel, needless to say, but still love. It's the only thing powerful enough to make people do stuff that crazy."

"Love? But he wanted to kill her."

"Oh, yeah, but what's weird about that? It's classic stranger stalking. Look, put yourself in Manfred's shoes. He's a simple guy, not much going for him, no talent, no outlet for what's got to be a passionate nature. One day he sees her, in a photograph or on TV. He's smitten. Now there's a channel for his love. Maybe it starts small—he's a regular fan, like ten thousand others. He collects pictures, souvenirs of Trude Speyr. But that's not enough. The channel gets deeper, starts to wear away at the banks of his regular life. He starts going to her tournaments. He gives up his job, his friends, assuming he had any, his family. His fantasy life gets richer. He's only really alive when he's thinking about her, looking at her. In his mind they're together. But of course, in real life she doesn't know he's alive. After a while this becomes intolerable. He begins writing to her, trying to get close to her physically. Maybe he invades her space, steals little things, makes demands. She's terrified, naturally, but he reads this as rejection. In his mind, she was always nice as pie. Now the river is raging. It washes away the rest of his life. He's got nothing left but her, and she rejects him, worse, ignores him. He's got to make her notice him, or die. So he attacks. When he's killing her, *then* maybe she'll notice him."

She was watching Wolfe while she spun this out. He was following it all with more intelligence than she had seen in him before, or maybe she hadn't looked in the right places.

"It sounds like the Music Lover," he said in a quiet voice.

"No," said Marlene with absolute confidence. "The Music

Lover's completely different. The Music Lover is a sadist named Vincent Robinson. What he wants is to control and torment his victim. No love involved. He's got some crazy sado-mas thing going with the target's sister too, which I'm not even going to try to figure out. Basically, he's *aping* a stranger stalker to scare the vic and get his rocks off. He *feeds* off her terror. The psychology is completely different, and my feeling is, if I catch this guy in the act and dance on his head for a while, he'll back off and find someone else to play with. That type of guy is relatively easy to chase away from a particular individual. True obsessives are nearly impossible to discourage."

"Can't be cured, huh?"

"Oh, I said discouraged, not cured," said Marlene. "I'm a firm believer that if you want to change your life, you can. Most people don't. Obsessives rarely do, sadists never do. In my experience anyway. You know, how many shrinks does it take to change a light bulb?. One, but the light bulb—"

"Has to want to change," supplied Wolfe.

They smiled at each other.

"You have a nice smile, Wolfe," said Marlene. "You ought to crank it up more."

He blushed, much to her surprise, and then she checked her watch and stood up. "I got to go out to Edie's. You're sure you want to come to work tomorrow?"

"Yeah, I'm fine. Really."

"Can I send you anything tonight? Your motivational tape?"

She grinned. He reddened again. "No, thanks. I'm fine."

"Okay. Thanks again for saving my life. Now you're responsible for me forever, lucky you." She leaned over and kissed him on the cheek, which she found remarkably warm and dry, like a hot roll.

Marlene arranged for her VW to be towed to a garage to have its alternator replaced, and had a quick meal with Harry at a local clam bar. Then he drove her to the Sag Harbor marina and its informal ferry.

She found Edie Wooten and the dog in the grand, nicely shabby, dark-beamed living room of the rose-colored house. Sweety rose from his puddle of drool and came to greet her.

"How did you get along?" Marlene asked Edie.

"Oh, great, super," said Edie. She was sitting in a bluish chintz Windsor chair by the fireplace, which was filled with a bouquet of dried flowers. On the round coffee table before her were spread piles of music manuscript. "He followed me around all day like a lamb. I tried to feed him little treats from lunch, but he wouldn't take them."

"He doesn't take food from anyone but me, except from his dish at home. It's part of being a guard dog."

Edie smiled and patted the dog's flank. "He doesn't seem much like a guard dog. He seems like a big lovable lunkhead."

"And you can't tell that you're a world-famous cellist except when you're playing the cello. You can only tell he's a guard dog when he's guarding."

Marlene sat down in the wing chair opposite and eased off her new sneakers, which pinched. Oddly, she felt entirely at home here; she decided it was the absolute unpretentiousness of the unassailably rich.

Marlene asked, "Anybody come by today?"

"No. They keep pretty much to themselves in Ginnie's house. I saw Ginnie at the pool today with Vince, though. We didn't talk." She seemed sad for a moment as she said this. "The pool is neutral territory. Technically, it belongs to me, but I let them use it as long as they behave themselves when I'm there."

"How did they seem?"

"Oh, you know—hungover, druggy. Look, I hate to be rude, but I have some arranging to do and some more practice . . ."

Marlene stood up. Yes, and you don't want me to pump you about your sister and her boyfriend. "That's okay, Edie. Can I call my daughter from here?"

Of course it was all right. There was a phone in her room.

Lucy answered, for which Marlene was grateful. She did not particularly want to speak to Karp at this juncture. Lucy had reached the age when speaking on the phone was a treat and not a burden. New York Telephone was considering a new substation for her and her gang of preadolescent girlfriends. She was full of chatter about the end-of-school party (for which her suspension had been mercifully rescinded), about which boys were particularly annoying and how they had been put in their place, the doings of the various little Chins, Woos, Mas, and Lees with whom she consorted, this mixed in with flashes from the front—there was a perpetual mob of newsies at the door, who had lately been joined by black pickets carrying signs about Daddy, and no, Daddy wasn't a racist, then on to her plans for the summer (she wished to attend Chinese day camp) and finally, "When are you coming home?"

"Soon, kid. When this business is over out here."

"Daddy said you're living on an island."

Marlene agreed that this was the case, and described the many glories of Wooten I.

"Can I come out there? With Daddy?"

"Well, Daddy's pretty busy now and so am I. I still have a couple of more days of guarding Ms. Speyr. The tournament isn't over yet."

"But after," Lucy pressed, "after, can I come out?"

"Sure, Luce. I'll have to ask Ms. Wooten, but I'm sure it'll be fine."

"Would you *really* ask her?"

"Really, really," said Marlene.

Rohbling now entered the endgame, each side with a single major piece left to play. For Waley this was Dr. Bannock, the psychiatrist who knew the defendant best. For Karp it was Dr. Perlsteiner. The two men could not have been more different in their mien or appearance. Erwin T. Bannock was six feet tall and athletic, in his early fifties, with a full head of dark hair nicely graying at the sides. He was dressed in a beautifully cut tweed suit, a three-piece, with a paisley tie and shiny brown cap-toe shoes, an outfit just casual enough to distinguish him from the lawyers, and suggesting (as he meant it to) a British gentleman who had through some quirk found himself at Johns Hopkins and decided it would be a lark to become a psychiatrist. He had a soft, reassuring voice, and the habit of pausing for three beats before answering a question, as if summoning the information afresh from some vast store kept behind that broad, tanned forehead.

Waley proposed to stipulate Dr. Bannock's sterling record in the interest of saving time. Karp refused, got a glare from the judge, ignored it. The jury had to hear about the doctor's education, his awards, his membership on the appropriate boards.

Bannock was an essential witness for the defense, not only because he knew the defendant best, but because he had been treating Rohbling throughout the period of the murders. He had met with him three days before Mrs. Hughes had been killed, and two days afterward.

Waley took his position before the jury and began slowly to wring from Dr. Bannock his expertise. Karp scribbled notes in the private shorthand he had developed in law school. With the part of his mind not thus engaged, he became conscious once more of his revulsion toward this sort of expert witness. Theoretically, and perhaps at some time actually, an expert witness was supposed to be a servant of the court, explaining complex matters to the jury. This largely remained the case with experts like city engineers and ballistics technicians. But psychiatrists were invariably mere pimps, their substantive knowledge hollow and entirely for sale.

Waley was taking his witness through the psychiatric treatment provided. Bannock said that Jonathan Rohbling was out of his mind, a paranoid schizophrenic, in fact, with multiple-personality disorder as the cherry on top. A schizophrenic family, the Rohblings: the tyrannical father, the neurasthenic mother, the powerful figure of Clarice Brown, loaded with love-hate ambiguity, combined to produce the psychotic break. Jonathan thought he was a black man named Jared Brown, the true son of Clarice, hence the makeup, hence the trips to Harlem to blend in with his people. Significance of the blue cloth suitcase? Ah, yes: Dr. Bannock had determined that Clarice Brown packed her things in just such a suitcase when the Rohblings had dismissed her.

Bannock also recounted his take on the actual murder. Jonathan wanders Harlem, lost and lonely, driven to find a warm maternal replacement for Clarice. He shows up at a church supper, befriends Jane Hughes. She invites him for coffee; she is lonely too, is attracted in a maternal way to the handsome, religious youth. Once in the apartment, he switches to his "true" self, the son of the beloved, hated, Clarice. He starts treating Mrs. Hughes as his mother, fantasizing, speaking to people who are not there. Mrs. Hughes becomes frightened, asks him to leave. He brandishes the suitcase, opens it, engages in a dialog with the mammy-mistress doll. Mrs. Hughes is terrified, shouts for help. He pushes her to the couch. He is in a panic. *Clarice is going to abandon him again!* He holds her down with the suitcase; without the suitcase she cannot leave. Symbolically, of course. In actuality, the cloth suitcase smothers her. Now, in his mind, she won't leave him. So lost in unreality is he that he has no idea that he has killed her. He continues with his pleasant conversation, picks up the famous ashtray, imagines that she gives it to him as a present. He puts it in his suitcase and leaves.

So, because of his suffering from a mental disease, paranoid schizophrenia, he didn't really *understand* that he had killed Mrs. Hughes? Waley's voice was filled with wonder at the power of science. No, came the answer. He had no idea what he was doing? No, he was dominated by his psychotic ideation. Or that what he was doing was wrong? No. In a sense, Jonathan Rohbling was not even there. Thank you, Doctor. Your witness.

"Dr. Bannock," Karp began, "you've testified that the defendant has a mental disease called paranoid schizophrenia, and that you were treating him for that disease. What was that treatment?"

"Well, with schizophrenia the best we can hope for is a reduction in the symptoms through the use of drugs. Halperidol is used, the thiothixines, and for more refractory cases, chlorpromazine and clozapine."

"And what was the defendant in fact taking at the time of the murder?"

Bannock pursed his lips, paused for his usual moment. "I can't say what he was actually taking. I had prescribed sixty milligrams daily dosage of Navane, which is a thiothixene antipsychotic."

"When you last saw him, before the murder, as you testified, on April seventeenth, had he been taking his medication?"

"I can't say for certain, obviously. He said he was."

"In your professional opinion, was he?"

A longer pause. "No."

"So, on April seventeenth, the defendant, your patient, was an unmedicated psychotic there in your office, was he?"

An impatient wrinkling of the noble brow. "It's not as cut and dried as that. He may still have had some drug in his system."

"I see," said Karp. "But to all *appearances* he was normal, he was not in blackface, he did not think he was this Jared, he was not having conversations with imaginary people, he showed none of the symptoms you have described, correct?"

"Yes."

"He presented the aspect of a drug-controlled schizophrenic then, this is what you're telling us, Doctor?"

"That is correct."

"You didn't think on the afternoon of April seventeenth that he could not comport his behavior to the requirements of the law, did you?"

A clever man, Dr. Bannock. He saw the trap closing and thought for a moment on how to avoid it. "It's not that simple. The underlying schizoid state does not—"

"Just answer the question, Doctor," said the judge.

"No, not at that time," said Bannock grumpily.

"Because if he had been manifestly incapable, you, as a good citizen and a doctor, would not have allowed him to roam the streets, isn't that so?"

"Of course."

"Thank you," said Karp. "So that was Wednesday. On Thursday, since, as we have heard, the defendant, in disguise, appeared in Harlem, met Mrs. Hughes at a church affair, be-friended her, made a date for Saturday, kept that date, and killed her, are you therefore saying, Doctor, that in three days he somehow lost that substantial capacity to comport his behavior to the requirements of law?"

"Yes, with schizophrenics we often see periods of near-normal-appearing behavior."

"I see. Now, then, you've testified that you also saw the defendant on the Monday *after* the murder for his regular appointment. The twenty-second of April. How did he seem then?"

"He appeared calm and normal."

"So are you telling us, then, that he appeared to have no mental disease on the seventeenth, trots out a mental disease on the eighteenth, kills Mrs. Hughes on the twentieth, still in the grip of a mental disease, and then appears normal in your office two days later?"

"No, not exactly. The disease is always present, but it can take different forms, mild or severe, depending on both internal and external factors. Some triggering event often causes the actual psychotic break, and the—and the aberrant behavior."

Karp heard the little stammer, observed some moisture on the noble brow, and was glad. "What triggering event, Doctor?"

"Well, the situation, the presence of a black woman of the correct age, middle-aged or older, the blue suitcase, the opportunity . . ."

"So the presence of all these would trigger this psychotic break?"

"Yes. Would tend to."

"Doctor, if you look around the courtroom, you will see several women of that description. There is even one on our jury. The blue suitcase is right here. Yet Mr. Rohbling is sitting calmly in his seat. How do you explain that?"

"The situation, I mean here, a courtroom, is not appropriate for the situation in which we would see the psychosis actually evinced."

"Do you mean that if he rose from his seat, grabbed the blue suitcase, and tried to smother Mrs. Finney there in the jury box, the court officers would stop him?"

"Yes, but what I meant was that a certain situation of intimacy is necessary to trigger the response."

"Intimacy, I see. You mean, he has to be alone in an apart-

292 / *Robert K. Tanenbaum*

ment, say, with a helpless woman before he becomes incapable of comporting his conduct to the requirements of the law."

"Well, in effect, that is the case."

"In simple terms, he only goes crazy and kills when he can get away with it, is that what you're saying?"

"That is the effect, but in the event he is not thinking in those terms. He—"

"Thank you. How terrifically convenient for Mr. Rohbling! He only becomes an insane killer when he can escape the consequences of his act."

"Objection! Argumentative. Not a question."

"Sustained. Jury will disregard."

"Doctor," Karp resumed quickly, "your testimony—this business about Jared, and Clarice, and Mr. Rohbling's mental states—is entirely based on what Mr. Rohbling has told you, isn't that true?"

"Yes."

"You haven't been able to look into his head, say, with modern instruments of any kind, or do any definitive blood or tissue tests that would independently establish this diagnosis of paranoid schizophrenia?"

"No."

"Why not, sir?"

"Because there are no such tests. The indicia of the disease are straightforward, as I've testified. The flatness of affect, the retreat into hallucinatory fantasies, the inability to form normal social bonds, are diagnostic for this disease."

"Yes, thank you, Doctor. You're a scientific man, do you know what Occam's razor is?"

This caught the witness off guard, as it was meant to. He frowned and said, "In a general way. I believe it's the principle that says that if you want to explain something, some experimental result, then the simplest explanation, the one making the fewest assumptions, is the one likely to be true."

"Yes, very good, that's my understanding exactly," said Karp, beaming. "So, Doctor, since we have on one hand an elaborate set of assumptions about some mental disease, based on another set of assumptions of how this disease was generated during the defendant's youth, based on the defendant's word alone, with no independent verification, and on the other hand we have the alternate possibility that the defendant is spinning a line of malarkey to escape punishment, wouldn't Occam's razor practically force us to believe that you are being fooled?"

Karp was rewarded by the flush that blossomed on the witness's cheeks. "Absolutely not!" he declared.

"Pray tell, why not, sir?" said Karp gently, as to a child.

"Because I'm a psychiatrist. I've had years of training to distinguish malingerers from genuine sufferers, in addition to nearly twenty years of experience with all types of mental disease. I know what I'm talking about!"

"Do you? Tell me, Doctor, how many of your patients, in your whole career, have been paranoid psychotic murderers?"

The witness was startled by the question. His mouth opened but nothing came out.

"Counting them up, are you?" put in Karp.

"Your Honor, I protest this badgering," cried Waley.

"Mr. Karp, have a care!" growled Judge Peoples.

Karp voiced an apology and waited.

Bannock cleared his throat. "Mr. Rohbling is the only one."

"The *only one!*" exclaimed Karp in mock amazement. "Do you tell us, sir, that the defendant is the *only* patient you have ever had that was facing a charge of murder and might have a powerful reason to prevaricate as to his symptoms?"

"Yes, but that's—"

"Then, isn't it true," said Karp, lowering the pitch and lifting the volume of his voice so as to sound as much like the Lord of Hosts as possible, "that your testimony as to the defendant's so-called disease, and his ability or inability to comport his conduct to the requirements of the law, is worth nothing? Zero?"

"No, no, my experience can be generalized to . . . the present case and, of course, I'm familiar with the literature—"

"The literature, I see," said Karp, his tone contemptuous. "I have no further questions for this witness."

Naturally, Waley rose for redirect, to repair the damage Karp had done to his star. Once again the jury was treated to a look inside Jonathan Rohbling's skull, courtesy of Dr. Bannock. The on-again, off-again nature of his disease was explained as entirely consistent with paranoid schizophrenia. Mr. Rohbling was not going to attack a member of the jury because he was taking antipsychotic drugs. When he was taking these drugs, he was free of the violent impulses that characterized his disease. The drugs were uncertain in their influence, were they not? Of course. They affected different people differently. They even affected the same people differently at different times. Therefore, it was perfectly consistent with science that Mr. Rohbling could be a good little boy on a Thursday and a monster on Friday and a good little boy the following Monday. Of course, and this was delivered with a dose of psycho-speak equivalent to six hundred milligrams of Thorazine; the jury was stunned, gaping, *psyched.*

Nevertheless, Karp came right back on re-cross. Doctor, you contend that the defendant was not under the influence of his medication when he committed the murder? He was not. But he was drugged at your appointment before and your appointment afterward? Probably. Then a colloquy on the pharmacology of Navane, or thiothixine, its effects, the absurdity of assuming that its effects could be turned on and off like a lightbulb over the course of a long weekend. Karp had done his homework, or Collins had. He waved research reports. He quoted. Then the finale: Doctor, do you know of a single other case, *in the literature,* where a paranoid schizophrenic committed a violent act attributable to his disease and then appeared normal to a psychiatrist three days before and two days after that act? Answer the question. The answer was no. Thus Karp ran out the clock, which was, at least in part, the point. The judge halted the proceedings at five-thirty, which meant that Karp could start with a fresh jury when he presented his rebuttal witness the following day.

Outside the courtroom, in the hallway, a roped corridor had been set up, leading from the door to the D.A.'s private wing of the building, an aisle now manned, at the D.A.'s express order, by four burly court officers and a group of gigantic cops from the Tacticals, beyond which seethed the yowling press corps, down which Karp strode like the Prince of Wales.

TWENTY

M arlene awakened to birdsong and the sweet voice of the cello. She lay in bed for a few minutes listening, cozy within the bedclothes (an actual featherbed, the first she had ever slept in) watching gray-blue light streak the patterned wallpaper. The room was of a comfortable smallness, as a bedroom should be, and full of old, slightly shabby, lovely things—real lace curtains, a wardrobe inlaid with flowers and cupids, the brass bedstead on which she lay. She mused, as often before, on the insoluble mystery of family life, on how this marvelous environment, so secure, so tasteful, could have produced an Edie and a Ginnie Wooten. The cello swelled to a peak, stopped in midphrase, and after a brief pause, began again from the beginning of the movement, the second of Schubert's *Rosamunde* quartet.

With a sigh Marlene heaved out of bed, washed, dressed, armed herself, and went down to the kitchen, where Bridget Marney supplied her with egg, toast, excellent coffee, and conversation about geraniums and dogs. Ms. Wooten was not to be disturbed in the mornings: the iron law of Wooten Island, to which no conceivable danger might make an exception. Marlene fed Sweety his two pounds of kibble, walked him, and put him on guard. Mr. Marney, a male version of his wife (pleasant, sixties, weather-worn), arrived just as Marlene was finishing her second cup, and led her to the boathouse, in whose damp shade lay a half dozen craft: a couple of Boston Whalers with fifty-horse outboards, a slim wooden rowing boat, a dory with a center-mounted diesel, a racy wooden speedboat, and a forty-foot Chris-Craft in mahogany, circa 1925. They took the speedboat.

Twenty minutes later, Marlene was at the marina dock. She waited, smoked a cigarette, watched the faint breeze pimple the still water of Sag Harbor. A horn sounded. To Marlene's surprise, it was not Harry come to pick her up but Wolfe.

"I'm surprised to see you," she said as they drove off. "Are you okay?"

"Fine. Good," he said in a tone that did not encourage exploration. He seemed to regret their brief intimacy in the hospital. Clearly, he was one of those men who wish not to think that they can ever be anything but big, strong, and ready for action. As they approached the tennis club, Wolfe said, "Harry wants me to go with the tour. The client—"

Marlene felt a quick stir of irritation, which she stifled. Edie hadn't mentioned Wolfe, and despite what Marlene had told her husband, she felt herself entirely capable of guarding Wooten by herself. She grunted assent and got out of the car.

A dull day on the courts passed. There were no copycat attacks. In the tournament, Trude Speyr came in second to a Yugoslav woman who had not been threatened with mutilation and death, which Marlene thought not surprising. Harry was busy arranging the rest of the tour, which Wolfe would join as chief bodyguard—next stop, Short Hills, New Jersey. Marlene made herself at home in Mort Griffin's office and got Sym on the phone to check messages and then spoke to Tranh, who seemed to be holding everything together rather better than Marlene herself did when she was there. After listening to his report, Marlene said, "Sounds great, Vinh, you're a national treasure. Harry will be back late today to take over. Anything else?"

"No, I do not believe so. I was somewhat surprised to see that the machine gun was missing from its place. I had thought that you did not approve of such weapons."

"I don't. When did you notice it was missing?"

"These past few days. Since you left for the tennis match."

"Shit! Dane probably swiped it back. I'll talk to him."

Marlene next called the garage, where a man told her that it was not merely the alternator that had gone but the coil and a considerable, but yet to be tallied, number of spark plug wires, and did she really want to put that kind of money into the car. She did.

Then she called her loft, where she spoke to Posie, who wrenched at her heart with blandly told tales of the twins' narrow escapes from poisoning, scorching, sharp instruments, and other immolation, and held them each up to the phone so that they could whine, babble, and fret into the instrument, and scarify further their mother's heart. Lucy was, in comparison, an oasis of good sense. She discounted heavily the tales of disaster, said everything was fine, that meals were regular, the loft was reasonably neat, don't worry, and can I still come out to the island when you're finished guarding?

"I think it'll be okay, Luce, but we have to check with Ms. Wooten."

"Is there swimming?"

"I think there's a pool."

"Oh, great! I'll bring my red Speedo."

And more in that vein, until she signed off and Karp came on.

"Disaster upon disaster, I hear," said Marlene.

"Exaggeration," said Karp lightly. "We hardly know you're gone."

"I believe it. How's the trial?"

"Trying," said Karp.

"I see. You going to win?"

"Doubtful. I'm pushing not to lose. What's happening with Dr. Dope out there?"

"Hasn't made a move yet. I may have to stir him up a little."

A pause. "That sounds like a good plan, Marlene," said Karp in a tight voice. Spiky, spiky. They quickly ended the call, by mutual agreement.

Well, that was depressing enough, thought Marlene. My sons are being raised by a hippie slut victim, my marriage seems to be in the toilet, my daughter . . . well, my daughter seems to be moving into the role of Family Sane Person. Maybe I should ask her advice. These and other increasingly maudlin and self-pitying fancies occupied her as she twirled back and forth in Griffin's expensive leather swivel chair, and toyed with her split ends, until her reverie was interrupted by the entrance of her partner.

"I was looking for you. They're gone," said Harry.

Marlene returned to good-little-soldier mode. "The star?"

"The star, the Germans, and Wolfe. I'm going back to the city. You got your car back?"

Marlene explained about the VW.

"You could rent one, no, here's a better idea. You could use Wolfe's. Ask the kid for the keys."

Marlene did so. Wolfe's car was immaculately kept, smooth-running, and it had that terrific stereo. Marlene chose *Greatest Hits of the '70s* for the drive back to Sag Harbor. "Best of My Love" by the Emotions; "I'm Not in Love" by 10cc; "Love Will Keep Us Together" by the Captain and Tenille. Who could forget them! Marlene was slightly hoarse, but with a mood much improved, by the time she pulled into the marina. There she found Mr. Marney loading groceries and propane tanks into the Wooten speedboat, a happy accident. While he worked, she ran to a tourist shop near the marina and bought a black nylon tank suit (size five), rubber zoris, a cheap straw hat, and a straw carry-all. It was starting to turn hot, and Marlene thought she would spend the day by the pool.

The body still drew looks, Marlene found. When she walked out onto the pool deck at Wooten's Island, she was rewarded by a rustle of interested movement among the group of oiled degenerates gathered around the shallow end, the kind of stir you see among crocodiles when a gazelle comes down to drink. Marlene noted this, and noted also the presence of Ginnie Wooten and Vincent Robinson. The others were typical rich trash, all slim, smooth, tanned, and damned. She settled her things on a wooden lounger near the deep end, walked to the diving board, and dived in.

The air was hot, the water delightfully cool. Marlene did three easy lengths and then emerged, dripping, her suit a glistening second skin. It had, naturally, worked its way up between her buttocks, but she did not bother with the traditional coming-out-of-pool finger flick, but left them attractively in view as she walked back to her lounger. She spread a towel, lay down, put on her sunglasses, and waited. In five minutes, she heard the lounger next to hers creak and a voice say, "I came over to see if you needed help getting your ass back into your suit."

"No, thank you," said Marlene, recognizing the voice. "We meet again, Doctor."

"A line from every horror movie," said Robinson happily. "I should tell you that displays of forbidden flesh are frowned on at this pool. Little Edie insists on it; otherwise, we would dispense with suits altogether. Also, no fucking in the pool during daylight hours. Those are the rules."

"Thank you, Doctor. I stand corrected."

"Would you like to fuck me in the pool tonight?"

"No, Doctor, I'm working," said Marlene.

"Oh, right. Little Edie's stalker. How tragic for her! Well, then, for the nonce I'll have to content myself with studying your remarkably generous pubic bush. Is that your Italian heritage, I wonder?"

"Sicilian. I wouldn't be surprised."

He laughed. "Meanwhile, what about a drink?"

"Is there a bar?"

"Indeed there is. Fully stocked, right there under the awning by the cabanas. What can I get you?"

"You can get me a tray on which there is a bucket of ice, a sealed bottle of tonic, a sealed bottle of Gilbey's, a lime, a little knife, and a glass."

Robinson laughed again. "Oho! She's afraid of being drugged, is she? Drugged and dragged into the shrubbery for obscene delights. That's your husband's influence, I imagine."

One of the disadvantages of having only one eye is that you can't check things out from the corner of your blind side. Marlene shifted her position so that she could look Robinson in the face as she said, "Yes, he thinks you murdered your nurse with drugs."

Robinson smiled delightedly, as if she had just told him she liked his eyes. "Yes, I know he does. He had that nigger cop following me around half the winter. I suppose I should be insulted. I mean, really, the least he could've done is send a white man. I saw him on television recently, your hubby, pounding some little jig. I almost warmed toward him. He really is quite a gigantic Jew, odd, because we always say, 'little Jew,' don't we. Does he have an absolutely gigantic willy?"

"Gigantic enough," said Marlene. "*Did* you kill your nurse?"

"Probably. She was certainly growing tedious enough to deserve it. One thing I can't abide is a tedious woman. Like little Edie, for example. Oh, I'm forgetting our drinks . . . !" Robinson lifted his arm and snapped his fingers twice.

To Marlene's surprise, Ginnie Wooten rose from among the group at the shallow end and trotted over to them, wobbling slightly on heeled sandals. She was wearing a red thong bikini on her skeletal body. Marlene noticed that she kept her eyes down while Robinson gave his order, and that there were two fine chains running from her crotch down each leg to ankle cuffs.

"A serviceable slave, actually," said Robinson as she walked away to the bar. "Of course, she's not a real slave, so one's, let us say, palette of outrages is limited, but one mustn't complain. I noticed you looking at her little chains. They go up to studs embedded in the labia. A constant reminder and also, of course, the slight, continual sexual irritation. Very effective in producing the proper attitude."

Marlene watched his face, which she still found attractive, although now in a horrifying way, like the sick attraction of subway tracks or a loaded gun. She had never seen an expression like his on a human face before: the eyes avid, bright, intelligent, utterly without any recognizable human emotion. It was like looking at a mantis. His mouth was fixed in a meaningless smile. Marlene found it hard to imagine why, when he walked down a street, people didn't spontaneously drop what they were doing and tear him to pieces.

"Why did you become a physician, Dr. Robinson?" she asked spontaneously.

"For the drugs, of course," he threw back. "And the power. The only power that means anything is power over the human body, preferably one body at a time, and we doctors have that par excellence."

"So you didn't take the Hippocratic oath?"

Robinson giggled. "No. Sadly, I was ill that day."

Ginnie came back with a tray containing the media for making gin and tonics and placed it slowly, drugged-careful, on a small folding table. As she bent over, Robinson said something into her ear. She smiled, turned her burnt eyes briefly on Marlene, and walked off.

"I just told her that I was thinking of us all going over to the big house tonight and tying you up and letting her use her manicure set on you. Snip, snip. Make us a little drinkie there, would you?"

"No," said Marlene equably. "And I think I'll pass on mine too."

"Oh, I hurt your feelings! I'm always doing that, I don't know why. And we should be friends, you know. We're very much alike."

"You think so."

"I do. I've been looking into your career. Both of us make our own rules, both of us do just as we please, the only difference being that you're a hypocrite, and feel obliged to justify your actions—how many people have you killed?—as being in service of some notional higher good, whereas I do what I like merely because it pleases me. The will is all."

"The Marquis de Sade," said Marlene.

"Exactly! If you let yourself go, I think you could be one of his more complete and proficient devotees."

"But he ended up in jail, didn't he? As will you."

"Oh, really? And who is going to put me there? Your big jewboy?"

"Yeah, as a matter of fact. One thing I've learned, Doctor, in my years of dealing with scumbags, is that they are all *au fond*, whatever their pretensions, mere assholes. They all make mistakes, they all get caught, if not for one thing, then for the next, and so will you. You'll love Attica, by the way, especially once the word about your racial attitudes hits the cell blocks."

Robinson gave her his boy-pulling-wings-off-flies grin. "Why, I think you really believe that! What a quaint idea: crime does not pay. But nothing pays better. Haven't you heard that every great fortune was founded on a crime? A case in point is young Rohbling. Do you really imagine that he'll spend a single day in jail? Of course, to be fair, I'm not nearly as well fixed as the Rohblings, but I intend to change that quite soon."

"Really? How?"

He laughed and said in a fake whisper, "No, that's a secret. Ginnie knows. Why don't you ask her? You're such a favorite of hers."

Suddenly, Marlene was overcome by a boredom so oppressive that it seemed to darken the sun. She had met more than her share of bad guys, and they were universally bores. The violent criminal, almost by definition, is grotesquely self-involved, but Robinson seemed to her to occupy a class of his own. Talking to him was like watching a bad movie as a goof, fascinating in its awfulness for a while, until you realized that there were more rewarding things you could be doing.

She stood up abruptly, stripped her towel off the lounger, and thrust it into her straw bag.

"Going somewhere?" Robinson asked, standing as well.

"Yes, away from you."

"But why? I thought we were having such a nice conversation."

"No, you didn't. You were annoying me and annoying your girlfriend by talking to me, and loving it because you're a sadistic little shithead."

Robinson's smile grew tighter. He reached out and grabbed Marlene's left wrist. He said, in what was meant to be a commanding voice, "Sit down, you stupid bitch!"

Marlene sighed and instead of pulling away from him, as he

had expected, went toward him, jamming his calves up against the lounger frame. Then she pulled the .45 out of the straw bag and jammed it hard into his belly.

"How crude," he said disdainfully, releasing her. She took the gun away from his belly and then, almost without willing it, and not pausing to justify it through the Principle of Double Effect, she flicked her wrist and snapped the muzzle of the weapon into his groin, and when he flinched, she dropped her shoulder and shoved him backward over the lounger. His head knocked against the fieldstone terrace with a satisfying coconut sound. She saw the look on his face. Pain, rage, but also triumph. As she walked away, she felt sick at heart.

"Dr. Perlsteiner," said Karp, facing his first and only rebuttal witness, "could you tell us something of your background and qualifications?" This was why he had declined the stipulation of expert qualifications; he loved this part.

Perlsteiner said, "I received my medical education at the University of Heidelberg in Germany, and then did postgraduate work at various hospitals in Berlin, and then I went to Vienna to be certified as a psychoanalyst."

"And who was your teacher in Vienna?"

"Sigmund Freud."

As always, a stir went through the courtroom. Even the most benighted recognized the magic name. In the pissing contest among shrinks that made up an insanity defense trial, this was the unmatchable squirt.

Karp took him through the rest of his résumé: private practice in Berlin, escape from the Nazis, capture in France, the concentration camp, the new life in America, long service as a forensic psychiatrist at Bellevue. Then:

"Have you examined the defendant, and the record of his behavior preceding and after the murder in question?"

"I have."

"As a result of this examination, did you reach any conclusions as to whether Jonathan Rohbling, at the time of the murder of

Jane Hughes, lacked substantial capacity to comport his behavior to the requirements of the law, by reason of mental disease or defect."

"Yes, I did."

"And what were they?"

"I concluded that he did not lack that capacity. He knew what he was doing and that it was wrong."

This was the formal rebuttal, what the People had to show beyond a reasonable doubt. Karp paused for a moment to let it sink in.

"Doctor, tell us, on what do you base this conclusion?" asked Karp, and off they went. Perlsteiner had a good courtroom voice, carrying but not harsh, and with a slight accent that recalled, for the older jurors, Albert Einstein and the actors hired to play distinguished scientists in the movies. Rohbling, he concluded, although by no means playing with a full deck, was not suffering from schizophrenia, paranoid or otherwise. How could he tell?

"By his competence," answered Perlsteiner. "I will explain. Schizophrenia exhibits in many forms. It is a labile disease, and in fact, we often now speak of 'the schizophrenias,' plural, do you see? But it is a true disease of the mind, just like polio is a disease of the motor nerves. If you suffer from schizophrenia, you can't use your mind properly, just like, if you have polio, for example, you can't use your legs. So, when I hear of a person who dresses himself up, who prepares his clothes, his wig, his makeup, just so, who travels on the subway, to what is an alien culture, for him, and passes himself off successfully as a member of that culture, who befriends a respectable elderly woman, who makes his escape after committing a crime, who eludes the police for some time, who recalls a psychiatric appointment and attends it, and presents a facade of normality strong enough to deceive a psychiatrist, then I say to you, whatever this man is suffering from, it is *not* schizophrenia. Schizophrenics are, typically, nearly helpless people."

"And what in your opinion is Mr. Rohbling suffering from?"

"Well, he is compulsive—obsessive-compulsive syndrome, to

be technical. Infantile, narcissistic. He feels bad about himself, and why not? He's a young man, he has no discipline, he doesn't work, he doesn't go to school. His father has contempt for him, ignores him." Perlsteiner shrugged. "It makes him feel better, disguising himself. Now he is in control."

"And why, in your opinion, did he kill Jane Hughes?"

"Oh, impossible to say. I would not even guess at the psychology."

Karp accepted this as a welcome departure from Dr. Braddock's encyclopedic understanding of Rohbling's motivation, and moved on to a point-by-point refutation of the defense's psychiatric testimony, from which it emerged that Dr. Perlsteiner (and by extension, Dr. Freud) did not think much of modern American psychiatry. The business about the disease switching on just when it was convenient—nonsense! The disease was variable, true, but once florescent, it did not wane back to normality for short periods in the way proposed. Never. He deplored especially the tendency to medicalize every nasty character trait, and to attribute antisocial acts to dark compulsions, traceable, of course, to childhood trauma. Thank you, no further questions.

Waley's cross-examination was brief. One of the signs of a great cross-examiner is knowing when not to do it, as here. Perlsteiner was a strong witness and a sympathetic one. To try to grind him down would invite unwanted comparisons with the Gestapo. So Waley took only a few artistic cuts. Dr. P. was how old? Seventy-four. Not on the American Board of Psychiatry? Not a member of the New York Psychiatric Institute? No promotions in the past fifteen years? Few publications? Why was that, Doctor? Waley drew a brief sketch of a distinguished doctor who might have been great *once* but was clearly past it, out of step with modern psychiatry. Karp thought it was the right move for Waley; it was what he himself would have done. How much the jury would discount Perlsteiner's testimony and how much they would rely on the presence, wit, and character of the dueling shamans, a contest in which Karp thought Perlsteiner was unbeatable, was at present unknown, but Karp thought, from his observation of the jurors, that the good guys had picked up a few points. Perlsteiner stepped off the stand. The evidentiary phase of *People* v. *Rohbling* was finished.

Karp now required a police escort to carry him home. A blue-and-white preceded his usual unmarked car to the Crosby Street loft, and the two cops in it made a lane through the pickets and news crews to the door of the newly installed elevator. He summoned it with a key and rode up, carrying the usual take-out dinner, tonight a bucket o'chicken.

In the loft, gloom prevailed. No one had been in or out for days. The twins were cranky. Zak had a rash, Zik some undefined ailment inclining him to clingy weeping. Posie was keeping them minimally cleaned and fed, but the rest of the loft was starting to resemble the East Village crash pad that was her natural habitat. A burnt pot sat on the stove, and the kitchen was full of its rank scent. Lucy was glum. Her efforts to maintain some vestige of normal home life—setting the table, making a crude salad—broke Karp's heart.

"Is this going to be over soon, Daddy?" she said in a small voice. She had eaten enough to maintain a starling, and pushed her plate away.

"Yeah, real soon, baby," he said. "I'm sorry about all this."

"I miss Mommy."

"Me too."

She sighed. "I need a break. This is just like jail."

Marlene came back from the pool and showered and washed her hair, although the soap did not reach where she really felt dirty. She put on a thick terry-cloth robe she found hanging on a hook, wrapped a towel around her head, put zoris on her feet, grabbed her straw bag, and went downstairs.

She sat in an Adirondack chair on the lawn in front of the house. She lit a cigarette, but crushed it after a few puffs. She felt full enough of toxins. The dog came trotting out from the back of the house, and came up to her and placed his massive head on her lap, looking up at her worshipfully. Marlene stroked the dog's head and closed her eyes. She tried to remember St.

Teresa's famous chapter on resistance to evil, but the words of the saint were useless to her, too far away in time and situation. Marlene was not a contemplative nun. She wished devoutly for a lap on which she could place her own head and be stroked and told that everything was all right. She missed her family. She wept briefly, and then let her mind go empty. Bees buzzed, sparrows twittered in the rafters, a gull called, the wind came soughing through the grass and the pines off the shining Sound. In the house, the cello began to play, something elegant, classical, full of confidence in the ultimate order of the universe, Haydn perhaps, or Boccherini. Music, nature, her peculiar brand of religion: these performed their usual blessings. Marlene took the towel from her head and let the breeze dry her hair. She slept for little over an hour.

Later, dressed, she ran up and down the rough beach with Sweety, until she was tired and hungry. Meals at the big house were taken, democratically and *en famille*, in the huge tiled kitchen with the Markeys. Tonight: tomato soup, crab salad, and cold asparagus, ice cream—WASPy, bland, but nourishing food. Neither Marlene nor Edie had much to say, and table talk was dominated by domestic trivia and commentary on food and weather. During the meal they heard the sound of a heavy engine starting up away in the direction of the boathouse.

"That'll be Ginnie and her friends with *Bonito*," said Markey. "She told me to get it ready. Some kind of party. Said she'd be gone most of the night and not to lock the boathouse."

Marlene recalled that *Bonito* was the big yacht and became conscious of a mild relaxation around the table, which she shared, provisionally, if she assumed Robinson was off the island for the night. Conversation became lighter, Marlene trotted out some horror stories from her speckled past that seemed amusing now, and Edie described the foibles of a number of famous people. After dinner, Edie spent a good hour on the phone, speaking with her agent and people in various world capitals. Marlene phoned home and spoke to Posie and Lucy. Daddy was taking a nap, should we wake him up? No, honey, let him sleep. I'm coming out to see you, okay, Mom? Sure, honey, pretty soon.

Marlene and Edie chatted after dinner, both politely avoiding the big subject. Marlene mentioned Lucy and how much the child wished to see a house on an island, and Edie extended an invitation, at some vague date in the future, when the current unpleasantness had (presumably) been resolved. At ten-thirty, Edie went off to bed. Marlene prowled around the immediate grounds with Sweety and found all quiet.

She woke from her usual light sleep in the small hours to a creaking, scraping sound. Steps? She waited, but there were no further noises. She could hear the dog snuffling and pacing the hallway, as she knew he did several times in the night. He was clearly not concerned, and therefore there was no one in the house who should not be. She drifted back to sleep.

Just after dawn she was jerked awake by a shrill cry. She raced into Edie Wooten's bedroom, where she found her client, sitting in bed, her face white as the lined counterpane, staring at the foot of the bed, on which lay a single dark red rose. The note attached to it read, "Soon."

TWENTY-ONE

Karp listened to Lionel Waley's closing statement for the defense in *Rohbling* rather as a great operatic tenor might listen to another one reaching for the high note and hitting it just right—that is, with a mixture of admiration and bile. The state of New York favors those who represent it by providing that the closing arguments for the defense precede those of the prosecution, and there is no rebuttal allowed. Karp would have the last word. Waley had therefore not only to make his own argument but to predict what language Karp would use and discount it in advance. Which he was doing, or trying to. Karp took notes, and adjusted in his impossibly crowded brain the phrases and sequence of presentation of his own closing so as to counter these preemptive strikes. Waley was saying, in effect, "The prosecution will say blah-blah, but you know that wah-wah is true." Karp would have to do the opposite, but retrospectively. This is one reason why the closing arguments in major criminal trials, although written-out and outlined, are not memorized speeches but are given extempore. Another is that as he speaks, the lawyer is reading the jury, seeing what cuts sharply, what moves the listening faces, and what does not.

Waley was expatiating on the law as it applied to the case and interpreting, in a way favorable to his client's cause, the charge that the judge would give to the jury when the closings were finished. He could do this because jury instructions in criminal trials are almost entirely boiler-plate exercises, pinched by actual statute and acres of precedents, besides which, Judge Peoples' instructions were notable for balance and fairness.

"The law assumes competence, it assumes rationality," Waley was saying, "but it allows for tragic cases where rationality and competence do not exist. A criminal act requires a criminal actor, that is, someone who understood what the law required and made a conscious and knowing decision to break it. It is the burden of the prosecution to show beyond a reasonable doubt, ladies and gentlemen, beyond a reasonable doubt, that Jonathan Rohbling, at the moment of committing the crime with which he is charged, *did not lack* substantial incapacity to comport his conduct to the requirements of law. In simple language, it is for you, the jury, to decide on the basis of the evidence you have heard whether there is a reasonable doubt that Jonathan Rohbling was in his right mind on the evening of April twentieth in Jane Hughes's apartment. If you have such a doubt that because of his mental disease he did not know what he was doing, or that it was wrong, then you must find him not guilty by reason of insanity."

Karp made a note. Not that great, Lionel, he thought, all those negative constructions are confusing. But he knew that in the course of his speech Waley would repeat that essential argument many times, with many illustrations. He would try to demonstrate that the testimony of his shrinks *constituted* reasonable doubt. If a trio of top psychiatrists testify the guy's crazy, well, then . . .

The argument was standard and specious, and Waley was presenting it as well as Karp had ever heard it done. He wondered briefly if Waley really believed that Rohbling was insane under the law, and decided that he did. That was his art, his genius as a defense attorney: he could manipulate his beliefs to suit his case. He *was* stricken by the tragedy of J. Rohbling, madman, and if he could make the jury believe it along with him, he had won. Karp took notes, listened, waited. It would be some hours yet before his last licks.

"He must have tossed it in," Marlene was saying, "from that window. He climbed up the ivy, your window was open, and he flipped it in. You're on the west side of the house and the wind was from the east—it still is—"

"I thought the dog was supposed to stop anyone from getting in," Edie Wooten protested. She had stopped crying, but her eyes were still moist and red. She was hunched in bed like a kid with the chicken pox, dabbing her face with tissues and then tearing them into shreds.

"Nobody got into the house, Edie, that's what I'm trying to tell you. If he had tried to open the window enough to climb in, the dog would've heard him. As it was, I heard something in the night and so did Sweety. He must have tossed the rose and note and run off."

"So what do we do now?"

"Same as before, only now I think we'll put Sweety in your room at night."

"You think he'll come back?" She bit her lip, hands to face, classic terror.

"Of course. He has to. He's obsessed. And we'll get him."

"So . . . what? I'm the *bait*?"

"Afraid so. Unless you want to spend your life running, this is it."

Edie wailed and pulled the covers over her head.

Marlene left her then and walked around the house with Sweety. She checked the ground under Edie's window, but found little disturbance. Robinson must have been particularly careful, or maybe he had sent Ginnie.

In the boathouse, she saw that *Bonito*, the big Chris-Craft, was in its berth, looking tatty, with lines tangled and bottles and articles of clothing strewn on its decks. There was a noise from below decks. Sweety gave his warning growl.

A young man Marlene did not recognize staggered out of the main cabin hatchway. He was wearing nothing but white tennis shorts and a gold razor blade on a chain around his neck. His face, tanned and handsome though it was, showed the signs of a bad hangover. He stared at Marlene and her dog blankly for a moment, then groaned and said, "Jesus shit! Where the hell *is* everybody?"

"Probably back at Ginnie's house?" Marlene offered.

"Oh, Ginnie! She took off with Vince. Hell if I know where she is." He blinked at her. "Do I know you?"

"I don't think so."

"I didn't fuck you last night, did I? No, it was somebody . . . you got anything on you? Uppers? No? Coke? Fuck! I am *fucked up*! Started in Danceteria, somebody said, Ginnie Woo's on a fucking boat, now where am I? Some place on the Island. These aren't my shorts."

"Vince knows how to throw a party, hey?" said Marlene.

"Oh, fuck, lady! The guy is out of his mind. I say that, *I'm* fucking out of my mind and I'm my *father* compared to Vince. Last Thanksgiving? Twenty of us, private seven-two-seven, Marrakesh. Jesus shit! Four days. Fucking Arabs never saw anything like it."

"On Thanksgiving I thought he would've taken you to Turkey, not Morocco."

"Turkey? What the fuck's in Turkey? Nah, forget it! Fuckin' Turks're real down on fun, man . . . Christ, you got any aspirin, Empirin, Darvon . . . shit! You don't got shit."

The man staggered back below. Marlene left the boathouse and went around to the dock. She wondered where Robinson and Ginnie had taken off to last night, and there was something else in what the jerk had said that disturbed her, but she couldn't quite locate the itch. She went back to the house.

Waley's closing statement took up the whole morning, and at the end of which only the most wide-awake observer would have known who the victim was in the case. For Waley the "real" victim was clearly the defendant. Unloved. Abused. Insane. Jane Hughes might just as well have been hit by a runaway truck. Waley ended with an impassioned rendition of his original theme: don't compound this tragedy by punishing a young man who needs medical help.

Karp went on in the afternoon. He fixed with his eye a juror in the first row, Mr. Domingo Corton, welding-machine operator, fifty-four, whom Karp had noticed nodding in agreement during Waley's performance. He would speak like this directly to each juror in turn, giving each one that portion of his argument he thought would tell the most, based on his assessment of that juror's personality and the extent to which he thought they favored either side.

"Ladies and gentlemen of the jury, this case is not about the sad life and personal troubles of Jonathan Rohbling. This case is about the brutal murder of Mrs. Jane Hughes, the beloved mother of five children, the grandmother of seven. You have heard a great deal of testimony from distinguished psychiatrists, which Mr. Waley has just ably recalled for you, as to the defendant's mental state at various times in his life. This testimony may be interesting or not, but it is important that you realize that it is *not* the critical evidence in this case. Judge Peoples will instruct you that you must convict Mr. Rohbling of murder unless you find that owing to a mental disease or defect he was substantially incapable of comporting his conduct to the requirements of the law. That's a fancy way of saying that you have to find that when he killed Jane Hughes, he did not know what he was doing or that it was wrong. How would we know this, what the defendant's mind was like at the moment when he killed Mrs. Hughes? Well, with all due respect to the psychiatric profession, no test or method has ever been devised that will tell you what is in someone else's head at a particular time. It is beyond the ability of science."

Mr. Corton was now nodding well enough for Karp too. He shifted his gaze to Mrs. Bertha Finney, sixty-four, retired postal worker, the jury's lone female black elder.

"So how *do* we tell? Members of the jury, this is no great mystery requiring years of graduate school, medical school. You know from your own lives that the major evidence indicating mental state is behavior—facial expression, speech, both tone and content, and action. We don't need a psychiatrist to tell us if a loved one is upset or our boss is angry. Human society *depends* on our native ability to determine what is going on inside a person from the way they behave. Now, sure, there are frauds, there are cheats, there are con men in the world, but these people also depend on our ability to read mental states from behavior—they are skilled at *imitating* such behavior so as to give us the *wrong* idea of their sincerity."

Switch to Julio Meles, twenty-nine, courier service manager, refresh smile.

"Now, let me assure you that if some poor soul being treated for schizophrenia wandered out of Bellevue in his underwear and pushed Jane Hughes under a train, raving all the while, and waited for the police to arrest him, the odds are very good that we would not be here in a courtroom today. The state of New York has no problem accepting a plea of not guilty by reason of insanity when the behavior of the accused clearly warrants it. We are not in the business of persecuting the sick and helpless."

Karp turned his attention to Earlene Davis, forty-one, restaurant cashier.

"But we know that such is not the case with Mr. Rohbling. We *know* it in the teeth of all the wild theories of all the psychiatrists that Mr. Waley can find in the telephone book and hire for generous fees, because we *know* how Mr. Rohbling *behaved*. You'll recall me asking Dr. Perlsteiner about how he knew that Jonathan Rohbling did not suffer from schizophrenia, and he answered with one word: competence. Everything we know about the defendant's behavior in the days preceding and following the murder of Mrs. Hughes shows competence, and not only that. We also see decision, alacrity, and guile. But let me make it absolutely clear, ladies and gentlemen . . ."

Karp made it absolutely clear to Lillian Weintraub, fifty-nine, housewife.

". . . I am not saying that Mr. Rohbling is a model of mental stability. Here I find myself in agreement with Mr. Waley. I have no doubt that Mr. Rohbling is a sick man. But that is not the point. The People are not obliged to show that Mr. Rohbling is a well-balanced, happy person, able to live a full and rewarding life. I am certain that Judge Peoples will instruct you as to that.

But there are many types of mental illness. Drug addiction and alcoholism are mental illnesses too, listed as such in Dr. Lewis Rosenbaum's big *DSM III* book, which we all saw earlier, but we do not for that reason excuse the junkie who mugs or the drunk who kills with his car."

Karp focused on Theodore Spearman, the retired NYU chemistry professor promoted to the jury from alternate, a man who might be expected to know about proof.

"No, all we are obliged to prove, and what we *have* proven, beyond a reasonable doubt, is that Jonathan Rohbling planned to kill Jane Hughes, that he costumed himself carefully so as to inveigle himself into her confidence, that he sought her out at her church, that he preyed on her decency, posing convincingly as a young black student lately come to the big city, and so got himself invited to her apartment, that he kept that appointment with murder at her apartment, that he killed her, knowing that he was killing her, for Jane Hughes fought hard for her life, she did not go easily as he pressed his suitcase down on her face, smothering her to death. And we have further proven that he escaped stealthily from the murder scene, and that when he was confronted by Detective Featherstone, as you heard, he cleverly and guilefully denied ownership of the suitcase, knowing that it contained damning evidence connecting him with the crime. Ladies and gentlemen, is this the *behavior* of an out-of-control maniac who doesn't know the difference between right and wrong? *Give me a break!*"

Pause. Switch to Carmen Delgado, thirty-one, dry cleaner. Karp took a deep breath, summoning the beginning case into his head. He would now review all the significant evidence as it applied to the theme he had just laid out for the jury, boosting his triumphs, ignoring his slips, telling him a coherent, convincing tale that would stick, he hoped, to their minds more tenaciously than the one Waley had told in the morning.

Late in the second hour of this grueling work, he noted out of the corner of his eye a young black woman he recognized as a clerk-typist in the bureau office enter the courtroom, walk up to the barrier dividing the well of the court from the spectator seats, attract the attention of Terrell Collins at the prosecution table, and hand him a folded piece of paper. The jury noticed it too, and their attention wavered for an instant. Karp suppressed a flush of rage. By far the gravest sin that any employee of the district attorney's office could commit was to interrupt in any way a closing argument. Death in the family was no excuse, nor was the outbreak of nuclear war. Karp raised his voice a hair, pumped out a little more charisma, brought the jury back to full attention, and plowed on. He would have someone's ass for this. Afterward.

Karp in his office, drained, rubbing an icy can of Coke across his eyes.

Collins was there for his usual postmortem, this the very last one. He could tell by the twitching of his boss's jaw that something was wrong (talk about *behavior*!), but he didn't have a clue as to what it was. He thought that the closing had gone splendidly. Karp had brilliantly defused the whole dueling-shrinks aspect of the case, finessing Waley's strongest card. The press— they had been yelling something about another granny-killer victim, but they had rushed down the gantlet so quickly that he hadn't been able to make out what it meant.

Karp chugged three-quarters of the soda and snarled, "Now, what the *fuck* was that business with passing papers in the middle of the goddamn closing?"

"Hell, Butch, I don't know. Look for yourself. I wasn't going to get into a damn discussion with the woman, so I just took what she gave me."

Karp read, "Fulton says call Homicide 28th IMMEDIATELY."

Karp punched in a familiar number. Fulton came on the line right away, as if he had been waiting by the phone.

"You heard yet?" the detective asked.

"Heard what? For fuck's sake, Clay, did you tell my office to interrupt me in *court*?"

"I did. Get this. A woman named Margaret Evans did not show up for work this morning. When a co-worker checked on her at one-fourteen this afternoon, she found her in her apartment, dead, with a blue cloth suitcase over her face. M.E. says it looks like smothering. Time of death, last night sometime. Woman is black, age 58, two kids, four grand kids."

"Oh, shit!" said Karp. "And the press has it already? How the hell . . . ?"

"Somebody tipped them, is what I heard. How we going to play this, Stretch?"

Karp did not reply for a moment. He was trying to figure out if there was any way of keeping this news from the jury, and decided that there was not. Had he known about it sooner, he might have been able to make a case for sequestration, but by now the jurors were at home, sitting in front of the tube or looking at the evening paper.

"I want you to handle it, Clay," he said at last. "You need me to call zone command or the Chief of D., I will."

"No problem. By the way, I checked. He was in Bellevue, in case you were wondering."

"Oh, *that's* a relief," said Karp. "I guess we should thank God for small favors. What's your thinking, off the bat?"

"Off the bat? A copycat. Rare, but it happens. A psycho, or someone who just wanted to whack his mother-in-law, but was stuck for inspiration until the trial. So we'll do the usual canvass, check on the relatives, the love life, the neighbors. Who knows, it could be a grounder—"

"It's not a grounder, Clay," said Karp, his tone flat and resigned. "Have you thought about the possibility of something nastier?"

"Like?"

"Like, Jonathan's got a pal, a disciple? My shrink called it his hobby. Maybe there was a club."

"Maybe you're getting paranoid in your old age," said Fulton. "We're talking about Rohbling here, son. The lone pine tree. Kid don't have a friend in Jesus, he got no friends at all. Oh, yeah, this'll amuse you. You know where the vic worked?"

"Don't tell me . . . for Rohbling, right?"

"Uh-uh. For that sweetheart you had me trailing around after last winter."

"Robinson?"

"Yep. She was a medical-records specialist. Small world, huh?"

"Tiny. What was Doctor Death doing the night of, by the way?"

"Oh, he's clean. According to his office, he was out on some little island in the Sound. Wait a second, I got it written down her somewheres . . ."

"Wooten Island," said Karp.

"That's it." Pause. "Wait a second, how the hell did you know that?"

"You said it was a small world. Don't ask," said Karp.

Karp's mood was not improved when, upon arriving home, he found the press thicker and more importunate than ever, the Evans murder having lashed them into a frenzy of speculation, and the pickets louder in their invective for the same reason. Thus, when he discovered that his daughter was missing, had been missing since noon, he was not his ordinary calm and reasonable self. He was cruel and abusive to Posie, in the most intemperate language. She wailed and ran to her room, from which issued the sound of disorganized packing. The twins burst into sympathetic tears. In the midst of this shrieking hell, while Karp was attempting to form some productive thought as to what to do next, the telephone rang. Karp let the machine pick it up and heard Marlene's voice saying, "She's here."

Moving as fast as he had ever moved on a basketball court, he raced to the phone and snatched up the receiver.

"Marlene? Jesus, I was going crazy!"

"I bet."

"Oh, God, I'm fucking shaking here."

"What's going on? It sounds like crying."

"Yeah, well, I yelled at Posie." He put his hand over the mouthpiece and called out the news to Posie, who came out smiling through the tears. Karp apologized, and the girl, who, like the sages of the Orient, dwelt in the eternal Now, swept the weeping twins up and away with kisses. Into the phone Karp said,

"Marlene, tell me you didn't plan all this out without letting me know."

"Of course not. It was a misunderstanding. I told Lucy that when my business was finished, she could come out here and spend a day or two, and she thought that meant the tennis thing, so when I told her it was finished, she arranged everything."

"*Arranged* . . . ?"

"Yeah, she came out with Tranh. Of course, he asked her if I was expecting her, and of course she said yes, which was true as far as she could see, and they took the train and a cab and the livery boat, and here they are. Tranh is paralyzed with embarrassment. Edie Wooten was a little surprised too. Lucy, of course, puts the whole thing off on me. And when I pointed out to her that you didn't know and would be going crazy, she said she left you a note, and then she said, oops, I forgot the note, sorry. The brat is incorrigible."

I wonder where she gets it from, thought Karp, fuming. "So you'll send her right back?"

"Well, as long as she's here, she might as well spend a day or so."

"What! Are you out of your fucking mind!" Karp yelled. "You're guarding that woman against a dangerous stalker, and you're going to keep Lucy there?"

"Well, you know, I made just that point to Lucy," said Marlene in a distinctly cooler tone, "and do you know what she said? She said that if a stalker could get past me, and Tranh and the dog, we better hang it up."

"Marlene, that's ridiculous!"

"And, she said, you're grumpy because you're losing your trial and everyone's miserable at the loft, and that's why she decided to come. She said, and I quote, I don't want to stop liking Daddy."

Karp could not think of a suitable riposte to this. Marlene resumed, after a moment of silence, "How *is* the trial going?"

"Down the toilet. There's a killer copycat-ing our defendant, but the jury's going to think . . . God knows what the jury's going to think. I thought it was even money on a hung, and maybe a tiny chance of a win, still, but . . . you know the background on this was always that he was a serial killer. We couldn't try it that way, but it was in the air, the jury understood that—you know how it is. Now, with this out, it sours the case. They're not thinking we got the wrong guy or anything, but maybe he had help, it's not straightforward anymore."

"I'm sorry, honey," said Marlene with genuine sympathy, mixed with relief that the subject had changed from parenting to the law. "And you worked so hard. Do they have any leads on the copycat?"

"Not yet. Woman seems to have been employed by your pal Robinson, by the way. I thought that was significant."

"Is it?"

"Apparently not, since he was away on your island paradise at the time of the murder last night."

"No, he wasn't," said Marlene. "He took off with his merry band last night on a yacht, and I know they made it to the City because I talked with a guy who started the evening clubbing downtown."

"Well, well," said Karp. "The plot thickens."

"It does indeed," said Marlene.

"Daddy was mad, wasn't he?"

"Furious. But I calmed him down. Did you apologize to Tranh?"

"Yes. I said that the dishonor was mine. He said I was an ignorant monkey, not worth drowning."

"I concur with that. Never again, Lucy, I mean it, although . . ."

"What?"

"I suppose I should take pride in your resourcefulness. At least you didn't get lost."

"I'm socially precocious," said Lucy with a casual drawl.

"Yes, and intellectually retarded. Now that you're here, how do you like it?"

"I love it. It's like a fairy castle on the sea. Could we go swimming now? I have my suit on underneath."

"No, it's too late," said Marlene. "Tomorrow. And wipe that expression off your face! You're lucky I don't tie you up in the cellar."

That evening they dined in the paneled dining room. Tranh leaped into the kitchen and whipped up a *moule marinière* with a bushel of local mussels. Lucy put on her Perfect Little Girl act, charming the pants off Edie and the Marneys. Tranh sat by the cellist, regaling her, in French, with anecdotes about old Paris. He had, it seemed, worked in a bistro frequented by Darius Milhaud and Paul Claudel. For a pick-up dinner under siege, it was a great success.

Afterward, Tranh and Marlene slept in shifts, but no incident disturbed the night. In the morning, during the sacred hours of cello practice, Tranh stayed by the house with the dog, while Marlene took Lucy down to the beach with her carry-all full of blanket, gun, sandwiches, and a thermos of lemonade.

The day was cloudy, however, with the wind picking up from the east, speckling the bay with little whitecaps. They swam until they were chilled and then walked along the beach, selecting choice pebbles and various interesting pieces of jetsam, until they came to a point that looked over the two-mile channel to Sag Harbor.

They had gone only a little way back when Lucy said, "There's someone near our stuff." Marlene squinted, but could make out only a shadow, like a stick figure, near their blanket. It must be Tranh, she thought, and wondered whether anything had gone wrong at the house. She quickened her pace. As they came closer, she saw, and the sight produced a gut wrench of fear and revulsion, that it was Robinson. He was reclining next to their blanket, dressed in white duck slacks, navy lisle shirt, and huaraches.

"Ah, the lovely Mrs. Karp," he called out gaily, "and who is this? A little Karp? How charming!"

"Get lost, Robinson!" Marlene snarled.

" 'Robinson'? Dear me, yesterday when you assaulted me, it was 'doctor' and very polite with it. It must be the immigrant crudity surfacing." He turned his gaze on Lucy, and Marlene felt her flesh prickle. "Manners are very important, little girl. For example, it's considered rude in the best circles to hit men in their wee-wees with your gun."

Marlene stooped and yanked up their blanket. "Fine, we'll leave. Take the thermos, Lucy."

"Oh, but aren't you going to introduce me to *Lucy*?" said Robinson. He rose and took a step closer to the girl.

"Yes. Lucy, this is Dr. Vincent Robinson, a vicious, evil man. You are not to ever talk to him, and if you see him coming, run away."

She took Lucy's hand and started to walk back toward the house. Robinson followed close behind Marlene, crowding her, his mouth inches from her ear. "What a thing to say!" he murmured. "Really, I love children. Their bones are so flexible. I like it when they sit on my lap. Do you think Lucy would like to sit on my lap? No? Maybe later."

They reached the cut in the dunes where a path led back to the big house. Marlene could smell his cologne and feel his breath warm against her neck.

"You have absolutely no idea what you're in for, do you, my little wop? A bodyguard? What a joke you are! You're like a dog that's run into the street just about to get squashed by a truck, you and kikey Ike, and your little mutt bitch—"

Marlene placed two fingers in her mouth and let out a piercing two-tone whistle. In seconds the dune grass was rattling with the passage of a large animal, and Sweety emerged onto the path. Marlene turned and pointed at Robinson. "Sweety, *iddu é 'n nemicu*," she said. Sweety made a sound like oil drums rolling down a gangplank and showed Robinson all his pretty white teeth. Robinson's tan lightened a shade. "If that dog touches me, I'll sue you for every cent you've got," he said. "I'll break you—"

"No, actually, you won't," said Marlene, "because if he goes for you, you won't be able to pee, much less sue. In fact, I think it's you who've gotten in over your head, Vince, not me. Now go away! We don't allow degenerates on this side of the island."

As she spoke, Sweety, his back hair bristling, was inching closer, snarling softly and slavering. A gob of dog drool fell on the naked arch of Robinson's foot. He forced his face into a not-very-convincing superior smile, nodded, gestured touché with his hand, spun on his heel, and left.

"You should've sicced Sweety on him, Mom," said Lucy as they walked together up to the house.

"No, actually, I'm pretty pleased with the way I handled that. The thing about violence is you want to avoid it whenever you possibly can. It takes something out of you when you use it. At first it's hard, and then it gets easier, and then you don't notice it at all. Or like it."

"Like that man," said Lucy.

"Yeah, like him. The other thing is, you don't want to use it in dribs and drabs. Either you don't use it at all, or you use it with overwhelming force."

"What you did on the street, in the fair."

"Uh-huh," said Marlene. Suddenly she felt weak, exhausted. Though the day was cool, her throat felt rough and parched, as if she had just fought a battle on the desert. She plopped herself down in one of the Adirondack chairs, and took a long drink of lemonade from the thermos. She offered it to Lucy.

"No, it's too sour. Can I go in and get a Coke from Mrs. Marney?"

Yes, she could. Lucy trotted away. Staring after her, Marlene wondered why she had just given her daughter a lesson in applied violence, why Lucy could shoot a pistol and box at an age when her peers were tinkling out little Mozart sonatas or learning how to float on their toes to *Swan Lake*. Was this crazy or the acme of sanity, given the state of the world? Marlene couldn't decide.

She sat there for the better part of an hour. Mr. Marney came out of the house, grumbling to himself and pulling on a yellow slicker. He waved to Marlene as he went past. Shortly thereafter, she heard the sound of the big speedboat starting up, echoing loudly in the boathouse, and then the sound of a group of chattering people on the path to the dock, and then the sound of the speedboat pulling away. Ginnie and her pals must be off. Marlene wondered if her interaction with Robinson had prompted the exodus. She didn't really care, and in any case the little shits could be back at any time. They seemed like insects in their flitting from one pleasure dome to another. Still, she felt some resolution of this affair was at hand. Either Robinson would go on to other tortures, or he would try again and she would catch him.

Tranh came out of the house. Marlene watched his peculiar light, shambling, round-shouldered walk, which always looked to her as if he were carrying a burden. He made almost no sound as he crossed the gravel path.

"Excuse me, Marie-Hélène, but the repair shop has called. Your car is completed. They wish to hear when you will collect it."

Marlene looked up at the sky, which was lowering. "It's going to pour later. Let's do it right now," she said. "We'll drive over to Southampton in the Wolfe-mobile and you can drive the VW back here, and then you can take Lucy back tomorrow in Wolfe's car. Oh! Can you drive a . . . ?" Marlene gestured shifting a manual shift. Tranh responded with a remarkable Gallic facial expression combining injured pride with a negative assessment of the intellectual capacity of the interlocutor. Marlene laughed, Tranh brought out one of his rare grins, and they both went inside.

Marlene and Lucy were in Wolfe's Caprice, driving back to Sag Harbor, the VW, ransomed for an outrageous fee, trailing behind, the windshield wipers clearing the steady drizzle from the windows. Marlene and Lucy were singing along with the Eagles tape. Marlene felt good. There seemed to be some new energy vibrating in her body, and the familiar lyrics were somehow more profound and full of a deeper meaning. The last song, "You Can't Hide Those Lyin' Eyes" finished amid general merriment. Lucy popped out the tape.

"Are there any more tapes?"

"*Hits of the Seventies?*" Marlene offered.

"Yuck!" Lucy popped the glove, came up empty, looked on the floor behind the front seat.

"Here's one," she said, retrieving it.

"That's not music," said Marlene. "And put your belt back on!"

Lucy did so and looked at the plain black tape. The label had nothing on it but a numbered date. "What is it, then?"

"Oh, it's like a lesson. Wolfe listens to it while he drives. It sort of helps him to be . . . I guess, better at his job."

"I want to hear it," said Lucy, and thrust it into the slot.

Click. Hiss. "You're wrong, it is too music," said Lucy.

Marlene jammed on the brakes so hard that her rear wheels fishtailed and Tranh had to swerve to avoid her as he pulled up on the shoulder behind. She turned off the engine and dashed back to the trunk. With shaking hands she inserted the key and jerked up the lid, revealing two long boxes of tape cassettes. She inspected a few, but knew beforehand what they were: commercial tapes and bootleg tapes from concerts, everything Edie Wooten had ever recorded.

Tranh came running up. "What is the matter? Has the car broken down?"

"No, and there's no time to explain. We have to get back to the island immediately." She slammed the trunk down and ran to take the wheel. The Caprice roared onto the road, tires shimmying on the slick pavement.

"What's wrong, Mom?" asked Lucy as the car passed a truck at seventy in the face of incoming traffic, and the outraged horns blared.

"What's wrong is I'm an idiot," said Marlene tightly, half to herself. "Of course it was Wolfe. It was sticking in my face from the time I read his application. He was a security guard at Tanglewood, and the Music Lover letters started just after that. I let him into her apartment—of course he had the keys, he could come and go as he pleased. The night in Juilliard, same thing. Christ! I saw Robinson, and it never occurred to me that—shit! And when he came in the other night, he didn't have to climb any walls—Sweety would've licked his hand. Conway Twitty, my ass!" She actually banged the heel of her hand against her forehead. She was puzzled about what she was feeling. A disaster like this . . . but somehow she found it hard to take seriously, as if a barrier had appeared between her and the world of feeling.

"Wolfe is really a *bad* guy?" asked Lucy, confused.

"Yeah, and he's probably sitting in there right now because we left her alone with my famous guard dog. I was so damn *focused* on Robinson and that stupid sister . . ." She giggled, and Lucy shot her an odd look.

It was pouring when they reached the marina, and a sharp northeasterly wind was whipping up a strong chop in the channel. Wooten Island was invisible in the gray. The manager of the marina had wisely shut down for the day, put his rental motors away, and battened down his day sailers and Boston Whalers. In such situations visitors to Wooten Island were supposed to call from a pay phone at the foot of the marina dock so that Mr. Marney could come in with the island speedboat. Marlene did so and got a "temporarily out of service" recording.

She explained the situation to Tranh, after which he said, in French, "You are not to blame, Marie-Hélène. He was a plausible villain. I had no suspicions myself, and I am suspicious of nearly everyone. In any case, I presume you do not wish to involve the police."

Marlene felt a surge of gratitude. Somehow Tranh understanding this made it all right. Police. It would be a zoo. Heiress held hostage by hired guard. End of business. Karp, his anger and disapproval. But now, she thought, it would all work out, simply and neatly. She felt full of power, as if rays of energy coursed from her head. She could even see the rays, a pale purple tingling to rose at the edges. She felt a warmth in her limbs and stomach, as if anticipating some good thing. The nasty day suddenly seemed brighter. "Right," she said. "Our mess, our cleanup." She laughed. Tranh looked at her strangely and said, "I will prepare one of these boats," indicating the seventeen-foot Fiberglas day sailers.

"Oh, a sailboat," she cried. "We'll sail to the isle. Can you sail?"

Again the quizzical expression, blended now with worry. "I am not sure. I have only sailed from Nha Trang to Luzon in the

Philippines. But the boat was smaller." He jumped down into the white craft, hauled the sails out of the cuddy, and began to bend the mainsail to the mast. "Lucy! Come help me!" He lifted the child down from the dock. He handed her the jib and showed her where it snapped to the forestay and jib sheets. Marlene was dancing along the dock, kicking at puddles. She studied the iridescence of some spilled oil. It was amazing that she had never noticed that you could make pictures in the spilled oil. No, not make pictures, the oil was *showing* her messages, vital messages, messages of cosmic significance, if only she could work them out. She stared into the glistening pool. Images of battles and palaces appeared; weird hierarchical figures swam to the surface and mouthed oracles. Yes, all of this she had thought to be reality was merely a cover, and made sense only if you knew the secret. The interplanetary secret. She dropped to her knees, studying it, full of wonder. It was all perfectly clear.

A man grasped her arm, a man who was Tranh yet not Tranh, who had a golden face and coruscations of red fire darting from his head. She let him lead her to the ship. How clever of them to disguise the star vessel as an ordinary sailboat! She went aboard and allowed herself to be placed on a seat in the cockpit. There was a small figure there too, shining like mother of pearl, speaking to her in a language she could not understand. She smiled back at the figure and closed her eyes so she could help to navigate across the stars.

"Lucy, listen to me," Tranh said in Cantonese as he cast off the lines and kicked the bow away from the dock. "Your mother is not well. Has she taken a drug or fallen and hit her head?"

"No, I don't think so," said Lucy in a quavering voice. "She just had some lemonade and a ham and cheese sandwich that Mrs. Marney made."

"And did you eat this food too?"

"Uh-huh, but the lemonade was too sour."

"Did you meet anyone on the beach?"

"Just that doctor, the bad one. He was waiting for us by our blanket. Sweety chased him away."

"*Wah!* This must be the answer. Some drug. Lucy, she will

not be able to help me with Wolfe, and I will not be able to do all necessary things by myself. So you must be a brave girl and help me." He had her get herself and her mother into life jackets, dropped the centerboard, and showed her how to work the jib sheets. Then he sheeted in, and the boat began to move rapidly across the bay in the stiffening breeze.

When they were past the stone breakwater, the boat took the full force of the surge and the twenty-five–knot easterly wind that was blasting up the Sound. Lucy gave a little cry as the boat heeled over on its beam ends. Tranh steadied it, eased the mainsheet, and set out on a broad reach toward Wooten Island. Marlene rolled off her seat and onto the deck of the cockpit. Her eyes were still closed, and she had a blissful smile on her face. They were all soaked to the skin from the rain and spray, and Lucy had started to cry, the tears invisible against her wet face.

The island was still lost in the rain, but Tranh had a superb sense of direction. Many times he had taken boats through the mangrove marshes of the Mekong Delta at night, in the teeth of enemy patrols. When he judged it proper, he tacked, Lucy letting fly the jib sheet at his command. The boat whipped about. Marlene rolled languidly across the deck to the lee bulkhead. A gray mass appeared ahead of them, and in a few minutes Tranh spotted the flagpole at the foot of the Wooten Island dock.

Tranh brought the boat alongside, tied its bow and stern lines to cleats, rummaged through Marlene's straw bag for her pistol and spare magazine, and lifted Lucy out of the boat. Marlene he covered with a spare sail and left her where she lay, smiling to herself between Proxima Centauri and Arcturus.

TWENTY-TWO

Tranh led Lucy through the sparse pines, keeping well away from the paths. It had been some years since he had done this, and then it was in a thicker and warmer forest, but he found that he recalled the art of moving through woods against an unseen enemy. He worked his way around to the west of the big house, toward the boathouse. There was no sound but the rain on its tin roof, no motion not made by the gusts. He left Lucy at the wood line with a comforting word, and taking his Russian pistol in hand, he darted across the narrow lawn and slipped into the building.

All the boats were in their places, but as he walked along the wooden decking built around the basin, he could smell the stink of gas and saw that the surface of the water was thick with greenish oil. Someone had poured the gas out of all the gas cans and opened the drain cocks on the big cruiser, spilling its diesel fuel. But the speedboat was loosely tied at the far end of the boathouse dock, its prow pointing out to the Sound. Tranh jumped down into the boat and made a quick inspection. There were two suitcases in the cockpit. Tranh opened them. One was neatly packed with men's things. The other was full of women's clothes, roughly stuffed in. The craft was fueled and ready to go. Its engine was still warm. Someone was planning an escape by sea. He popped the engine coaming and examined the Chrysler six.

The boathouse had a small repair shop, a workbench with tools and supplies. From a pegboard he took a coil of thin steel wire and a roll of duct tape, and stuck them in his jacket pocket, along with the distributor rotor he had taken from the speedboat's engine. He found an old greasy blanket and a tarpaulin on a shelf, and he took them too.

He came out of the boathouse and found Lucy where he had left her. She was pale and shivering. He slit the blanket and the tarp with his knife and made a rough poncho out of it and slipped it over the child's head. He led her back into the pine wood.

He smiled at her and smoothed the damp hair off her forehead. "Little sister," he said in Cantonese, "now we must be soldiers for a little while. In my country, during the war, girls the same age as you were soldiers and they did very well, and you will do very well too. Wolfe is planning to escape with one of the boats, and he plans to take Wooten-*sìujè* with him. So, he must come down this path with her, and we will prepare an ambush for him. Do you know this word, ambush? No? We lie here in wait, and when they come out we will capture them."

"With our guns?"

"Just so, with our guns. Now, we must examine the ground and see where is the best place."

The Music Lover finished tying up Edie Wooten with adhesive tape. The Marneys were tied up similarly and locked in the cellar, as was the dog, who had been perfectly friendly throughout. It was going very well. The summer storm had been a good break, because it would have been difficult to handle Marlene, Tranh, and the little girl all at once, and now they were off the island with no way to return in time to stop him. He certainly didn't want to hurt anyone without it being absolutely necessary, especially not Marlene, who had been kind to poor dumb Wolfe.

He left Edie lying on the couch and went to get the cello. Reverently, he caressed the miraculous finish, and reflected that the instrument was much like himself. Stradivarius had taken mute spruce and sycamore and willow, and with varnish and glue had made it into something divine, just as the dull material of Jack Wolfe, a hick security guard, a hopeless loser, had been transmogrified by the power of Edie Wooten's playing into the Music Lover, the perfect audience, soon to be the eternal and only audience.

He lifted the cello and placed it carefully into its case, and put the bow into its velvet clips. Now, should he take the cello down to the boat first, or the musician first and then her instrument? Perhaps he should ask Edie? No, it was important to show decision. He went over to her and said in his music lover voice, so much deeper and more cultured than Wolfe's voice, the voice of an announcer on WQXR, "I'm going to put your cello on the boat now. I'll be right back."

"Please don't hurt me," she whimpered.

That was puzzling. His brow wrinkled. How could she not understand? She had been telling him to do this in everything she played. "Of course I'm not going to hurt you, silly! I love you. You just rest here for a minute. Be right back."

He hoisted the cello and slung Marlon Dane's MP5 on his free shoulder. The cello was lighter than he had expected. It seemed, indeed, lighter than the machine gun. He walked out the front door, swung right and down the garden path to the boathouse.

"You see, little sister, there is the path he must follow to the boathouse," explained Tranh. They were squatting in the wood line to the west of the house. "It leads through the rose garden and then sinks between two banks and then rises and curves around before it goes down to the boathouse. You see how I have wired and taped your mother's pistol to the tree there. It is what we call a fixed gun. It is very useful when you have few troops. We have very few troops, only you and me, but if we are clever, we will win. Now, this wire will fire the gun when you pull it. Take it in your hand. You will crawl under the bush. Do it now! Now lift your head over the stone wall. Can you see the path?"

"Yes. A little of it."

"And that white rose bush at the end. Can you see that too?"

"Yes."

"Good. This is very important, so listen. When Wolfe passes that bush, not before, you duck your head behind the wall, all the way down to the ground, and you pull your wire twice, then wait one breath, then twice more. I think that when he hears the bullets pass him, he will drop down behind that low bank for shelter, and fire back at the flash and sound of our gun. I think also that he has a machine gun, so you will hear a very loud banging, and you will also hear the bullets passing overhead. They will make a sharp noise like firecrackers, and pieces of wood and leaves may fall down on you. Will you be frightened?"

"No," said Lucy; then, after a pause, "A little bit, perhaps."

"Yes, that is normal, but you will still do what is required."

"Where will you be?" she asked.

"I will wait at the rear of the house. When I hear your shot, I will come up behind him and capture him."

That was the plan. Tranh thought it a good one. He really had no doubt that Lucy would do what she should, but as always, the most unpredictable part was the behavior of the enemy. When fired on, Wolfe had four choices. He could go to the ground at the convenient sunken path Tranh had left for him, in which case Tranh would come up behind him and stick a gun in his back. Or he could run back to the house, and Tranh would be between him and the house. Or he could run to the boathouse, in which case he would be trapped, with nowhere to go.

As he took up his position he considered the fourth option and the critical angles of the situation. It was near, perhaps too near, but the child was well hidden, and Wolfe would be confused and deafened by his own firing. And there was nothing else to be done. He waited, squatting, watching.

A door slammed. Heavy steps on the gravel path. Wolfe emerged from around the corner of the house, carrying a cello case, and started down the rose garden path. Tranh slipped along the side of the house in a crouching lope, concealed by the rose bushes.

Two shots sounded. Tranh felt a momentary pleasure. An excellent child, though a girl! Then a burst of three from the MP5, a heavy tread, another burst of three. Bad. Wolfe was doing just what Tranh would have done in the same situation. He was charging the ambushing gun, firing controlled bursts. Tranh took off in pursuit.

The Music Lover had to admit that Wolfe had some useful skills. As soon as the shots were fired, he did the right thing, just as in Vietnam. Run toward the ambush, is what the experienced troops used to say, and although it was scary to do it, the guys who did had a better chance than the ones who dropped where they were, because the V.C. always had mortars or heavy weapons zeroed on the most obvious cover.

Whoever was firing from the wood line shot again, high. The Music Lover saw the flash against the rain-soaked leaves. He fired another burst and kept moving. Now he was in the woods. He crouched behind the tree and waited for his ears to stop ringing from his own firing. He listened, but heard nothing but the rush of wind and the patter of the rain through the woods, and his beating heart.

The plan was still in effect, though. He would take down whoever it was and go on as before. Crouching, he moved through the bushes. There it was, a glint of metal, the muzzle of a semiautomatic pistol.

The Music Lover fired a long burst at where the man holding the gun would be. To his surprise, the gun stayed where it was. He moved forward. He came close enough to see that the pistol had been taped into the crotch of a maple sapling. A wire was wrapped around the trigger. He traced it straight back to another tree, where it took a turn and went off to the left and down. He tugged it. It went slack. The Music Lover saw that the wire disappeared into some bushes ten feet away. He raised his weapon.

From behind him a voice said, "Put down your weapon! Surrender!"

The Music Lover whirled around. He saw the Vietcong standing there, a thin, wet Vietnamese man in the black clothes they all wore, with his pistol held straight out. The Music Lover tried to bring the machine gun up, but before it had moved an inch, the first of three bullets struck him in the chest.

He fell back onto the wet forest floor. It was all a dream, he thought. I never got out of that ambush. Twelve years, the crummy security jobs, the transforming music, the woman, the plan, cutting that guy's throat, I dreamed it all. I'm still here in Cu Chi. He thought, how totally fucking far out! Wait'll I tell the guys! He filled his lungs to yell for the medic, and died.

It was eight the next morning before Marlene could talk sensibly. She came up out of the dream resentfully, reluctant to leave the glittering space opera whose wonderful denizens seemed able to answer the deepest questions that afflicted her soul. And unlike a regular dream, this one stayed in her memory, each detail sharp as crystal, although she could no longer understand what they meant.

"Camel spent off the water," she said to Tranh. "It's not less than the sixth, more than the vision. Belanthey is the absolute key."

"Marie-Hélène," said Tranh, "can you understand me? Do you know where you are?"

The French was somehow able to penetrate through the last seductive vapors of the drug. She blinked, sighed, saw the man, knew him, knew herself, recognized the room she lay in as her bedroom at Wooten's. Her mouth felt all at once unbearably dry. She asked for water, drank.

"I was out of action for a while, wasn't I?"

"Yes, for nearly an entire day. I believe it was Robinson that put some drug in your lemonade."

A frightened look. "Lucy . . . ?"

"She is well."

Then memory flooded back. "My God! Wolfe, Edie, what . . . ?"

Then Tranh had to explain what had happened, editing around Lucy's part in it, which he did not feel Marlene was yet up to absorbing. There would, apparently, be no trouble with the authorities, who had already come and gone.

"The Wootens apparently can do no wrong in this locality," he said. "The police arrived, they were polite, they removed the corpse. Miss Wooten explains Wolfe was simply an insane stranger, shot by a security guard. It is fortunate that she speaks excellent French, or it would have been impossible for me to convey the nuances of the necessary fabrication. Wolfe's association with your company was not mentioned, the press was not notified. So it ends."

Marlene felt her nose burn and her eyes overflow. "Poor Wolfe! I still can't believe it. He was . . . there was something so . . ." But she could not explain, not to Tranh, hardly to herself, what the dead man meant to her. It was tied in with her brother, and the fucking war, and the men she hired and the men she hurt, all the sweet, slow, violent lost American boys.

She stopped crying and asked, "How is Edie? I should go down and see her."

She made to get out of bed, but Tranh gently prevented her. "Mlle. Wooten is fine, and it seems that she is not to be disturbed in the mornings for any cause. Listen!"

The cello's music drifted up from below, sonorous and sad.

"I spoke with her last night at some length. A strange story. Would you like to hear it?"

She would. Tranh said, "He spoke to her about her music. Wolfe. He said he knew that she was speaking to him in a way that no one else could understand. Apparently, he was quite knowledgeable about the instrument and its repertoire. She was amazed despite her terror. A sensitive man. It was at root a kind of jealousy, as if by playing to an audience she was betraying him, like a woman who shares her body with many men, and so he had decided to kidnap her so that she would play for him alone. The things he had taken from her, the recordings, these were no longer sufficient to slake his passion." And more in this vein.

They talked for some time, remembering Wolfe as a comrade, a stranger, a puzzle beyond their comprehension. "He was a soldier too," said Tranh musingly. "A good one, an infantryman. In Vietnam."

"How do you know? Did you see his record?"

"I saw him move. I remembered."

A number of things now came together in Marlene's mind: Tranh's isolation from the normally cohesive Vietnamese community, certain things he had let drop, his peculiar skills, the Russian pistol Lucy had seen . . .

"You weren't one of *our* Vietnamese, were you?"

After a moment he shrugged, smiled faintly, and answered, "No. But Tranh Vinh was. He died on the ocean, during our voyage. There were twelve of us on a fourteen-foot sailboat. I took his papers."

"Who are you, then?"

"No one, to tell the truth. A casualty of the war, perhaps like Wolfe, or your brother. Yes, I know about him. He comes to the office occasionally when you are not there. I give him small sums. We talk about the war."

"Does he know?"

"No. Only you know. And, you know, sometimes it is hard for me to recall that there was once such a person as Pham Vinh Truong, who studied in Paris, who taught mathematics in a lycée in Saigon, who had a wife and a daughter, who joined, reluctantly, the National Liberation Front, who was a major in the 615th Battalion of what you call the Vietcong, whose family was killed in a bombing raid, who, after the war, was deemed insufficiently devoted to the state, and was imprisoned and reeducated, who escaped by sea, and who . . ." He stopped and let out a long sigh. "I suppose it was Lucy that led me to this latest chapter in what seems even to me to be an absurd life. She reminds me so much of Nguyen. Not her appearance, of course, but in spirit, her air. I will deeply regret losing her acquaintance."

"Why should you lose her acquaintance?" Marlene asked.

Tranh seemed surprised at the question. "Because, I assumed, that now that you know my history, you will not wish to employ me. But I hope that you will not feel obliged to inform the authorities of my—"

"Don't be absurd!" said Marlene, waving her hand dismissively. "I can't possibly do without you. For the business with long division alone I owe you lifetime employment. Besides, the war is over."

It is not, thought Tranh, but he said only, "Thank you, Marie-Hélène."

By nine, Marlene had showered, scrubbed most of the foul taste from her mouth, dressed, went down to the kitchen, heard Mrs. Marney's version of the story (clearly the most exciting thing that had happened on Wooten Island since the Montauk Indian raid in 1687), fended off the substantial breakfast offered, hugged her daughter, heard *her* version of the story, was appalled and grateful, and sat down at the kitchen table with toast, coffee, and a cigarette.

Mrs. Marney had a little color TV in the kitchen, tuned to some morning news show from the city, with the volume turned down to a barely audible murmur lest practice be disturbed. On it a well-groomed woman was interviewing a distinguished-looking older man. Marlene paid it little attention. She still did not feel herself. The colors of the morning were still too bright, the sounds—the sighing of the cello from the music room, the sound of the birds outside the kitchen window—were still too poignant, chance remarks still resonated with covert meaning. Acid, she thought. The fuckhead had slipped her a really immense dose, probably mixed with more exotic indoles.

The TV switched back to an anchorman. He was saying something about a riot. Tape of a night scene, the city, uptown, a gang of black youths, flames from a shop, an overturned car. The anchorman came back, something about the rain suppressing what could have been an even worse riot in the wake of the Rohbling verdict. Marlene's attention focused on the faint voice. A shot of the distinguished-looking man who had just been interviewed, speaking to reporters in a lobby of the Criminal Courts Building. Lionel T. Waley in white letters across the screen. Marlene felt a chill, one that increased as she saw her own husband shying from a mob of reporters. She got up and ran to the phone.

Karp was in his bed, playing with his sons. He had his knees up under the covers, and Zik and Zak were having a hilarious

338 / *Robert K. Tanenbaum*

time climbing up this mount and rolling down it to Karp's chest, where they were rewarded with a loud raspberry on the tummy. Karp was having a hilarious time too. He couldn't think of anything he wanted to do more, at this point or into the indefinite future. The phone rang, for the thirtieth time that morning, and as before, he let the machine pick it up.

"Butch!" called the tinny voice. "Pick up! It's me."

Karp reached a long arm over and lifted the receiver.

"Marlene! How are you this fine morning? Want to talk to your sons? Boys, it's Mommy."

"I saw the TV. What happened?"

"What happened? Mr. Rohbling was declared not guilty by reason of insanity by a jury of his peers, is what happened. How are you, dear?"

"We're fine. I'm coming home."

"No kidding? What about your client?"

"That's finished. The guy's dead."

"Well, that'll teach him not to mess with my wife," said Karp.

"Are you all right?" asked Marlene nervously. She might be doped up, but there was something about her husband's tone she did not like.

"Never better," said Karp.

"You're not depressed?"

"I *was* depressed, but now I'm fine. I am also no longer the Homicide Bureau chief."

"Jack fired you? The bastard!"

"Not at all. The fact is, I bet the farm on this one, and I got whipped, fair and square. He warned me he would have to cream my butt if we lost, and he did, with his usual Irish charm. I am going to be the Special Assistant to the District Attorney for Special Projects."

"What the hell is that?"

"Nothing. A job with no responsibilities and a low, low profile. With a paycheck, however."

"Jesus, Butch! What will you *do*?"

"I don't know. I think I'll spend some time hanging around here with the kids. This motherhood racket is a piece of cake. I don't know why women complain all the time. Yeah, maybe I'll just hang loose and do my toenails, and read *Goodnight Moon* and let you shoot all the bad guys. By the way, did you whack this latest guy personally, or did that fall to one of your minions?"

"A minion. Butch, are you *really* okay? You sound, I don't know, kind of wacky."

Karp considered this seriously for a moment, while he licked, nuzzled, and otherwise amused his children. Then he said, "I guess, what it is, when you stretch the rubber band far enough and then let it snap back, it tends to get a little tangled. I made a big mistake, and I should pay the freight. To tell the absolute truth, I feel like somebody just lifted a Mosler safe off my chest. I mean, it's been years since I haven't been worrying about something, fighting something, stressed out to the max. You know?"

"Yeah, I do," she said, with feeling.

"And Roland and Guma took me out last night to commiserate, and Roland was the one who got hammered, because even though he's such an ambitious bastard, he still felt bad about the trial."

"And he'll pick up the bureau."

"I expect so. God knows he's lusted after it long enough. And he'll do a good job. I'll tell you something, Marlene, when the foreman stood up there—he was that NYU professor *I* put in there, the alternate—and read the verdict, I felt this incredible sense of relief. Do you think I set all this up? Insisting on running this trial. Just to get a rest?"

"It wouldn't completely stun me if it was true," said Marlene. "I saw Lionel T. on the tube, by the way, pontificating. Apparently, justice was done."

"Maybe it was," said Karp. "Rohbling's going somewhere where he won't have much access to elderly black ladies, maybe not for twenty-five to life, but a good long time. I will say Waley was gracious in victory. A real gentleman, and a lesson in how to run a trial. But I'll get him next time."

"That's my old Butch!" said Marlene. "Speaking of getting, I have a suggestion for your first special project."

"I'll entertain it."

She described her recent contacts with Vincent Robinson and what he had done to her. Karp was silent for a few seconds. Then he said, in quite a different, a sterner voice, "I think it's time Dr. Robinson was suppressed."

"On what charge, Counselor?" asked Marlene.

Karp laughed, a muffled sound, because Zak was trying to sit on his face. "Oh, charges! This is Special Projects, honey. We don' need no stinkin' charges."

Karp had a nice office to go with his new job, one just down the hall from the district attorney's, with the old-fashioned sort of furniture and a good three-window view. Its former occupant was a man named Conrad Wharton, who had been, under the *ancien regime*, one of Karp's most implacable enemies. Sitting in Wharton's special oversize chair, behind Wharton's special oversize rosewood desk, made Karp prone to unwonted fits of giggles.

It was now four days after the verdict in the Rohbling trial. The press had gone on to other things, as had the militants. Karp was cheerily back at work, a rested, smiling Karp, a different man from the fearsome, hulking scowler he had lately been, and already launching his first special project.

To this end he had called a meeting in the D.A.'s conference room. Around the long oak table sat those interested in the malefactions of Dr. Vincent Fiske Robinson: Paul Menotti, the U.S. attorney, more grumpy than usual at finding himself off his own turf; Cynthia Doland, his lovely shadow, crisp and demure in a pale off-white linen suit; V. T. Newbury, representing Fraud; Lieutenant Clay Fulton, in charge of investigating the murder of Margaret Evans, in which Robinson was a suspect; and Karp, at the head of the table.

Karp said, "We're still waiting for one more person, but I think we can get started. Lieutenant Fulton will bring us up to date on the status of the investigation. Clay?"

Fulton took a cheap memo pad out of his breast pocket, thumbed through it, and began. After sketching in his surveillance of Robinson the previous winter and what it had yielded, he moved on to the more fruitful recent inquiries.

"First, we know Robinson was in town on the night Margaret Evans was murdered. He was club hopping off a yacht. They docked at City Island, where a stretch limo met them and took them into Manhattan, and carried them from place to place. We interviewed most of the party. Some say Robinson was there with them throughout; others think he might have slipped away for a while with a woman named Virginia Wooten. What I gather from their accounts was that everyone was doped or drunk enough that they wouldn't have noticed an elephant wandering away for a couple of hours."

"What does this Wooten woman say?" Menotti asked.

"I don't know because we haven't had a chance to talk with her. She seems to have disappeared." He paused to let this sink in. "On the other hand," he continued, "she could be any-where and show up tomorrow. They don't call these folks the jet set for nothing. Moving to the victim: Margaret Evans was a medical-records specialist responsible for, among other things, the pharmaceutical records at the St. Nicholas Medical Centers dispensary on Amsterdam Avenue and One-oh-fifth Street. She'd been working there for eight years, and her colleagues considered her a good worker. A decent, honest woman, one of them said. On the night she died . . . hello, Marlene."

Marlene paused at the door, then walked in. Karp introduced her as a private detective with some special knowledge of Vincent Robinson. "Ms. Ciampi has agreed to help us out *pro bono*," said Karp. "Marlene, I think you know everyone but Paul Menotti from the A.G. and his assistant, Cynthia Doland." Marlene shook hands and sat down.

Fulton continued from where he had left off. "On the night she died, Evans made herself dinner and ate it alone. At about ten-thirty she opened the door to the people who killed her. No signs of forced entry. I say people, because one of them was a woman. She left some short blond hairs in the apartment. A man out walking his dog noticed a couple he hadn't seen around be-fore walking out of Evans's building around eleven. He wasn't close enough to get a good ID, but it was definitely a man and a woman. Both blonds. So it certainly would've been possible for

Robinson and this woman Wooten to travel uptown, get into Evans's apartment on some excuse—I mean, he was the victim's boss, practically—kill her, and get away downtown without being missed by a bunch of dopers."

"Why'd he kill her, if he did?" asked Menotti. "I have to say this is pretty speculative."

Fulton said, "She was going to rat him out. We played the black woman's voice from the hot-line tape to some of her relatives. It was her."

In the ensuing silence, Karp said genially, "V.T., maybe you can add something here."

"Well, first, in the last two months," said V.T., "there has been a very substantial increase in the street supply of prescription drugs in the City and along the East Coast. This is mostly d-amphetamine, Percodan, Nembutal, and Quaaludes, all drugs with a healthy street market. During that same time period, the St. Nicholas Med Centers filled prescriptions for thirty thousand Percodan tablets and fifty thousand Dextramphetamine caps. The service area seems to be unusually prone to painful afflictions and weight problems. Their books seem to balance, though: a bona fide patient for each piece of scrip. But there's no doubt it's a racket, and a big one too. We have a watch on a numbered account in the Caymans that we think is associated with Robinson. Major increases in the same period."

"That's still pretty vague," said Menotti. "You won't even get an indictment on that showing."

"Did you show it to him?" V.T. asked Fulton.

"No," answered the detective, "I was saving it for now. This was found in Margaret Evans's purse."

He passed a plastic evidence pouch across the table. In it, Menotti saw, was a slip of paper with his own name and his office phone number written on it. "I don't recall she ever called us," he said. "Do you, Cynthia?"

"I don't think so," said Doland, "but if she called the hot line, she could have called here too. It could have been anonymous. I'll review the logs, see if she did."

Karp said, "Fine. Okay, Marlene here has a view of Robinson that might be helpful. Marlene?"

"I've spent some time around this man in connection with another case," said Marlene. "Vincent Robinson is a sadist. I mean that in the technical sense. He derives pleasure from causing pain, and he's frank about it. He thinks he's a superior man and has the right to do what he likes to anyone. He is from a well-off family but has the ambition to become enormously rich in his own right. Needless to say, he is totally amoral. He runs with a group of people who fancy themselves decadents. They indulge in sexual fantasies of the sadomasochistic variety and plenty of drugs, dispensed by Robinson, of course. These people are harmless ninnies, except, possibly, to themselves, but Robinson is a truly dangerous man. For one example, he knew that I would be facing an armed and possibly dangerous stalker, and he slipped some psychedelics into a thermos I was using. For another, if he is our killer, the use of the blue suitcase to smother Mrs. Evans was no accident. He wanted to get back at Mr. Karp here for investigating him, and thought copying Rohbling's style would help confuse the jury. Which it did. His weak point, in my opinion, is his desire for notice, to be admired in his awfulness. I think he uses Virginia Wooten for this. She is essentially his slave, and he keeps her docile through the use of drugs and sexual cruelty. I like her for the accomplice here. I also think she would also know just about everything useful to us about Dr. R."

"Yeah, that's why he sent her to Timbuctu," said Menotti. "Well, there doesn't seem much point in going on, until we have Wooten to talk to, and since we have no idea where she is . . ." He left the thought hanging and began to make leaving-the-meeting motions.

"Oh, I think one of us knows where she is, or could make a good guess," said Marlene. "How about it, Cynthia? Want to help us out?"

Everyone stared at Marlene and then at Doland, who colored slightly and gave a good imitation of a baffled innocent.

"Is this a joke?" Menotti rumbled.

"No. The last time I saw Ms. Doland, she was dressed in a white confirmation dress and white patent mary-janes—no, that's a lie. I saw her last just the other day at Wooten Island, with Ginnie Wooten and Robinson. Nice white bikini, no mary-janes. The time before that, I should have said, she was beating up a guy in a sex club so he would come on her shoe. You're one of that gang in your off hours, honey. I came in here this morning and saw you, and I swear, if it hadn't been for that crisp linen suit and your prissy look, I probably wouldn't have recognized you. Maybe your boss will want to talk to you about how come it's been so hard to pin anything on Robinson. Maybe some discreet leaks? But right now the only thing I personally want to know is: where is she?"

There is a great deal of difference, Marlene reflected some weeks later, between being tied up for fun and being tied up for real. She observed this to her husband, just after he had informed her that Ginnie Wooten had made a full statement implicating Robinson in a dense slate of crimes, including the murder of Margaret Evans. They were in their kitchen, putting groceries away.

"Yeah, Ginnie didn't much care for jail," Karp was saying. "I can't say for certain, but I think they arranged for her to be in a cell with a broader ethnic and sexual orientation than she's used to up on Park Avenue."

"Our beautiful mosaic," said Marlene. "And she spurned it?"

"I'm afraid so. They may have made fun of her whatchama-callit's . . . you know, those things in her crotch. May have hurt her feelings, poor kid. I really think that Robinson thought she'd take the whole rap for him, but Roland offered her a sweet deal and she jumped at it."

"They arrest him yet?"

"The warrant's cut. Roland said he'll call when they have him wrapped. Want to come to the perp walk? We can hold hands and wave to him as he slithers by."

"No, I don't want to see his face again," said Marlene quickly, and knew that it was true and knew why: that leap in front of the subway train attraction, the foul suck of the sadistic, that dwelt in her own soul, that she fought every day, that Robinson had recognized and gloated over. She felt a chill and shook herself.

"What's wrong?" asked Karp. "You looked funny."

"I don't know," she said lightly. "Someone walked on my grave."

And as she busied herself with humble domestic tasks that evening, and cast her mind back over the dreadful and bloody year she had just spent, the idea floated into her mind of a party, a truly gigantic and memorable party, symbolizing . . . she did not quite know, but something—escape, survival, the crazy dance of her life. She would invite *everybody*, which was feasible now that they had the elevator. She would invite a gang of Jamaican dopers and killers she knew from Brooklyn, and ask them to provide the music, and a Mexican shelter operator and cutthroat feminist, also a killer, and old Dr. Perlsteiner, and a crazy reporter, an old pal from college, if she was in the country, and everyone from her company, Harry and Sym, and Dane, and the Homicide Bureau and the Rape Bureau to party with the criminals, and an elderly British demolition expert she knew and Karp's old Aunt Sophie (maybe they would get it on?) and of course, the D.A. himself, and everyone in the building, of course, and her whole family, including her crazy vet brother, and Tranh the reformed Vietcong, who would cook shrimp balls and fried dumplings and other delicacies in a giant flaming wok, while Lucy and her gang of girlfriends carried around plates of smoking goodies, and everything washed down with gallons, crates, of champagne. And, of course, Father Dugan, and ask him to bring that Irish kid, Kevin Mulcahey, along, because if the kid couldn't get laid at *this* party, he might as well check into the seminary. Posie, for one, would suck him out of his clothes in a New York minute. She imagined herself gazing over the throng, explaining to the priest who everyone was, all the impossibly conflicted fragments of her life so far, the lions and the lambs cavorting. Maybe he would have something interesting to say, no doubt in Latin.

And let's have that doctor too, Davidoff, the one whose misadventure had caught Murray Selig's eye and started the long, slow demise of Vincent Robinson.

Karp would enjoy such a party, the new Karp, the new relaxed, home-at-six Karp, with whom Marlene had for the last few weeks fallen again in love, owing to the time, the bland, missionless time together alone, which (in a good marriage) is to marital bliss what steroids are to lifting weights.

These pleasant daydreams were interrupted by the ringing of the phone. Karp said, "That'll be Roland," and picked it up. He spoke for ten minutes, and when he got off there was an odd look on his face.

"Well?"

"Oh, they picked him up with no trouble. Brought him in, he gave them the finger and asked to call his lawyer. No surprise there."

"And?" She was observing him closely. He was leaning against the counter, idly tossing a can of soup in his hands, with his gaze fixed on infinite nowhere.

"Oh, nothing," he said. "Roland just mentioned that Robinson had retained Lionel Waley."

Marlene set her jaw, flared her nostrils, and, in a voice of brass, said, "Don't. Even. *Think* it!"